Tina's Promise

By

Gerda Osiecki

This book is a work of fiction. Places, events, and situations
in this story are purely fictional. Any resemblance to actrual
persons, living or dead, is coincidental.

ISBN: 1-4107-7620-4 (e-book)
ISBN: 1-4107-7619-0 (Paperback)

Library of Congress Control Number: 2003095431

This book is printed on acid free paper.

Printed in the United States of America
Bloomington, IN

1stBooks - rev. 08/14/03

Thanks to my husband Bert, Linda and Carol, our daughters and Catie our grand-daughter for all their encouragement and support.

1

A shrill, ear-splitting shriek pierced the darkness. Sirens? Fire? Eyes opened wide, Tina was confused. Where am I? What's happening? As the dim light from the transom allowed her to focus, it registered. She was in a London hotel. The continuing noise was from an ugly English telephone mounted on the far wall of her room. It was half past five in the morning—her wake-up call.

Stretching and relieved to find that she'd made it through another restless night, Tina sprang into action. A quick shower, dress, hair, makeup and she was ready. It was the first day of her new life. To become a whole person again, it was necessary to start over.

Tina Cappo had crossed the Atlantic finding herself far from the comfortable life she had known in St. Louis. The brutal murders of her parents eighteen months before had left her homeless, destitute and alone. She had grieved, but now, although vowing to find those responsible, it was time to move forward.

In the time elapsed since the murders, Tina had learned to accept the fact that her loving family and their St. Louis hotel, the only home she'd ever known, were gone forever. Having had to drop out of college with no marketable skills, Tina was, nevertheless, a survivor. Being well read and having an interest in foreign lands, she applied for an entry level job at a travel agency. Then, when the opportunity presented itself, she trained to become a tour guide. This was the day of reckoning. The first group of tourists were about to descend on her.

Tina was beginning a new life, but thoughts of what had happened bringing her to this day were always in back of her mind. Her problems had begun when she and her college roommate were visiting in South Africa. They had promised to spend their summer vacation with Mara's parents and had been in Capetown about three weeks when Spencer Cappo, Tina's father, called with upsetting news.

Shortly before Tina's departure, Spencer had been presented with a proposition to invest in twin hotels being sold in Chicago. He'd been searching for such an opportunity and believed this offer warranted consideration. The pros and cons had been discussed prior to Tina's leaving, but Spencer had promised that a final decision regarding the properties would be held off until the family was reunited. It was a decision not to be taken lightly. They would be borrowing against their family-owned hotel as well as investing their life savings.

Listening to her father as he spoke, Tina sensed that Spencer was ready to go ahead with the purchase of the hotels in spite of the promise he had made. Questions she asked were met with a "testy" response. Clearly Spencer did not want to hear any arguments from his daughter.

"Forget about the hotel while you're on vacation, Tina. We've got everything under control. Your mother and I have confidence in the way Larry is handling things and so should you. Need I remind you that Larry helped make our hotel what it is today and that you are planning to marry him after graduating from college? You must know that Larry is working hard to serve our best interests."

"Of course I believe in Larry, Daddy, but why can't this wait until I get home?"

"The sellers want a yes or no now, Tina and we believe it's a good deal."

"But you're putting the hotel and your savings at risk. What if something goes wrong?"

"Sometimes it's necessary to take a little risk, Tina."

Spencer reminded Tina that the Carillion, when turned over to her mother, had been a small comfortable hotel—a stopover for salespeople and tourists heading west. "Your grandfather recommended we take Larry on. He knew we'd have to modernize if we expected to compete with the hotel chains moving in. I remember his exact words: 'Larry has a degree in Hotel Management. His ideas and suggestions will bring more tourists and salespeople to our hotel.' We took the risk and you know it worked for us. The Carillion is now rated among the finest in St. Louis. We've earned a five star rating and much of this is due to Larry's efforts."

"Larry's judgment has served us well, I know, but you're planning to mortgage the hotel as well as invest all your savings into something that will no longer be under family control. I worry about that. Have you discussed this with your attorney or accountant? They are our friends as well as consultants. You could count on them to be objective and unbiased in giving professional opinions."

"I've gone over everything with Larry. Believe me, Tina, we know what we're doing."

"I know Larry wants the best for us and it is our future as well that is at stake, but can you trust the people you'll be partners with, Daddy? Furthermore, do we really need to do this? We're comfortable in St. Louis. Why would you want to get involved with strangers in Chicago where we are outsiders? How does Mom feel about what you're doing? Is she ready for the headaches that could be part of the deal?"

"Larry is one of our family, Tina. He's the son we never had. Your mother is comfortable with the idea. Having witnessed Larry's ability and loyalty over the years, she agrees that we can depend on his judgment. To be honest we're both grateful that he hasn't wanted to move on to bigger challenges. Mother and I are not getting any younger you know. We've given our lives to the St. Louis Carillion, but there is another world out there and it would be nice to have the freedom to explore some of it while we're able."

"I understand, Daddy, but would you please run this past the professionals."

"Nothing is going to change, Tina. We will continue to operate our hotel, but will take advantage of the services and expertise that the Chicago legal and accounting staffs have available. Remember we're thinking about your future. You'll need an income after you and Larry are married. The Chicago hotels will be very lucrative in time. Trust me, the Chicago purchase will be advantageous to us all."

"It sounds like you've made up your mind and nothing I say will change it."

"Even if we did not expand into other territories, Tina, I've come to realize that the St. Louis Carillion is no longer the Mom and Pop enterprise it once was. Yes, our attorney and accounting friends have served us well in the past, but this is more than anything they can handle. Branching out into Chicago, they would have to be versed in Illinois law. The people we'll be working with live and are established in Chicago. They know the ropes. It's a good deal, Tina. I can't risk losing out by procrastinating."

"You're talking about making a drastic change and I can't help feeling uneasy. I like things the way they are, Daddy."

Knowing he had not won over his daughter, Spencer added, "It was my intention not to tell you until your return, Tina, but I've been seeing a doctor. Preliminary tests indicate that I need heart surgery."

"Heart surgery? When did this happen? Why didn't you tell me?"

"Now don't get excited, Tina. I'm only mentioning it now so that you understand why I'm anxious to go forward. Knowing experienced attorneys and accountants are working with Larry while I'm laid up will be beneficial and less stressful for me."

"Why did you let me go to South Africa knowing you were having problems with your health, Daddy? There's no way I would have left had I known. I'm sure everything will work out all right, but I want to be with you and will catch the next flight home."

"No Tina! Don't spoil your vacation. I'm okay with whatever happens. There are more tests scheduled which may change the doctor's diagnosis."

"The diagnosis doesn't matter. I couldn't stay here another minute knowing you're in trouble. I'll call Mom as soon as I know the flight number and time of arrival."

Tina arrived in St. Louis two days later. Her mother and father tried to minimize their concern, but Spencer was scheduled to go into the hospital the following day for further tests. While Spencer's physical problems were uppermost in Tina's mind, she was disappointed that Larry was not in St. Louis to welcome her home. As usual, he was out of town.

When her mother picked Tina up at the airport, she couldn't help but complain. "Larry's never where I am anymore. It's almost as though he plans it that way. We're supposed to be getting engaged in a few months. One would think he'd want to be with me once in a while."

"Larry has a great deal on his mind these days, Tina. He's running around Chicago on our behalf. From what I understand, there are meetings every day. We're grateful that Larry is accepting all this responsibility while your father is going through a rough time."

"Is Larry angry that I went to South Africa with Mara? You know I couldn't break my promise to her. Even if I had spent the summer in St. Louis, there's no guaranty Larry would have been here with me."

"He's not angry, Tina. He wanted you to go and have a good time."

"Before you know it, I'll be back at school. Vermont is a long way off and I won't be coming home again until the holidays in December. I wanted so much to see him."

"Things happen, Tina. Right now Larry has to be in Chicago. You can't believe what it takes to put something like this deal together. It's especially difficult when most of the people involved are out of state."

"Personally I don't think you and Daddy need the headaches, but if it's what you want, there's no sense in my arguing any longer."

Trying her best to reassure Tina, Terry spoke about the importance of having two hotels in Chicago. There would be a Carillion East and a Carillion West. "It's exciting to think we're building on the humble beginnings of your grandfather's St. Louis Carillion. True, we'll be in partnership with the former owners for a while, but your father plans to buy them out in a year or two."

"You don't think it's risky, Mother?"

"The St. Louis Carillion is ours. It will always be our home, Tina. We are not giving up ownership. When you and Larry get married, you'll be managing the Chicago hotels. When we're ready to retire, all the properties will belong to you both. Your job now is to finish school—and be a little patient."

"I'm trying, Mom, but I miss Larry and need him to reassure me. It's been so long since we were together."

"It's your father who needs him right now."

"I know, but Larry could at least call."

"He will, Tina. Your father is relying on your fiancée to handle a major acquisition and you should be proud that Larry is so capable."

Tina really wanted to have a face to face talk with Larry. She had so many questions that needed answering. Telephone calls between them were frustrating because Larry always seemed to cut her short. "I have to go, Tina. I'm expected at a meeting or I have another call." There was always some excuse to cut her off in the middle of a conversation—especially when her questions became personal.

Larry did call a few days later. "I'll be back in St. Louis before you leave for the fall semester," Larry promised. "Then we can talk. By the way, I've missed you, Baby."

"Before you hang up, what's going on Larry? Tell me what's happening with those Chicago hotels."

"Nothing for you to worry about, little one. It's grown up business. I promise you and I will have better things to talk about when we do get together."

Setting aside her worries about the hotels, Tina turned her attention back to her father and the impending surgery. Tests proved that Spencer would need a triple by-pass. The procedure was scheduled for Monday of the coming week.

Over the next several days the family suffered the agony of suspense, but to everyone's relief, Spencer came through the surgery with little complications. By the time Tina was due to leave for the fall semester, she felt secure in the knowledge that all was going well. Eager to reunite with Mara and catch up with all the happenings of her school friends, Tina put her concerns about Larry and the hotels aside.

Larry never made it to St. Louis before Tina had to leave for school. He did, when he phoned, promise to visit her soon. Meanwhile, aware that she had a great deal to learn about surviving in an age of fierce competition, Tina decided to pursue studies that would help her fit into the family hotel business. She would prepare herself to be a helpmate to Larry just as her mother was to her father and her grandmother had been to her grandfather. Optimistically she said to Mara, "Larry and I will get married, find success in all we do and then live happily ever after."

Their Junior year began and the two carefree friends were happy to be together again.

2

To understand the Cappo family and Larry, as well as the events that lead to Tina's arrival in London, it is necessary to go back in time.

Tina was the only child of Spencer and Theresa Cappo. They lived in the penthouse of the hotel that had been in the family for many years. It was convenient. Tina had known no other home. The Hotel Carillion was centrally located, very near the St. Louis Arch—known as the Gateway to the West. A few feet and one could be on the promenade walking beside the Mississippi. A tram to the top of the arch would provide a spectacular view of the city and the riverboats waiting for cruisers and gamblers.

The Hotel's conference rooms and ballrooms were popular and booked well in advance for conventions, weddings, parties and special occasions. The Carillion was committed to giving superior service and had an excellent reputation. Rooms and suites were tastefully furnished. In addition to offering a complete menu of gourmet foods that were prepared under the direction of a Parisian chef, there was celebrity entertainment and dancing every Thursday through Sunday night.

The floor below the penthouse was sectioned into apartments for long-term residents who were accustomed to seeing Tina just about anywhere. Most felt sorry for the lonely little girl. Quiet and polite, Tina was liked by all. One of Tina's favorite residents was an elderly lady who had a small dog—a beautiful orange Pomeranian.

"May I take Tippy out for a walk, Mrs. Bonte?"

"Tippy would love that, Tina. When you get back you must join me for some cookies and milk. I like hearing you talk about your teachers and friends."

"And I like visiting you."

"It must be lonely for you, Tina. I notice you never bring friends into the hotel. Is it because they live too far away?'

"My books are my friends, Mrs. Bonte."

"I have noticed that you always carry a book under your arm. Do you have other hobbies or special interests?"

"I take piano lessons and play the violin in the school orchestra. That keeps me pretty busy. The orchestra is required to be at all school assemblies and special events. Right now we're practicing to play for a high school production of 'Pirates of Penzance'. Rehearsals are going great. The performances are scheduled for May 28 and 29. I can get a ticket for you if you'd like to come."

"I'd love to see that play, and remember it from when I was a little girl in England, but you know I hardly ever leave this apartment. I can't unless someone helps me. The show needs a soprano with a good voice. You must tell me what you think when you come back from walking Tippy."

Tina loved animals but had none of her own. Her parents felt it would set a bad precedent. Pets in the hotel were not to be encouraged even though they had made an exception in the case of Mrs. Bonte who was confined to the apartment for reasons of poor health. Mrs. Bonte had been a tenant in the hotel for years. She'd moved in shortly before Tina was born and had seen her grow from a pretty baby into a lovely young lady.

Studying her, Mrs. Bonte recalled that she had often combed and French braided Tina's silky black hair. It was very long now—almost long enough to sit on. Today it was pulled back into a ponytail.

What a beauty she is, Mrs. Bonte thought. That hair, those curly black eyelashes surrounding big blue eyes, and she is so petite—she'll be a heart breaker some day.

Tina was accustomed to the hustle and bustle of the busy hotel. People were always coming or going. All were cheerfully catered to by the family and staff. To them, every wish was a command. While often seen wandering about in the hotel, Tina learned early that she must be quiet as a mouse. She could be seen, but not heard.

It was Tina's habit to carry a book wherever she went. Her parents were always busy leaving her to fend for herself. Guests would often find her eating alone in the elegant dining room. The book was her security blanket. Reading enabled her to forget that she was alone. It also prevented her from "people watching," a favorite occupation.

"It isn't polite to stare at people," Terry reprimanded when observing her daughter's reaction to some of the more bizarre outfits or behavior of their guests.

Tina loved to read. Her favorite books were those that took her on adventures in foreign lands. She would quickly lose herself in the exciting places with the strange names.

"I read about a place in Spain called Pamploma, Daddy. Did you know that people come from all over the world to race angry bulls through the streets of this small town? Many are run down or gored by the animals and end up in the hospital with bad injuries. Some people have even died."

"Pretty stupid, in my opinion," answered Spencer, "but it is a very popular festival that takes place in July. Hundreds of people come from everywhere to take part in the wild game of trying to outwit the bulls. I understand there's a 900-yard run from the corral to the arena."

Another city that fascinated Tina was Istanbul, Turkey. Having seen pictures, Tina asked her father if he'd ever been there.

"Yes, Tina I have. It's a fascinating place. Remember that video we saw recently featuring the Topkapi Museum?"

"The one where the thief lowered himself from the ceiling to steal the jeweled dagger? How could I forget? I was so afraid they'd catch him."

"Did you know that the museum was originally a place where rich sultans kept their harems?"

"Were they slaves?" Not waiting for an answer Tina began to talk about the Bazaar in Istanbul. "There are rows and rows of shops selling jewelry. It would take me a hundred years to decide what to buy with so much to choose from, but I'd like to go there some day."

"I'm sure you will," replied Spencer, impressed that his young daughter was already interested in a world so far removed.

"Look, Daddy, at these pictures of the beautiful Mosques. The book says that someone goes up in those tall minarets several times each day calling the men to pray. Once they are inside, the men roll out prayer rugs and kneel facing Mecca. Did you know that women aren't allowed to worship in the mosques and that men have to bathe their feet leaving their shoes outside? Look at them all lined up. I wonder how they can find the right shoes when leaving to go home."

Books were Tina's answer to loneliness and boredom. While her classmates lived in communities where there were children to play with, she had to make do with what was available in the hotel. Imagination had to be her best friend.

When Tina turned fourteen, Spencer and Terry found they had a little more freedom allowing them to plan short vacations. They had hired Larry Hermano two years before and felt secure in leaving the responsibility of running the Hotel to him.

They visited the National Parks—Grand Canyon, Yellowstone, Bryce, Zion, Yosemite were all on the family's "must see" list. For Tina, Yellowstone National Park was the most exciting. There was the Geyser Basin with Old Faithful, the Grand Canyon of Yellowstone, the magnificent waterfalls and, at the extreme northern end, Mammoth Hot Springs which was described as a cave that was inside-out.

Larry was always willing to take on the responsibility of running the hotel in the family's absence. In fact he encouraged them to take time off whenever Tina was on school vacation. The Cappo family was pleased that their protege was dependable and ambitious.

Larry was very personable. He had a smile and kind word for all including the staff. One couldn't help but like him.

"He's the best person I've ever worked for?" said the chambermaid after he had complimented and then teased her by asking if she had a sister.

Mary, who worked in the kitchen and didn't want the chambermaid to think she was special added, "He's nice to everyone." The bellboy agreed.

Larry's good looks were an asset when it came to pleasing the lady guests. Most turned their heads when they noticed Larry in the lobby and made some excuse to attract his attention.

"Good evening, Madam. Is there something I can do for you? You have dinner reservations? There's a cab waiting out front. Have a good evening." Or you might find him giving directions to someone new in town. "Let me show you," he'd say drawing lines on a map. Larry couldn't do enough for guests of the hotel and they appreciated the service.

Larry Hermano was over six feet tall. While not into contact sports, he kept himself in top physical condition by visiting the hotel gym three or four days a week. He looked really sharp in exercise wear and knew it made an impression on anyone who shared the facilities. A good swimmer, he was often found in or around the hotel pool sharing pleasantries with guests.

"I was the baby in the family," Larry confessed one day when speaking to Spencer. "There are twelve years between me and the next youngest—a sister. There were seven children. By the time I came along, most of my brothers and sisters were on their own. They all work very hard. One of my sisters is a file clerk, a brother repairs cars, another works for the Sanitation Department. My youngest brother, Joseph, is a mailman. There are a dozen nieces and nephews. In spite of all the hours they work, there is never enough money. I was a good student and wanted to do more with my life."

It was rare that Larry spoke of his family. Spencer listened attentively as he continued, "My family was proud of me and supported my ambition. They made it possible for me to attend college. I love my family. They are good people. I owe what I am and what I may become, to them. Thanks to my family and the chance you've given me, I'm going to become somebody."

Tina, just as everyone else, liked Larry. Their paths often crossed during the day. Sometimes he took time out and joined her for a snack or a swim in the hotel pool. He'd tease her on occasion, but mostly would compliment her on how she looked. If the truth be known, Tina had a schoolgirl crush on Larry even though he was ten years her senior.

"Hi, Doll," he'd say as they passed in the lobby or met in the elevator. "That's a really sharp outfit you're wearing. You look like a movie star."

At times Larry would invite Tina for ice cream or a soda and she'd tell him about her dreams for the future. She'd hate it when they were interrupted. "Got to go, little girl. Duty calls," he'd say adding, "See you later, alligator." Tina's response as he ran off was always the same—"After a while crocodile." Then she would sadly return to her lonely world.

Tina was not particularly interested in boys. Attending an all girls school, she had little occasion to meet or interact with the opposite sex. The only men in her life were Spencer and Larry. Although Larry had more important people to fuss over, he enjoyed teasing the very young and innocent daughter of his employer. Sitting

15

across from her as they had diet cokes, he owned that Tina was growing up and that she was very pretty. With her fair coloring, she would never need makeup. Her dark hair and beautiful eyes would turn heads wherever she went.

Interrupting his thought, one of the entertainers stopped at the table to say "hello." When she left, Larry remarked, "One day you'll be coming in here made up and dressed to kill just like her, Tina. You won't have time for me then because men will be falling all over themselves to be near you."

"I will never look like that," Tina replied. "Stage people are always acting—long after the show is over."

Although they couldn't do much about it, Tina's parents understood that their daughter was lonely and in need of friends. In another year she would be looking into colleges which would surely help Tina emerge from her cocoon and become the lovely butterfly they knew was underneath.

"I'd like to have our daughter working with us in the hotel after graduating from college," said Terry. "After all, It will belong to her some day."

"She should be taking courses in Hotel Management, Terry, but it's wrong for us to pressure her. Kids can be stubborn and often resist the advice of their parents."

"While it's been our dream, Spencer, we must remember that Tina has lived her whole life in this hotel. We can't blame her for wanting to spread her wings. If we leave it to her, she might eventually make the decision we hope for on her own."

Spencer had, on several occasions, tried to feel Tina out about her preferences as to school location and courses of study. Her grades were excellent. Being accepted into a college of her choice would not be a problem.

The time for decision was getting closer when Spencer asked, "Have you given any thought about where you'd like to attend college, Tina?"

"Not yet," she answered. "But there's still plenty of time."

"Do you know what studies you'd like to pursue? Schools have specialties you know. Some might be better than others if you have a particular interest in mind. This last year in high school will go quickly. It won't be long and you'll be sending out applications. Have you asked the advice of your guidance counselor?"

"I have to set up an appointment, but right now the only thing I'm sure of is that I don't want to get lost on a gigantic campus. I'd rather be a big fish in a little pond. As to what I want to do with the rest of my life, I haven't a clue. I want to make friends, join a sorority and have fun. I want to learn and make you proud of me. That's all I will commit to as of now."

In truth Tina just wanted to escape the surroundings that had kept her sheltered and naive. She had a great deal of growing up and living to do before making decisions about the future. It was why she was considering distant colleges, She wanted a school that would allow her to explore options.

The college Tina ultimately chose was one in Vermont. The brochure promised everything she thought would be to her liking. There would be only about three thousand students on campus. Deciding on a major would not be required until her Sophomore year.

Tina graduated from high school that June. She was the class Salutatorian. As a reward, and aware of Tina's interest in foreign travel, Spencer and Terry gave her a European vacation.

"Your mother will go with you. The tour we have chosen is similar to 'Around the World in 80 Days." It's an overview of many countries. The difference is you'll have only thirty days. You and your mother had better pack roller-skates."

They went to England, France, Belgium, Germany, Italy and Spain. "Would you believe it, Mom? Like in the movie, we'll be in Belgium on Tuesday."

While Spencer's family vacationed in Europe, he and Larry had some serious man-to-man discussions. "You know, Larry, it's always been my ambition to buy a second hotel. What do you think of the idea?"

Larry had been looking for new challenges for a long time. He felt it was time that his dreams were brought to fruition. At last, Spencer was opening the door.

"I think it would be great if you bought another hotel Spencer. You might want to consider Chicago, however. With the big chains moving here, the hotel situation in St. Louis is pretty well saturated. Imagine a St. Louis Carillion and another Carillion in Chicago. I'm sure the reputation we already have would assure success."

The excitement in Larry's face and voice was contagious. "Who knows, maybe in time, there could even be a third Carillion somewhere," was Spencer's response. "Perhaps you should start looking around, Larry. You've been with us long enough to know what I want and can evaluate properties. I'll hold the fort here. If you find anything interesting, I can check it out when our wanderers return from Europe."

That's all the encouragement Larry needed. He left for Chicago a few days later and came back with descriptions of properties that were available. One or two of these looked very promising. Spencer could hardly wait for Terry and Tina's return to get their opinions.

Tina and her mother had a wonderful time together. They shared experiences never to be forgotten. It was truly a whirl-wind trip ending too soon, but Tina promised herself to revisit many of the countries more leisurely in the future. She could not have guessed the future would become the present only two years later.

On their arrival back in the States, Tina and Terry were anxious to share their experiences with Spencer. He too was eager to tell his wife and daughter about the talks he'd had with Larry.

"Thanks Dad for a wonderful trip. I kept a log so I wouldn't forget anything."

"Before you start, let me tell you what's been happening here."

"Okay, you go first!," said Terry. "Once Tina gets going, you won't have a prayer."

"Larry and I were talking one day and I mentioned that I'd like to buy another hotel. He thought it was a great idea. It appears he's been getting restless and looking for more responsibility."

"I know we've occasionally thought about it, but are you telling me that you're serious, Spencer?"

"Yes I am, Terry. If we're ever going to do it, now is the time. Larry has located some properties in Chicago that he feels have potential. As soon as we get Tina settled in college, I plan to check them out."

"I can't believe you want to take on more work, dear. It's so nice to finally have a little leisure time and I had hoped you and I could get away once in a while. With Tina in school we could have that second honeymoon. As I recall, we never had the first one."

Vacations just for the two of them would be nice but, being practical people, there was the matter of money. The next four years—more if Tina went on for a master's degree—would mean tuition, room and board, travel and expenses for incidentals. This would probably be followed by a wedding. There was also Larry's restlessness to contend with. The Cappos might lose him to something more challenging if Spencer did nothing.

Terry knew of her husband's dreams and understood, but would have preferred to put the matter of a second hotel on a back burner for the time being. Her priority at the moment was to help Tina get ready for college. The last two weeks of summer would go quickly and there was much to do. Tina would need a wardrobe suitable for Vermont winters. In addition she'd have to shop for bedding, towels and toiletries.

Tina planned, over the weekend, to call Mara Konigswahl, her assigned roommate, about color schemes. She expected to take her stereo, computer, television and VCR. It was unlikely that Mara would bring such items since she was coming from Capetown, South Africa.

"We'll practically be setting up an apartment," Tina said "and I want everything to be perfect."

"I know how exciting this must be for you Tina. It will be the first time you're away from us. We will miss having you around, but are happy for you. You'll have a great time."

"I can't wait, Mom, but will miss you too.

A little choked up, Terry continued, "Dad told me to set up a checking account for you. You will need to buy books and incidentals. For emergencies, you should also apply for a credit card, but be careful that you don't put us in the poorhouse."

"Very funny, Mom. I'll try hard not to."

Tina was eager to meet her roommate. They had talked briefly on the phone and Tina had found her to be cheerful and animated, but there were many questions left to be answered. Would there be contrasts in their work habits? Was Mara serious about school or merely looking for a good time away from home? What did Mara look like? Was she pretty, short or tall, heavy or thin? Did she smoke or drink? Worse, was she into drugs? Most of all, could they become friends or would each go their separate ways finding they had nothing in common. Only time and living together would tell.

3

The school year was about to begin. It was moving day. Not an inch of space remained in the family car as Tina left home for college. Other arrangements could have been made but Spencer and Terry insisted on driving her to Vermont. If an excuse was needed, they wanted to help their only child settle in. Truthfully, they would miss Tina and knew the distance would prevent frequent trips home. It was only natural that their daughter would slowly grow away from them as new experiences were encountered. While in their hearts they understood the change would be good for Tina, it was difficult letting go knowing their lives would never be the same.

On the plus side, with Tina settled, Spencer could again concentrate on his ambition—that of building a hotel empire. It was no secret that Larry was becoming frustrated with Spencer's vacillating. Only last week they had had an argument. "You send me out to look for opportunities, Spence. I come back with good properties to look at, but that's where it ends. I'm spinning my wheels."

"It's my hotel and my life savings that are at risk, Larry. I don't want to rush into a commitment without giving it considerable thought. You can't blame me for that. After we get Tina settled, I'll get serious. I promise then to give your suggestions my undivided attention."

The drive to Vermont was long requiring two overnight stays. On the morning of the third day they reached St. James College.

"It's just like the picture in the brochure. Don't you love the way the ivy grows up the brick walls, Mom?"

"Yes, Tina, I've always been partial to the Victorian look. It makes me feel comfortable, cozy and warm."

"Looks like everyone is moving in at the same time," was Spencer's comment as he witnessed the commotion. "The place is a madhouse."

When entering the Administration Building, they could see that the interior had recently been redecorated. Fashionable color tones prevailed. Ample draperies with pleated valances were of mauve, turquoise and green printed chintz. Deep plush turquoise carpeting covered the floors and the walls had been done in a pale mauve burlap. Everything had been carefully coordinated. In many ways it reminded Tina of their own Hotel Carillion which had recently gone through a similar facelift. The Cappo family felt comfortable from the moment they entered the building and again when they reached Cedar Hall dormitory, where Tina would spend the next four years.

Spencer, Terry and Tina met, and immediately became enchanted with Mara. Speaking with an accent, Tina's roommate professed that she was an "Afrikaner." She explained that they were Dutch settlers who had come to South Africa years before. "Africaners," she said, were largely responsible for the country's growth.

"My parents have lived in South Africa since they were married." I was born there as were my brothers and sisters. There were two sisters before me. After ten years, Mum decided it was too quiet in the house. She missed the diapers and formulas and convinced my Dad to try for a boy. Surprise! Nine months later there were triplets—three boys. Good thing Dad is part owner of a diamond mine."

Herself an only child, Tina had difficulty visualizing so many children under one roof. "Guess you were never lonely or bored," she said, sighing.

"Bored? What's that? Every day in our house is like being at a three-ring circus."

Although English was Mara's native language, the accent was new to the ears of the Cappo family. They would have encouraged her to talk all day, but discovered she was also a good listener and able to draw people out. Sensing that Tina was shy and reserved, she jokingly said, "Look at us, Tina. We're like Mutt and Jeff. I'm muscular and big while you're small boned and tiny."

Tina laughed. It was true. Terry, who was helping to organize her daughter's belongings, said, "I'd say you are tall and well endowed, Mara. As for you, Tina, you're petite."

"Mara's right, Mom. We're different as night and day. Her eyes are almost black while mine are light blue. Mara's hair is short and so blonde it looks like flax. Mine is long and dark as pitch. I wonder about the computer that matched us up."

"One that needs re-programming, but we'll show them, Tina. I know we'll be a good team."

Chuckling, Terry added, "You could always bill yourselves as 'the odd couple'" The hearty laughing brought curious passers by into the room. "What's so funny?" they asked as introductions were made. Within five minutes it was as though all the dorm residents had been friends forever. Terry was satisfied that her daughter would be happy at St. James College.

When Spencer came into the room hoping to pry his wife loose—they were facing a long trip home—he said something about adopting Mara. "We'd like you to think of us as your American family. You'd be our second daughter."

"I'd like that very much, Mr. Spencer. Having a family while so far from home would mean a great deal to me."

As they said their good-byes, it was clear to all that Mara needed the warmth of Tina's parents as much as Tina needed a new and outgoing friend.

It had been a long day. The girls prepared for bed, but before dousing the lights, talked a little about their plans for the future. Tina was undecided, but Mara had a pretty good idea of the studies she wanted to pursue. "I've always been interested in dirt and want to be an archeologist," she said.

This was a far cry from anything Tina could imagine herself being interested in. She thought the pyramids of Egypt were a sight to behold, but digging in the hot sun hoping to find another crypt like that of King Tut—one that had not been looted—was something else. Tina had no clue about a career choice. For her this was an opportunity to live and explore. Decisions about the rest of her life could wait. "In the end I'll probably wind up like my parents in the hotel business," she confessed, "but for now I need space to find myself."

Both Tina and Mara agreed that they'd be changing their minds many times before committing themselves to life decisions. They could not know, that in the end, fate would be making many decisions for them. As the lights were turned off, the girls made a vow. "No matter what happens to us, we'll always be there for each other." A strong bond had been established. It was a bond that would see them through the days and years to follow.

The official school year started on Monday. The two friends were quickly absorbed in classes, homework and research. It proved to be very different from high school. The college library became a second home as course requirements were very demanding. On rare occasions they would get together with classmates to play cards, but the college had high standards and most of their group took assignments seriously.

Living in the dormitory, they quickly learned to accept minimal privacy. Friends shared not only dorm rooms, but bathroom facilities, clothing, confidences and just about everything not nailed down. Their classmates and dormitory occupants, having come from all corners of the United States as well as abroad, had different likes and priorities, but they were all compatible and respectful of each other. Many became good friends.

Saturday nights could be counted on for "letting loose." Ascott was the typical small college town. On Main Street there was a movie house featuring second or third run films and a few bars. A favorite hangout was the one that had a juke box and small area for dancing. Sometimes there would be too much beer consumed, but Tina and Mara were underage and drank only diet soda. They did not need alcohol to have a good time. Being with young people was enough stimulation.

On a night out, Mara could be counted on as the life of the party. With Tina in tow, they were always surrounded by friends. They were very popular. Mara was loved for her innovative ideas for having fun and Tina for her loyalty, kindness and willingness to help anyone at any time. While jokes were made about the Mutt and Jeff look-alikes, it was all in good spirit. The girls had no problem laughing at themselves. Mara and Tina preferred being in a group when relaxing from their studies. They had never before had the opportunity to interact with young people and thoroughly enjoyed the college camaraderie.

There were many good memories from that first year at St. James College. Tina and Mara pledged to the same sorority, Delta Lambda Nu. The chapter was dedicated to helping single parent children who lived in the area. Whenever time allowed, they would take the children on outings, or to the library where they would spend hours reading to and with them. It was very rewarding to witness their enthusiasm and to know they were doing something to help. Both Mara and Tina were idolized by the children. Little girls attempted to imitate their every move while boys used every trick in the book to get special attention.

When calling home, it was evident that Tina was growing up. "Beer's bitter but not half bad if you have it with pizza," she said one day to her mother who almost had a fit. "Relax, Mom, I'm kidding. They won't serve us anything but coke and you know Mara and I don't need alcohol to have a good time."

Relieved, Terry asked? "Will you be coming home for Thanksgiving?"

"We only get four days off, Mom. I don't think we'd better. The flight home for such a short time wouldn't warrant the expense and there's a paper I have to work on. I'll be busy until Christmas recess at which time Mara and I will be coming home. It will be different not being there on turkey day. I'll miss you and Daddy, but we'll find something to do. Mara will keep me company. Don't worry. We'll be fine."

"The holiday won't be the same without you, Tina, but I think you're right. As for Dad and me, we're happy that you and Mara are adjusting so well to being away."

Learning that the girls would not be going to St. Louis for the Thanksgiving weekend, Alex Turner, a classmate, invited them to his parents' farm. The farm was but an hour's drive from the college and lonely classmates were always welcome in the home of John and Jesse Turner.

"My brother, Stanley, wouldn't miss a holiday and will be there too," said Alex. "He always brought his friends home for the holidays when at St. James. My parents became accustomed to sharing the holidays with young people who were temporary orphans. They wouldn't know what to do if the guest rooms weren't occupied by our friends."

"We'd love to come," said both girls simultaneously.

"I'm so glad you agreed to go," said Mara to Tina when they were back in the dorm. "In case you haven't noticed, I think Alex is really nice and he seems to like me too. Wouldn't it be great if you and his brother hit it off?"

"Stop right now, Mara! You're always trying to set me up with someone. You know my heart belongs to Larry even though he doesn't seem to know I'm alive."

Stanley Turner was an engineer who lived and worked in Boston. To say he was impressed with his brother's new friends would be an understatement. It was evident that Alex had more than a platonic interest in Mara and that was fine with Stanley whose eyes were immediately focused on Tina. From the moment she entered the room something happened. Could this be the soulmate he'd been promised?

After the introductions, the girls were escorted to the cozy guest room on the second floor. It was a large room with a fireplace that had been lit to take out the chill.

There were two double beds on which were white chenille spreads and many fluffy pillows. Draperies had been drawn back to let in the sunshine. There were family pictures, which the girls planned to study at their leisure, everywhere. Leaving the friends to settle in, Alex and Stan asked them to come to the family room for a tour of the house when ready.

They were in a big, old farmhouse that had been modernized. All the rooms were spacious and welcoming. Mara and Tina felt right at home. Ending in the kitchen, they went to work helping with the food preparation. There was a great deal of clowning around, but with many hands, the last minute chores were completed. While waiting for the turkey to come out of the oven, they conversed over drinks and snacks.

The Turners made it possible for Tina and Mara to be part of a family on this their first holiday away from home. They really appreciated the home-cooked Thanksgiving dinner. After eating and participating in the cleanup, the two couples went for a walk. Tina and Mara were introduced to the farm animals. Having been assured that the animals were pets and not destined for the table, the girls agreed life on a farm could be fun.

Alex and Stan kept the girls on the move every minute of the weekend. It had snowed, which was a real treat for Mara. A good part of Friday and Saturday was spent outdoors. The girls were taken out on snowmobiles and also did some cross-country skiing.

"Let's have a snowball fight," said Stanley as he picked up a handful of snow and aimed it at his brother. Winter activities were new to Mara having come from a warmer climate, but all enthusiastically got into the spirit when snowballs found their marks. The grand finale came with the construction of a snowman. Dressing him in whatever clothing they could spare, he was quite a sight. Down to their sweat shirts, they were cold and anxious to get indoors where a blazing fireplace waited. Cups of hot chocolate were offered and appreciated.

It was a very special weekend and over too soon. Tina would have to work double time on her term paper to make up for time lost, but it was worth it. As Alex prepared to drive the girls back to school, Stanley kissed Tina's cheek and asked for her address and phone number.

"I'd like to spend a weekend at the college—that is if you're free and I can get away from my job. It's my alma mater and will bring back memories. I'm sure Alex would let me bunk with him."

"That would be nice, Stanley. I hope you can work it out." Although Larry was always uppermost in her thoughts, Tina was pleased that Stan would want to keep in touch. He was kind and thoughtful and certainly fun to be with. They'd had a great time together. While a midget next to his six foot height, they made a striking couple and she had felt protected in his presence.

"Alex told me Stan has a great future in the company he's working for. In addition, he's good looking and comes from a warm, loving family. What's not to like?" asked Mara after they left the Turner home.

Tina had to agree, but there was Larry Hermano— Larry, who probably hadn't even noticed that she was missing from the hotel.

4

Stan visited, called and sent cards. Tina liked the attention, but thought of him only as a good friend. It was Larry who was in her dreams. Mara, on the other hand, had no doubts about Alex.

"He's the man I intend to marry some day," she confided.

"What makes you so sure, Mara? How do you know Alex is Mr. Right?'

Although sheltered all her life, Tina had learned about birds and bees, but remained puzzled when listening to her friends who seemed to be falling in love every other minute. "How do you know when it's real and not just infatuation?" she'd ask. The best explanation she could get was that there would be a brass band and fireworks. Was there such a thing as one-sided fireworks? Certainly Larry was barely aware of her existence.

"How did you know Alex was the right man for you, Mara?"

"I knew from the moment we met. Alex was across the room and making his way toward me. As we looked at each other, there was magic. Right then and there I'd have followed him to the ends of the earth. Good thing he didn't ask since neither of us will be going anywhere but school for a while."

Tina welcomed his attention, but knew she didn't feel sparks when with Stanley. Understanding her need to experiment with a new-found freedom, Stanley was content to be patient.

Tina and Mara went to St. Louis for the Christmas holidays. Spencer was a bit under the weather, but attributed his ailments to indigestion resulting from stress. "As you know, Tina, I've had Larry looking for hotel properties to invest in. He's eager and anxious for me to make a move. I know he wants and needs more responsibility and that he is coming up with possibilities, but the final decision rests on my shoulders. While it's something I've always wanted to do, there's a great deal to think about. The thinking keeps me awake at night. As a result I'm always tired."

"It's not like you to be so tired, Daddy. You should see a doctor."

"Not necessary! All I need is sleep and I'll be good as new. Maybe I'm getting old."

"You're not old and it won't hurt to get a checkup."

"If it makes you feel better, Tina, I've asked Larry to put his search on hold for a while. He's back helping me with the work around here."

"Good, but I imagine he's disappointed."

"He is, but there's no rush about buying another hotel. The word is out that we're looking and the right thing will come along eventually."

Although busy with hotel matters, Larry made it a point to be extra nice to Tina and Mara while home on Christmas break. Believing at first that Mara was the cause, Tina was surprised to discover that it was she who had Larry's attention. No matter where she went, Larry was in front of her, smiling. It was as though he was aware of her as an adult for the first time.

"I believe he's flirting with me," she said to Mara.

"Sure looks like it to me, Tina. Play your cards right, and who knows what might develop. Your dreams may come true after all."

In her thoughts, Tina compared Larry to Stanley. She had to admit that Larry was smooth. He was a charmer often performing for the benefit of an audience. While moody and even ruthless with suppliers at times, he was worldly and street smart. Stanley, on the other hand, was an up-front kind of guy. What you saw was what you got. He was dependable and predictable and held Tina on a pedestal. In short, Stanley was a lovable, loyal teddy bear, while Larry was exciting. What young girl doesn't like excitement?

Larry asked many questions about school. Was she seeing any boys? "You must be careful, Tina. College guys are always out for a good time. I know that because I've been there. They prey on innocent young girls. You need someone who will look after you—someone who is mature."

Was Larry hinting that he might have some plans for her? She was flattered and what young girl wouldn't be at the prospect of having such a handsome "older man" as a suitor—especially one she had adored since childhood. Thoughts of Larry brought tingles up and down her spine. Was that what the girls meant by brass bands and fireworks? Yes, Tina was sure it was love she felt.

33

Hopefully Larry was starting to get the same feelings for her.

Their winter break ended and the girls were back at school. Stanley and Tina continued corresponding and there were frequent phone calls, but they hadn't seen each other in quite a while. Soon would be the Easter recess. There was another invitation to the Turner farm. Stan could only get away for the weekend, but the girls accepted and enjoyed every minute of their stay. They'd worked hard and were ready for a break.

Unlike Alex and Mara, who were head over heels in love and already making wedding plans, Tina and Stanley remained "just friends." Stan would have liked to be further into a relationship, but instinctively knew that Tina was not ready for anything serious at this time. He was prepared to wait.

The girls planned to spend their summer vacation with Tina's parents in St. Louis and the time was quickly approaching. "Can't wait to see your parents again, Tina, but I must confess that I'm getting homesick for my family."

"We'll visit them next year, Mara. I know that must seem like a long way off, but you know how quickly this year has gone."

Spencer was ailing that summer, but tried to hide it from everyone. There had been little further action regarding the purchase of hotel property. Since the last time the girls were in St. Louis, Larry had been asked to take over many of Spencer's duties leaving him little time for researching the market. On occasion he'd made recommendations to Spencer, but all were rejected on the basis of location, cost or some other reason. Nothing had turned Spencer on and Larry was fearful that his plans might go up in smoke. It was almost a year since he and

Spencer had discussed the possibility of purchasing another hotel.

I'd better be ready with a backup plan, Larry thought. Perhaps I should think seriously about little Tina. Call it an insurance policy. Marrying her, I wouldn't have to worry about my future. With those thoughts in mind, when Tina and Mara arrived for their summer vacation, Larry went all out. Although busy with hotel business during the day, he often joined the girls at the pool. At night he escorted Tina to shows presented in the hotel. After the entertainment, they usually went dancing in the disco lounge. Tina was ecstatic. Her dreams, at last, appeared to be coming true.

Mara was always asked to accompany them and would quickly find someone with whom to dance, but it was watching her friend that made her happy. Tina's romantic notions about Larry were materializing at last. It was time, she thought, that Tina learned what it was like to be cherished and loved. When Alex came to visit in August, things were perfect. The couples double-dated and enjoyed being together.

Summer was drawing to an end. Tina would shortly be back at school beginning her sophomore year. She was a beautiful, young girl and Larry knew he should be concerned about competition. He'd learned that Alex had a brother who was very interested in Tina. Certainly there would be others. Although it wasn't in Larry's nature to be demonstrative, he knew Tina would want to see signs of affection and managed a few kisses. Her reaction proved to him that she expected more. If he was serious, Tina would want him to act like a lover.

"I guess he's afraid to scare me and that's why he's holding back," said Tina to her friend. "Don't forget he's older, Mara. He probably thinks I'm too young to have feelings and desires."

35

"Don't compare him to what you hear from girls dating guys who have hormones running amuck, Tina. Larry's too mature for kid stuff. He'll get bolder when he realizes you're grown up enough to think about marriage."

One night Larry arranged to be alone with Tina. Without preliminaries, he took her hand and slipped a ring on her left hand, fourth finger. It was a large ruby in a lovely gold setting. Larry called it a friendship ring. Tina was surprised and spontaneously wrapped her arms around his neck. Larry found himself kissing Tina's lips, but then pulled away. Tina could not hide her disappointment. "Why is it that you always put me on hold?" she asked.

"You're young and innocent, Tina. I like you that way. We have something special and it's tempting, when you seem so eager to experience life, to go further, but I don't want you to let anyone, not even me, talk you into having sex prematurely. That kind of love should be reserved for the marriage bed. I expect we will marry one day and hope that day will be your first love experience."

"I'm not a baby, you know," replied Tina with a deep sigh.

"Maybe not, but I think of you as my little doll and want to protect you even if it is from yourself."

"I'm not a doll and I won't break either."

Larry was a master at sweet talk when he wanted to be and Tina was pacified. Who said there had to be fireworks? It should be enough that Larry was hinting at marriage. Tina was in love and Mara was happy for her friend. Personally, Mara preferred someone like Alex who was affectionate, but she realized no two people were alike. Different strokes for different folks, she said to herself. Thinking of the future, the girls talked about the possibility of a double wedding after graduation.

Tina's parents were aware of what was happening. It was as though Larry had suddenly been awakened from a deep sleep and found their little girl. Where previously Larry had thought of her as a child always underfoot, Tina now appeared to be his queen. Spencer and Terry were delighted. They had wanted Tina in the business and had groomed Larry. Like a fairy tale, they could envision a happy ending. Hopefully their daughter and Larry would wait until after Tina's graduation to marry and that a suitable hotel could be purchased by then—one that Tina and Larry would manage.

About a week before school was to start again, Larry had a call from an agent in Memphis about a hotel that was up for sale. At Spencer's request, he left St. Louis to check it out returning just in time to see Tina off to the airport. Both girls found it difficult to leave the summer behind. They would not be back until Christmas recess. Tina had tears in her eyes as Larry took her aside and said, "We'll get engaged the Christmas of your senior year. Wait for me, my pet."

"Then can we get married in June?" asked Tina, drying her eyes. What could be better she thought—a graduation diploma and a marriage to my dream man. Tina couldn't wait to tell Mara. Like Mara, she was engaged to be engaged. She was going to marry the love of her life.

"Wouldn't it be great if we both got engaged at Christmas, Tina? Imagine the two of us showing up after the holidays with rings on our fingers. I feel sorry for Stanley though. He loves you very much and has been patiently waiting for encouragement from you. What will you say to him?"

He'll be hurt, but I'll tell him the truth. As you know, it's always been Larry for me. People fall in love and can't help with whom. It just happens. I'm so happy and hope Stan will understand and wish me well. I don't know about you, Mara, but I can't wait until we're seniors."

5

Having committed herself to a future with Larry, Tina decided it was time to get serious about a course of study. She discussed her options with the guidance counselor and began to fill her schedule with subjects relating to hotel management. Larry was pleased when she told him of her decision.

"Your father wants to buy another hotel—one you and I can manage when we get married, Tina. He'll be tied up with all the parties scheduled for the holidays and has asked me to research the field. I'm afraid I'll have to be out of town a great deal. As you know my excursion to Memphis turned out to be a wild goose chase. In truth, I'd prefer a Chicago location. Wouldn't you?"

"Dad relies on your judgment a great deal and I know he keeps you on the run. I keep asking him if he's feeling okay, but he brushes me off. He seems to be tired all the time. Is he hiding something from us?"

"You know your father. Sometimes he overdoes it. I'm always trying to get him to slow down. He likes to forget that I'm on board to look after the hotel and his interests."

Tina was worried about her father, but when she talked to her parents, they continued to assure her that their purpose in sending Larry out on his own was to give him experience. They felt he needed and wanted the responsibility. "I'm just a little tired," said Spencer when questioned. "It's not unusual to be tired at my age."

"Your father will soon be sixty-five, Tina. Most men want to retire at that age," Terry added, smiling at her husband.

Temporarily consoled, Tina planned on a trip to St. Louis during Easter week. She was anxious to see Larry before leaving with Mara for the promised summer in Capetown. While there had been several letters and a few phone calls since Christmas, Larry was not very good at small talk on the phone. He certainly didn't come across as being comfortable with expressing affection. Tina was frustrated and wanted to be reassured. She was sure he'd do better when they were face to face. She knew, from Larry's last letter, that he had something to tell her about a recent visitor to the hotel. Hopefully that would not be all Larry wanted to talk about. Tina was hungry for intimacy, if only in their conversations.

Not having seen each other in several months, Tina was sure Larry would be at the airport to greet her. She was disappointed when it was her father who came to pick her up. Not aware of Tina's letdown, Spencer, excitedly, told her about their visitor.

"You won't believe this, Tina, but we've been presented with a great opportunity. There was a guest staying at the hotel last week. He was on his way to Las Vegas. The first night he was here, Larry, socializing in the lounge as was his custom, introduced himself as the hotel manager. One word led to another and Larry learned that this man, Anthony Luppo, and a partner were owners of two hotels in Chicago. The hotels were about to be put on the market to be sold.

"It seems the hotels are run down and in need of renovating requiring an infusion of cash. Apparently Luppo and his partner, having other investments, are over extended at the present time. When told that I am the Carillion's owner and interested in buying another hotel, a suggestion was made that I become a partner. That way they wouldn't have to sell right away and I'd have a foot in the door. I plan to meet with these people and have a look. It could be the opportunity we've been looking for."

Trying to overcome her disappointment about Larry, Tina replied, "Buying outright or buying into is a big difference, Dad."

"Yes, Tina! Larry and I were up all night and agreed that we would buy them out in a couple of years thereby having the best of both worlds."

"But until you buy them out, who'd be in control—us or them?"

"Now don't get excited, Tina. Larry's in Chicago asking questions. He's seen the hotels and tells me their locations are perfect. There's one on each corner of the city center. We'll, of course, go over the books and have inspectors look at the buildings, but Larry is very enthused. There are many things still to be resolved, and it will take time, but it looks like the hotels are a find."

"You know how I feel, Dad. I don't like the idea. You have enough on your hands as it is. If you really are bent on expanding your holdings, I can only warn you to be careful. Don't rush into anything. There's a great deal at stake and a wrong move at this stage of your life isn't necessary."

After this discussion, Tina returned to Vermont for the last weeks of the school year. She had not seen Larry while at home and was very disappointed, but put her mind to her studies. In a few weeks she would be flying with Mara to South Africa. While she'd have preferred, under the circumstances, to spend the summer with Larry in St. Louis, Tina's promise to Mara was a commitment she would honor.

Larry did call twice before classes ended. While sharing her feelings on the telephone, Larry said, "I'll miss you too, Baby, but time will go quickly. They'll keep you busy over there and I'll be commuting back and forth to Chicago. There wouldn't be much time for us even if you were here."

Sighing as she hung up, Tina said, "It's time I stop feeling sorry for myself, Mara. Larry's busy and doing the best he can. We'd better concentrate on our trip to South Africa. We have our tickets, but I'm waiting for my visa. Are your papers all in order, Mara?"

"Yes, but I want to bring little gifts for everyone and have to think about what to pack."

"So do I. Will we need to get shots?" asked Tina shuddering. "I hate shots."

"I don't think so. It's only suggested if you venture into the hinterlands where there is danger of disease. Maybe we'd better check with the embassy though."

Mara's parents had not seen her in two years. They were excited and making plans for the girls' arrival. Although letters were written and photos exchanged—not to mention the long distance phone calls—nothing could take the place of a visit. They needed to hug their daughter and look into her smiling face as she told them about the man she loved and life in America.

Though premature, her parents would want to talk about the wedding that was to follow Mara's graduation. Most likely the couple would be married in Vermont. If that were the case, only Mara's parents would be attending. Other family members and friends would be disappointed, but Mara's mother promised a second celebration in the future. The newlyweds, she thought, might even be persuaded to include a stopover in Capetown when on their honeymoon.

It was about a week before they were to leave when Larry called from Chicago. "Things are moving along nicely," he said. "The two hotels I'm looking at need work, but are located in prime areas. I've met and talked with many people and they all agree that this is a once in a lifetime opportunity. Tony Luppo is offering a good deal. I've been looking over the books and discussing financial arrangements. Everything checks out, and I'm very excited, but your father keeps dragging his feet. I really don't know what more he expects or wants me to do. Maybe you could talk to him, Tina."

"He should go slowly with this, Larry. It means putting the hotel and my parent's life savings on the line? To be honest the whole idea scares me to death, and I wish you would all forget about it."

Tina was busy with exams the last few days of school and not giving much thought to what was going on at home. As far as she knew, Spencer was still looking and Larry was always out of town trying to find more convincing arguments to go ahead.

"The offer is very attractive, Tina," said Spencer when he called. "Getting involved with two more hotels would mean hard work in the beginning, but by the time you and Larry are ready to manage them, it should be a piece of cake."

Tina talked to her mother, who admitted to being apprehensive knowing they would be investing everything they had worked for, but was told that it had always been Spencer's dream to own another hotel. "I'm ready to stand by whatever decision your father makes," Terry said.

After listening to her parents, Tina could only assume that Terry and Spencer knew what they were doing—that they wouldn't be considering the proposition if there were doubts or problems with financing. Regardless, Tina was uneasy.

A last minute call to Larry did not relieve Tina's anxieties. When asked, Larry admitted that his work required a great deal of socializing in Chicago. He was vague when questioned, but talked at length about the important people he'd been meeting. He said nothing about their plans for the future.

Attempting to get Larry to say something of a personal nature, Tina changed the subject. "Guess what Mara and I did today," she said. Before Larry could answer, Tina continued. "We went window shopping. I know we're a little ahead of time, but we looked at engagement rings and wedding gowns." Larry did not take the hint. He didn't even make a joke about it. He's probably moody because I'm going away, she thought, but when asked if he would prefer that she stay home, Larry replied, "I'll be busy and out of town most of the time anyway, Tina. It's only six weeks."

"If only I could be with you, Larry. I really need to be held and reassured that you love me. We never talk—at least not about things that are important to me. All I know is that you're having a great time in Chicago. I'd cancel this South Africa trip in a minute if I could count on your being in St. Louis for a few days. I miss you Larry."

"I miss you too Baby, but you promised and must go with Mara. You'll be back before you know it. We'll have

43

a couple of weeks before school starts again to make up for lost time. Go now and enjoy yourself. Send me a postcard now and then. Don't forget that what I'm doing in Chicago is for our future."

Larry had hung up, but the phone remained in Tina's hand as she thought, Couldn't he at least have said, "I love you, Sweetheart?" She longed to hear some words of endearment, but conversation with Larry was always the same. He seemed to be uncomfortable with sentimentality—or could he be trying to tell her something?

Tina called her father that evening. "I feel great," he said answering his daughter's question. "I'm waiting for a call from Larry. He left for Chicago a while ago and is prepared to talk terms with Mr. Luppo and his partner. The hotels need renovating and redecorating and we're trying to work the figures into a bottom line cost to us. The present owners seem to be amenable to the idea of remaining as partners until we buy them out a year after contract signing."

"You're sure this is what you want, Daddy? A partnership?"

"We'll be mortgaging the Carillion and using our savings, Tina. A temporary partnership arrangement, under the circumstances, is probably the best for us all. We believe this is a 'win-win' situation. Opportunities like this don't come along every day."

"Please don't do anything until I get back from South Africa, Daddy. I'll have a little time before school starts and we can talk things over then—all four of us together."

"Nothing will happen while you're away, Tina. Although we have confidence in Larry, for he has both your well being and ours at stake, we're still a long way from any positive decisions. Things like this don't get resolved overnight. Go and enjoy your vacation with Mara. Together with Larry, we'll take care of things at home."

It was too late to change plans, but Tina had bad vibes about leaving the States. Although she kept her concerns about Larry and the hotels to herself, Mara knew that her friend was unhappy. Under the circumstances, she would have been uncomfortable as well. True, Larry was handsome and worldly and had a great future, but it was difficult to understand his treatment of Tina. He appeared always to be wrapped up in himself and indifferent to Tina's needs and concerns.

"Well, Tina thinks he's wonderful and that's all that matters," said Mara to Alex as they walked to the dorm after class. "When I first met Larry, I thought he was really nice even though a little old for Tina. Now I'm not so sure he's right for my friend. She wants affection and he seems to find that hard to give. He's not like you, Alex. You're always considerate, loving and willing to listen. I know it's wrong to compare the two of you, but for Tina's sake, I wish Larry could be more like you. I can't help feeling there's something missing in Larry and Tina's relationship."

"Tina thinks the sun rises and shines on Larry. It's not up to us to make judgments. After all, not everyone can be as sexy and wonderful as I am," teased Alex.

"I suppose that means I should appreciate what I have in you, Alex."

Tina, had been in love with Larry all her life and there were blind spots. "Yes, he treats me like a baby, and is always preoccupied with business," Tina said when talking to Mara, "but he's helping my father who is not feeling as well as he pretends. Dad is bent on this idea of expanding so that Larry and I have it made when we get married. Instead of being annoyed, I should be grateful that Larry's knocking himself out. With my father so vulnerable, we could be taken advantage of by those Chicago people. Remind me to stop worrying. What will be will be."

Tina could not know that Larry had his own agenda. His goal was to be sole owner of their hotel one way or another. Initially, wooing and winning Tina as a means to getting this accomplished hadn't been a bad idea. Sometimes the end justifies the means. However, with the plans he now had underway, that would no longer be necessary. He would own the Carillion without having to marry the boss's daughter.

Larry had spent years winning the Cappo's confidence. Now Spencer was in his hands and at the mercy of the would-be partners in Chicago. It had helped Larry's cause that Spencer was ailing. Wanting to keep this fact from his wife and daughter, Spencer had gradually relegated more and more authority to him. By the time Tina and Mara were ready to leave for South Africa, it was Larry who was making the important decisions. He'd been in close contact with his advisors over the years, and with the appearance of Anthony Luppo at the hotel, the end was in sight. Larry was in the driver's seat. The Carillion would soon be in his hands. It had been easy.

Mara's family was a delight. Mother, father and the boys lived in a big, old house near Capetown and appeared to know everyone. The first thing on the agenda was a "welcome home" party for Mara where Tina was introduced to family, friends and neighbors. The girls were wined, dined and taken everywhere. They went to small villages where the local tribes entertained and to Kruger National Park, a huge game preserve, where lions, elephants, leopards, rhinos and buffalo were free to roam. South Africa is a photographer's paradise, and except for some uneasiness about home, Tina enjoyed being part of Mara's world. It was very different from her own.

Days went quickly. While Mara expected to spend the entire summer with her family, Tina had made separate arrangements. She wanted two weeks of quality time with Larry before starting the new semester at school.

The second week of vacation had just begun when Tina was called to the phone. It was Spencer telling her, among other things, about his impending heart surgery.

The announcement came as a complete shock. Abruptly putting an end to her vacation, Tina booked a seat on the first flight home. Having called her mother regarding the time and date of arrival, she hoped that Larry would be waiting at the airport. Disappointed again, she found Terry waiting to pick her up. Her mother explained that Larry had left the night before to attend some important meetings and that he didn't plan to be back before the start of her school year. Tina was heartbroken. After a few days Larry called.

"I'm sorry, Tina. Everything suddenly came to a head, but should be settling down soon. I'll come to visit you in Vermont. We'll have a few private days away from everybody."

There were several other calls from Larry, but someone was always waiting for him somewhere making it necessary for him to be brief. Tina was sad, but preoccupied with Spencer's surgery and recovery. When classes began and she was together again with Mara, there was much catching up to do. Tina told her about Spencer's surgery and shared her feelings of frustration about Larry. Mara wanted all the details and was sympathetic, but then it was back to course demands and college routine. They were juniors. In less than two years they'd be graduating. Soon they would be engaged and looking forward to getting married.

School had been in session two weeks and there had been no word from Larry. No phone calls, no letters—

absolutely nothing. When calling home, she learned that
her parents had not heard from him either. In their voices
Tina could tell that they were concerned. When questioned,
Spencer admitted that there had been rumors. Larry had
been seen in Chicago nightclubs with unsavory looking
people and appeared to be spending money freely. When
phone messages were left unanswered, Spencer learned
that Larry had checked out of the hotel. There was no
forwarding address.

"Have you called Jake Lewis, your attorney?" Tina
asked, panicking.

"Yes, but he told me that there was nothing he
could do since I'd given Larry Power of Attorney. He said it
was like giving him a blank check."

Ten days later Tina received the call that would
change her life forever. Jim Lowe, their accountant and
long time friend, would have given anything not to be the
messenger of the terrible news.

"Tina, is Mara with you?"

"No. She's at the library. What is it? Is something
wrong? You sound like you have a cold. Is my father all
right? What do you want with Mara?"

"Nothing, but I hoped you wouldn't be alone. It's
your mother and father. Your parents are gone, Tina."

"Gone where, Jim?

"Not gone, Tina. What I'm trying to tell you is that
your parents are dead."

"Oh my God! What happened? Were they in an
accident? When? Oh God, they can't be dead. Tell me

they are in the hospital—hurt, but not dead. Tell me they're not dead, Jim."

"I'm so sorry, Tina. It wasn't an accident. Your parents were shot in their bed as they slept. They never knew what happened. A maid found them this morning. Looks like an intruder got into their suite. The safe behind the reception desk was broken into as well. Police are everywhere. They're trying to locate Larry."

"He's not there?"

"No one knows where he is, Tina. You'd better get here as fast as you can. Ask Mara to call me when you have a flight. I'll be at the airport to pick you up."

Jim hung up, but Tina was frozen on the spot. She was in a daze. Their accountant's words kept going through her head, but her brain wouldn't accept what he had said. Her parents murdered? Who would want to kill them? The phone in her hand fell to the floor. Her shock turned to hysterics and that is how Mara found Tina on returning from the library.

Kneeling beside her, Mara took her friend in her arms. She understood only the words: "They're dead."

"What did you say? Who's dead? What are you talking about? What happened while I was at the library? Talk to me, Tina!"

"They're dead."

"Who's dead? Tina, who died?"

"Spencer and Terry—my mother, my father."

"Were they in an accident? Maybe they are just hurt and in the hospital."

Gerda Osiecki

"No Mara! My mother and father are dead. They were murdered. Jim called."

"Murdered? That's impossible. Who would murder your mother and father? Come, sit on the couch while I call Jim back. There must be a mistake."

After talking to Jim, who confirmed that there was no mistake, Mara took charge. How could a few hours change everything so drastically? She made arrangements for the first available flight which landed in St. Louis around eleven o'clock. Jim was at the airport to drive the two devastated and speechless girls to the hotel. In the lobby they were met by Barry White, the detective in charge.

"Miss Cappo, I can't tell you how sorry I am to have you come home to this tragedy. I know it's a terrible shock to you, but hope you understand that I have to ask some questions."

"Why would anyone want to kill my parents? Where is Larry?" asked Tina through a fresh flood of tears.

"We hoped you would tell us where Larry Hermano could be reached, Miss Cappo. When did you last hear from him?"

"I don't know where he is. He hasn't called me."

Explaining that the vault at the front desk had been broken into and that valuables belonging to guests were missing, Detective White asked about the keys. "Who would have keys, Miss Cappo?"

"I don't know. I don't know anything," she answered. "Larry should be here. Did you call Tony Luppo? He should know where Larry is."

"Can't this wait, Detective White?" Mara asked. "You can see Tina's beside herself. She's in shock. We could both use a cup of tea."

"I'm sorry to be so insensitive, but I hoped Miss Cappo could help us. We can't seem to find anyone—not Larry or the people he was dealing with. It's like the earth just swallowed them up. Our best shot in the solution of any crime is the material we can gather in the first twenty-four hours. After that the trail gets cold, but you're right, Miss Konigswahl. My questions will wait until tomorrow. Please see that Miss Cappo gets some rest. If she does think of something, have her get in touch with me immediately."

Jake Ellis, their attorney and Jim, their accountant, did what they could to get things calmed down at the hotel. Mara had taken her grief-stricken friend to the penthouse apartment where the wives of Jim and Jake and some of the hotel staff tried their best to comfort her. They were friends, but none could respond when she searched their faces pleading for answers. "Why," she cried? "Who would want to do this to my parents? They had no enemies. They were the kindest people in the world and liked by everyone."

People were accumulating in the lobby. Guests were shocked to learn about Tina's parents. Those that had belongings in the safe were trying to get the attention of police officers while others were concerned that a mad man was on the loose. Were they going to be the next victims?

When the police left the murder scene with whatever small clues they could find, arrangements had to be made for a double funeral. Mara had taken care of the burial arrangements as Tina remained in a state of shock. Tina had few relatives, but those that could, along with friends and staff, came to sit with her at the wake. She spoke to no one and couldn't swallow the food that was offered. There was no consoling Tina in her grief.

Larry was nowhere to be found. Life goes on, but for Tina it would never again be the same. My parents aren't coming back and neither is Larry, Tina repeated over and over again as she sat alone in darkness. I loved Larry, but know now that he never loved me.

Tina was hardly surprised when Jake called a few days after the funerals to say, "There's no money left, Tina. The savings accounts, the investments and the hotel—everything is gone." Tina was penniless and homeless. The hotel belonged to the bank or some unknown entity. She would have a week to vacate the apartment in which she had spent her entire life.

"Mom, Dad and I were naive and stupid," she said to Jake. "We never knew what hit us. Together with Larry's friends in Chicago, they wiped us out."

"Spencer had the Carillion mortgaged to the hilt, Tina. He never consulted Jim or me. We didn't know or we might have been able to stop him. There's no doubt they cheated your father, but from all we can see, it was done legally. I wish there was something we could do to turn it around, but there isn't."

"I've accepted the fact that Larry stole everything from us, but I can't believe that he would kill. There has to be another explanation for my parents' murder, and if it takes a lifetime, I promise to find the answer."

Mara hated leaving Tina after the funeral, but had to get back to school. Knowing the penthouse, that had been home to Tina, must be vacated, a relative—an aunt living in Milwaukee, offered temporary sanctuary. Aunt Joan was a loner and a recluse. She and Tina's parents had never been close, but Tina accepted her invitation.

"I don't care where I go," said Tina to Mara when they parted. "I have to get away from here."

After about two months in Milwaukee the tears subsided, but the anger remained. Tina couldn't continue to live off her aunt's sympathy and was determined to come to grips with her life. She had already dropped out of college since there was no money to continue her studies even were she able to concentrate. Determined to move on, where could she go?

Mara called often from school. She wanted Tina to come back to Vermont. "I'll move out of the dorm and we can live off campus together," she said.

"I miss you, Mara, but I can't come right now. First I have to find a job and learn to support myself."

There wasn't much work to be had in the little college town, but Mara scoured the want ads hoping to find a job for her friend. One day she learned that a travel agent near the college was looking for a clerk typist. She convinced Tina to send a resume. Perhaps it was her experience with travel or the extensive reading she had done, Tina interviewed for and was offered the position. Mara found an efficiency apartment off campus and the two friends moved in. They were together again.

While Tina could now absorb herself in work and pay for her keep, she couldn't escape the vision of her parents being murdered as they slept. She lived with the nightmare of the caskets being lowered into the ground and promised herself that she would do everything possible to find those responsible. Detective White continued to keep in touch, but there were never any answers.

"We're running into dead ends everywhere, Miss Cappo. It's as though Larry and Tony Luppo never existed. The Chicago hotels are there all right and they are up for sale, but no one at either of the hotels has ever heard of Luppo or Sergio, who was rumored to be his partner. Tell me, Miss Cappo, how are you holding up?"

"I can't stop thinking about what happened, Detective. Everyone tells me that time will heal. It hasn't and it doesn't—if anything my nightmares are getting worse. While I have a typing job at the present time, I keep hoping to find something more challenging. I need work that will be demanding and exhausting so that I can find sleep at night."

Mara did get engaged to Alex on Christmas Day of her senior year. It reminded Tina that this was to have been her special day as well. The dream she had once had about a happily ever after was long forgotten. "God knows where Larry is," she said to Mara, "but some day our paths will cross. I don't know where or when, but we'll meet again."

"You've never heard anything from or about him?"

"No, Mara—nothing! And the hurt won't go away. Let's not talk about it. It's bad enough that I keep rehashing things in my mind. Thank God I have you and my job right now, but I can't keep relying on you to be there for me. Soon you and Alex will be married and ready to begin your lives elsewhere. I'm happy for you both, but I must begin to think about where I want to go next."

"What about Stanley? He's crazy about you and is waiting for you to give him some encouragement."

"I know. He writes to me and wants to see me, but I don't know if I'll ever be ready to trust a man with my heart again. Even if I could think of Stanley as more than a friend, it would be as though I'm turning to him on the rebound. I respect him too much for that."

"You can always move in with us when we get married," said Mara.

"I couldn't. Not only would I be intruding, but I wouldn't be breaking the chain of dependency. No, Mara, I'm going to work hard at this job and take whatever training they offer. What I would really like, some day, is to go out of the country. Maybe I'll be a tour guide. You know I've always been anxious to travel and see the world's wonders. There must be courses I can take."

With this in mind, Tina began to take hold of her life. She had a purpose again. Mara agreed that a new all-consuming direction would be good and did whatever she could to encourage her friend. Although hired as a clerk-typist, Tina often assisted agents in the office therefore learning a great deal. Tourism held a fascination for her and in January Tina found herself enrolled in a course given specifically for tour guides.

May 15 was graduation day at St. James College. It was to have been a celebration for Tina as well. However, it was only Mara who had made it through the four years. Mara's parents had flown in from Capetown - not only for the graduation, but for a wedding that was to take place a week later. While the wedding had originally been planned for June, a new exciting job required that Alex report to work the day after Memorial weekend. The newlyweds would be relocating to Chicago after only an overnight honeymoon.

Tina did not go to the graduation. It would have been painful for her not to be up there with her classmates receiving a diploma. Instead she was completing her tour guide training with the Cartrite Agency. She would be crossing the Atlantic to begin her first touring assignment at the same time Alex was scheduled to start his new job in Chicago.

Tina was Mara's Maid of Honor and Stanley, the Best Man. The couple had arranged for a small wedding with the reception to be held at the Turner farm. Mara's parents were the only guests from the bride's side. There would be a second reception in Capetown as soon as Alex earned enough time off for a vacation.

It was a lovely day for a wedding. The bride was beautiful and the groom so proud as he watched her slowly walk down the aisle on the arm of her father. The two families had bonded over the ten days Mara's parents had been the Turner's guests. Mr. and Mrs. Konigswahl were happy for Mara and satisfied to know they would be leaving her in loving hands.

Mara's parents were anxious to see Tina again. So was Stanley who had never gotten over his feelings for her. Everyone understood the sadness behind Tina's smile knowing she must be thinking of all the terrible things that had happened to change her life.

Whatever happened to those dreams we had on that first day at college, Tina wondered as she helped prepare Mara for her honeymoon getaway. Hugging Mara, Tina whispered, "I'm so happy for you. I know you and Alex will have a wonderful life."

"When you get back from England we'll have an address, Tina. We want you to stay with us. I have your itinerary and will leave a message at the desk so that you can reach me wherever you are. I love you, my friend— almost as much as I love Alex—and you know we'll do anything we can for you wherever you are."

"Truthfully, I don't know how I'll get along without you, Mara, but I have to try. I may want to get a place of my own in Chicago—a place to hang my hat when I'm not out tour guiding. Hopefully it will be near you and Alex and, who knows, maybe I'll run across Larry."

"Forget Larry, Tina. He's not worth your little finger. Stanley is still crazy about you, and except for his little brother, there isn't a nicer guy. Be nice to him."

"I won't let myself hurt him again. He's too good for me," replied Tina trying to show a bravado she didn't feel as Mara said her good-byes.

Tina remained at the party for a while after Mara and Alex left. She was her usual warm, friendly self and even danced with Stanley, but her thoughts kept returning to what might have been. Her heart wasn't in the festivities.

"I've got to get away. You understand that, don't you, Stan."

"Yes, I understand you've been through a terrible trauma, Tina. You must know that you have the whole Turner family in your corner. If you ever need or want us, we're here."

"Thanks, Stan. It's very reassuring knowing that I can count on you all. You can't imagine how it feels to be so utterly alone. I'll be in touch when I get back in a few months."

Stan held Tina close and gingerly kissed both cheeks as he, reluctantly, left her at the airport gate the next morning. He knew she had to find a way to take control of her life. Hopefully a stint out of the country would do it for her. He would be waiting.

6

The screeching telephone having accomplished it's purpose, Tina was awake. It was the fourth day in June. Going to the window, pulling back the drapes, she saw—absolutely nothing. It was a typical London dawn. The fog was so thick that the street in front of the hotel was invisible.

Mustn't forget the umbrella today, she thought. Even if it doesn't rain, it will come in handy as a beacon for my tourists to follow. As Tina showered and dressed, she continued talking to herself. "I really need to believe this job will keep me challenged. The nightmares are not getting any better and I don't remember when I last had a good night's sleep. If only Detective White would call. At least I'd feel they were still actively working on finding those responsible for the death of my parents."

Tina had arrived in London from America just two days before. Most of the last forty-eight hours had been spent reviewing her own carefully researched notes as well as last minute instructions from her employers, the Cartrite Travel Agency. The tour, her first, was scheduled to last twelve days. This morning's priority was to get in touch with someone named Alan Ritter. He would be her tour bus driver.

"Good morning Mr. Ritter. This is Tina Cappo. You were expecting my call! Could we meet for breakfast in the coffee shop downstairs in about half an hour?"

"Glad to hear from you, Miss Cappo. I'll be waiting. You'll recognize the uniform."

"We'll be working together. My instructions are to be at Heathrow Airport by nine a.m," said Tina wanting to sound very professional.

"Good! It will give us time, before gathering up all our tourists, to get acquainted. After breakfast I'll drop you off at the airport so that you can check on the flights."

A few minutes later, having met and introduced themselves, Tina and her driver were seated having breakfast. Both looked very crisp and business-like in the Cartrite colors of navy blue, red and white.

Tina brought Mr. Ritter, her driver, up to date on the information she had received from the agency. There would be fifty-one vacationers by the time all were collected. Supposedly their flights would arrive over a three-hour period. Most would be coming from Australia and New Zealand, but a husband and wife with two children were listed as residents of Dallas, Texas. There were also two last minute cancellations that were immediately booked by a couple from Long Island, New York. Flying from Germany to London, they had hoped to connect with a tour of England, Ireland, Scotland and Wales—one that would fit into their return travel arrangements. They were lucky. Two elderly ladies, who needed special assistance, were also on the roster. They were from South Africa.

In accordance with the census data in Tina's notes, all of the group were English speaking, but she was warned that there would be accents difficult to understand. It was also expected that Tina would be encountering fatigue on the part of her charges due to the great distances from which they had come.

"From what I've heard, Mr. Ritter, Australians usually book tours back to back since flights from 'down under' are very costly. Preparing to 'going on holiday,' Australians often accumulate months of free time. This tour could conceivably be the third or fourth leg of a long hiatus."

"Imagine living out of a suitcase week after week."

"It's no different from what we do, Miss Cappo, but we call it 'making a living.'"

"Right you are. Well it's nice to know language won't be a problem. My records indicate that everyone speaks English. Helpful, also, is the fact that I'm somewhat familiar with the tour having taken it myself about two years ago."

"We're scheduled to take on a city tour guide tomorrow, Miss Cappo. Is it okay if I call you by your first name?"

"It would be less cumbersome. The name is Tina. And you are Alan. Hello again, Alan."

"Friends call me 'Al', but Alan's fine. The city guide's name, by the way, is Jessica Rudman. I've worked with her many times. She really knows London and will make it easy for you to get started."

"According to the route laid out by Cartrite, we won't be missing any of the traditional tourist attractions. Buckingham Palace, The Tower of London, No. 10 Downing Street, The Changing of the Guards, Westminster Abbey, Trafalgar Square, Madame Tussaud's Wax Museum— they're all on the list. With the city guide on board, I'll be free to get to know the people and that should take some of the pressure off. You probably know this is my first assignment. I am a little nervous. Who am I kidding, a little nervous? I'm very nervous."

Alan thought her monologue amusing. She'd been to England before? He planned to ask her about that another time. As for now, however, he was busy concentrating on the most beautiful eyes he had ever seen. They were big and ice blue. Looking into them was like looking into her soul. They held him captive. This woman, he thought is gorgeous—a knockout. What have I done to get so lucky? Aware that he was staring and making Tina uncomfortable, he composed himself and said, "Don't worry about a thing, pretty lady. I've done this tour many times and could do it backwards if I had to. If something does go wrong, I'll put on a Beatles tape or pass around some goodies. There's always a bucket full of hard candy at the front of my bus. I haven't lost a passenger in a long time."

Tina thought of the times when she was the pampered tourist. The roles had been reversed. Her job now required that she cater to the whims of others. She hoped her charges would be patient and that they would like her. People, however, paid to be pleased and would expect an above-average experience from the Cartrite Agency. Tina wanted to do her best for the tourists, the agency and herself.

"Always be prepared for the unexpected," warned Alan as they rose from the table to leave the coffee shop of the hotel. "You, me and the tour group will be staying in this hotel for two nights. Then we start on the sight seeing tour our customers paid for. You and I will practically be living together. Hope you can tolerate a short, chubby, guy who likes to talk."

"I'm easy to get along with, Alan. However, while we're on the road, I'll do the talking. Your job is to get us safely from one place to another. That doesn't mean I won't turn to you for help and advice regularly. I'm sure our charges will come up with questions better answered by a real Londoner."

"You've got a deal, Tina. May I conclude that I do have a suggestion before we separate. You'd better call the airlines for their latest estimates on flight arrivals. It looks bad out there and I suspect there will be many delays."

Grateful for Alan's suggestion, Tina left the table to make the necessary calls. Enroute to her room, she thought about her bus driver. He was young—about the same age as herself. Judging from the ring on his finger, he was married. Why would a handsome, happily married young man, want to spend his life on the road?

Alan's warnings, and those of her fellow tour guides to be prepared for the unexpected, were quickly substantiated. On calling the airlines, Tina learned that flights were delayed. Apparently fog conditions had played havoc with all the schedules. She caught up with Alan who had, after their breakfast meeting, returned to his hotel room.

Explaining that flights were delayed, Tina said, "None are expected before 4 p.m. So much for what we went over this morning. We'll have to rearrange everything and go to Plan B which we haven't worked out. Any suggestions? See! Already I find myself needing your help."

"First tell me what you have in mind. Then we can decide if your ideas are workable."

"As I see it, we're fortunate in that the group is scheduled to spend the first two nights in London. Rooms are reserved no matter what time we get the tourists checked in. This afternoon and evening was to have been free to explore the neighborhood or take a rest."

"Sounds good, so far. Then what, Tina?"

Had all gone as scheduled, Tina would have met the planes as they arrived, directed the tourists to waiting vans and accompanied them to the hotel. Under the current circumstances however, Tina thought it best for Alan to share in the responsibility of welcoming the tourists as groups arrived. There would certainly be missed connections. Vacationers would be tired and upset having been up many hours. "While I get one group settled, you could wait for the next. Does that sound logical to you?" Tina asked.

"Both logical and practical," answered Alan.

"Tourists will expect, on arrival, to be met by someone representing Cartrite. They won't want to hang around the airport any longer than necessary."

"Some may need help changing and understanding English currency," Tina interrupted.

"Yes, and there will be a scramble for luggage. Some might need to make phone calls. That's always a challenge in a foreign country. Two of us might not be enough, Alan."

"We'll work it out, Tina. The important thing is that each plane is met by one of us."

Alan and Tina worked well together. They were a good team. By 11:30 that night all had been given their room assignments. The weary tourists were instructed to meet in the hotel coffee shop the next morning at seven. There they would have a buffet breakfast and orientation meeting.

Although tired, due to her early rising and the non-stop activity of the day, Tina again could not sleep. Thoughts of her dead parents took over the minute her head hit the pillow. She got up, and rather than pace the floor, turned on the television. Hours later she took the sheet and blanket from the bed retreating to the lounge chair prepared to spend what was left of the night. If only Detective White would call to tell her that the killer had been caught and was behind bars. It would bring closure allowing the nightmares to stop. Exhausted, Tina tried counting sheep, but all she saw were tourists—an occupational hazard she was soon to discover.

Actually Detective White had been taken off Tina's case. "You're spending too much time on that Cappo matter," his captain had said. "It's been over a year and you're nowhere. The leads, if there were any, have dried up. You're off the case as of right now—today."

"What do I tell Miss Cappo, the daughter?"

"Tell her anything you want. Pretend you haven't given up, but that you've got other, more pressing, assignments. I want you to report to Lt. Johansen. He needs your help."

There goes that screeching telephone again. That can't be the morning wake-up call already, muttered Tina. What happened to last night? Well my gal, it's time to rise and shine. While you're at it, you might try getting a grip. In case you haven't noticed, you do an awful lot of talking to yourself these days.

Circulating among her group at breakfast a half hour later, Tina was pleased to find smiling faces. All had apparently slept well, were enjoying a good breakfast and appeared to be ready to begin a new adventure with her as their fearless leader.

"Any problems or complaints that you know of, Alan? No? I guess that means we're off to a good start."

Calling everyone to attention as they ate breakfast, Tina said, "Sorry to interrupt. Hope you all had a good night. There is a busy day ahead for you. You may remember, from our brief encounter last night, that I am Tina Cappo, your tour guide. If you have any problems or questions, please bring them to me. I will try my best to help. With me is Alan Ritter, our bus driver. At the front of the hotel is a big blue and white Laker Bus on which is printed the number 201. Take a really good look at us. We three will be with you for this entire tour."

Explaining that they, along with other busses, drivers and guides, would be making frequent stops, Tina warned, "Getting on the wrong bus could be a disaster. You might end up in Italy and that would make all of us very unhappy. We promised the Cartrite Agency that you'd be returned to your native countries when this tour is over.

"We'll be boarding the bus at 9:30 this morning. Please always be prompt when given a time and place to meet. It isn't fair to have your fellow passengers sitting on the bus waiting for late-comers. Our tour bus has been given specific times to be at special points of interest. If not on schedule, we will not be allowed admittance."

Continuing, Tina explained that the group would spend the next two days visiting London's highlights. "Our first stop will be to pick up Jessica Rudman. She will be our local guide. Knowing London, you will find her both interesting and entertaining. When leaving the bus, please try to stay together. Miss Rudman will take the lead. I'll bring up the rear—along with those of you who are camera fanatics.

"There will be a two hour lunch break today. Alan will leave you in the vicinity of Harrods Department Store. You will be on your own and tempted to spend the two hours shopping, but you'd better plan some time to eat. Dinner tonight will be in the main dining room of the hotel, but not until seven o'clock. You'll be very hungry if you don't have something between now and then. We will be back at the hotel by six enabling you to freshen up. After dinner the evening is yours. Some of you may have made arrangements to go to the theater.

"I believe I've covered everything. Now finish your breakfast. We'll see you on the bus at 9:30." Surprising both Tina and Alan, the entire group was waiting for them while the luggage was still being loaded. Told to sit wherever they wished, Tina said she would post a seating schedule for future days. "So that everyone will get to sit at the front of the bus, seats will be changed each morning and afternoon."

The two days in London went off without a hitch. No one got lost and there were no problems that Tina couldn't resolve. Alex was amazed at how efficiently Tina took control. If the novice tour guide was nervous, she surely hid it well. Where did all that poise come from, he asked himself. She's young—more like a prom queen than someone having all this responsibility. She should be in college, dating boys, and having fun. Alan resolved to learn more about the beautiful tour guide that had entered his life.

Alan didn't know that Tina was just as curious about him. Here was a young man, handsome and married. Why would he want to be away from his wife for weeks at a time?

Tour guides and their drivers have a never-ending responsibility when enroute. After settling tourists at mealtimes, most will look for an out-of-the-way table for themselves. Respecting their need for relaxation and privacy, most tourists will amuse themselves with small talk Having come from all over, they will have much to share.

In conversation at their secluded table the first night, Tina told Alan that she had nearly lost Mrs. Brown in Westminster Abbey. "She wasn't with the group when I counted noses. I went back and found her watching people doing brass rubbings."

"What, may I ask, are brass rubbings?" was the puzzled response from Alan.

"Do you remember, when you were a kid, placing tracing paper on a penny and rubbing over the high spots with a pencil to get an impression? People do the same thing with embossed brass coverings on caskets kept in historic churches or head stones in cemeteries. In Westminster Abbey it's necessary to get a permit. When visiting you will see many interested people rubbing on parchment paper which, when finished, will be taken home to be framed. Apparently it's Mrs. Brown's hobby."

"Where do you get your trivia, Tina? I've been on this route three months and never before has anyone asked about brass rubbings. You never cease to amaze me."

"There's more, Alan! Wait 'till you know me better." Realizing that she was beginning to sound flirtatious, Tina changed the subject. "Tomorrow we really get this show on the road. I've already told our charges to have breakfast and be ready to move by eight o'clock. Bags will be picked up while we're in the coffee shop. Don't know about you Alan, but I've had enough for the day." Rising from her chair and waving to those still remaining in the dining room, she said, "Goodnight all. See you in the morning."

Days three and four were long days of travel. There was some sightseeing along the way, but the miles were mostly interrupted by refreshment and pit stops. As Alan drove through the beautiful English countryside, Tina circulated brochures and was a wealth of information having been on a similar trip with her mother. Tina was amazed at how much she had retained of the lectures given by the tour guide in charge at that time.

Gerda Osiecki

"Notice the quaint houses with the thatched roofs. It's just like every English movie I've ever seen," said Tina to her resting group.

"Is that a stork's nest up there on that roof to the right?" asked Mrs. Stone who was sitting behind the driver.

"There are a few nests in this area, but the inhabitants seem to have gone elsewhere for the season. Haven't seen any storks around here lately," answered Alan.

"I'm going to pass around some literature about Stonehenge which is our first stop this morning. I'm sure most of you have seen pictures of the mysterious stone circle of eerie monoliths. People believe that Stonehenge was the scene of an ancient place of worship. The stones reach up to twenty feet in height and can weigh as much as 350 tons. No one knows for sure where they came from or how they were able to get these gigantic stones to remain upright. Anyone here willing to hazard a guess?"

Most were asleep or too tired to respond. Tina said, "Alan has brought some tapes. I'm sure you'll enjoy listening as you sit back and take in the beautiful scenery. It will be about two hours before we make our next planned stop. If you'd rather close your eyes and nap, we'll all understand. We did have an early call this morning."

The group was getting acquainted and conversation between rows and across aisles was animated. Everyone had something to share—where they came from, what other trips they had been on, where they were going next, children and grandchildren at home. The subject matter had endless possibilities. Eventually they were all dozing and it was quiet.

"We certainly have a good group on this tour," said Tina to Alan that night at dinner. "They are cooperative and seem to all get along."

"It's your magic touch, Tina. My last two tours were trips from hell. Believe me, this group is exceptional, but it's because they respect you. It's amazing, but you tell them to be somewhere at a given time and there they are. We haven't had to wait for anyone. In fact most are at the bus before I open the door."

"It's the people, Alan. They listen and respect each other. Any tour guide would look good under those circumstances. I'm sure it has nothing to do with me threatening them. They can't really believe I'd let you take off leaving them behind."

"Don't be so modest, Tina. You've got us all hypnotized. It's not just our tourists. Whenever we meet up with other drivers and guides, they flock around to get your attention. Admit it! You've got something special. Maybe it's that cute Missouri accent and then there's that little girl quality about you. I believe most of the tourists on this trip think of you as a daughter or granddaughter that needs to be protected from the mean old world. Tell me, oh fearless leader, what brought you here? I certainly want to know more about you."

"It's a long story, Alan, and it is late. There are phone calls to make and I'm ready to call it a night."

"Remember, Tina, I'm here and a good listener."

"Goodnight, Alan. See you at breakfast."

Mara, as promised, had left a phone number at the desk of the hotel where Tina was staying. Message in hand, Tina went to her room and immediately called back. Although it was three o'clock in the morning Chicago time, Mara was happy to hear from her.

Gerda Osiecki

"What's happening?" asked Tina after the usual preliminaries.

"Not much. We're temporarily quartered in a hotel and looking for an apartment or a condo."

"Detective White promised to call me if there were any new developments. I'm on the road and know it's difficult for him to keep up with me. Did he contact you, Mara?"

"You've only been gone a few days, Tina."

"I know and I'm sorry I woke you, but it's good to hear a familiar voice."

"I'm glad you called. Are you getting any sleep, Tina?"

"Not much, but they tell me I'll sleep when I get tired enough. Believe me, I'm beyond tired and should start to sleep any day now—maybe while I'm supposed to be lecturing on the bus tomorrow. Aside from not sleeping, I'm doing okay. The tour is going better than expected. The people are well behaved. Maybe they feel sorry for me being new at this, but they are cheerful and cooperative. Hope all is well with you and Alex. I'll call again in about a week. If there's anything I should know about, try to reach me. Sorry I woke you. Now go back to sleep, Mara. Thank you for being there and listening to me. I miss you."

Mara knew Tina well enough to suspect that the nightmares were still with her. Promising herself that she would call Detective White in the morning, she rolled over and tried to recapture the dream Tina had interrupted. She was alone in Chicago and lonely. Alex and Mara had just about settled into the hotel when her brand new husband was sent out of town. In the dream Alex had surprised her by coming home earlier than expected and was about to kiss her.

70

Tina, Alan and the tour group spent the next day crossing Wales. The highlight for most was the short stop at a tiny town that had the distinction of having fifty-eight letters in it's unwieldy name. All bought the official town banner after hearing the children spell and repeat,

Llanfairpwllgwyngyllgogerychwyrndrobwllllantysiliog ogogoch.

"Try saying that three times fast," challenged Tina.

By nightfall they had crossed the sea to Ireland where they would be spending a few days.

"They claim there are forty shades of green covering Ireland's landscape," said Tina as the bus unloaded, amid raindrops, at the hotel. "Does anyone know why?"

"The rain," said one of the men. "It's a secret they won't tell outsiders, but it's the rain. Here they prefer to call it 'mist'."

With her group back on the bus, Tina explained that they would soon be at Blarney Castle. "I hope some of you will climb to the top. You'll want to tell your family and friends that you kissed the Blarney stone. It is said that you'll be blessed with the skill of flattery if you do. Sounds good, but whatever you do, don't lean over too far."

Upon their arrival at Blarney Castle, Tina asked, "Are you ready?" Since most of the group were elderly, there were few takers, but Tina, Alan and several other brave souls did the tourist thing which meant hanging backwards over an opening high atop the tower.

"Come on, Tina. You didn't come all this way not to give the stone a big kiss," teased Alan.

"But half of me will be hanging over that edge."

"Hopefully the right half, Tina. Actually it looks worse than it is. I'll hold your ankles and won't let you fall. Come on! Be a sport. You'll be given a fancy certificate for your bravery and be able to include that valuable document in your scrapbook."

"Okay! I'll do it, but then it's your turn, Alan. You too have to kiss that Blarney Stone."

"Most people tell me that I'm already full of Blarney, Tina. Truthfully, there are things I'd rather be kissing."

Sarah and Agnes, the two elderly ladies from South Africa smiled. "Don't they make a cute couple, Agnes? Have you noticed how they look at each other. Why don't they forget about kissing that old stone and get right down to what they really want to do?"

"Who do they think they're kidding, Sarah. My guess is they are already sleeping together."

"You're such a gossip, Agnes."

"And you're a busy body, Sarah. But isn't it fun to watch them. Remember when…"

"Cut it out Agnes. That was a long time ago."

It was a good show for those who had climbed to the top of the Castle. Those that didn't participate, watched from below, and for them that was scary enough.

Back on the bus, the group was treated to a tape of Hal Roach, the famous Irish comedian. His one-liners kept everyone laughing. When the tape ended many were anxiously preparing to tell their own favorite stories. The line, "That's a good one—write it down," was heard frequently for the next several days.

Evenings in Ireland were spent visiting the local pubs where talented live comedians entertained with unique Irish humor, and of course, there were always the performing Irish step dancers.

"I dare you to try dancing without moving your body, Alan."

"Only if you get up there with me, Tina."

"Didn't I tell you, Sarah? Look at the two of them. They think they're fooling us. If they aren't already sleeping together, they should be."

"You read too many of those trashy novels," replied her friend.

"I've saved the best for last," said Tina to her group that night. "Tomorrow we will do the Ring of Kerry, but you must all promise to pray tonight for good weather. Alan tells me he hasn't ever seen it although he's been there many times. Like he said, 'It mists a lot around here.' You'll be happy to know that there will be time for souvenir shopping. Some of you have wanted to buy Waterford crystal."

They were awakened to a beautiful day. The greens were greener and the sun was shinier. "You must have taken my advice and prayed for a miracle. Have you ever seen a more spectacular view? We'll have about two hours. There will be time to take pictures, walk around and have some refreshments. Alan tells me the scones here are the best he's ever had and he claims to be an expert in the food department. When we leave here, it's off to Dublin, our last stop in Ireland."

It was a rough crossing back to the mainland and many of the group were seasick. Tina and Alan were kept busy bringing those in trouble on deck where fresh air seemed to help. All were happy to touch land when the ship docked. They would spend two days in Scotland.

The first day brought the group to Gretna Green. The little town was famous for performing hurried marriages. "In America we would call them 'shotgun weddings'." Tina explained that they'd all be part of an imitation wedding. "Do we have a couple who will agree to dress as bride and groom?"

"How about you two?" was the response from Sarah. "You and Alan are young and fit the part better than any of us."

Being good sports, Tina and Alan allowed themselves to be dressed in wedding attire. Others in the group pretended to be participants and guests. There was an irate father with a shotgun, a weeping mother, a bunch of pretend kids and lots of snickering relatives. They were all recruited from Tina's tour group. A picture was taken and, as expected, everyone purchased a copy for remembrance.

That night, at the local pub, they were treated not only to bagpipes, but dancers in kilts, Scottish jokes and Haggis, the local delicacy.

"Tastes like paste," said Tina.

"Do you know what Haggis is made of?" asked Alan.

"Haven't a clue, Alan."

"Haggis can be found only in the mountains of Scotland. It's a strange looking animal having two short legs on the left side and two long legs on the right. Because of that configuration, the animal runs counterclockwise on mountain trails. The only way to catch a Haggis is to stop short in front of one. Frightened, it will change direction. With the short legs now on the wrong side, the Haggis falls off the mountain and becomes a delicacy for a Scottish chef to prepare."

"You'd better try that story on someone more gullible," laughed Tina.

"Listen, Tina! They're playing my favorite Beatle song. Dance with me."

Tina hadn't danced in a long time. It felt really good to be in the arms of a strong, young man. While they danced, Alan sang softly in her ear:

> Close your eyes and I'll kiss you.
> Tomorrow I'll miss you.
> Remember I'll always be true.
> And while you're away
> I'll write home every day...

Now don't get carried away, Tina thought. Alan is married, and you're getting over a king-sized hurt. That's a very bad combination.

The dance over, they walked back to the table. Trying to cover up the feelings Alan's singing had provoked, Tina asked, "What do you think is going on with our couple from Los Angeles? Look! They can't seem to keep their hands off each other."

"They might be newly married, Tina."

"Or be having a secret rendezvous."

"That could be. After all they are far from home and unknown to anyone on the tour."

Gerda Osiecki

Alan had dreams of such an escape with Tina. Holding her in his arms as they danced was exciting. Would she go away with him some time in the future or was she committed to someone? He couldn't help but ask, "Is there a special person in your life, Tina?"

"No, Alan! There's no one."

"It's hard to imagine someone so lovely could have escaped being in a special relationship, but I'm happy to hear it."

The conversation was getting much too personal and Tina thought it best to change the subject. "What's on the agenda for tomorrow, Alan?" she asked.

Alan's sixth sense told him that he had hit a nerve. Tina had problems—problems that she preferred not to share.

"Tomorrow we go back to England. Our first tour is almost over. Before you know it, we'll be meeting the next group and beginning again. Luckily the agency gives us a weekend off between tours. We need some time for personal business."

"Right, Alan! Aside from catching up on calls and correspondence, I'm looking forward to some much needed sleep." Personal things for Alan, she suspected, would be to spend time with his wife—that is if their home was anywhere near London. To Alan, she said, "We'd better round up the troops and get them back to the hotel. It's been a lovely evening. I've almost forgotten this is a job."

"Believe it or not, Tina, I'm actually looking forward to our next four tours. In the past it was only the weekends I lived for. Could it be the company?"

"I thought it was because of the scenery, Alan."

"The scenery never changes, Tina. The tour guides do. Some are average, but then you came along. I'm not alone in believing you're the most beautiful sight us poor bus drivers have seen in a long time."

"Stop it, Alan. You're embarrassing me."

"You can't deny what happens every time I stop the bus—you're immediately surrounded by the competition. I'm always tripping over guys trying to get near you."

Tina's face turned crimson at Alan's continued compliments and quickly directed her attention elsewhere. Not quickly enough because busybody Sarah had overheard part of this interchange and couldn't wait to tell everyone. It was no secret that there was electricity in the air when Tina and Alan were together. All were amused and did their share of gossiping. It was part of the fun to speculate about their relationship. Were they or weren't they an item?

The last day of the tour involved getting everyone to the airport for their return trips. Happy but tired vacationers had completed their evaluations. Comments had been favorable. They appeared to like the food, the accommodations and the service. Both Alan and Tina were given envelopes containing generous gratuities and many had included complimentary notes of thanks.

Exhausted tourists had exchanged addresses, and Tina was left with the impression that there were friendships made. Starting out, Tina had been fearful and insecure. Having successfully made it through the first assignment, she was now satisfied with herself. It was a job well done and she had enjoyed the experience. Yes, Tina felt good. Things were going to work out all right.

The first order of business for Tina on Saturday morning was to call Detective White. "He's on vacation," she was told by the desk clerk. "Detective White tried to reach you before leaving. He said something about wanting to meet with someone while on vacation—someone who might be able to shed some light on your case."

Tina hung up curious to know who Detective White had gone to see. Was it possible that the police finally latched on to something meaningful? Having left a phone number where Detective White could reach her, she'd have to wait for his call back.

The weekend was over. After reviewing the material from Cartrite Travel outlining the details of the next tour group, there were chores to take care of. Fortunately her long hair only needed frequent washing. There was no need to spend hours at a beauty salon. Everything in her wardrobe was wash and wear as well as wrinkle free. Uniforms made it easy. With a little luck, Tina hoped to find an hour for television. Then the cycle would begin again.

According to the data received, the new group of vacationers would be young. They were college students on hiatus. Most were taking a break before beginning masters programs in the fall semester. The tourists were from Canada. While the itinerary would remain the same, Tina expected the young people would interact and participate more enthusiastically in the social events planned each evening.

Every tour is different and Tina expected there would be new challenges to face or problems to solve. These young people would not be content with long speeches on the beauty or history of Great Britain. Having experienced it herself, she knew they would want excitement instead of lectures.

It will be enjoyable being with people my own age, she thought. I expect they'll be full of vim, vigor and vitality which should make it easier for me. I'm sure all will want to kiss the Blarney Stone and participate in the Gretna Green marriage ceremony. With everyone clowning around, it should be a fun experience.

Monday morning and all flights were verified to be on schedule. The tour went smoothly and the students, as expected, were prepared to let loose after grueling months of study. They weren't so lucky as the previous group at the Ring of Kerry. Where that group had been able to enjoy the beautiful view of the cliffs overhanging the ocean, these tourists encountered real, honest to goodness, rain. No one seemed to notice. The only problem Tina had with this group was that they had a tendency to wander at night.

"They are never where they're supposed to be when I call the room or knock on doors," said Tina to Alan at dinner.

"You don't suppose they're mixing it up, do you?"

"Mixing up what?"

"You know! Maybe they're swapping rooms and exchanging roommates."

"Well they're old enough if that's what they want to do. They don't pay me to be a chaperone."

Alan could tell Tina was relaxed about her responsibilities to the tourists and the agency that employed them both. She laughed more. They kept their banter at breakfast and dinner meals light hearted and upbeat. The mood of their young charges was catching.

Alan loved music and liked to sing. His good strong baritone voice was often to be heard while driving through the picturesque countryside. Starting with a soft hum, it wasn't long before he'd be singing full voice with all the young people joining. Whenever there was music at night,

Gerda Osiecki

Alan and Tina would dance. Was he holding her closer each time? No, Tina! He's a married man. It's your imagination working overtime.

7

It was a memorable tour for all. The vacationers, escorted to the airport, were saying their "farewells" to small groups separating for final destinations. Tina and Alan had done all they could for their comfort and convenience. They needed and were ready for a well-deserved two-day weekend.

Driving back to London, Alan said, "One of the men gave me two tickets to 'Phantom of the Opera,' Tina. Seems he couldn't use them and suggested I take you. Could I convince you to go with me to the matinee performance on Sunday?"

Tina wondered why Alan would not be going with his wife. Perhaps she has other responsibilities or maybe they live too far away to make the trip, she thought. Answering, she said, "The reviews have been great and I'd love to go with you, Alan. There's some catch-up paper work and telephoning I'll have to make time for this weekend and I'm sure you have things to do as well. Do you think we can accomplish everything that needs doing on Saturday?"

"Never fear! Alan's here! You'd be surprised how fast I can make us work when there's a purpose. When we get back to the hotel let's have an early dinner. My suggestion is that you get a good night's sleep to prepare for a busy day tomorrow."

When the phone rang on Saturday, Tina was startled. It had been another night of tossing and turning. She had intended to call Detective White the first thing in the morning. Instead, it was almost noon and he was calling her.

"How's it going, Miss Cappo? he asked. They told me you called last week. I wanted to be sure not to miss you again."

"You were on vacation?"

"I was for a few days. What's happening there? Are you okay?"

"I'm all right, I guess. The job keeps my mind occupied and that's good. It's the nights that are the worst. I get flashbacks of my parents in those twin coffins. It must have been five o'clock this morning. before I finally dozed off. As a result, I just got out of bed. Tell me, has Larry surfaced? Is there anything new?"

"Nothing, Miss Cappo, but we haven't given up. We'll find him one of these days. Meanwhile I do want to ask a rather delicate question."

"Go ahead, ask me."

"My question may upset you."

"The objective is that we find Larry. If it will help, I'll answer whatever questions you have."

"My understanding, Miss Cappo, is that you and your parents had a long association with your manager, Larry. Weren't there plans that you would marry him?"

"Yes, he was with us for many years. I had a crush on him even as a small child. When Larry proposed, I was delighted and so were my parents."

"After you said 'yes' would you say Larry participated or was enthusiastic about making wedding plans? Did you ever get the feeling that something was missing? Was there anything suspicious about the way Larry treated you?"

"Just that we were rarely together. I would have liked more private time with him, but he was busy doing my father's bidding. As you know, my father wanted to buy another hotel—one which Larry and I were to manage after our wedding."

"Is it possible that Larry was deliberately making himself scarce?"

"You're leading up to something, Detective. What are you trying to tell me?"

"There's no sense my beating around the bush. Is it possible your fiancée was avoiding you to hide the fact that he was gay?"

"Gay? You mean homosexual? Of course not. That's impossible. I told you we were going to get married. We were in love. I can't remember when I didn't love him."

"It's been done before, Miss Cappo. Some people are very skilled at keeping secrets."

There was a long silence as Tina tried to process what Detective White was suggesting. Then she said, almost in a whisper, "Maybe that's why he was always putting me off. How could I have been so stupid?"

When the words registered, it was as though a bomb shell had hit Tina's foundation. She tried to hold back her feelings, but her eyes filled to overflowing. Although he tried, there was nothing Detective White could say or do that would console her. He could only listen as she continued, "He was always out of town when I came home for school breaks telling me it was for our future. He said we'd have the rest of our lives to be together. All lies? Was he only pretending so as to gain my parent's trust?" Without waiting for an answer, Tina asked: "What makes you think that Larry is gay?"

"We've been questioning Larry's card playing buddies, Miss Cappo. As far as we can tell those were the only friends he had in St. Louis. There was one man we talked to—his name is Jameson. Did you ever meet him?"

"Larry always played cards elsewhere. I never met any of his friends. He didn't talk about them or mention their names."

"This guy Jameson is homosexual. Although claiming never to have had a personal relationship with Larry, Jameson told us that it takes one to know one. His theory is that Larry carefully kept his liaisons away from the St. Louis area for fear of discovery. You never had any suspicions?"

Shaking her head and beginning again to choke up, Detective White continued, "I have very little to go on, Miss Cappo, and could be grasping at straws, but there's that Tony Luppo fellow. I think he and Larry were friends and that Tony was behind much of what happened after he was introduced to your father. If it turns out that they are both homosexual, Tony could have been Larry's inspiration as well as lover."

Trying hard to keep her emotions in check, Tina interrupted, "Judging from his treatment of me, your theory is beginning to sound feasible, Detective. How gullible can a person be? To think I believed him when he said he wanted to abstain from sex until our wedding night to keep me pure. He wasn't abstaining. It was just sex with me that he didn't want. What a fool I've been."

"Don't blame yourself, Miss Cappo. You're not the only innocent victim taken in by a skilled con-artist. They like to prey on nice people. I'll find Larry and when I do he'll pay for what he did. That's a promise."

Detective White could hear in Tina's voice that she was about to break down. "Are you okay?" he asked.

Anxious not to further humiliate herself, Tina responded, "I will be. Thanks for calling. If there's nothing else, please excuse me. I've got to go." Placing the phone on the receiver, Tina fell into a chair. The flood gates opened.

How could Larry have been so cruel? In retrospect, Tina should have realized something was wrong. It was obvious that Larry had been avoiding her for quite some time—long before the tragedy of her parents' death and his disappearance. They had trusted him while he laughed and made fools of them all.

The more Tina thought about her conversation with Detective White, the faster the tears fell. She couldn't bring herself to stop crying or even to move. Why would Larry have destroyed her and her family? They had always been good to him.

It was several hours later when Alan entered Tina's room to deliver a message from their employer. He knew immediately that something was very wrong. Curled up in the lounge chair, staring into space, Tina appeared to be in a trance. Her hair was uncombed and she was still in her bathrobe. Her eyes were red and swollen. From the dried streaks remaining on her cheeks, she had obviously been crying.

Shocked, Alan asked, "What happened, little one?"

Tears turned into sobs. Tina couldn't get the words out. Her entire body was shaking. She obviously was in pain. Sympathetic and wanting to do something to help, Alan took her into his arms. Catching the corner of her mouth, he kissed her tasting the salt from her tears. Without thinking he found his way to her open lips, then her eyes, her neck and her finger tips. As Tina responded, he sensed that she needed him, and he certainly wanted her. It felt so right to pick her up and carry her to the bed where he gently removed the robe and short night gown underneath.

What happened next could only be explained by Alan's built up need to make love to her. He had been attracted to Tina from their very first meeting. His fantasies took over. As for Tina, she'd been betrayed by her first love. The call from Detective White had left her emotionally destroyed. If only for her self esteem, she needed to know someone wanted her. Apparently Larry never had. He intended only to use her.

"Oh, Tina, what have I done?" asked an alarmed Alan when a painful cry came from the salty lips he was kissing. "I didn't know. I had no idea this was your first time. Forgive me for hurting you. Say something! Please, Tina! I wanted you so much."

"It's okay, Alan—not your fault! I needed you too. Larry said we should wait for our wedding night to have sex. I waited, but it turns out he never intended for us to be married. It was all a lie."

"Who is Larry, Tina? He's not worth your tears, but tell me about him. It will make you feel better if you let it out."

Holding the sobbing Tina on his lap, Alan put aside the temptation to take her again. It would have been easy considering her vulnerability, but he liked and respected her too much to use her as, apparently, Larry had. She would end up hating all men and that was the last thing he wanted. Instead, recognizing that what Tina needed most was consoling, he kissed away the fresh tears rolling down her face and encouraged her to talk.

"Tell me about it, Tina. What is it that has caused your unhappiness and all these tears? I've watched you and knew someone or something had hurt you."

"How did you know? I thought I was being upbeat and cheerful."

"You do put on a good performance each day for the tourists and for me, but your room is next to mine. Walls have ears. I know you don't sleep. Your radio is on all night. I often hear you crying."

"Do I disturb you?"

"It disturbs me to see your beautiful face turn sad when you think no one is looking. So many times I've wanted to come into your room and take you in my arms. Only the fear that you'd throw me out, restrained me. Tell me, Tina, what can I do to make things better. I want to help you."

Through fresh tears, Tina answered, "I guess I do owe you an explanation. Let me start by saying that there was a man I planned to marry. His name was Larry. He was an employee in the hotel my parents owned. Although he was ten years older, I had a crush on him, and was the happiest girl on earth when he suggested we plan a future together."

"I take it, something went wrong."

"You might say that, Alan. He turned out to be a con artist." Tina hesitated before continuing. "We were to get engaged at Christmas and planned a June wedding after my graduation from college. It was every young girl's dream. Apparently my dreams were not Larry's. He never intended for us to get married. There were other objectives in Larry's mind."

"What happened, Tina? What objectives?"

"My parents were interested in buying another hotel—one that Larry and I would manage after our wedding. My father wasn't feeling well at the time and encouraged Larry to go scouting around for something suitable. Supposedly Larry found a deal that interested my father. In spite of protests from me, my trusting Dad mortgaged our hotel and invested all the money we had into a partnership with some people who had two hotels in Chicago. As it turned out there were no hotels. It all came to light when my parents were found murdered."

Trying to keep up with Tina as she spoke, Alan asked her to slow down. "You're telling me your parents were murdered? No wonder you have nightmares. Did Larry have something to do with the murders?"

"All I know is he disappeared and the police are looking for him. It's been two years. Our hotel was taken over by creditors. There was no money for me to finish school. Life as I knew it, was over."

"And that's how you ended up in London as a tour guide."

"Yes, but that's not the whole story>"

Seeing that Tina was again ready to break down, Alan said, "I'm so sorry. Although I can see how painful it is for you to talk about what happened, please go on, Tina. Let it all out. It will help and I'm here to see that it does."

Again pulling herself together, Tina repeated what she had learned from the morning's telephone call. "The detective working on my case called this morning hinting that Larry was homosexual—not even a real man. It seems he could not love me or any woman. His interest was in other men. That's why he was always putting me off whenever I looked for or tried to show affection. I thought it was because of my young age. How's that for being naive? Oh Alan, I need to know that it isn't my fault. Kiss me. Hold me. Make love to me."

This time there were no cries of pain—just contented moans. It sounded like a kitten purring. Holding each other close, both finally fell asleep. Tina couldn't remember when she had slept so well. The break of dawn found Alan again ready to take her and an aroused Tina eagerly responded. Neither wanted the night to end, but both had work to do if they were to see "Phantom" that afternoon.

After quick showers, they dressed and had room service send up breakfast. Between mouthfuls, they talked. Alan had a million questions and Tina did her best to answer him explaining that the mystery of who was responsible for her plight remained a question mark. It was then that Tina remembered the ring on Alan's finger. She had been so self-absorbed that all thought of his being a married man had escaped her.

"Oh Alan—I'm so sorry." Taking his hand, she said, "Forgive me. I didn't mean to make trouble for you. We must forget this ever happened."

"What? Of course it happened. I wanted it to happen and you did too."

"I should never have involved you in my problems, Alan. We flirted a little and it must have looked like I was coming on to you. Then, finding me hysterical, it was only natural you would react as you did. I got carried away."

"Let's say we both got carried away, but I'm not sorry—not for one minute."

"I have no regrets for myself, Alan. Where I was an immature child, you've transformed me into a grown woman. It was about time and I'll always be grateful to you. However you have a wife and I had no right to cause you to forget that."

"Wife? What wife? Whatever gave you the idea that I'm married?"

"You wear a ring. It looks like a wedding ring."

"Have I ever said anything about a wife, Tina? The ring on my finger was my father's. It was all I had of him when he died. I always wear it. I'm not married, Tina."

"I thought you were married, Alan. I really did."

"Well I'm not. That's why I took this job. I like the freedom of coming and going where and when I want. My father married very young and was tied down with responsibilities until the day he died. That kind of life is not for me. Today I'm a bus driver. Tomorrow I might want to be something else. I like it that way."

At first Tina was bewildered that someone she had spent a most important night with could treat sex so casually. After some thought, however, she was relieved. Somewhere she had heard that sex and love were not synonymous. She reasoned that they both had needed each other, but for different reasons. While there might be other nights, time would eventually take them in different directions. Alan would most likely continue to do his thing in England whereas she had a mission to accomplish. She had promised to avenge the death of her parents. That, Tina knew, could lead her anywhere.

"I think we'd better take time out to glance at the packet received from Cartrite, Tina. Also, I did come in here yesterday with a message for you. Someone by the name of Mara called. She left her address and phone number in case you needed to reach her. Do I want to know who Mara is?"

"She's a very good friend—my roommate in college. I'll get back to her. Now let's get the paperwork over with. After I make my calls confirming reservations it will be time to leave for the theater. We must get there before the chandelier falls."

"We'll pick up Chinese food on our way back to the hotel. As for this evening, I've already got plans for us."

Suspecting what the plans might be, Tina said, "Just be sure you schedule in a little sleep time. We've got to be wide awake in the morning when the next group of fifty enthusiastic tourists arrive. They must not suspect that we've been bad."

"I'll be good in public, but after hours, will make no promises."

The third and final Great Britain tour was routine—uneventful until they were on the ferry going from Fishguard to Rosslare, Ireland. Not familiar with doorstops on board, Janet Adams fell coming out of the ladies' restroom. On inspection, there was a pretty deep cut on her forehead. In addition, trying to break her fall, she had twisted her wrist. The small infirmary on board was able to take care of the head wound, but no X-ray equipment was available to determine if the wrist had been fractured. A side trip to the emergency room of St. Catherine's Hospital was suggested by the staff nurse.

"Is the hospital much out of the way, Alan?"

"It will likely cost us half a day—an hour each way plus whatever time it takes in the emergency room. If not life threatening, you wait and then wait some more."

"It's our responsibility to see that Miss Adams is examined and taken care of. She may opt to cancel out of the remainder of our tour. In that case I'll have to arrange for her transportation home. Whatever happens, changes will have to be made to our itinerary. Let me talk it over with her and the other tourists."

The ferry was just about to dock when Tina gathered her charges around her. Miss Adams immediately made it clear that she planned to continue on the tour under any circumstances. Popular with her fellow travelers, there was a resounding cheer.

"Good! That's settled," said Tina. "I'll call the hotel and ask them to hold dinner for a few hours. I'm afraid we'll have to forgo our scheduled lunch stop at Waterford. That may be a disappointment to some of you, but for those interested, there will be other opportunities to buy crystal."

"While you're in the hospital with Miss Adams, I'll look for a place to have lunch," said Alan. "We've only had a snack and the troops will be hungry."

Back on the bus all were sympathetic to Miss Adams who was feeling no pain thanks to a little pink pill. She made jokes about being clumsy and promised to call for assistance dressing, if necessary. "Always willing to help a lady in distress," said someone from the back of the bus. There was no shortage of young men ready, willing and able to get involved.

About an hour later, the bus with occupants was at St. Catherine's hospital. Tina accompanied Miss Adams to have her injuries taken care of while Alan drove off to find a suitable lunch stop.

"You're doing good, Alan," someone said. "Now go find us a deli."

"Better make that a pub," shouted another passenger. "Delicatessens are a New York thing."

X-rays proved that Janet had indeed suffered a fracture. After immobilizing her wrist, Tina and her patient left the hospital to find the group waiting for them in the parking lot.

"Thanks for being so patient with me," Janet said. "They fixed me up. I'm glad it wasn't my arm that was broken. Look at all these bandages just to fix a fractured wrist."

"We should all give thanks to our bus driver" said one of the ladies. "He found a pub whose owner happily supplied lunches. Not only were the sandwiches good, but the proprietor allowed us to use the shady area in back of his house for a picnic."

Everything had worked out better than expected. It was a contented group that continued toward Blarney Castle where they spent the remainder of the afternoon. The incident was much discussed and would be remembered as one of the highlights of the trip when telling their friends back home.

Tina and Alan rehashed the day's events that night after dinner. It had been a long day and they soon found themselves headed for Tina's room. Sharing a bed at the end of each busy day was something they both looked forward to.

While making every effort to keep their relationship private, it was difficult to fool everyone. "They think we don't know where they go at night," said Ida Cerna, "but it's a free country. More power to them." Tina sometimes caught the knowing looks of their tourists, but Alan was oblivious.

The final Great Britain tour was uneventful and quickly coming to an end. Both Tina and Alan, being from different backgrounds, had begun their relationship fully believing it would be temporary. While it lasted, they would continue to seek comfort in each other. That had been the plan, but each day found them more deeply involved. One night Alan said, "I can't bear the thought that it's almost over. You're planning on two weeks in America, but I wish you would spend them here with me. Do you really have to go?"

"I don't want to leave you Alan, but you know I must. There's unfinished business waiting for me at home. Detective White might be more diligent if I was there nagging him. Being out of the country for a while was good for me personally, but hasn't done anything to help me find the murderer of my parents."

"You don't even have an address, Tina. Where can I reach you? I can't allow you to just disappear out of my life."

"I know where you are, and you can reach me at my friend Mara's until I find an apartment of my own."

"Near the home office?"

"No! I'd like to be in the vicinity of Chicago. That's where Mara and her husband live, and it's where Larry seems to have found a second home. I might possibly run into him or some clues."

"I understand, but let's not talk anymore about you leaving me. There's so little time left. It's going to be terrible letting you go."

"I'll never forget you, Alan. You've changed my life and I'll always be grateful. Thank you for allowing me to be a woman."

"It was my pleasure." replied Alan trying his best to keep it light.

"Don't laugh, Alan. I was a child when we met—not willing to trust anyone. Thanks to you I can now hold my head up and face the world with confidence."

"If you find Larry, then what?"

"He betrayed me and cheated my parents, but I don't believe he murdered them. There is an explanation for all that happened and I won't rest until I find the answer."

Tina and Alan tried to make the most of any private time they had left. Both rationalized that it was primarily sex and companionship they had shared—not love that would last a lifetime. Neither was yet willing to make such a commitment. Alan would continue living in England and Tina's roots were in America even though she expected to be away much of the time.

In spite of good intentions, Tina and Alan's last days together proved to be more sentimental than either of them had anticipated. Alan, who had wanted no commitments, was having second thoughts. He had never before felt so strongly about anyone. While a loner by nature, he found himself wanting Tina to remain with him. Perhaps he could settle down after all, he thought. But what about Tina? Was she ready for anything more.? Alan could understand her wanting to put the ghosts to rest. Unfortunately, the ghosts were in America. Rationalizing that a temporary separation might be best for all, Alan said, "This isn't the end, Tina. We'll start again whenever you're ready. Meanwhile, promise me you'll write. I need to know you're okay."

"I will and don't worry. I'll be fine. The gang is having a farewell party downstairs, Alan. We're supposed to be there and had better get going."

"It's our last night. I've asked room service to send up champagne and sandwiches. If we sneak away after a reasonable time, I think our tourists will forgive us. They may not even notice we're missing."

"Don't fool yourself, Alan. They watch us like hawks."

"They've already been partying with some drinks under their belts, Tina. By the time we duck out, they won't know we're alive, and even if they do, who cares. It's our last night. When I give the signal, take my lead and follow me upstairs. I've got serious plans for us."

"Promises, promises! Remember, we have an early wake-up call. Getting everyone on their flights is always a challenge."

"You'll be leaving as well, Tina, and that's a bigger problem for me. I don't know how I'll be able to say 'good-bye.'"

"Don't make me cry, Alan."

"No time for that, my sweet. There's a party downstairs waiting for us. Are you ready to join them? Don't forget my signal when I think it's safe for us to leave."

8

Tina was back in America. In Boston, her first order of business was at the Cartrite Agency. There she turned in her paperwork. The agency was pleased that Tina's first tours had gone well, and was anxious to reassign her to the Greek Islands. She was granted two weeks' leave to take care of personal matters before the start of the tours.

The agency had been overwhelmed with reservations when advertising a new Greek Island package. As a result there would be two busses for the land portions of the itinerary. Tina was expected to host one group while Alice Renkin, a woman she'd met during training, would be the tour guide on the second bus.

Since the tour included several flights and a cruise, drivers and escorts for land and city excursions would vary from day to day. Upon landing in Athens, the one hundred tourists were to board another flight to Cairo, Egypt, there to spend three days. On returning to Piraeus, all would board a ship for a seven day cruise of the Greek Islands. The tour was to terminate in Istanbul, Turkey. There would be four back to back tours—each fully booked.

Confident that she was thoroughly briefed in what was expected of her, Tina left for Chicago the next morning.

An anxious Mara was waiting at the airport. After vigorous hugs both tried to talk at once. There were many questions to ask and so much news to share.

"I won't be able to concentrate on driving, Tina. Let's have a cup of coffee here in the airport. A muffin might be in order as well since it will take at least an hour before we get to our condo."

"Okay by me, Mara. They only gave us peanuts on the flight from Boston."

Seated in the terminal, Mara said, "You look wonderful, Tina."

"So do you, Mara. Marriage certainly agrees with you. How's Alex?"

"He's terrific. The honeymoon just goes on and on—that is when he's in town. When he's on the road, which is often, I'm lonely. However, it's you I want to hear about. Something is different. The sadness is gone from your eyes, but it's more than that." As Tina blushed, Mara continued, "Why you're glowing, my friend. I think you've got some explaining to do. That occasional postcard we received from you left much unsaid. Time to confess, my friend."

Obviously trying to change the subject, Tina asked, "Have you heard anything about Larry, Mara?"

"No, I haven't. I know I'm staring, Tina, but you look so good. It's as though you've come back to the living."

"Going away for a while was the best thing I could have done, Mara. Yes I'm still determined to avenge the death of my parents, but I feel stronger, and am at last ready to put my life back on track."

"Dare I hope that you're here to stay?"

"No. I'm going to continue guiding tourists for a while. The money is pretty good, and you know, traveling has always been one of my true passions."

"How long before you have to go off again? You'll be staying with us, of course. Alex and I wouldn't have it any other way."

"Thanks, Mara. I'll take you up on that offer until I find an apartment. Hopefully there will be something available in your neighborhood."

"I'd like that, but with you traveling all the time, why wouldn't you just stay with us when you're in town?"

"Because you and Alex are newlyweds and should be alone together. If that isn't enough reason, I need to put down roots somewhere. About my next assignment, the agency has given me two weeks to get my house in order. With all I have to do, that time will go very fast."

"I'll help you, Tina. Together we'll find an apartment nearby."

Tina wanted an apartment in the Chicago area not only to be near her friend, but because Larry had spent so much time there. She hoped to run into him somewhere and pin him down for answers to all the questions haunting her.

"It's going to be so nice having you with us even for a little while, Tina. Now, however, let's talk about you and your adventures in England. Did you meet anyone exciting?"

"Well, there was this bus driver," answered her red faced friend. Mara was amused and prompted for details.

"Sounds like a special bus driver. Go on!"

"His name is Alan, and yes, he was more than just a bus driver."

"I knew there was something different about you. Don't you know secrets between friends are not allowed? Tell me about Alan, your bus driver."

"We worked really well together."

"There's more than just work involved here, Tina. Don't even think of holding back on me. How old is this Alan? Are you planning to see him again?"

"He's about my age, quite good looking and short like me. He knows his way around and I really grew to depend on him. Alan liked to tease, but always in fun. It helped take my mind off the problems at home."

"And?" prompted Mara.

"We flirted, but it was all innocent until the day that Detective White called suggesting Larry was gay. Alan came into my room and found me hysterical. I was a basket case."

"What was that you just said, Tina? Larry gay? Says who and when did this happen?

"One of Larry's card playing friends—someone I never met, said so. He told Detective White that Larry was a closet homosexual. After the way he behaved toward me, it didn't take much to convince me that he was telling the truth."

"Yet he asked you to marry him? Why would he do that if he was gay? That's really low."

"I don't have any proof, but it all fits—the way he was always making excuses and insisting that I remain untouchable. It wasn't natural and I should have guessed. Anyhow, when Detective White called me, I really went over the edge—my parents murdered, everything they had gone, Larry's disappearance and then to find out he couldn't ever have loved me."

"A call like that would put anyone over the edge, Tina."

"Alan found me in pretty bad shape. He didn't know what had happened or what to do with me. Trying anything he could think of to comfort me, he took me in his arms and kissed me. One kiss lead to another and then another. Before we knew what was happening, we were in bed where I willingly gave up my virginity."

Mara was shocked, but understood completely. Her friend had been terribly hurt—first by the loss of her family and home, and then by Larry's indifference and behavior. She needed to know that someone could love and want her.

"It was a fling, Mara, which lasted through the remaining weeks of our tours. Being with Alan was what I needed. He was exciting and wonderful."

"When it comes right down to it, Tina, there's nothing more comforting than to be in a man's arms. I'm happy for you. No wonder we heard so little from you the last few weeks. It had to be difficult for you to leave your Englishman behind."

"It was, Mara. We probably won't see each other again, but I'll never forget Alan and what he did for me."

"Time will tell if there is to be an encore with your bus driver, but there's no doubt in my mind, that Alan was good for you. You look wonderful."

"You aren't disappointed in me, Mara?"

"Never! After all you've been through, it was time for some happiness in your life."

Realizing that they had been talking for a long time, Mara said, "We'd better start for home. Alex will be wondering if you missed the flight."

"You're right, Mara, but I'm really happy that we took this opportunity to talk—just the two of us. Alex might not understand if he knew that I succumbed to the first man to cross my path."

The two friends continued their chatter while on the drive home, through dinner and long into the night. Tina had not yet adjusted to the time change, but finally crashed when there was no more response from Mara. Tomorrow would begin her search for an apartment. She would also contact Detective White.

It was almost noon the next day when Tina woke up. Mara, knowing Tina's plans to find an apartment, was going through the classified section of the newspaper. On hearing footsteps, Mara looked up and said, "You're finally awake and hungry, I presume. Alex warned me about keeping you up so late last night. He's well acquainted with jet lag."

"I really was tired, Mara, but it wasn't just due to jet lag. Some of the blame must go to the fact that Alan and I were burning the candle at both ends pretty steadily before my departure."

"Don't apologize! You're entitled! While you're having breakfast or lunch, since it's almost twelve o'clock, you can look over some of the ads I've clipped out of the local paper."

Although Mara's preference was that Tina live with them when in town, she could understand Tina's need to have a place of her own. The important thing was that she'd be nearby. They could do things together. They might even find Larry if they combined forces. After all wasn't she Dr. Watson and Tina, Sherlock Holmes?

"Don't know what I'd do without you, Mara. You're a gem putting up with me."

"Hey! Remember our promise that first night at college? We said we'd always be there for each other."

"Yes. But it's so one-sided. You're always the one helping me."

"You are my family, Tina. You and Alex are all I have on this side of the hemisphere."

"Would your parents consider relocating to the United States?"

"No! They'd never leave South Africa. My brothers and sisters are all settled in Capetown. All their friends and relatives live there. Mom and Dad would be very lonely here. The best I can hope for is a visit now and then."

Three days later, Tina found an acceptable apartment. It was a small one bedroom walkup in a quiet neighborhood about a mile from Alex and Mara's condo. She paid two months' rent and then began a search for furniture that would be functional and not terribly expensive.

As they went from store to store, Tina said, "I'm so excited, Mara. No longer will I be a homeless person. The apartment is close to your condo, but I'll try not to become a nuisance."

"You could never be a nuisance, Tina. I'm delighted to have you nearby."

There were some pieces of furniture that Tina found to her liking, but she said, "It's unlikely that anything I order would be delivered before I have to leave on my next tour."

"Don't worry, Tina. They can call me when your purchases are ready for delivery. I'll wait at your apartment and check everything out so that you won't come back to an empty apartment."

"Thank you again, Mara. I'm always in your debt." Tina bought a couch and lounge chair and then found a small oval table with chairs that would fit well into her combination living-dining room. "Now," she said, "I must go back to your condo and call Detective White. I want him to know where I am."

The detective was happy to receive Tina's call. He'd already made some unsuccessful attempts to find her. "It's important that we meet before you take off again," he said. "I'll be in Chicago for a few days next week. Can we get together?"

"Sure, but give me a hint. What's important? Do you have a lead on Larry's whereabouts?"

"It might be nothing but a hunch, Tina. We'll talk about it when I see you."

"I've rented an apartment, but haven't moved in yet. It would be best if we met at one of the hotels in town." They settled on the Downtown Regent, five p.m., the following Monday.

On Monday, the day of the planned meeting, Mara drove Tina to the Regent Hotel and then went to meet Alex for dinner. He would be leaving for California on business the following morning and they had gotten into the habit of eating out the night before his departures.

Since Officer White was not in sight when she arrived, Tina left word at the desk, picked up a newspaper and sat in the lounge to wait. An article in the paper caught her attention. It was a story about a Milwaukee family that had died—burned when a fire gutted their apartment. The apartment was in a large building previously owned by the couple. According to the reporter, the building had been taken over by a group of investors. The victims had been in the middle of a court battle and had refused to vacate the premises.

Tina was so engrossed in the story, which seemed to parallel her own, that she lost track of time. Glancing at her watch, she was surprised to find it was after six o'clock. What happened to her five o'clock appointment with Detective White? She would wait another fifteen minutes. Something urgent must have come up. At half past six Tina gave up, hailed a cab and left, fully expecting the detective would call her at Mara's condo later in the evening.

When Mara and Alex came home, anxious to hear the details of her meeting, they too were puzzled. Tina told them about the newspaper article and all agreed that the circumstances were too similar to be entirely coincidental.

"I can't understand why he hasn't called. Do you think he's involved in that Milwaukee case, Alex?. Maybe that's what he wanted to talk to me about."

"You could be right," Alex said. "He'll surely call with an explanation in the morning. I'll be leaving before seven tomorrow and it's getting late. Mara wants to help me pack and I have a few surprises for her so we'll say good night. See you when I get back, Tina."

"Thank you Alex—for everything. I hope you know that you and Mara are my favorite people."

"It's a pleasure having you here. Both Mara and I wish you didn't feel it necessary to move into a place of your own, but we understand. All I ask is that you try to keep my beautiful wife busy whenever you can. I don't like being away so much, but there are a few more years of travel ahead for me. A person has to pay his dues in this kind of a job. Thankfully, Mara understands."

Mara rose early to see Alex off. After kissing him good-bye, she picked up the morning paper and sat down to have a second cup of coffee. The headlines caught her in mid-swallow. A police officer had been killed. It appeared to be a mob hit. Something told her—she didn't have to read on to know—that the officer in question was the same Detective White Tina was to have met the night before.

Mara stared at the article trying to fully comprehend what she had read, when a sleepy-eyed Tina appeared. From the expression on Mara's face, she knew instantly something bad had happened.

"What is it, Mara? You look like the world just came to an end."

"You won't believe it, Tina! It says here in the paper that your Detective was shot last night."

"Detective White? That can't be true. I've got to talk to him. Where is he? Which hospital is he at?"

"He's dead, Tina."

"How can he be dead, Mara? We were to have met last night."

"According to this article, they think the shooting was mob related—that he was stepping on some toes."

Tina was speechless. After a long silence, she asked, "Who, now, will help me find Larry?" Mara could not give her an answer. After much thought, Tina continued, "There's a similarity between what happened to the

Milwaukee family and that of my parents. I believe that is what Detective White wanted to tell me."

"Would anyone have known about your scheduled meeting with him yesterday?"

"I don't know. It's possible he was shot to stop him from getting to me."

"Or maybe they, whoever they are, believe he'd already talked to you. You too could be a target, Tina."

"Me? That's possible, but I don't think anyone knows about my job—nor could they have gotten wind of where I am living. How could they when I don't even know the address myself?"

"I never thought I'd say this, but it's good you'll be leaving in a few days, Tina. It might not hurt to contact Detective White's precinct in St. Louis and tell them of your suspicions. With the death of one of their own, there should be investigations. Write them a letter and I'll mail it for you after you've safely gone on your next tour."

"That's a good idea, but promise you won't do anything to endanger yourself, Mara. I'd never forgive myself if anything happened to you. Suppose you did run into Larry on the street one of these days, what would you do?"

"There's nothing I'd like better than to come face to face with him, Tina. I'd get the low down on the creep and wait for your return to strangle him. Don't worry about me. I can take care of myself—look at how big I am. As for you, little one, only Alex and I know where you live, who you work for and where you're going. Officer White might have had some phone numbers, but that wouldn't help anyone locate you overseas. If anyone does contact me, I'm deaf, dumb and blind. I'll keep you informed if there are any important developments."

"Larry knows you, Mara. I hope he doesn't realize you and Alex are living in the Chicago area."

"He probably assumes we've settled in the East. That's where we attended college and, of course, Alex's parents live in Vermont."

The following days were a whirlwind. Together the friends cleaned the apartment in preparation for furniture that would be delivered. Tina expected to be back in about two months and that would be the official moving day.

All too quickly came the morning of her departure. Tina had just finished packing the last of her bags and was about to lock up and tag them when the doorbell rang. She couldn't believe it, but Stanley, Mara's brother-in-law and Tina's good friend and beau from college days, was standing at the door.

"Stanley—what are you doing here? I thought you were in Boston. How good to see you."

"I knew you would be leaving today. Alex updates me on your comings and goings even though Mara tries to keep your secrets. Brothers are like that. You can't trust them."

"It was no secret, Stanley. There was so much I had to do in my two weeks off. Finding and furnishing an apartment takes time, you know. I planned to call when in my own apartment, but that won't be until my tours in Greece are over."

"I'm worried about you, Tina. That newspaper article about Detective White bothers me. It's very strange and I think there's more to it than is being reported. I'm on my way back to Boston, and if it's okay with you, would like to accompany you as far as New York. It would make me feel better to know that you are safely out of Chicago."

"You're a good friend, Stan. To be perfectly honest I am looking over my shoulder a lot these days and would welcome your company. Thanks for caring. I'd certainly enjoy not traveling to New York alone."

Instructing Stanley, as they departed for the airport, to watch over her friend, Mara kissed them both. "Hurry back Tina, and be careful."

"Don't worry, Mara. I'll see that she boards the plane for Athens before I get on my connecting flight to Boston. As for you, be good and keep your doors locked and bolted. A person can't be too careful these days."

"I'm thinking about getting myself a big dog—one that bites. See you in a few weeks, my friend. Can't wait for you to get back."

Stanley and Tina had a great deal of catching up to do while enroute to New York. They hadn't seen each other in a long time. While Tina feared an encounter with him would be awkward, it was evident that Stan bore no grudges. They could be friends even though their carefree relationship had ended with her choice of Larry as a soulmate.

"Tell me about your experiences taking tourists through Great Britain, Tina. Do you really like what you're doing? It must be difficult living out of a suitcase and sleeping in a different bed every night."

"For now, it's something I have to do, Stan. The job keeps me busy and that's good. It allows me to block out the tragedy of my parents' deaths for a few hours each day. Dealing with all the different personalities and experiences can be a challenge, but I like people, and have always wanted to see the wonders of the world."

Tina told him about situations she had encountered in her travels. Some were quite amusing. He laughed with her and it felt good—almost like old times. Obviously she did not mention her relationship with Alan.

"Our world gets smaller all the time," she said. "This morning I was in Chicago. We're about to land in New York and tomorrow morning I'll be in Athens hoping to connect with the other crew members. There's a great demand for this trip. We ended up with one hundred tourists going on each tour."

After landing in New York, they had only a short time before the boarding of Tina's flight. A hug, a friendly kiss on the lips and promising to write, Tina was out of sight. Turning to leave, Stan could not deny his feelings for her. He had never stopped loving her and hoped she would wake up one day recognizing him as more than a good, loyal friend. He was willing to wait. Patience had always been his strong suit.

Turning and about to walk away, Stanley's attention was drawn to two men standing nearby. They were staring at Tina as she passed through the gate and appeared to be having a discussion about her. While it's true her looks could turn heads, this was a different kind of interest—more than just the reaction of men ogling a beautiful woman. I'm getting paranoid, he thought as he turned to catch his flight. The men stopped talking and began to walk in the same direction. Were they following him? Nonsense! Your concern for Tina is making you a little crazy, Stanley. Next thing you know, you'll be looking under the bushes.

9

The airport in Athens was total chaos. Having left New York seven hours behind schedule, Tina missed the connecting flight to Cairo. It was there that she was to meet and welcome most of the new group of tourists. Fortunately Alice Renkin, her counterpart, was already in Cairo, and had managed, along with the bus drivers, to get the earlier arrivals settled in the hotel.

"Glad to see that you and the rest of our tour group made it," said Alice greeting them with a relieved smile. She had been concerned about handling so many people on her own.

"Sorry to be late. I thought we'd never get off the ground in New York and then that delay resulted in our missing the connecting flight to Egypt."

"Well you're here now and all is well. Do you know what happened at J.F.K.?"

Tina explained that people were boarding as scheduled when suddenly everything came to a halt. Passengers were told only that there was a serious problem with the airplane. The carrier was in the process of requisitioning another 747 which would have to be made ready for the eight hour flight overseas. The airline expected a delay of two hours since luggage and meals would have to be transferred. All were given food vouchers and told to wait for the next boarding announcement.

Two hours later passengers were again ready to begin boarding only to find that the second aircraft also had problems. A third 747 had to be located and prepared. Luggage and meals were transferred one more time. Again a two-hour delay. Passengers were moaning, groaning and complaining all to no avail. Some decided to give up their travel plans entirely. "Two strikes and you're out" was the mantra. The seven passengers traveling with Tina were courageous, however, and remained for the successful final liftoff. Upon landing in Athens, all confessed to having been very uneasy about the "seaworthiness" of aircraft in general.

"Thank goodness you were here, Alice. Knowing you were on an earlier flight saved me from having a complete nervous breakdown."

"Fortunately I checked and knew you'd be delayed. Hope you don't mind, but I took it upon myself to have our two groups meet for a short briefing at nine tonight. The roster has been checked and all one hundred passengers are present and accounted for. You'll have fifty-two on your bus—forty-eight on mine. By the way, Tina, where'd you pick up that hunk bringing up the rear?"

"I opened my eyes and there he was. His name is Jason Thomas. The roster lists him as thirty-two years old. He's traveling alone, but that doesn't mean he's available. Would you want him on your bus? It can be arranged."

"No!. He's all yours. I've already picked the man for me."

"Well, back to business! I understand we'll be on our way after a seven o'clock breakfast. Omar Rami and Faro Hassan are our city guides. They have scheduled a full day of sightseeing. The morning will be devoted to the Cairo Museum."

Interrupting, Alice told Tina that the group would be having lunch in an outdoor restaurant in the country. On the way, the tourists would see Bedouins living and working along the fertile banks of the Nile River. Omar and Faro planned to make quite a few stops before the busses would return to Cairo. Among them would be the bulrushes where Moses was said to have been set adrift.

"It's a good thing our city guides are in charge the next few days," said Tina, yawning. "I've never been able to sleep on a plane and can't wait to hit the sack. Could I ask you to take over tonight's briefing, Alice? I promise to be a new person after stretching out on a real bed for a few hours."

Breakfast behind them the next morning, all were ready to get on with the day's adventure. First was the museum. Omar was on Tina's bus. He had a little problem with English, but knew his way around the exhibits. Obviously he'd heard the questions a thousand times and was well prepared.
.

"Is that really solid gold?" asked a lady from Baltimore staring at the glass-enclosed sarcophagus. The mask of gold was an embossed replica—the head of Tutankhamun, the boy king. The tomb had been found in the Valley of the Kings.

Most of the tour members were fascinated by the museum's contents and Omar's commentary but, as in every crowd, there are those who would rather spend time shopping for souvenirs.

"Where can I buy a Cartouche?" asked an elderly woman from New York. She was already wearing more jewelry than anyone should own, let alone take on a tour.

"What's a Cartouche?" asked another lady.

"A Cartouche originally was a large stone or tablet, either oval or oblong, providing an area for an inscription in hieroglyphics," answered Omar. "Visitors often ask to have their names translated into hieroglyphics and then have the symbols mounted on a silver or gold plaque that can be worn on a chain. It's a popular souvenir of a visit to Egypt."

"I must have one," said Mrs. Reif. "Where can I get a cartouche with my very own name?" Omar was suddenly surrounded by a chorus of interested shoppers. "How long does it take to get one made up?"

"There will be time for you ladies to shop. You will go to the Bazaar before leaving Cairo. There you can buy anything you want. Trust me, I know the good stores." It was pretty clear that there would be something in it for Omar if he brought business to the right places.

Driving through the city of Cairo was an experience that fascinated everyone. Where else could one see men in white sheets, attached by long ropes to camels and donkeys, maneuvering through traffic—or veiled women balancing baskets filled to overflowing on their heads? There was a near accident caused by a man who appeared to be wearing loaves of bread on both arms. The bread had big holes in the center causing one of the tourists to remark, "Look at those king-sized bagels."

All laughed, but were speechless as the bus toured the market place. It was over one hundred degrees in the shade yet whole quarters of meat were hanging from hooks outside the shops. The passing multitudes were not disturbed by the swarming flies who were enjoying the feast offered by the butchers as well as fruit and vegetable stands. Omar explained that the natives had no problem with flies. "They go away when you go home," he said.

When learning that "home" could be anything, the tourists were even more astounded. According to Omar, there were entire families that lived on the streets. Others camped in tents over graves in the cemetery—these wanted to be close to loved ones who had died. Fortunately rain or cold weather is a rarity in Egypt.

Life was certainly different here. Everyone had something to say except Jason Thomas who sat quietly by himself apparently oblivious to what was going on around him. He appeared not to be interested or preoccupied. Attempts to include him in conversation fell on deaf ears. Tina wondered why he had chosen a tour that was obviously of no interest to him. He's strange and moody, she said to herself. It's best to ignore him.

Leaving the city, the busses followed the Nile where they saw natives working with water buffalo. It was interesting to watch. They'd had an early breakfast and were beginning to feel hungry when the bus driver turned into a narrow path that lead to an outdoor restaurant. Omar told them that they would be served shishkabob along with some native vegetables and watermelon.

When Alice arrived with her group, Tina said, "I don't know what happened to my appetite, Alice, but it seems to have left me after seeing all those flies in the market place. I know the food in our hotel is safe and we've had no problem with it, but we're out in the open here. Something tells me I should pass on this banquet."

"It doesn't look very appealing, I admit, Tina, but when in Egypt, one should do like the Egyptians."

"The Egyptians have lived here a long time, Alice. They have, no doubt, developed an immunity to whatever parasites may be hanging around. I'm hungry, but some canned soda should get me through until dinner. This off-the-road outdoor stopover makes me very uncomfortable."

After lunch they visited what was thought to be the oldest of the pyramids—Sakara, the Step Pyramid. Then there were stops at the forty-foot statue of Ramses II and the bulrushes. It was very hot. Arriving back at the hotel, the tired tourists had time only to freshen up. Then they were to depart for dinner and the evening's entertainment which would be in a huge tent. Inside the tent were long couches facing low tables on which dinner would be served. In the center was a dance floor where belly-dancers performed.

Prior to entering the tent, they were treated to a performance of dancing horses. The evening should have been an Arabian Nights delight except that many of Tina and Alice's tourists were complaining of stomach cramps. By the time dinner was served, most had excused themselves and gone back to the hotel.

It seems the groups had succumbed to "Pharaoh's Revenge." Only a few hardy souls survived to make an appearance at breakfast the next morning. By the time the busses were to leave for the day's outing, only twelve had survived. The remaining tourists were not in any condition to ride the camels to CHEOPS, the Great Pyramids of Giza, or the Half Lion-Half Man, SPHINX.

Alice was also among the missing. "Glad I didn't eat lunch yesterday," said Tina as she gathered together what was left of the tourist groups. "Come, everyone," she coaxed leading the way. "Find a camel you like and let's go. You didn't come all this way not to be able to boast that you rode a camel to the pyramids."

Watching Mrs. Reif, who was first to mount, Tina shouted, "Hang on! Camels get up back end first and move as soon as they are sat on." Her warning came too late. Turning to Mr. Reif, Tina added, "I don't think your wife heard me. Fortunately she was holding on to the saddle horn. She could have gone right over that camel's head."

Tina wasn't so sure she should have encouraged this side trip when she saw how frightened everyone looked as they watched Mrs. Reif try to get her balance. There was no turning back however. The Bedouin camel drivers were already contemplating the tips that would ensure safe passage.

"Protect yourself against the Evil Eye," they said with their hands outstretched, but Tina had warned them not to pay until they were at their destination. It was not uncommon for a camel driver to take the money and run— that is, take a person off the camel and leave him or her stranded wherever they were at the time.

The few tourists that remained had little choice, at this point, but to get on the camels. They were soon a small parade headed for the pyramids. As the group began to relax, there could be heard nervous laughter. Arriving at CHEOPS, about half an hour later, all were happy that Tina had encouraged them to take advantage of the opportunity. While smelling of camel, all had survived and were pleased with themselves.

"You'll want to go inside CHEOPS even though there's not much to see," said Tina. "Everything in these pyramids has either been looted or found a home in museums. The finest collection of pyramid treasures, as you know, is in the Cairo museum."

Since it was extremely hot in the sun, Tina had no problem getting her small group to accompany her into the pyramid. Lighting inside was very dim. Cleat-like steps and planked walkways needed to be cautiously traversed single file. Tina's tourists had finally gotten to the last slippery incline when the dim lights went out completely. In total darkness, all were captive not daring to move in any direction. Panicked, some began to shout for help and others resorted to four letter words. Without illumination, it would be impossible to go forward or retrace one's steps. It was about ten minutes before the lights were back on. At that point a few brave souls risked the remaining steps into the center of the tomb, had a quick look into the empty room and left, fearing another blackout.

"Was that someone's idea of a joke?" asked reclusive Jason Thomas as he passed a toothless, smiling Bedouin. All were amazed that Mr. Thomas had finally spoken, but continued along the path that would take them outside. The sun felt wonderful after having been in the damp, musty-smelling pyramid. Turning, expecting to see their leader, they found that Tina was nowhere in sight. Was she still in the pyramid? Had the lights gone out again?

Turning to the old Bedouin, the group shouted, "You must find our guide." There was no reply—just a grinning face staring back at them.

"He doesn't understand us."

"Let's find someone who does," said Mrs. Andrews, desperately looking for help. There was no one around.

At that moment, Tina emerged. "Where were you?" all shouted at once. "We were looking for someone who would go back in there to find you. You're bleeding! There's blood on your forehead. What happened to you?"

"Is everyone out? Are you all here? I'm fine. It's just a scratch. When the lights went out someone ran into me throwing me off balance. With the wet sand under my feet, I slipped. That's what I get for not wearing walking shoes. I must have hit my head on something. The next thing I knew, you had all disappeared. It's such a relief to find you out here together."

"You had us worried," said Mrs. Reif. Everyone around here just grins when you say something to them. We didn't know what to do."

"You did good. As you can see, there was nothing to worry about. Now let's go back to the hotel for a little rest before dinner. Tonight we see the Sound and Light Show at the Great Pyramid. I know you'll find the story, together with the lighting, very thought provoking."

"You had to be there," is what those that were fortunate enough to see the Sound and Light Show reported to the still suffering tourists who had missed the presentation. "It was as though the sphinx was able to speak. Can you imagine the tales she would tell the world if she really could talk?"

Spending some time in Cairo the following morning, all the ladies stocked up on Cartouches—at a stand highly recommended by Omar and Faro. Then the two groups were flown back to Greece, where they would board a cruise ship out of the Port of Piraeus. Some of the tourists were beginning to feel better, but all were happy to be on the ship where they would have ready access to private bathrooms.

"Have you had any complaints from your group about toilet seats?" asked Tina when she met Alice in the hall.

"I know there are problems with mine. Every time I sit down—and since I'm still suffering from Pharaoh's Revenge, that's quite often—the toilet seat shifts and comes off the hinges. At this point it's cracked and I've called the steward for a replacement."

"I'm glad it wasn't only me that had to call the steward. How about dinner tonight, Alice? I'd like company, but are you up to eating?"

"I'm feeling a little better and willing to give it a try. Just no more shishkabob, please."

As they walked down the hallway, Tina said, "Don't look now, but aren't those toilet seats lining the walls? Could it be that the whole ship is having problems?" The next morning, looking through the porthole, Tina found there were discarded toilet seats floating everywhere. They had been thrown overboard like Frisbees.

A new rash of complaints from the passengers on board followed the toilet seat incident. It was the ship's maiden voyage after being refurbished. Instead of white towels and wash cloths usually found in bathrooms, all dark colors had been purchased. Depending on the color of the day, tourists, after using the wash cloths, had faces that were blue, green, red or purple. Apparently procurement had neglected to check if the linens were colorfast.

"Judging by the first day of this cruise, I think we're in for an exciting experience," said Tina to Alice who agreed wholeheartedly.

Toilet seats and linens were substituted and all was forgotten by the time the ship docked at Mykonos, the first port of call. Mykonos is famous for it's windmills and is a vacation resort frequented by the rich and famous.

"Where is Petros, the Pelican?" asked Mrs. Stern. "I've read about him in guide books and he's supposed to be here."

"I believe that's Petros over there with all those people. He's resting on top of a coil of rope," answered Tina.

As Mrs. Stern approached, someone said, "Don't let the closed eyes fool you. Petros the Pelican bites."

Needless to say Mrs. Stern had to test the warning and found, to her dismay, that he did. The pelican bit her finger and it hurt. "We'd better clean that wound," said Tina shaking her head as she tried not to laugh. "When we get on board, the infirmary can take a look at it."

The next port of call was Santorini. Tina remembered that the approach to this island was spectacular and asked her charges to be on deck before breakfast. What, from a distance, appeared to be snow covered mountains, was transformed, as they watched, into a glistening white village 885 feet above sea level. Donkeys were waiting to take the spellbound tourists up the switchbacks to the village of Thera where shopkeepers waited with great anticipation. Just as spectacular was the view from the village. There below was the beautiful Aegean Sea on which rested, what appeared to be, a miniature boat. It was their cruise ship.

There was another stop at the Island of Crete. The group was taken to the Palace of Knossos which described as one of the most impressive sights in the Mediterranean. Last of the Greek Islands on the agenda was Rhodes where the group trekked up a rocky path to the Acropolis of Lindos—there to visit the Temple of Athena.

The cruise ship then set sail for Turkey where they would disembark at Kusadasi for a bus tour to Ephesus. "I can't believe the history that is all around us or that people centuries back were so advanced in technology," said someone fascinated by the bath houses and the amphitheaters.

"Is it true that Noah's Ark came to rest on Mount Ararat?" asked someone. This prompted many others to comment, "To think our steps are retracing some of the ground that the Apostles walked on. Cleopatra too. St. John the Baptist is buried here. Both St. Paul and St. John preached in this area. They say the Virgin Mary spent her last days here. I heard that St. John brought the Virgin Mary to Ephesus after the Crucifixion."

Everyone had something to add. Tina summed it all up by stating, "There are many theories about the happenings in this part of the world. It is credited with being the Cradle of Christianity."

"Aren't you happy that I persuaded you to take this trip? It's like going back in time," said Mrs. Stern to her husband.

"Thank you, my Dear. I'm always happy, but appreciate that you're there to remind me."

"You must admit, your wife picked a winner with this tour," said someone in the group who had overheard the conversation.

The opinions, questions and observations came from all directions and Tina was happy to see everything through the eyes of her tourists. The trip had started off with some headaches. There were missed connections, stomach cramps, her fall in the pyramids, broken toilet seats and colorful showers. All these incidents, however, would be translated into amusing stories when back home with family and friends.

They were a compatible group although Jason continued to be a mystery. In spite of all the efforts made by his fellow travelers, he refused to warm up to anyone. Most had come to the conclusion that he was a loner needing his own space. He was, as usual, not at breakfast the next morning when Tina addressed her group.

"We're now in the Sea of Marmara. I'm sure you've all heard of the Dardanelles. You'll want to go on deck when you've finished eating. The skyline of Istanbul will soon be visible through the early morning fog. Our captain has promised to sail the ship past the city to the mouth of the Bosporus from which point we can look into the Black Sea. I think you'll agree that it's as though we're entering a make-believe Hollywood set."

"As the group gathered on deck, one of the ladies said, "I believe I can see some of the minarets in the distance."

"Did you know that Istanbul is known as the most Asian of the European cities?" asked Tina of the group standing nearby.

"It's difficult for me to think of Turkey as European," said one of Tina's audience who then asked if they would be permitted to enter the mosques.

"We'll visit the Blue Mosque which is famous for its mosaics and St. Sophia which was once a Byzantine church. It was converted into a mosque, but is now a museum. You will see that some of the Muslim symbols have been removed to allow visitors to see the Christian images that were once underneath."

"Do we have to wash our feet and leave our shoes outside when we enter the mosque?"

"The worshippers do, but for us it is only necessary that we cover our shoes with slippers provided at the door," replied Tina. "Our itinerary calls for almost two days in Istanbul and I'm sure you'll find it not nearly enough. The city is enchanting - probably because it is so unique. You'll wish you had time to explore on your own and we hope that you will come back some day. There is so much more to see, but a tour, such as this, can only cover the highlights."

"I know I'd like to come back and to Egypt as well. Being under the weather while there, I missed a great deal. The next time, I'll also want to take the Nile Cruise that goes to Aswan, Luxor, Karnak and Abu Simbal," said Mr. Pepper.

"I'm sure the Cartrite Tour Agency can accommodate you whenever you're ready, Mr. Pepper, and I wouldn't mind going along as your guide."

Upon arrival at the seaport in Istanbul, the group boarded a bus for a city tour. The traffic was comparable to that on New York City streets. Everywhere could be seen 1942 Chevrolets—apparently a favorite automobile in Turkey. The first scheduled stop was at the famous Topkapi Palace. A guided tour through the Harem and the Museum, which housed the treasures of the Sultans, took several hours.

"I remember the Topkapi Museum from a movie. Wasn't that where someone stole the jeweled dagger?" asked Mrs. Jennings.

Ignoring the question, an eager shopper asked, "When do we go to the Grand Bazaar?"

"You'll have about two hours to shop in the Bazaar tomorrow afternoon. In the morning we'll be visiting the mosques. On the way we will see the Obelisk that was brought to Istanbul from Egypt. Also nearby is the Serpentine Column that found it's way here from Delphi."

"They didn't have modern equipment in those days. How did they get these monuments from Egypt and Greece all the way to Istanbul?"

"I'm sure our city guide will try to answer all your interesting questions. Now, about the Bazaar, I want to give you fair warning. First, shopkeepers will try to lure you into stores to look at carpets. If you go with them, you'll have no time for anything else. Second, the merchants in Turkey expect you to bargain. They will offer you a cup of coffee. It is very strong. They will be disappointed—even insulted—if you refuse to drink a little. It's a game they play before bargaining can begin. The owner of the establishment will start off by naming some outlandish price for the item being considered. You are expected to counter with a ridiculously low offer. The fair price will usually be somewhere in the middle."

"But we only get two hours. Why so little time? How can a person shop, bargain and drink strong coffee in two hours.? I'm sure most of us would want to have a whole day."

"I know how you feel, but it's all our schedule allows. We must be on the busses by five p.m."

"What you're telling us is that we should buy whatever souvenirs we need quickly and hope for some time, when that's done, to browse."

"Come prepared with a list and hit the souvenir shops that have everything. If you're serious about buying jewelry, know what you want and be careful. I'm sorry there's only two hours, but we cannot be late. Look at it this way, with less time to shop, you'll be going home with some cash in your pockets. You might even thank me for that."

After an early dinner, Tina, Alice and their tourists were bussed over the Galata Bridge to a Turkish night club where they were to be entertained by authentic Turkish belly dancers.

Upon arrival they were ushered into a dark room smelling of strong tobacco. Ready for them were long tables already set up with watered down drinks. No sooner were all seated when the show began. Thinly veiled women with fake jewels in their belly buttons twisted, turned and gyrated to strange sounding music. Admittedly the dancers were more shapely than those in the Egyptian tent, but the setting didn't compare. Knowing they would have an early wake-up call, the group left immediately after the performers finished dancing. Drinks were mostly untouched. It was obvious Tina, Alice and their American tourists were not ready to trust the establishment—shades of Pharaoh's revenge, perhaps.

"It was probably due to the Arabian Nights setting in Egypt, but this evening couldn't compare," were comments made by those who had been able to attend both.

After departing Istanbul there were but two days remaining on the tour and these would be spent in the vicinity of Athens. Boarding the bus for a visit to the Acropolis and the Parthenon the first day, Tina, as usual, counted noses. One of her group was missing. Jason Thomas, the handsome recluse was late. Going back into the hotel lobby to call his room, Tina was given a note by the receptionist. It was from Jason and stated that he had left the tour.

"Something has come up and I am returning to America" was the cryptic message.

"Strange," said Tina when returning to the bus. "The tour would have been over in two days. Leaving early, he'd have to make special travel arrangements and that is expensive. Well, he's gone and it's none of my business. I never understood why he chose this particular trip in the first place."

"Good riddance," said Mr. Johnson who admitted to having had several run-ins with him. "He won't be missed."

Although their last evening in Athens was free to explore the Plaka on their own, Tina's people chose to stay together and asked that she be their leader through the streets of this famous tourist attraction. Bouzouke music could be heard coming from every little hole in the wall and it was infectious.

"Let's try this taverna, Tina. It isn't too crowded and they're playing NEVER ON SUNDAY, one of my favorite songs," said Mrs. Anthony who could always be counted on to infuse life into a party.

"I'd like to have some of that stuff they call 'Ouzo'. From what I've heard it could turn even me into Zorba the Greek," said her husband doing a few dance steps to the music.

They were no sooner seated when most of the group rose from their chairs to join in the circle of dancers already on the dance floor. Who could resist the music? The vacationers were ready to let loose. "There's just so much mythology, history and culture a person can digest," said Mrs. Anthony. All enjoyed the camaraderie—and the Ouzo.

Tomorrow, the last day, would include a bus tour to the Poseidon Temple and the Oracle of Delphi. After that they would leave for the airport—their vacation, over.

Seeing everyone off at the airport was bittersweet. The group had bonded and remained in a party mood. Most stopped at the Duty Free shops for bottles of "Ouzo." They claimed it was for medicinal purposes. As for Tina and Alice, there would be very little free time between saying "good-bye" to the departing tourists and "hello" to those newly arriving.

"I must make some phone calls," said Tina to Alice as they breathed a sigh of relief that all their responsibilities were on their way.

"Me too, Tina. Don't know about you, but I'm tired. Even though it's an easy tour since most of the time was spent baby sitting, we were constantly on the move."

"Cheer up! Only three more tours to go. Think we'll make it?"

"One thing I know for sure, Tina, there will be no more lunches in off-beat places for me, and not for my people either. Omar and Taro, if again our guides in Egypt, will be disappointed, but we eat in the hotel or not at all."

"Bottled water too," added Tina.

"Amen to that, my friend! This tour had a rough beginning, but you see how quickly everyone forgets the mishaps. By the time our people departed, there was only praise for us and the tour itself. Evaluations and the generous gratuities proved everyone went home feeling good about the itinerary Cartrite provided."

Both girls retreated to their rooms as soon as they were in the hotel. Tina's first priority was to call Mara. It was six o'clock in the morning when Mara's phone rang.

"Sorry to wake you, Mara, but I wanted to call before the new vacationers start arriving. Once that happens, I'm lucky to find enough time for the bathroom. How is everything? You and Alex okay? Anyone been looking for me?"

"We're fine. We miss you. How about you?"

"It's been an interesting tour. I'll tell you all about it when I see you. Meanwhile, I'm anxious to know if the police are doing anything after getting my letter. Has anyone tied that Milwaukee case to mine? What's happening?"

"There hasn't been much in the paper about the Milwaukee fire, but the St. Louis police are really upset about the death of Detective White and seem to be going all out to find his killer. If they have any leads, they're not letting on to the press. I did get a call from someone though—Officer James McDonald is his name. He said that he's been reading up on your case and wants to meet with you when you get home. He doesn't know where you are or that you are working. He thinks you're on vacation and I didn't contradict him."

"Maybe a new broom is what we need, Mara. It's possible Officer McDonald will see things from a different perspective and meet with success instead of dead ends. If he calls again tell him I'll see him when I get back."

Tina and Alice's remaining tours went very well. There were always the complainers, but they managed, somehow, to pacify even the worst offenders. Someone on the third tour fell while on board ship. Again it was a door sill—this time coming out of the shower. Several stitches to the chin were needed and this was quickly and efficiently taken care of by the ship's doctor. There were also instances when Tina had to rescue someone in her group from an over enthusiastic shopkeeper.

By the time the four tours ended, both Tina and Alice had their fill of Egypt, Greece and Turkey. The trips were repetitious as were those in Great Britain. However the British Island tours found Tina in the arms of a handsome bus driver at day's end. The Greek tours, in contrast, had been strictly business.

Alan had written several times wanting Tina to request another round of tours with him. "I'd like us to be together again, Tina. Never thought I'd miss you so much."

"I miss you too Alan and it's tempting," she responded "but we both know it wouldn't work out in the long run. Better let it go knowing we'll always be friends. I'll never forget you and what you did for me."

"Don't know about you, Alice, but I, for one, am looking forward to the slow season. There will be a few months before we're needed on the road again and I'm anxious to get back to my new apartment. Everything there was left in a state of disarray and I have a great deal to do if I want to turn the mess into a home."

"I know what you mean, Tina. Can't wait to get home to friends and family myself. You might know, just before leaving on this assignment, I met this really nice guy. He impressed me and I think the feeling was mutual. I'd like to get to know him better. Hope he's still around. Nice guys are hard to find these days and they don't hang around long. They're either married or don't want to be."

"Tell me about it," said Tina with an expression that spoke volumes.

Tina never spoke about the men in her life. Alice was curious, but not one to pry. Instead she said, "Dating has become such a hassle. You meet someone, and before you know it, they're pressuring to get you in bed. You're always left wondering about their last partner and it's embarrassing to ask."

"I'm afraid I haven't had much experience Alice. Oh, I did have a boyfriend. We were engaged to be married, but it turned out he was gay. Finding that out didn't do anything for my self esteem. Maybe I'll meet Mr. Right someday. My friend Mara did. She's got a great husband."

"Does he have any brothers?'

"Yes, but hands off. I'm thinking of taking a second look at him for myself," said Tina beginning to see merit in the idea.

"Where will you be when you get back to the States, Tina? I'd like to keep in touch."

"I don't have a phone yet, but will call you as soon as I'm settled. Can't wait to prepare my own meals and that's strange because I don't know how to cook. I don't even know if my range works, but you can visit and be my guinea pig any time you find yourself in Chicago."

"Have you put in for your next assignment?"

"My first choice would be Italy, but it's questionable if they'll give me what I want. This tour covered a lot of territory. It didn't require a great deal of work on our part since city guides had most of the responsibility and that's good. They've grown up with all the mythology and history, and know just how to make those ancient times come to life."

"True, Tina! We would have had to do all kinds of research, and even then, bore our tourists to death. Personally I think we had plenty to do without the lecturing responsibility. Think of all the airports and ports of call we had to deal with. We were always counting and looking for people who were straggling to get that last photograph."

"Any tour loses something after the first time around, Alice. It will be good to be back in the States."

It was time to part. As they hugged and prepared to go to separate gates, Tina said, "Good luck with that nice man you left behind."

"Thanks!" Alice replied. "Let's try to work together again some time. Call me."

10

Tina was home at last. Her very own first home. Mara had temporarily set up the apartment understanding that Tina would have her own ideas.

"It looks great, Mara. You did a terrific job. Hope you won't mind if I change things around a little. I've always been one to move furniture and stuff until it feels comfortable. However, once something has found a spot, it usually stays there forever."

"Sounds good to me and of course I don't mind. You're planning other purchases, and for now, I simply spread things around to fill up spaces. Sorry I can't stay Tina, but Alex is coming in from Europe this afternoon. How about dinner with us tonight?"

"Could I have a rain check, Mara? I'm tired and you know how they keep feeding passengers on flights. I never know if I've had breakfast, lunch or dinner. Tonight all I want is tea and toast."

"I understand, but make yourself a cup of tea now. Then close the blinds and take a long nap."

Tina's number one priority after breakfast the next morning was to contact officer McDonald of the St. Louis police department. He'd left many messages with Mara and seemed anxious to meet with her.

Calling from a phone booth since her telephone had not yet been installed, Tina identified herself.

"Is it really you, Miss Cappo? I thought you wanted us to solve a murder," was McDonald's curt response.

"What has my being away got to do with whether or not you solve crimes, Officer McDonald?"

"I've been trying to reach you for weeks. Your friend kept telling me you were on vacation. My understanding was that you were destitute—left without a dime. I'd like to know how one can go on an endless vacation without money."

Ignoring the officer's remarks, but inwardly seething, Tina coldly responded, "Mara said you wanted to see me. I can be in St. Louis next week unless you want to meet me here."

"Next week? That's the best you can do. I thought this was important to you."

"It is, Officer McDonald. Then how about tomorrow at one o'clock? Will that be satisfactory?"

"It will have to be," he said unceremoniously hanging up the phone.

Tina was not impressed with Officer McDonald. He was rude and she'd like to have told him where to go. However he did want to see her and might have some new information to share.

At precisely one o'clock the next day, Tina was at police headquarters in St. Louis. She had her defenses up and was prepared to dislike McDonald. When a tall, extremely good looking man came toward her, introducing himself as Officer McDonald, it was difficult to imagine him to be the same person she had spoken to on the phone. His bright smile gave a lie to everything she had expected. He took her by the hand and ushered her into his office. Leading her to a comfortable chair, he offered hot coffee and tempting deli sandwiches.

"Please, Miss Cappo, sit down and join me for lunch. I didn't have breakfast and am famished. I suspect you are as well. You must have had to catch an early flight."

Still angry that he had been so obnoxious on the phone, Tina pushed aside the plate he was offering and replied, "No thanks! This isn't a social call. You wanted to see me. What was so important that I had to drop everything and get to St. Louis? Tell me, Officer McDonald, why am I here."

"Relax, Miss Cappo. To be truthful I don't have much to tell you other than that your case was reopened and placed in my hands. After reading through all the material, I was curious about you."

"That's it? You had me fly down here just to satisfy your curiosity? There had better be more. Does the renewed interest in my case have anything to do with Detective White's murder?"

"Yes because he had gone to Chicago to meet you. Your letter asking that we look into the similarities between the Milwaukee case and yours, was also an important factor."

"It's about time someone in your precinct woke up."

"Come now, Miss Cappo! Lighten up! Don't make me eat alone. I ordered for both of us. There's plenty and it's embarrassing to be feeding my face while you're giving me those frigid looks."

"What did you expect? You weren't exactly Mr. Congeniality yesterday."

"I apologize. My only excuse is that I've been buried in work. Your case is an old one and had been put aside. Leads, if ever there were any, are cold and therefore difficult to retrace. To be perfectly honest, I resented your being away on vacation when my boss wouldn't even approve a day off for a ball game."

"For your information, Officer, I was not on vacation unless that's your definition of moving people around Egypt, Greece and Turkey every two weeks. By the time I finished the fourth tour of the same itinerary, it could hardly be called a vacation. I make a living guiding tourists. Sometimes I get tired too."

Accepting his apology, Tina proceeded to ask questions. She wanted to know where Detective White had left off in his investigation. Had he confided in anyone? Were there any notes that McDonald could follow up on.?

McDonald explained that Detective White was not much of a talker—that he kept to himself and was secretive about his comings and goings. According to the precinct captain, White had been instructed to give up on the Cappo murder case. As seen from his notes, however, it was apparent that he had continued investigating on his own.

"Detective White's notes," McDonald said, "revealed that he had contacted Kevin McCarthy, a retired Chicago police officer, who told him about a gang of kids known as 'The Uptown Boys.' It appears Detective White was planning to meet with McCarthy in hopes of locating some of these gang members. Following up, I've scheduled a meeting with McCarthy next week. It is my intention to pick up the pieces left when Detective White was killed."

"Sounds like a long shot, but if Detective White was interested, it might not hurt to see how far you get."

"That's what I thought. It's worth a few hours of my time if Barry was on to something relating to those old street gangs. If I could get my hands on one or two of those 'Uptown' kids referred to, we might all learn something."

Realizing it wouldn't be easy to find anyone after all the time elapsed, Tina changed the subject. "I am very sorry about Detective White. He was always patient with me in spite of the fact that I was a trial to him. Did you know we had an appointment to meet the night he was murdered? I waited for him at the hotel over two hours unaware that he had been shot. Did he leave a family?"

"He was married. It is said that he and his wife were very close. There were no children. Mrs. White is a lovely, courageous lady. She owns a business keeping her financially solvent and busy. I understand the wives of fellow officers visit her frequently."

Apologizing for not being more helpful, Tina explained that Larry Hermano, although he had worked many years for the hotel, was a mystery. Apparently he shared only what he wanted people to know. A personal question was always diverted by a joke or an anecdote pertaining to growing up in a house full of older siblings.

"In all the years he was with us, we never met any of his family. He played cards with some friends, but to my knowledge, neither they or any family member ever came to our hotel."

"You have no idea where he lived before your father hired him?"

"I asked, but Larry never gave a straight answer. He had a knack for avoiding questions. Instead, he'd tell a joke and we'd end up laughing forgetting that a question was left unanswered."

"Sounds to me like a person with something to hide."

"In retrospect, yes! Would you believe I planned to marry Larry after graduating from college? We were going to carry on the family business. My parents loved him and were overjoyed. He was family. They opened their hearts, home and personal life to him. How stupid we all were."

"Don't blame yourself, Miss Cappo. Larry must have been planning what happened for a long time. Con men aren't usually that patient, but your friend had a lot to gain."

"Do you think Larry's using a different name and that's why he hasn't turned up?"

"Possibly, but Larry Hermano could have been a fictitious name to begin with. Speaking of names, Miss Cappo, may I call you Tina?"

"Why not! Now that you've forced me to have lunch with you, we might as well be sociable."

Knowing Tina had a plane to catch and happy that she was no longer angry, McDonald said, "I really appreciate your coming here on such short notice. There should be more to tell you after I see McCarthy next week. Since I'll be in Chicago, could we meet for an early lunch? McCarthy isn't expecting me until three o'clock and my flight gets in at eleven. I could be at the Downtown Regent by noon."

"Okay, but that's where I was to have met Detective White the day he was shot. I hope it's not an omen."

Before Tina left McDonald's office, she asked that he keep her address and phone number off the record. "I'd rather no one knows that I'm living in Chicago."

Tina had about a week before her scheduled luncheon with Officer McDonald. No longer the ogre he appeared to be that day on the telephone, she was actually looking forward to seeing him again. In the meantime, she and Mara had shopping to do. Tina was still searching for a television, two lamp tables and an occasional chair.

Mara was only too happy to accompany Tina on her shopping excursions. It was such fun being together. They'd have lunch or dinner and share their experiences and feelings. Neither of them was ever at a loss for words.

"What was he like?" asked Mara after Tina had gone to St. Louis and met Officer McDonald.

"He turned out to be a pleasant surprise, Mara. From our phone conversation, I expected to hate him—that he was a male chauvinist grouch—but he was actually quite nice. I believe that Officer McDonald will do his best to find the murderer of my parents."

"Glad to hear someone's taking an interest. It's about time. What happened to bring about the change in attitude?"

"It was Detective White's papers that peaked Officer McDonald's curiosity. Among other things, his notes referred to some street gangs in Chicago. Detective White didn't elaborate on why these gangs interested him or how they fit in to the murder of my parents, but something must have triggered his wanting to know more about them."

"Maybe that's what killed him. Did Officer McDonald have anything more to add?"

"He wanted me to know that my case had been reopened. While having lunch in his office, there were endless questions. I had a hard time answering. All I could tell McDonald was Larry told amusing stories about his childhood and that he always spoke of a supportive family."

"I'm sure he wanted names and addresses of family members."

"Yes, but I couldn't help him. McDonald was astounded when I told him that Larry had never had visitors—not in all the years he was with us—and that he always avoided personal questions. The look on McDonald's face implied that we should have taken warning from Larry's evasiveness. We should have, I know now."

"Perhaps it was all a lie, Tina—right from the very beginning. The person your grandfather recommended to your family could have planned everything that happened a long time prior to his showing up at the St. Louis Carillion. Think about it! If he could successfully invent a past, it would never haunt him in the future."

"Officer McDonald agrees with you, Mara. He too believes that Larry was planning the takeover of our hotel for a long time."

Asking if Tina had another appointment with Officer McDonald, she said, "He's coming to Chicago next week. We're meeting at the Downtown Regent."

"The Regent? Haven't you had enough of that place? There are other hotels in Chicago, you know."

"You forget we're strangers around here. It was the only hotel with a restaurant that came to mind at the time. Anyhow, Detective White wasn't shot there. The hotel is not at fault."

"Yes, but you had an appointment with him there that night. It still gives me the creeps when I think about it. Getting back to Officer McDonald, however, what does he look like? Is this going to be another tall, dark and handsome man in your life?"

"You're incorrigible, Mara."

"I just want to see you respectable like me, Tina. Have I told you lately that it's great to have you around? It reminds me of those carefree days at school when all we had to worry about were our grades."

"Wish we could turn back the clock, Mara. Life was so simple then."

Tina's telephone was installed that afternoon. The first to call was Stanley. He was working late and angling for an invitation to Tina's new apartment. He had not yet mentioned it to anyone, but his company was about to open a satellite office in the Chicago area. Stanley was interested and more than willing to relocate. He'd be near his brother and sister-in-law, but more importantly, he'd be able to see more of Tina. There were two problems, however. The first was that his boss might have other plans for him, and the second, that Tina might prefer he remain in Boston.

"It's that bad penny again," he said. Tina immediately recognized Stan's voice. "Mara told me you were back, but I decided to let you have a few days to yourself. She gave me your number. Are you settled in yet?"

"The apartment is beginning to shape up, and if I say so myself, is starting to look lived in. I wonder, Stan, if anyone really understands how much it means to me to have a place of my own. Even the penthouse that I lived in my whole life wasn't a real home you know. Everything was so formal. It was like living in a fish bowl."

Having come from an entirely different family situation, Stanley couldn't quite relate, but understood. Although Tina was surrounded by people all the time, they were transients and she was expected, always, to be on good behavior. This had to have been difficult for a little girl. "Perhaps I can help you forget your solitary childhood," Stanley said adding, "I'd like nothing better than to be your knight in shining armor."

Tina laughed reminding Stan that it might be difficult with him living in Boston and her in Chicago.

"Did I forget to tell you that I made a deal with my boss? After describing a blue-eyed, raven-haired beauty I knew in Chicago, he's decided to open a satellite office in your neck of the woods."

"In Chicago? You're kidding me."

"Afraid not. I made such a fuss that he's going to let me help get the new office up and running. You'll be stuck with me whenever I'm in town. For starters, how about next week?"

"You really are full of surprises, Stan. I'd like to say 'yes' but made an appointment with Officer McDonald, the new police officer assigned to my case. He's going to be in Chicago for a few days and I don't know how much of my time he'll want. I must be available."

"I understand and can be patient a little longer. Is this McDonald looking into anything specific?"

"He's coming to see a former Chicago police officer. According to notes left by Detective White, this man might be able to shed some light on my case. McCarthy, this retired officer, seems to think there was some cover up about things that were happening about ten years ago."

"Obviously it's important that you be there for Officer McDonald, but I'm not letting you off the hook. I'll call you over the weekend and we can work something out for the following week. Meanwhile get some rest. I want you wide awake when I come to see you in that new apartment. It's been a long time. For now goodnight and sweet dreams. Stay out of trouble if you can."

"You've got it. Good night, Stan."

Tina was about to leave her apartment to meet Officer McDonald when the phone rang. Who would be calling? Mara knew she had an appointment and so did Stanley. She had given her unlisted number to Officer McDonald in case he needed to cancel or postpone their meeting, but he should be on his way by now. She picked up on the third ring, but there was no response to her "hello." Continuing to hold the phone to her ear, a chill ran through her. Someone, she felt, was on the other end of the line. You're getting paranoid, Tina muttered to herself. Whoever it was, he or she must have been frustrated about dialing a wrong number.

Tina called a cab and went on to her appointment with Officer McDonald. She was punctual and again found herself waiting. A half hour passed while she nervously sat in the lounge observing everyone coming in and going out. This couldn't be happening to me again, she said with misgivings. Where is he? The thought occurred to Tina that it might have been McDonald trying to reach her as she was leaving the apartment.

Tina almost gave up when she saw a man coming toward her. It was difficult to recognize him behind the beard and dark glasses. Happy to identify him as Officer

McDonald in disguise, she didn't notice, until he was almost beside her, that he was limping and had a cut on his cheek.

"What happened to you McDonald?" she asked. "Did you get into a fight with Mighty Dog? What's with the beard and the dark glasses? There's dried blood on your face."

"I often hide behind a beard and glasses. It's fun to see people's reactions. Had you fooled for a while, didn't I? As to the limp, I'm okay now, but when I entered my hotel room in preparation for this meeting, someone must have been behind the door. Whoever he or she was—it happened so fast I didn't see anyone—tripped me. I landed on the floor knocking my head against the desk. In the excitement the culprit got away. Nothing was missing or disturbed. I must have interrupted a burglary."

"My phone rang as I was leaving to meet you. I thought it was a wrong number because no one said anything. Do you think it could have been your intruder?"

"No! I had your phone number on the night table, but it wouldn't have meant anything to anyone since there was no name attached. You do have an unlisted number?"

"Yes, but what does that mean? Couldn't an address be traced if someone had access to a phone number?"

"It would be difficult, but anything's possible these days. I'm convinced, however, that whoever it was in my hotel room, has nothing to do with you. Do you have an answering machine, by the way? If not, I suggest you get one. You should be screening your calls."

"You're not helping me, McDonald. One minute you tell me everything is okay—not to worry—and the next warn me not to answer my own phone. My number is unlisted and known only to you and my friend, Mara."

"I don't want to worry or upset you, Tina. We're both probably imagining things. Let's just keep our eyes and ears open. Take notes and tell me everything that appears to be out of the ordinary. In case you're still worried about my unwelcome intruder, stay with your friend Mara for a few days. I'll reach you at her place if necessary. Get an answering machine as soon as possible, and don't pick up any calls. Let the machine do it's work from now on. Save the tapes. It may be necessary to trace a voice some day."

"You're frightening me again, Officer McDonald, but I won't be intimidated into giving up my apartment. Between the dead bolt and the other locks on the door, I'll be okay. Your idea about an answering machine is good, but that's as far as I'll go. I won't be a prisoner of my fears."

McDonald's late appointment with retired officer McCarthy allowed time for a leisurely lunch. As they walked to the restaurant, McDonald suggested that Tina call him "Jim." "You'll be seeing more of me in the future," he said "and it would be nice if we could be less formal."

"Jim it is!. Well this is it. I hope you're hungry and like spaghetti. I haven't been here before, but the restaurant has been recommended." Comfortably seated, a waiter brought the menu and, at Jim's request, a bottle of red wine. Taking a sip from the glass that was poured, Tina asked, "How are you doing with locating Larry's family? Found anyone?"

"Not a soul, Jim replied. "It's possible this 'family' he talked about never existed. Don't give up, however. Everyone has a history and Larry had to have come from somewhere. My gut tells me that Chicago was more to him than that staged chance meeting with Tony Luppo at your St. Louis hotel."

"I agree! Certainly it was his home away from home prior to the murder of my parents and his subsequent disappearance."

"There's no doubt in my mind that Larry has ties, obligations and connections in Chicago."

"Something McCarthy said?"

Jim explained that McCarthy had given him information about the kids he called "The Uptown Boys." It seems they appeared one day out of nowhere. He said it was about ten years ago when these well-dressed, soft-spoken boys were first noticed hanging around the streets. When confronted by him and other officers, they would quickly disburse. The local gangs hated these kids insisting they were trouble makers—that it was they, not them, who were responsible for the sudden increase in break-ins, burglaries and the numerous other complaints of residents living in the neighborhood. The local gangs claimed that they were being unjustly accused and that the new kids had connections because they were never brought in for questioning.

"These new kids came from uptown Chicago?"

"Who knows for sure, but McCarthy believes that there was something to the complaints of the local gangs— that they really were innocent of the accusations made against them and that the 'Uptowners' were the real perpetrators."

"Did McCarthy bring his theory to the attention of his supervisors? What happened?"

"Yes he did, but that's the strange part. Nothing happened except that McCarthy was transferred to another part of town. Shortly after he was given a desk job. Ultimately, having enough years behind him, McCarthy opted to take an early retirement package."

"Are you telling me that Officer McCarthy was removed from his regular beat because he expressed his opinion about the new gang?"

"A person might come to that conclusion."

"Now I understand why you're anxious to see retired Officer McCarthy."

"That and the fact that Detective White was interested in these gangs. McCarthy might remember some names. It's the best and only lead I've got right now. I must leave you, Tina. McCarthy's doing this as a favor to me and I don't want to keep him waiting. If there's anything important that comes of this meeting, I'll call you."

"Okay, Jim. Good luck and thanks for lunch. I'll get that answering machine."

That's exactly what Tina did on the way back to her apartment. It looked very impressive next to her new telephone. She was rapidly filling the apartment with all the comforts and essentials of daily living.

In the mailbox was a letter from Alan pleading that she ask for another Great Britain tour. "When are you coming back?" he wrote. "Have mercy on this poor, lonely bus driver. I'm ready, willing and able to give up my wandering ways for you."

It was nice to know that Alan cared about her and wanted to continue their relationship. Tina did miss him, but knew she was only beginning to live. This was no time for her to settle down. Between Stanley who would be visiting next week and Officer Jim who was very interesting, she no longer was alone. Besides, there were too many unresolved questions to answer. There would be no real peace until Tina could come to terms with the past.

"Have to admit, though, that my self esteem has jumped one hundred percent in the last few months," said a smiling Tina to her friend, Mara, when next they were together.

"That's what happens when a girl discovers she's desirable," replied Mara. "Larry treated you as though he owned you. He never appreciated you as a person. To him you were always a little doll - a doll he, apparently, didn't care to play with. No wonder you were so insecure."

Several days later there was someone at the door of Tina's apartment. Through the peephole she could see that it was Officer Jim. After undoing all the locks, he was admitted. "Jim! What are you doing here? How did you know where I live?"

"That's my secret. Thought I'd stop by since I was in the neighborhood. Nice apartment—very cozy and inviting. It looks like you've settled in. Appears to be a safe neighborhood. How about the phone calls? Anything I should know about?"

"Just the usual hang ups. No messages. Occasionally I forget and pick up the phone. That's when I hear background music and imagine it's heavy breathing. The only messages I've had on the tape are from Mara."

"Some people have phobias about talking to answering machines. They'd rather hang up."

"I guess you're right, but what's up? I didn't expect you."

"I'm due back in St. Louis tomorrow. As long as I was nearby, and had a little time, I decided to stop and tell you about my meeting with McCarthy."

"I'll make some coffee while you bring me up-to-date."

"Before I start, is there anything you want to tell me? Has anyone been bothering or following you?"

"Not that I've noticed." Bringing the coffee to the table, Tina prompted him to fill her in on McCarthy and what Jim had learned.

"Actually, there's not much to tell. Kevin McCarthy went with me to police headquarters where we asked to go through old files and looked at mug shots. We were surprised to learn, from the officer in charge, that Detective White had made the same request several days before being gunned down."

"Did he tell you if Detective White had learned anything going through the files?"

"No! If Detective White did, he kept it to himself. That was his way. Don't forget, he had been told to drop the case and was doing this research on his own time."

"How about you and McCarthy? Did you get anywhere?"

"We spent all day going through files and pictures. While having lunch, Kevin continued to talk about his troubles with the 'Uptown Boys.' He described them as a rogue group protected by someone of influence."

"Did Officer McCarthy find who he was looking for in the files or pictures?"

"Apparently not. Remember all this happened many years ago. We did get some names and addresses, but people move. Gangs break up and are replaced by others. What were boys then are now grown men. Many of them are good citizens today.

148

"So you wound up in a dead end?"

"Not completely. Several of the boys from the local gangs had further difficulties with the law resulting in more recent data. One of these, Enrico Gomez, is still in jail. We paid him a visit. He was belligerent at first, but when McCarthy told him we were interested in the kids that had caused his gang so much trouble with the police, he went ape. We couldn't shut him up."

"Dos lousy bastards wuz always gettin us in trouble," he said. "Dey wuz pinin tings on us alle time. We dint do nuttin. We tol de fuzz but dey dont believe us. Always dey blame us."

Jim was enjoying his performance as he imitated Enrico Gomez. "Scum dey all wuz. Dey dint hav leatha jackets wid names on like us. Sure us guys rolled drunks sos we could buy drugs 'n smokes but not dem. Dey was real bad. Dint need dough but want power. Dey robbed and beat people fo fun. Cops wuz always pullin us in fo tings dey don. Dey planted stuff on us. We wuz always gettin blamed. We tell de fuz but nuttin happens."

"We asked Gomez if he knew any of the kids by name or where they attended school. He claimed to know nothing more about them."

"Gomez said these new kids were bad. Bad in what way?"

"The local kids were accused by the police as being responsible for break-ins where people were tied up, beaten and sometimes left unconscious. McCarthy remembers that there was evidence of forged checks and charges on stolen credit cards as well as thefts against insurance policies. Cash, valuables and stock certificates were reported missing from homes. The local gangs had alibis when interrogated and Gomez insists, to this day, that the real culprits were the rich kids from uptown."

"So - what's next?"

"I've got to get back to St. Louis, but McCarthy will continue his search for others who might have had run-ins with the 'Uptown Boys.' We're both curious about the accusation that these 'Uptowners' had protection from police headquarters."

"In that case, you won't get much cooperation from the police."

"That's why we're trying to find members of the group. From them we should be able to get to their parents and learn where the pressure was coming from."

"Looks like you and Kevin McCarthy have your work cut out for you."

"You might say that, but we'll get them, Tina. Don't give up. How long before your next touring assignment?"

"I thought I'd have the whole winter off, but the agency called and asked me to do an Australia, New Zealand trip in about six weeks. I could use the money and it's only two tours of about twenty days each so I'll take it. Their seasons are the reverse of ours which means it will be summer when I get there. I've never been in that part of the world and will have to busy myself gathering material that will be of interest to the tourists."

"Before you leave for Australia, I'll want to see you and McCarthy again. He's still hopeful that we'll find something in the archives."

"I appreciate your stopping by to bring me this up-date, Jim. There's not much added information, but I'm optimistic that the murderer of my parents will one day be brought to justice."

"That's my mission, Tina. I want to solve this case and bring a smile back on your face." Capturing her hands and bringing them to his lips, Jim continued, "I will find the person or persons responsible for your tragedy, little one. You've suffered enough."

Overwhelmed by Jim's expression of sympathy, Tina turned her head. There were tears threatening to erupt. Not wishing to embarrass her, Jim released her hands saying, "I must leave now, Tina. My flight won't wait, but I'll call you."

"Good night, Jim," answered Tina as the door closed behind him. She stood exactly where she was and silently asked herself, When did I become his little one and how about the way he held and kissed my hands so intimately?

Jim heard the door click shut. Walking down the hallway to the elevator, he also had a question. Why didn't you kiss her lips, you fool? You wanted to and couldn't have had a better opportunity. Quickly retracing his steps, he knocked on Tina's door. She was standing where he had left her, and apparently, expected his return for the door opened immediately. Jim kissed her solidly on the lips and said, "That's better and another reason why you can expect another visit from me soon."

Watching him as he left a second time, Tina smiled. Things were looking up. Then she closed and bolted the door hoping to digest all that Jim had told her. Was Larry perhaps one of that group he described? She'd go over everything with Mara in the morning. For tonight, however, she decided to play soft music on the stereo and think about Jim's kiss. She was soon asleep, dreaming sweet dreams about a sheltered innocent that had been transformed into a desirable femme fatale.

Mara's call in the morning woke her. Over breakfast, Tina shared all the information she had, but was not yet ready to kiss and tell. She knew it would result in a barrage of questions. Mara would want to know how she felt about Jim compared to Alan in London or Stanley in Boston. She couldn't answer that question because she didn't know. It was all happening too fast. Just a few months ago she was a rejected fiancée—now she appeared to have suitors everywhere.

After hearing what Tina told her about the Chicago gangs, Mara would have liked to drop everything in search of the so-called "Uptown Boys." One of them would surely lead them to the despicable Larry. Tina had all she could do to restrain her.

"I won't let you get involved, Mara. Alex would have my head if anything happened to you and I'd never forgive myself. Besides, any attempts on our part could alert the very people Jim and Officer McCarthy are trying to find. We must let them do their jobs."

"You did say Officer McCarthy's retirement was not exactly voluntary."

"True, Mara, but he still has friends at police headquarters who have given him access to the files. He has to be careful however. Some of those who persuaded him to take early retirement might still have positions of power. They may be the same people that had made it so easy for the 'Uptowners' to remain anonymous."

"The more I hear, the more complicated and devious this thing gets. You're right, Tina, to let the professionals handle things. I know Alex will agree when he comes home this weekend and hears the latest."

"By the way, Stanley is coming to Chicago next week to visit. Maybe we can go out as a foursome like in the old days. What do you think? Any suggestions?"

"I think it's great that he's coming to see you. Getting the brothers together sounds good too. We could spend the day sightseeing Chicago. We've never taken the time to do the tourist thing, and the city is new to you and Stanley as well. After dinner we could take in a show. I'll check the papers for ideas. Will Stanley be staying at your place or ours?"

"That's a good question Mara. We'll have to wait and see what develops."

"In other words, you wouldn't have any problem with his staying at your place?"

"I'm a big girl now," Tina laughingly replied.

"Never doubted that for a minute, my friend. You know I'd like nothing better than to have you as a sister-in-law."

"Don't you think you're rushing things just a wee bit?"

That night Stanley called. "Hi, Princess. I'm all set and raring to go. My bags are packed—all that's needed is your word and I'll get the airline tickets."

"Everything is quiet here. I know you'll need to line up your business appointments and anytime is fine with me. Just let me know when you'll be coming so that Mara and I can meet you at the airport. Alex will be back in a few days. You two don't get much opportunity to see each other so we thought we'd do some things together—like in our college days."

"Wait a minute! I'll give my little brother only half a day. Remember, my primary reason for coming is to be with you. How about I get to Chicago Thursday in the early evening? Unfortunately I'll have to schedule some appointments for Friday. If you'd like, we can share part of Saturday with my brother and Mara. Then I'll have to head back to Boston Sunday night. Okay with you?"

"Sounds good to me. While I think of it, Mara asked if you would be staying at my place or with them. Any preference?"

"Need you ask? If you put me on the couch, would the neighbors mark the door with a scarlet letter?"

"I can always say you're my brother. I've never had a brother and that might be really nice."

"God forbid. The last thing I want to be is your brother."

"The couch it is then. I'll just have to take my chances with the gossips. Seriously, Stan, I'm really looking forward to seeing you on Thursday. Call me when you have the flight number and time of arrival time so that I can meet you."

"No, Tina! I'll take a cab. We'll have a quiet dinner—just you and me. You name the place."

After a few more words, Tina hung up. Stanley, obviously, wanted time alone with her. The prospect appealed to her as well. She'd call Mara and tell her that plans for a foursome would be limited to Saturday and that Stanley would be staying in her apartment. Mara would understand—probably even give her stamp of approval having, from the very beginning, done everything she could think of to bring her best friend and brother-in-law together.

It was Thursday and Stanley was at the door. What would the days ahead lead to this time, Tina wondered? She nervously unlocked the many bolts and stood in front of him. For, what appeared to be an eternity, Stanley didn't move.

Did she have egg on her face making him wish he hadn't come? "Enter, Stanley. I don't bite," Tina said practically pulling him into her apartment.

Standing on tip toe, since he was over six feet tall making her feel like a midget, Tina offered her cheek. With a broad grin, Stanley kissed both sides of her face. Then, circling her with strong arms and lifting her off the floor, he moved to her lips. They were so sweet and he lingered for a very long time. At last, setting Tina slowly back on two feet, he looked her up and down. "You're gorgeous," he said. "Let me feast my eyes on you."

After a brief moment, he made a move to take her back into his arms, but this time Tina side-stepped him saying, "Coffee's ready." Leading him by the hand into the small kitchenette, she asked, "Cream and sugar?"

"You're my cream and sugar, Tina. I thought you knew that."

"Does that mean you want it black?"

"What it means is that I don't want coffee at all. I want another one of those kisses and then we'll go out for dinner. Don't remember when I've been so hungry."

Tina found herself cornered in the little kitchen. The coffee had been poured into cups, but both were left standing as he again found her lips. She could feel his hunger and was relieved when he gently put her down saying, "Let's go eat, my Sweet. This big man doesn't do well on an empty stomach. By the way, I like what I've seen so far of your apartment. When we get back, I'm expecting you'll give me the full fifty-cent tour."

"There's not much to see. It's a small apartment as I told you on the phone, but it's mine - my very own."

They had dinner at a quiet little Italian restaurant around the corner. There was much to talk about. Stanley wanted details about her tour experiences and then Tina brought him up-to-date on the theories of Officer McDonald and retired Officer McCarthy. Both agreed that they were a long way from finding Larry. There were some things she didn't tell Stanley. She did not want to worry him about the phone callers that never left messages and certainly not that the handsome Officer McDonald was showing more than a platonic interest in her.

The serious talk ended and Tina found herself enjoying the camaraderie reminiscent of their carefree days at college. Stanley liked to tease and Tina could never quite figure out if there was a hidden meaning behind his words. Did he mean to seduce her or was he merely testing her reaction? The worst was that she did not know what her reaction should or would be. She knew only that he made her laugh—she was light-hearted and almost happy. Stanley made her feel comfortable and cherished. Momentarily at least, she could forget her troubles.

"No doubt about it! You can be very convincing when you put your mind to something," she said after Stan told the story of how he persuaded his boss to open a satellite office in Chicago.

"It was easy when I told him that having an office in Chicago would give the company prestige. How could he resist that argument?"

"You know what I think? I think you're a smooth talker and I'd better be careful."

"You're getting to know me too well, Tina. Let's go back to your apartment now. I want to practice some more of my repertoire?"

"Practice makes perfect, they say." Both Stanley and Tina enjoyed the repartee. Walking back to the apartment, hand in hand, was fun. They were two carefree young people out on a date.

It was late by the time they arrived back at the apartment. Stan would have to leave early to get to the new office. His boss had specific goals he wanted accomplished and would expect results from the trip even though he suspected his protege might have an ulterior motive for wanting to be in Chicago. While happy to cooperate when romance was at stake, Tina was not necessarily the boss's top priority.

"Could I talk you into some coffee now, Stanley?"

"Are you trying to keep me up all night? If that's your plan, I'm not going to be on that couch alone."

"No coffee, then. I've had fair warning. Here's a pillow and some blankets. What's your preference in the morning—eggs and bacon or bacon and eggs with your toast and coffee.

"Not so fast! Come here girl. Do you really think I'm going to let you escape to your room without so much as a goodnight kiss?"

"I'll buy that, but just one and then it's lights out. Promise?"

"You know I like teasing you, Tina, but there is no way I'd ever betray your trust. It's so good to be here and I would like you to invite me back as often as my boss can be prevailed upon to free me from my desk in Boston. Some day I'd even like you to ask me into your bed, but it must be

157

at your invitation and because you're ready to make a lifetime commitment. In case you haven't noticed, I'm very serious about you."

"You're too good, Stanley. My choosing Larry turned out to be a mistake and I know it must have hurt you. I don't want to hurt you again—neither do I want to make any more mistakes."

"People will always make mistakes. Hopefully they learn from them, Tina. For the record there has never been anyone else but you for me—not from the first day we met at the farm. I love you and want you, but I'm willing to wait for the day when the feeling is mutual. I'll wait as long as it takes. Right now I'm content to hold and kiss you. Now let's have that goodnight kiss so I can get some sleep."

It was a very nice kiss. Tina found it difficult to break away. "Now be off with you, little princess, before I change my mind."

Friday night, when Stanley returned from his day at work, he found Tina busily cooking dinner. They ate by candlelight and then settled down on the couch to watch television.

"Just like old married folks," he said.

"Really? You could have fooled me. I thought married folks went to bed after dinner."

"That's newlyweds. Want to play 'make believe?'"

"Promises, promises," Tina replied.

"Now who's teasing?" asked Stanley.

The evenings with Stanley were perfect. Neither Stan or Tina felt a need to pretend they were something other than what they were. There was no fear on Tina's part that Stanley would push beyond the boundaries she had imposed and there was no doubt in Stanley's mind that Tina wanted him to continue his visits to Chicago.

Tina and Stan met Alex and Mara for lunch on Saturday. The brothers hadn't been together in a long time.

"Looks like Mara is treating you pretty good," said Stanley. "I thought you'd have the brow-beaten look by now. You're married almost a year and even Mara seems to be thriving."

"Try it, brother. You'll like it. It's amazing what a guy can get used to. Socks and underwear get picked up and washed regularly, and take it from me, having a beautiful woman cook and serve your meals makes up for not being allowed to watch Monday night football."

"I might surprise you some day, big brother. Actually, unlike you, socks, underwear and home cooked meals are not my top priorities. I kinda' had other things in mind. Changing the subject, old Buddy, how's your job going?"

"You know how it is when you're low man on the totem pole. Stronson, Inc. has plants all over the world. From the way it's going, I think they want me to check out all of them before deciding my future. It's exciting getting to all the facilities they have scattered around, but it's also exhausting—and I really hate being away from Mara so much."

"May I interrupt this conversation for a minute?" asked Mara with a look that pleaded for sympathy. "I don't like it either. If I could find some archeological digs around, I'd go get me a job. Somehow I remember that was my goal when I spent all those years in college."

"When they send me to Egypt, Sweetheart, I promise to pack you in my suitcase. So what's your excuse, Stan? Far as I know you live and work in Boston. What are you doing here big brother?"

"There aren't any pretty girls in Boston so I asked my boss to open an office in Chicago. He'll do anything to make me happy."

"You two are impossible," laughed Tina. "Don't you want to talk about sports or something? Who do you think will win the World Series this year?"

"That's my gal, Tina. There's a game this evening at Wrigley Field. Anyone interested?"

"Let's go." was the unanimous reply.

After purchasing the tickets, they did some sightseeing around Chicago and then had an early dinner for the game was to begin at seven p.m. It was a perfect day made even better by the fact that the home team won five to four. The game ended quite late since it had gone into extra innings.

"Want to stop at our place for a night cap?" asked Alex.

"Thanks, but no. It's late and I think it's time I got this pretty lady home," replied Stan.

"You wouldn't have any ulterior motive in wanting to rush back to the apartment?" teased Alex.

"You're looking at your honorable older brother Alex. Would I ever have anything other than Tina's best interest in mind? Maybe we'll hold hands for a little while and then exchange some real friendly kisses, but then I'll see that she goes to her room. My job is to play watchdog on the couch. It's all on the up and up. Tina will have to marry me before I let her seduce me."

"Will you guys stop already?" Tina asked. "You're making me blush. Take Alex home, Mara, and put a gag on him. I'll do the same with Stan."

"Sorry, Tina. I guess it is time we stop teasing. Stan will be leaving tomorrow and I know how important the remaining hours are to you both. To be truthful, I don't get home much and it's time Mara and I also have some private time together. I'd like a little reassurance that she still loves me. Do you want me to take you to the airport tomorrow?"

"Thanks, but I'm hoping Tina will see me off. If she does, you can't blame me for wanting to be with her as long as possible. I really enjoyed our day together. We'll do it again soon. Now goodnight, you two. See that Alex stays out of trouble, Mara."

It was a beautiful night. There was a big full moon high in the sky and the delicious smell of autumn was in the air. Stanley's intentions toward Tina were honorable, but in truth, he'd really like to follow her into the bedroom this last night. Instead he suggested a brisk walk before going into the apartment. It might serve as a cold shower. Tina knew where he was coming from because she, too, was tempted. They walked at a fast pace for about an hour not talking very much. Tina imagined spending the night in strong arms that would erase all her bad memories, whereas Stan thought of wooing and winning the only woman he had ever loved. Not being able to walk all night, they eventually found themselves back at the apartment.

"What a day, Tina. Going to the game was a great idea. Tell me! Where did you learn so much about yelling and screaming?"

"Everyone else was doing it. I just followed the crowd."

"You're a little imp, you know. Pretending to understand sports is a sure way to any man's heart."

"Oh, it is? I was told that the way to a man's heart was through his stomach. Does that mean I won't have to learn how to cook?"

"You know darn well that the way to my heart only requires that you let me kiss your sweet lips whenever mine are in the neighborhood."

"And when you're not in Chicago, may I ask whose lips you're kissing?"

"None could compare, so why bother."

"Do I bother you, Stan?"

"You can bet on that, Tina."

"How about some refreshment before I go to my room?"

"You're all the refreshment I need, Tina," said Stanley as he drew her close and kissed her very thoroughly. His height caused her to be lifted off the floor. She was, therefore, at his mercy when it came to the duration of that kiss. When finally setting her down, he pushed her gently through the door singing softly, "Goodnight my love. Sleep tight my love."

Tina, smiling, closed the door behind her. Once on the other side, she had some trouble with her own resolve. Her relationship with Alan while in England came to mind. Sleeping beside a strong man had been very comforting. Sex wasn't bad either. However, she knew that Stan would want more from her. He would expect and deserve commitment on her part and that meant she was prepared to love, honor—and settle down. Determined not to hurt him again, she had to be sure.

It was a restless night for both although neither Stan or Tina would admit to their thoughts and feelings the next morning. Instead they shared a leisurely breakfast of eggs, sausage and toast planning some neutral activities for the day. Stan would be taking a seven p.m. flight back to Boston.

They went to a movie in the afternoon. Neither could later remember the name of the film or even the subject matter. While holding hands, their eyes often met. Stanley thought about the night before. Should I have gone to the other side of that wall last night? Had I taken the chance, would it have caused Tina to close the door forever?

Meanwhile Tina mused, Maybe I'd know if Stan was truly Mr. Right had I invited him into my room. Well it's too late now. When we leave the theater, there will be time for only a quick dinner—then we're off to the airport. Conversation over dinner was stilted. Tina was already feeling lonely and Stan wished that she would board the plane with him.

"You'll be leaving soon for your Australia and New Zealand tours. When do you go?"

"My schedule calls for me to leave here on October 3l—that's about three weeks from now. Do you think you'll get back this way before then, Stan?"

"You can be sure I'll try. Too bad Australia flights take off from the west coast. It would have been great if I could have met you in New York for a few days before your departure."

"I'll really miss you, Stan."

"I hope so, Tina. They say 'absence makes the heart grow fonder.' I'm counting on it being so. Maybe you'll miss me enough to know that we were meant to be together."

It was a tearful parting at the airport. Stanley said he would call every day, and after a long kiss in spite of amused onlookers, he disappeared through the gate and boarded the 727.

Sighing as she left, Tina was sure her apartment would never be the same again. Stan had brought it to life in only a little over three days. When would she see him again? Maybe she'd surprise him one day before leaving for her overseas assignment. We'll see, she said to herself. This feeling of emptiness might go away when I get back to the real world.

11

As expected Mara called Tina the first thing Monday morning.

"Well?"

"Well what?"

"Did you say 'yes'?"

"To tell the truth, I was tempted, Mara, but the man got away unharmed."

"You know Stan's crazy about you, Tina."

"Truthfully, Mara, I almost wish he'd have broken down the door that separated us last night, but then it would have been even more difficult to send him back to Boston. Am I hopeless?"

"Crazy, yes—hopeless, no. I know you want to be sure of your feelings, but sometimes the only way to find that out is to go for it. To change the subject, what do you want to do today to take away the lonelies?"

Knowing she'd need clothing suitable for Australia's summer season, Tina suggested that Mara join her on a shopping spree.

"Sounds like fun, Tina. The shops here are already into fall and winter clothing. You'll have to hit the clearance racks. There should be good buys around and we both love bargains. I might even find something for myself. When we're done, plan on having dinner with us."

"I'd like that. My apartment feels a little empty right now. Are you sure Alex won't mind sharing you this evening?"

"Are you kidding. He'll love having two of us fussing over him. You know he doesn't get much pampering when he's away from home."

Dinner, after their long day of shopping, was simple, delicious and welcome. Mara was a very good cook. Sharing an evening with Mara and Alex was always a pleasure. They would watch television, play cards or just sit around and talk. When Tina was ready to go back to her apartment, Alex and Mara would walk with her. "We need the exercise," they always insisted.

This night was devoted to watching a show on television. At about half past eleven, the three musketeers were at Tina's apartment house. As they approached her door, they could hear the phone. "Come in with me," said Tina as she picked up the phone forgetting to let the answering machine take over. A strange voice on the other end of the line said, "Hello there! Nice to know you're back from shopping and safe at home."

"You've dialed a wrong number," Tina replied.

"Then how did I know you'd be alone tonight?"

Looking perplexed, Tina slammed down the phone. "What was that all about?" asked Alex, concerned.

"Jim told me to have the answering machine screen my calls. Unfortunately, I forgot. Some guy was on the other end saying something about my having spent the day shopping. Then he claimed to know that I'd be alone tonight and laughed. Very strange."

Alex and Mara were immediately concerned. "Come back to our house, Tina. We don't want you here by yourself."

"Absolutely not! This is where I live. What good is having an apartment if I can't use it. I'll only have a few more weeks and then will be living out of a suitcase again. I know you're both worried about me, but I'm a big girl and can take care of myself. My guess is that the call was made by someone randomly playing with the numbers on his phone. Lots of people go shopping and are alone at night. By dumb luck, this guy's call fit into my scenario. Next time I'll remember to let the machine answer for me. It's a good lesson."

"We'd both feel better if you were at our place, but if you insist on staying here, please lock up everything the minute we leave and don't open the door for anyone." Mara was not at all convinced that the caller had dialed a wrong number, but said she would call Tina in the morning. "Have the machine take the message and call me back."

Toward the end of the week there was mail from Alan. He was again driving tourists around England. Responding to the news that Tina had signed up for two Australia/New Zealand trips in November and part of December, he wrote, "I asked to do the tour with you, but Cartrite wouldn't let me take my bus overseas. Seriously, Tina, I miss you. I'd like nothing better than to have you back in my life, and my bed. Would you, perhaps, consider it?"

There was also a message on the machine from Jim in St. Louis. When Tina returned his call, Jim told her he'd heard from retired Officer McCarthy—that he'd made contact with another of the old gang members. This one, it seems, was now a respectable fire fighter who had vivid recollections of some encounters with the 'Uptown Boys.'

"John Jacobs is his name. He agreed to meet with McCarthy and me, but we've had some problems with schedules. When I'm free, Jacobs is not and when we're both available, Officer McCarthy has to be out of town. I really think the meeting should be with all three of us. The best date I could come up with was October 29. That's just before you take off for Australia."

"It would be nice to go away knowing something positive was happening at home. What made McCarthy think of John Jacobs after all this time?"

"Kevin McCarthy remembered a frightened little boy he'd chased one day and brought in for questioning. He was younger than the other gang members—not the usual cocky type with the wise mouth. He was released after a good lecture, but McCarthy continued to keep an eye on him. After talking with the kid's mother, she moved the family. The change in environment turned the boy's life around."

"Does McCarthy know where Mr. Jacobs is now?"

"Kevin remembered the mother's name and where she had taken the family. Fortunately she was still at the same address. Grateful for the break he had given John, she was happy to relay a message to her son who then made contact with Officer McCarthy."

"It's good to know that this lead is not another jailbird. He should be more believable, but being so young, do you think he understood what was going on at that time?"

"We can only hope. We'll know more after we interview him. I wish I could get up there before you leave Tina, but it's been a zoo here. My caseload increases every day and I have some court appearances to make."

"You're a busy man, McDonald."

"Need I tell you that meeting with this fireman isn't the only reason why I hope to be in Chicago before you take off again? I'll call you if I can work it out. It's a pain having an answering machine act as go-between, but you should play it safe. Have there been any more hang-ups?"

"A strange thing happened a few nights ago. I had just gotten to the door when I heard my phone. Without thinking, I picked it up and a man started talking. I believe it was a wrong number."

"What did he say?"

"Something about my having been on a shopping spree. When I suggested he'd dialed the wrong number, he laughed and hung up. I'm sure it was a chance caller being smart." Tina deliberately left out the part about her being alone. She didn't want Jim to know about Stan's visit. He would have given her the third degree. When put to the test, Tina preferred omission to lying.

"You're probably right. People get their kicks in strange ways, but it's important that you be watchful. Keep that tape and make a record of anything that might be out of the ordinary. This is a crazy world, and even if it has nothing to do with you or your case, there are certifiable nuts out there. I'd rather you didn't become a victim."

"Why is it that I feel safer when I'm out of the country?"

"It's the same all over the world, Tina. The only difference here is that this is where your parents were murdered."

"I guess I never told you about what happened to me in the Great Pyramid."

"No! You didn't. Tell me!"

"I was almost to the tomb in the center of Cheops in Cairo when all the lights went out. It was pitch black dark and very frightening. Someone pushed past me—pretty hard—and I fell ending up dazed with a lump on my head. It was probably someone who panicked in the total darkness, but it left me shaken and bruised."

"I'm sure it was an accident, Tina. People do strange things when panicked and it looks to me like someone lost control. Probably his or her only purpose was to get out of the pyramid as quickly as possible. Did the fall cause you to black out?"

"I was dazed momentarily, but what worried me was, when I got back on my feet, my people were gone. It was eerie to be in that damp pyramid alone. The dim lights, although again on, didn't help much, but I managed to find my way out."

"That incident would frighten anyone. I'm sure the person that bumped into you was as panicked as you were and that he or she meant no harm, but you never know. As I said before, 'there are crazy people out there.' A person has to be on guard at all times. There's a meeting about to begin and I must hang up now, Tina."

"Okay Jim, but keep me posted. Maybe I'll see you before I leave for Australia. If not, I'll be back around the middle of December."

"That's almost Christmas and a long way off. Sure you wouldn't like to come down to St. Louis for a few days? You could bunk with me."

"What kind of a girl do you think I am?"

"My kind, I hope."

"That's enough, Jim. End of discussion. What happened to that meeting you were going to?"

"Okay, Tina! You win, but I plan to do whatever I can to see you in Chicago before you leave. The memory of that kiss. when last I saw you, still lingers. Goodnight now little one. Sleep well and think of me."

Tina was not good at juggling suitors. Jim made it obvious that he was anxious to continue where he had left off when last at her apartment. The kiss had been nice. Tina had enjoyed it at the time, but had no serious plans for Jim—at least not yet. What would she do if he became more aggressive? Where Stan was content to be held at bay, Jim, she suspected, would not be so patient or tolerant.

"It's good my work will take me away from decision making for a while," she said to Mara when they were together. "Remind me not to meet any more guys—it's too confusing."

"Most women would die to be in your position," replied Mara who was enjoying the whole scene.

The next two weeks went quickly. Alan wrote asking that Tina come back to England. Stanley had arranged to call Tina every morning at half past eight with the intent of bypassing the answering machine. He was very busy, but was trying to get to Chicago before Tina's departure. Jim and Tina, meanwhile, played telephone tag. He'd call and leave a message. She'd return the call and he'd be out of the office. It was frustrating, but Tina rationalized that Jim would get through if he had something important to report.

One morning there was a call from Tina's tour agency. Her date of departure was to be advanced to October 29. The Agency explained that some of Tina's group had arranged for an optional two-day layover in Los Angeles. Having asked for a guide, the agency felt Tina should be the person to take on the responsibility.

This latest development would rule out any possibility of getting together with Jim since his meeting with John Jacobs and Officer McCarthy was scheduled for the 29th. As for Stan, he had been working on a deal to be in Chicago on the 30th. It would have been a one-day visit, but to Stan's mind, one day was better than nothing. Unfortunately with Tina's change in schedule, he'd have to settle for nothing.

"How do you like that, Mara?" Tina asked. "One day I'm worried about keeping three gentlemen friends apart, and then suddenly, there's no one to kiss me 'good-bye.' My departure date was pushed forward. I have to be in Los Angeles on the 29th and I guess it's only you who'll be around to see me off."

"Only me? What do you mean? Only?"

"You're my best friend, Mara. You know that, but with all the hunks threatening to knock down my door, I did think at least one would have gotten here to wish me well."

"They all wish you well and it's not over till it's over. There's still a week before you leave. With a little luck Alan will arrive from England, and while he's here, Stanley will drop in with an engagement ring and Jim will arrive handcuffed to Larry. You could have a reunion while you're kissing everybody 'good-bye.'"

"Forget it, Mara. I'll settle for you and Alex if he's not out of town."

Tina would be leaving in the morning. The bags were packed and ready to go. Mara and Alex had taken her to dinner and planned to drive her to the airport. Everything was in order. Now for a little sleep. Tina was just about to doze off when the phone rang. Who would it be? Tom, Dick or Harry—otherwise known as Alan, Jim or Stanley. So sure it would be one of them, she picked up the phone.

"Hi Babe. You don't stay home much, do you? Where are you off to this time?" said a raspy-voiced man on the other end of the line.

"What do you want? Who are you?" asked Tina recognizing the voice as the one who had called previously.

"I want you Babe," he sang. "Didn't I warn you to stop sniffing around? You're going to be sorry."

Tina put the phone down, but her insides were shaking. Someone who shouldn't have, had gotten her unlisted number. Could he have her address as well? If not, he was sure to get it soon. Unless he was guessing, It was evident that he knew a great deal about her comings and goings. In a panic, Tina dialed Officer McDonald. Surprisingly, he answered.

"I'm so glad you're there," Tina said explaining that she'd had a shock.

"Calm down, Tina. What happened? You're talking too fast. You sound upset."

"My phone rang. Thinking it was you, I picked it up. It was that caller again—the one we thought was a wrong number. It wasn't a wrong number, Jim."

"What did he say?"

"He threatened me."

"Tell me exactly what he said."

"I want you Babe," he said and then, "You'll be sorry if you don't stop sniffing around. Actually it was more like he was singing—you know that Sonny and Cher song, 'I Want you Babe.'"

"Someone's getting nervous, Tina. You must be stepping on toes. Good thing you'll be out of the country for a while."

"I think he knows it, Jim."

"What gives you that idea?"

"He asked me where I was going this time—like he knew I'd be leaving in the morning. For all I know, he might be watching my apartment right this minute. Let's face it Jim, information about me is getting out somehow. Maybe that intruder in your hotel room was looking for my phone number. I'm going to have the telephone company change my number again, but in addition, am planning to find another apartment when I get back. Although I've just moved in, I don't want to come back here."

"Can't say that I blame you for wanting to move again, Tina, but it's impossible to keep running. Bad people, If they want to, will find you no matter where you go. The best thing is to stay alert at all times and watch your back."

"I do and I will. Now that I think back, there was this guy on my last tour. He was a loner and very strange. He left the tour before it ended giving some lame excuse. Rearranging flights is costly. I have often wondered why he was in such a hurry."

"Tell me more, Tina."

"He was about thirty-two years old. His name, according to the roster, was Jason Thomas. None of us could figure out why he signed up for the trip. He didn't participate or appear to be interested in anything except that he joined us when we went to the pyramids—the day the lights went out and I was pushed off the narrow path."

"You could have been badly hurt that time, Tina. Are you sure having this job is necessary? If I had my way, you'd give it up and stay right where you are. I could come visit and we'd have a great time—just you and me."

"Dream on, Jim. This job is necessary for my survival and I do like what I'm doing most of the time."

"It's too late now, Tina, but be prepared for an argument as to the merits of your job when you get back. Meanwhile take my advice and refrain from calling or writing anyone. Arrange with Mara to be your only contact and be sure not to call her at her home number. I think you may be right in suspecting a leak and, until we know where it is, you should play it safe. Mara and I will work out some way to relay messages when necessary."

"Is my telephone number on record at police headquarters?"

"Not to my knowledge. I keep notes, but they are on my person at all times. Your official file has not been updated since you left St. Louis to live with your aunt after the funeral, but you never know. Anything is possible."

"Even my aunt doesn't know where I am, Jim. How could this creep know so much about me unless he has inside information? More and more I'm beginning to believe it has something to do with the person who got into your hotel room. He or she might have been following you to get

175

a line on me knowing you inherited the case and were given the file. Do all those working at police headquarters have access to confidential information?"

"The Captain, of course, would be aware of everything that goes on. We each have our own cases, but other officers know I'm working on finding the person or persons responsible for the murder of your parents."

"Do you think any of them could be taking orders from someone in the 'Uptowners' or could an 'Uptowner' have infiltrated the police department?"

"Now you're making me nervous, Tina. You may have a point though, and I promise to look over my shoulder from now on. Better yet, I'm due some vacation. How would you feel about my tagging along with you to Australia?"

"I think you'd best stay here and catch the bad guys—that is unless you think they'll be with me on the tour."

"Don't even joke about that possibility, Tina. Honestly, it would be fun doing Australia and New Zealand with you, but for now, I'll stay here and keep the home fires burning. Seriously, I can't imagine anyone would know where you're off to. Until a few days ago even you didn't know they'd have you leaving on the 29th."

Jim was disappointed that he couldn't get to say good-bye to Tina properly and told her so. He then advised her to hang up and get some sleep. "You're in for a big day tomorrow, baby," Jim said. "Have a good tour. I'll see you, doll face, when you get back."

Why did Jim's parting words sound familiar? It was Larry all over again. He too had always referred to her as a doll or a baby. Tina found it very irritating. I'm a person, not a doll, she protested getting ready to go to bed.

Although it was late, Tina decided to make one last call. Hoping that she would actually fall asleep, in spite of all the commotion caused by her mysterious caller, she wanted to preempt a call from Stanley. "Hello Stan," she said hoping that he was still awake and determined not to mention the mysterious phone call which would worry him needlessly.

"Tina! I've been trying to get you on the phone, but your line's been busy. I was just about to try again."

"That's what I thought. I'm really tired and have to be up early tomorrow, but wanted to say 'good-bye.' I hate that word. It's so final. German's have a much nicer way of saying 'good-bye.' They say 'auf wiedersehen' which means 'until we meet again.' I'll be back before you know it, Stan, and am looking forward to us being together then."

"I'd have made it to Chicago, Tina, if your agency hadn't pushed up that departure date. Need I tell you that I'll be thinking of you every minute while you're away."

"Better not. I wouldn't want to be responsible for you losing a cushy job that let's you goof off in Chicago whenever the spirit moves you."

"One of us is going to have to move sooner or later. You know that, don't you Tina?"

Ignoring the implications that went with Stan's remark, Tina responded, "It's so good to know that I have you in my corner. I'm not alone anymore and I can't begin to tell you how much that means to me."

"I'll always be there for you, Tina. In case you haven't noticed, I love you. Now goodnight, Sweetheart. Get some sleep. It will be a long day tomorrow."

"Goodnight Stan. I'll be in touch."

Tina preferred not to get into the complicated arrangements she had discussed with Jim regarding Mara as a go-between for purposes or relaying messages. She and Mara would work out the logistics on the way to the airport in the morning.

"Goodnight, my love," Stan said. "See you soon. I'll be counting the days."

Morning came all too quickly. It felt as though Tina hadn't slept at all. On the way to the airport, Mara was filled in on all the developments of the night before. She was appalled at the thought that someone was harassing her friend and agreed that Tina would have to move. Obviously, someone was on to her and, at the very least, wanted to frighten her.

"It's possible my phone line has been tampered with, Tina. The number is unlisted but I, like you, will get it changed as a precaution. I'll call your hotel in Australia leaving my new number and a post office box where you can send mail. About Stan and Jim, I'll work it out with them. Don't you worry about anything. Alex is away and I'll have time on my hands. Do you trust me to find another apartment for you in your absence?"

"I'd trust you with my life, Mara."

"Call me when you have the details about your return to the States. I'll pick you up. Try to enjoy yourself even though you're working and have so much on your mind."

"I hope my being out of the country will get that awful caller off my back. Once I'm with the tourists, I'll be too busy to think about him. I've never been to Australia or New Zealand. From what I hear, it's a different world and I could use some of that right now."

With some hugs and kisses, Tina turned to go through the security gates hoping, some day, to repay Mara for all her help and support.

12

As scheduled, Tina met and escorted the three couples who had opted for the two-day Los Angeles add on. They visited Disneyland and Hollywood and then it was time to collect the remaining arriving tourists for the start of the trip to Australia and New Zealand.

"We'll leave for the airport at about eight p.m. Eighteen anxious tourists will be looking for me there. Seven more will join our group in Sydney. The flight leaves at half past ten."

"I don't understand why we fly into Sydney only to catch another plane to Cairns and then, after two days, return to Sydney. Why don't we fly to Cairns in the first place?" asked one of the tourists in the group.

"I asked that same question of the agency. My understanding is that it has something to do with international airports as opposed to domestic. We don't get to choose."

"Why don't we have a stopover in Hawaii?" asked another member of the group who had come from New York. He was already weary of traveling.

Tina explained, while some flights refuel in Hawaii, theirs was non-stop to Sydney. She reminded her tourists that it would be a long night—about fourteen hours to Sydney and then, after a lay-over, another three-hour flight to Cairns. "I'd advise that you try sleeping, or at least resting, enroute. Did you know that Cairns is in the middle of a tropical rain forest? It is very close to the equator?"

The announcement to board the fully booked flight was heard over the public address system. Tina's tourists found themselves scattered throughout the 747 Jumbo Jet. While videos and meals passed the time, the night seemed endless. Having settled all her charges into their respective seats, Tina tried to relax. The fact that Carol Maguire had requested an emergency leave at a time when Tina was available, was a lucky break. Any of her fellow tour guides, had they not already been assigned elsewhere, would have gladly taken this assignment.

All Carol's notes, maps, connections, directions, suggestions and helpful hints were included in the folder from Cartrite and Tina had gone over the material during the flight's daylight hours. Her bus drivers would be responsible for most of the commentary, but Tina wanted to be prepared for questions. She would also need to know her way around the many airports involved. The tour included nine flights. There were also boat trips, two train rides and several optional excursions on the itinerary. It was expected that Tina would move her people through the maze efficiently—as though she was a native to each area on the agenda. Carol's notes and maps were a lifeline and priceless.

The flight to Sydney was over at last. It was an exhausted group that arrived Monday morning. The cramped quarters and turbulence made it difficult to move around during the night and everyone complained of aches and pains. Very few had been able to sleep.

Gerda Osiecki

Among the tourists meeting them in Sydney was a woman of about thirty-five who was legally blind. Although already on tour two months, she was traveling alone and needed assistance. It was her intention, after Australia and New Zealand to catch up with another group in China. The tour agency had made it clear that Tina would be responsible for her safety and well-being. This, she knew, would be an added challenge.

Gathering her people together while waiting for the aircraft that would fly them to Cairns, Tina reminded them that it was Monday. There had been no Sunday, but they would make up for having lost the day by having two Saturdays when returning to the States. Looking at the confused faces, Tina assured them that it would all work out even in the end.

"I know you're tired," Tina said, "but I'd like to take this opportunity to pass on some important information. First I want to tell you about the currency used in Australia. You're going to have to convert some of your American dollars. The bank here at the airport usually gives the best rate. While travelers checks and credit cards are acceptable everywhere, it's good to have cash for small purchases such as post cards, souvenirs and refreshments. I'd suggest about $50—certainly not more than $100 since you will have to convert back any money you haven't spent when leaving the country. The same will hold true when we go to New Zealand."

After circulating some coins and explaining their worth, Tina began her speech concerning customs. "It's necessary to go through customs and immigration in Cairns because that is our official entry into Australia. Have your passports, visas and travel documents available. We'll go through the line as a group. When cleared, you and your luggage will be taken to the hotel where you'll have some time to relax before leaving for the first item on our agenda—a ride on the 'Army Ducks' into the rain forest. 'Army Ducks are vehicles which were abandoned after

World War II. They were built to maneuver on both land and water. In the rain forest our guide will point out plants and animals indigenous to the area. Then, although thoroughly exhausted, you will have your first 'Aussie' dinner—roast lamb prepared on a spit. Not knowing or caring that you've lost a night somewhere and have been up thirty or more hours, you'll be expected to sing along with the restaurant's host as he leads you through the many verses of 'Waltzing Matilda.' Hopefully we can make it an early night since we'll be boarding a catamaran to Green Island in the morning where we'll have another full day of activity."

Observing the tired eyes and facial expressions of her charges, Tina added, "I told you, this is a tour not to be confused with a vacation. You came to see and do as much as could be squeezed into the time we are together."

The announcement to board the plane for Cairns was made and all were surprised to find they had been upgraded to comfortable seats in first class. What a contrast to the flight from Los Angeles where they were packed like sardines in a can. There were private television screens, champagne served with an excellent meal and space to stretch the legs for what was supposed to be a three and a-half hour flight.

The 727 started for the runway. We were again on our way. Not exactly. No sooner moving when the aircraft came to a complete halt. Passengers looked out the windows as mechanics ran from every direction. After half an hour sitting on the tarmac, it was determined that major repairs were required. With everyone remaining on board, the pilot taxied into a hanger. Two hours later, all was resolved. We were again underway. The three-hour flight had become more than five. There was no time, when we arrived at the hotel, to freshen up because the Army Ducks were waiting—also was the lamb dinner with the sing-a-long. It was an endless day as had been the endless night. All breathed a sigh of relief when finally in bed.

Gerda Osiecki

Morning came too soon, but a spunky group of travelers managed to again get on their way. "It's hard to figure the traffic around here," said Mrs. Dougal, one of Tina's group. "I'm afraid to step off the curbing."

"It's like in England." said someone. The travelers tried to convince the bus driver that he was on the wrong side of the road. He laughed, insisting that Americans were not smart enough to drive in a civilized country.

"It's best to look both ways before stepping off a curb," Tina warned. "Be careful as well of the foreigners renting cars. Not familiar with steering wheels on the right side, they do the craziest things. Even the natives here have a healthy respect for those guys."

"Roundabouts, known to Americans as traffic circles, can be a real challenge during 'peak hours.' It's fun to watch the foreigners maneuver them," said Dustin, the tour driver.

"What is the speed limit around here," asked a tourist watching the confusion in front of the bus.

"The rule of thumb seems to be that you are permitted to drive as fast as you want—until you crash," answered Dustin.

Green Island was a delight. After the hectic day before, all welcomed the opportunity to do only as much as they found comfortable. Some chose to relax in the beautifully landscaped swimming pool, but most opted for the glass bottom boat ride to the Great Barrier Reef known the world over for it's beautiful coral and exotic fish. After a great lunch one could take a swim in the clear aqua waters or, if motivated, there was snorkeling and scuba diving. Those not so ambitious could view the well stocked aquarium or spend time in the many souvenir shops. There was, on Green Island, something for everyone. After a wonderful day, all were safely returned to the hotel happy and content.

Another busy day began the next morning when the group boarded a train for a ride through the mountains to Kurandi. They had tickets to TJAPUKAI, an Aboriginal Dance Theater. This was followed by a ride to the airport where the group boarded a plane for Sydney. Many exciting excursions were planned for three days there—a tour of the city, dinner and performance at the world renowned Sydney Opera House, a trip to Koala Park Sanctuary and another dinner atop Sydney Tower's Revolving Restaurant with it's spectacular views. The final day included a lunch with entertainment on an old-time paddle wheeler. Every moment was planned for the tourists' pleasure. All were impressed but exhausted as each day came to a close. Hotel rooms provided television, but there were only two channels. One of these featured reruns of The Beverly Hillbillies. With such an exciting menu, most were content, after dinner, to go to bed early.

They were on a tight schedule. Most days required that bags be packed and ready for pickup before breakfast. While her tourists ate, Tina and the driver would gather, count, tag and load each piece of luggage on the waiting bus. On the way to the terminal, taking advantage of her captive audience, Tina would explain the procedure her tourists could expect at the airport as well as brief them about activities planned upon arrival at the next destination. When checking into a hotel, Tina's first responsibility was to get and distribute room keys. At a desk in the lobby would be posted information as needed. Upon leaving or arriving at airports or hotels, it was up to Tina and her driver to see that all luggage and passengers were accounted for and ticketed. The Cartrite Agency promised hassle-free travel. Tourists needed only to be punctual.

While Tina's travelers slept, ate or had free time, she was busy sending FAX messages, making confirmation phone calls, or arranging for special needs. While with the group, Tina would be explaining where to go, where to meet, what to be aware of, answer questions, and always, there were noses to count assuring that no one had been left behind.

Senior citizens were on the move and, therefore, big business to travel agents. Although it required her attention twenty-four hours a day, it was Tina's job to make everything appear easy and fun. For tour guides, it was always a challenge. A person would have to like what they were doing. Fortunately, Tina did. She was totally absorbed with her responsibilities leaving little time to think about anyone back home who might want to do her harm.

Due to the vastness of Australia, there were many inter-city flights and the group was in the hands of a new driver almost every day. The drivers were responsible for most of the commentary and were eager to share history, gossip and other tidbits of information. Each had his own style and the tourists were never bored. One loved to sing and the familiar "Waltzing Matilda," with it's many verses, insured audience participation whenever it came to the chorus. Other drivers liked to tell jokes. The humor could be pretty sick. After having driven through miles of roadway with nothing but sheep on either side, one bus driver asked, "Why did the ram go over the cliff?" Not waiting for a response, he answered, "Because he didn't see the ewe turn."

Someone from the back of the bus responded, "You're such a treasure, you should be buried," while another added, "You should be on a stage. There's one leaving in a few minutes." There was laughter followed by never-ending one-liners as the group warmed up and tried to outdo each other.

Driving for miles through the beautiful countryside, not only were there sheep—thousands of them—but herds of deer being raised for export as venison. One pasture was particularly interesting. There were hundreds of cows, different in that they were black on both ends with a wide white stripe encircling their middles. The tourists found the cattle unique and referred to them as "Oreo Cows." This required explaining since the bus driver had never heard of America's favorite cookie.

After leaving Sydney, the group again boarded a plane for Melbourne—Australia's southern-most city. To Americans it was difficult to comprehend that by going south they'd have colder weather. All of Australia is south of the Equator, therefore it is warmest in the north.

"We'll have an early dinner upon arriving in Melbourne and then a two-hour drive to see the Fairy Penguins. Wear warm clothing. It will be dusk when we get there and we'll be out in the wind about an hour watching the penguins as they leave the ocean to feed their young who are waiting anxiously in the brush. It's an experience you'll never forget. Fairy Penguins are about twelve inches in height and adorable as they gather in groups before daring to dash from the ocean to shore.

"It will be quite late by the time we get back to our hotel, but I'll give you tomorrow morning to sleep or explore on your own. In the afternoon we fly to Christchurch, New Zealand. Bags must be on the bus by two o'clock.

Tina explained that the group would have to go through customs in Christchurch and that she expected to have them at their hotel around half past one the next morning—this due to distance and time changes. "Expect an early wake-up call since we're scheduled to board the Trans Alpine Express at 7:30 a.m. The train will take us through the mountains. You'll be tired, but thank me when seeing the magnificent scenery."

The sleepy group made it through the short night and were given a box breakfast on a train that looked like the "Toonerville Trolley." As they passed through small villages, friendly people waved.

"At Springfield Station," said someone on the intercom, "you'll see Rosie, the Trans Alpine Express mascot. Rosie has been at this station for many years. Each time the train stops, the conductor gives her a meat pie. Over time, they say, Rosie has consumed hundreds of pies. The town's inhabitants have vowed to erect a statue in her memory upon her death."

While the passengers were on board enjoying the scenery, food and entertainment, their bus driver and coach traveled the narrow, curvy mountain road with the intention of meeting the tourists at the other end. From there the driver would take the group to the glacier area.

Our driver in New Zealand was of Scotch ancestry. His name was Arthur. He was very proud of his adopted country. It showed in the way that he held everyone's interest with stories about the rich and famous—also infamous—people who had or were still living on the South Island of New Zealand. He went out of his way to point out places and things that we certainly would have missed had we been sight seeing on our own. One day he stopped the bus so that we could watch some brave people bungy jumping off a high bridge toward the rushing cold water below. While our tourists were invited to experience the thrill, there were no takers. "Thanks, but no thanks," was the overall consensus as they saw a man, first stretched and then hanging by his ankles, just above the icy water beneath him.

The next day, after many hours on the coach, found the group in Queensland. Dinner that night was in a magnificent restaurant at the top of a mountain overlooking the city. The only access was by cable car. "What a view." "What a meal." "What a day," commented members of the happy group as they were driven back to the hotel later that night.

On the road again the next day, Tina commented about the mountains in the distance. "Arthur tells me that we've been extremely fortunate with the weather. Normally those mountains would be obscured by low hanging clouds."

"I repeat this tour every two weeks," said Arthur "and could count, on one hand, the number of times I've been able to show off these snow-covered mountain tops. Say a prayer that our luck holds out. I know some of you want to take the ski plane to the glacier on Mount Cook. The pilots won't risk flying if the weather is threatening."

"Some of you," said Tina, "have signed up for the optional boat excursion to Walter Peak's Farm tomorrow. If you have, you'll see trained dogs bring in the sheep and witness a sheep shearing demonstration. The shearers are so skilled that the wool removed ends up looking like one big blanket. You'll be invited to pet the animals and can catch the baby lambs if you're fast enough. Refreshments will be served at the farm and there will be entertainment as well as a sing-a-long on board ship."

While Tina would normally have stayed behind to do paper work, she decided to go with those opting for this side trip. To her delight, and that of all the others on the authentic old coal-fired steamboat, a group of local high school children entertained. Singing a Maori folk song complete with traditional hand motions to the accompaniment of a guitar, they were an unexpected treat. Because of the spontaneity, the performance was more appreciated than had they been professionals in a theater.

"Tonight will be your home visit with a real New Zealand family. I've assigned four or five to each host. You will be picked up in front of the hotel at six o'clock. Most of you have brought a small gift for your hostess and I know you'll enjoy the experience of meeting and talking with genuine New Zealanders on their own turf.

"Tomorrow there's a 5:30 wake-up call. Okay, I heard those moans back there. Remember we're on tour, not to be confused with vacation. You can sleep when you get home. The coach will take us to Milford Sound where we are expected to board a motor launch. While marveling at the spectacular scenery of Fiordland National Park, you'll enjoy a box lunch. We'll need a nice day so keep praying. It's worked for us so far."

Prayers were answered again. They couldn't have had a more beautiful day. The melting snow on the mountains resulted in cascading waterfalls everywhere. Seals relaxed on rocks and appeared to be posing for photographers. Some on the boat claimed to have seen crested penguins diving off the rocks into the crystal clear water. All agreed that Milford Sound was one of the trip's many highlights.

The tour was coming to an end and the remaining nights were to be spent in a hotel complex beneath Mount Cook, south New Zealand's highest mountain. What a location! It was like being in the middle of a fairyland. There was a photo opportunity to be found around every corner. After several side trips, it was on to Christchurch where the group would begin the return journey to the States. The plane was to touch down in Auckland on the north island and then Tahiti. There would be Red Eye flights from Los Angeles to final destinations. At each airport there were lengthy layovers.

"I will leave after getting you and your luggage on the plane for Auckland," said Tina. "Due to customs regulations, your luggage will have to be picked up and re-ticketed in Auckland by each of you personally. In Auckland it can be checked through to your final destinations, but again, on entering the United States in Los Angeles, you will have to claim your bags. As soon as you and the luggage are cleared, you will find a conveyor belt on which to place the checked baggage allowing it to continue on it's way. It sounds confusing, and I would like to help you through the maze, but a new group is arriving in the morning. There is no way for me to get back and forth from Los Angeles in time."

A flight back to Sydney, several phone calls, a little sleep and Tina would have to be ready to take on another tour.

I'd try to call Mara at the number she left, but don't have a clue as to what time it is in Chicago, thought Tina as she showered. To be honest I'm not even sure what day it is in America. If Mara had any news, I'm sure she'd have included a message. I do wonder if she found an apartment for me. Sure hate to think of starting all over again, but this time I won't have to do any shopping making it easier.

While Tina was busy with her tourists, things at home had been changing—not that anyone was about to alert Mara or tell Tina. There had been a big shake-up in the St. Louis precinct. Jim McDonald's captain had been replaced and he was assigned to work with a new partner - a female officer, Lucy Lombardo. Gossip said that she had come from Chicago. She was a sharp cookie and quite a looker. From the moment he laid eyes on her, Jim recognized that they would get along just fine. A week later the new captain called Jim into his office and said: "That Cappo case—forget it. You're not getting anywhere with it and the more recent homicides have a better chance of being resolved. No need for you to be spending time in Chicago when I need you here. Now get out there and prove that you deserve your new promotion. Congratulations, Detective McDonald!"

Jim was surprised and happy that his promotion had finally come through. He didn't like having to drop the Cappo investigation, but was not about to argue with his new boss, Captain Steiner. As a detective, he would no longer have Lucy as a partner, but they were good chums and he had every confidence he'd soon be making out with her. If he played his cards right, he could see Tina on the side since free time was his own. She didn't have to know that he was no longer giving his all to search for her answers. Yes, things were looking up for Jim McDonald— Detective James McDonald.

It wasn't long before Jim and Officer Lombardo were an item. They began, first, with a few drinks after work. Then they were dating and, by the time Tina was into her second week of the Australia/New Zealand tour, Jim and Lucy were well into a real hot romance. Lucy spent many hours in his apartment, not only were they making love, but they talked shop. It was only natural that the subject of Detective White's murder would come up. This was followed by speculation regarding the unfortunate demise of the family in Chicago which Lucy, having worked there as a police officer, was very much aware of. Before Jim knew it, they were looking at the similarity between that case and the one involving Tina's parents. Lucy wanted to know every last detail.

One day, after having had more than her share of drinks, she told Jim that Tina would never find Larry because he had been escorted to South America. When Jim seemed surprised that she knew about Larry, her explanation was that she had come across his name in some records that were filed.

As their relationship flourished, Lucy learned a great deal about Tina and of her persistence in trying to track down the killer of her parents. Unknown to Jim, she had searched and found notes in Jim's apartment and was, therefore, able to keep her contacts informed of Tina's every move. They knew of her new address, her unlisted number every time it was changed, who she worked for and that she was currently in Australia and New Zealand. Yes, there was a leak—a major leak due to Officer Lombardo who was using her charms to get whatever information she needed. Jim did not at first suspect since he was accustomed to being in charge when it came to women. Lucy was a new experience for him. By the time Jim woke up, he was in over his head. He had his promotion, but they, whoever "they" were, had him.

The new vacationers arrived on schedule and the tour began again. It was a smaller group and mostly couples. The days went smoothly—one after another. Tina was more confident about her surroundings and, consequently, there were few surprises.

The itinerary in Queensland, New Zealand again called for dinner on top of the mountain that could only be reached by cable car. This time Tina and Arthur, her driver, decided to join their tourists. The gondolas had a capacity of four. Tina and Arthur, bringing up the rear, were alone in the slowly ascending cable car. When meeting the descending counter-balancing gondola, Tina saw a familiar face. She jumped up from the seat shouting, "Oh my God. It's him."

Trying to hold Tina down in a cable car that was rocking dangerously, Arthur asked, "Who?"

Frantically waving her arms, it was as though she'd forgotten where she was or that Arthur was in the swinging car with her. Tina wanted only to crash through the door that electronically held them secure. When they reached the top, she bolted and ran wildly to the next car headed down leaving Arthur behind completely bewildered. Never having seen Tina so out of control, Arthur caught another gondola and followed as she ran up and down neighboring streets in despair. Thoroughly frustrated, Tina was in tears when Arthur finally caught up with her. She looked as though she had seen a ghost and was almost incoherent when he took her by the hand escorting her into a nearby cafe. The wine he ordered was downed in one gulp. It was only then that Tina calmed down enough to speak.

"Who did you see Tina? You freaked out. What happened?"

"I know it was him. He saw me too. I know he did."

"Who, Tina? Who did you see? I've never known you to lose control like that. I fully expected you to jump off the mountain to chase that man. Who was he?"

"It was Larry. I tried to catch up with him, but by the time I got down, he was gone. Not a trace of him anywhere."

"I don't know who Larry is, but are you sure it was him in that cable car?"

"I could see him clearly. When our eyes met, he was as shocked as I was. There's no doubt in my mind it was Larry."

"Slow down, Tina. Who is Larry and why would he want to run away from you?"

"It's a long story. I was once engaged to him. My parents were killed and all their assets stolen. At the same time Larry disappeared. He's involved somehow and I've been trying, for the past two years, to find him so that he could explain his part in what happened. Never did I expect to run into him while guiding a tour of vacationers half way around the world. Obviously he didn't expect to see me either—neither did he want me to confront him. There's no sign of him now. He's gone."

"We can check the airport and the train station. Come on. It might not be too late."

"I can't leave our tour group unescorted."

"They'll be busy eating dinner and then shopping in the gift store for a while. I'll leave word upstairs that we'll be back in the lobby to pick them up at ten o'clock. Meanwhile, let's see if we can catch up with this elusive Larry."

"Thanks, Arthur. We'll give it a try, but it would amaze me if he hasn't gone underground. I saw that look on his face. He was shocked and terrified at the sight of me."

"You should have seen your face, Tina. First I thought you were going to faint and then you turned into a maniac."

"We're wasting time. Let's go! I really don't think we'll have any success, but in the state I'm in, dinner would be wasted on me tonight—might as well continue searching."

As predicted, Tina was right. Larry had disappeared once again. Their search of the airport, train station and even driving around the streets of the city was to no avail.

That night Tina called Mara at her unlisted number even though it might be risky. She had to talk to someone who could sympathize with her situation. It was anyone's guess what time it was when she got through to her friend, but Mara welcomed her call.

"Mara," she blurted without preamble. "You won't believe this, but I just saw Larry."

"You must be kidding. No, you wouldn't joke about a thing like that, but when, how, where?"

"I was accompanying my group to a restaurant on a mountain top in Queensland that can only be reached by cable car. When meeting the gondola going down, I saw him in it. We stared at each other unbelieving, but it was him, Mara, and he knew it was me."

Gerda Osiecki

"Are you sure?"

"Absolutely. I caught the next car down, but he made a run for it. Arthur and I searched the streets, the airport and the train terminal for two hours. He was nowhere to be seen."

"Who's Arthur?"

"He's the bus driver taking us from place to place in New Zealand."

"Not another bus driver. What is it with you and bus drivers?"

"It's not like that—not at all what you're thinking. Arthur's a nice family man, happily married, just trying to help. He's old enough to be my father."

"Okay. I believe you. So what are you going to do now? Shall I call Officer McDonald and tell him?"

"I guess you should, but warn him to keep it to himself. Can't help but feel there's something or someone in the St. Louis police department working against me. No matter how fast I run, someone is always ahead of me. It's as though I'm in a race with myself. On second thought, maybe you'd better not say anything to Jim. I'll be home shortly and would like a few days to collect my wits. If Jim knows I'm home, and that I saw Larry, he'll be all over me."

"In more ways than one, Tina. By the way, I moved you into a new apartment. I think you'll like it and it's even closer to our condo."

"Did I ever tell you, Mara, that you're the best friend a person could have? The things you do to help me—it's impossible for me to express my feelings. A sister couldn't be more dear. I love you."

196

"Remember, Tina, we adopted each other and I love you too. Can't wait to see you. I'll pick you up. When and what's the flight number?"

"You'll be sorry you made that suggestion. I get in to O'Hare at six a.m., your time on December 15. Sure you want to be there?"

"If I had to stay up all night, you couldn't keep me away."

"Looks like I won't be due for another trip until sometime in March and I plan to spend most of that free time acting like a detective. Do I have a Doctor Watson?"

"You bet. Do you have a plan of action?"

"Well, first I want to hear Jim's account of what happened after I left. Then I'd like to meet retired Officer McCarthy. I'll also want to arrange a meeting with the two ex-gang members. Maybe I can pick up something Jim missed or is not telling me. I don't like feeling threatened in my own home and mean to put a stop to it once and for all."

"I'm with you, Tina, and can't wait to get started."

"You're the best, Mara. Now I must hang up, but I'll see you soon."

"Safe home, my friend. Good-bye for now."

13

It was good to be back. Mara was waiting, as promised. After collecting the luggage and stopping for lunch, Mara drove Tina to her new apartment. As expected from Mara's description, it was bigger and nicer than the one she had almost lived in before her tour assignment to Australia and New Zealand. It was definitely a step up. Mara again had all the furniture in place. The bed had been made. Pots, pans and dishes were washed and arranged in the kitchen cabinets. There were new towels in the bathroom. It was understood that Tina would later move things to her liking.

The telephone with an unlisted number had been installed and electricity was connected. The apartment was closer to her friend's condo. Mara had been very busy in her absence and was delighted to see the satisfied expression on Tina's face. She was obviously impressed. Tina's reaction, typically feminine, was to get emotional. Through tears, she said "thank you" over and over again.

Realizing Tina was exhausted, Mara told her to stretch out on the bed for a while. "I'll pick you up around seven and we'll have dinner. Alex is away. We can talk all night after you've rested."

"Could you stay over, Mara? I confess to being a little jumpy."

"I'd like that. Now lie down and close your eyes. I'll be back shortly."

A quick second look around the apartment and Tina did go to bed. She was just about to fall asleep when the phone rang. Tina was surprised to hear Jim's voice. Didn't Mara tell her the number was unlisted? How was it that Jim already knew where to reach her? More puzzling even was that he knew she had returned from her tour assignments. Perhaps Mara told him, she rationalized.

"I'm happy you're home, Tina. Can't wait to see you. How did it go?"

"It was a great experience, Jim. Everything went well, but it would have been nice to have had a little free time for myself. I never made it to the Australian Outback and the only Kangaroos I saw were in captivity. They really are cute. The little 'Joeys,' when tired or frightened, jump into the pouches of their mommies. As they grow older legs, ears or tails protrude because there is no longer enough room inside. It doesn't seem to bother Joey. His mommy is always there to protect him. I did get to pet a Koahla and hold a Wombat—very cautiously, of course."

Tina noticed that Jim wasn't particularly interested in her travels, but she rambled on. "New Zealand is beautiful. Mountains surround you, and everywhere, there are flowers. Did I mention the sheep? At last count there were millions."

Tina was wound up and Jim thought it best to change the subject. "Happy to have you back in the States, baby. Now tell me when do we get together?"

Ignoring Jim's question, Tina said, "Tell me about your meeting with John Jacobs. Was he of any help?"

"Not much. As a matter of fact, he was no help at all. It appears he was too young to be in on anything of importance. The interview was a waste of time in my opinion. Now back to you, doll—any phone calls I should know about?"

There was that offensive word again. Tina hated being referred to as a "doll." It irritated her so much that she didn't want to continue their conversation. More upsetting to her was the feeling that Jim was not being truthful. He appeared unwilling to talk about his meeting with Mr. Jacobs. Angry and in retaliation, Tina decided to withhold the fact that she had seen Larry—at least for the present.

"I really am tired Jim. Came home on the Red Eye from Los Angeles landing at six this morning. Your call caught me just as I was about to close my eyes."

"Okay baby, I understand. I'll call tomorrow and we'll talk about my coming to Chicago. Can't wait. Seems like an awfully long time since we shared that kiss."

Tina, annoyed, didn't respond as she hung up. She wasn't a baby and she wasn't a doll. Being addressed as such drove her to a point where she preferred not to talk or see Jim at all. Maybe I'll be more tolerant after a little nap, she muttered lying down, fully dressed, on the bed.

It was six hours later when Mara woke her from a deep sleep. After a quick shower and change of clothes, a ravenous Tina was ready for the dinner that Mara had thoughtfully prepared. Throughout the meal and until they turned out the lights of Tina's apartment, the two friends chatted. Talked out and sleepy, they agreed that Jim McDonald was no longer on their list of favorite persons. That thought remained with them at breakfast the next morning.

"Guess you should have stayed with your original impression of him, Tina," commented Mara. Aside from Jim's annoying habit of referring to her friend as "doll" and "baby," both girls were beginning to suspect that his interest in Tina had to do with getting into her bed. The murder of her parents didn't seem to be of much importance to him.

"We must come up with a strategy regarding the handling of Officer Jim," Tina said. "He wants to see me, but I think you and I know that it's not because of what happened to my parents."

"Right! He obviously wants to seduce you and is using your tragedy as a means to gaining entrance into your apartment."

"All I want from him, Mara, is information. Since he won't give it to me, I'm determined to meet personally with retired officer Kevin McCarthy. I've asked for his phone number and address, but Jim is evasive. I get the impression that he wants to keep us apart. Any suggestions? How do I get Jim to give me what I want without having him suspect that I have misgivings about him?"

"It would be best to get Jim to volunteer the information, Tina. Pretend that you're asking questions because you're curious—not that you're planning to take action."

"Jim's pretty smart, Mara. He is a police officer and will see right through stupid questions."

"Make him comfortable and relaxed. Give him a couple of strong drinks."

"Thanks pal. If I did that, I'd really have to run for cover."

"You know he'll get to your place expecting to bowl you over with his charm. You'll have to be on your guard from the moment he walks through the door. You must stop him in his tracks."

"And just how do you suggest I manage that?"

"Push him away and tell him you first want to talk about McCarthy and the visit with John Jacobs. While he's talking, you could include some seemingly innocent questions. Ask if Officer McCarthy still lives in Chicago? He might tell you he lives in the suburbs at which point you could ask him to be more specific. If he clams up, you'll have to try another approach. As you said before 'it won't be easy.' Good thing I have faith in you."

"It's important that I see Officer McCarthy, and to do that, I need his address."

"Jim might surprise you—especially if he knows you're determined. If he wants the visit to end up pleasurably, he may come to the conclusion that your way is better than no way."

"By inviting him into my apartment, I'm asking for trouble. That I know."

"Invited or not, he'll come. Remember, he's dropped in on you before."

"Right now he doesn't have my address. By the way, how did he get my new phone number? Did you give it to him?"

"Absolutely not. I haven't talked to him since finding your apartment and moving you in."

"It certainly is strange that he caught up with me so quickly."

"Thanks to computers, there's lots of private information becoming public these days. The police probably know more about us than we know ourselves. Whoever said 'Big Brother is watching' wasn't kidding."

Tina and Mara's strategy session continued, with only minimal success, all morning and until the phone rang. A cheerful Jim was again on the line.

"Did you sleep well, doll? I trust you're all done with that nasty old jet lag."

"Hardly. It's like I've been in outer space. I'm afraid it will take a little doing to get back to normal."

"You'd better put yourself on fast forward, Baby. I've got big plans for us. Can't wait to be with you and catch up on lots of things."

"Are you going to tell me you've solved my case and that the bad guys are behind bars?"

"Wish that were true, sweet pea. With all the craziness going on here at headquarters, I haven't had much time to pursue it."

"Crazy? Like what, for instance."

"You probably heard about the recent police corruption scandals in The Big City. When those kinds of stories become news, it opens Pandora's box. Before you know it, every city and every precinct is suspect and shakeups result. While you were away, St. Louis inherited a new Police Commissioner and he's looking behind every door so that we don't become the next headline. It's a real pain. But, enough of that. I have next weekend off. Think you'll be rested enough to have a visitor from St. Louis?"

"Really, Jim, I'm not fooling around. My nightmares need to be put to rest. You're not helping."

"I'm more than willing to help you rest, babydoll. Just say the word and I'll be there."

"Don't call me 'baby' and I'm not a doll. I'm serious, Jim. You can come, but I want you to tell me all that you know about these people you've been talking with. I'd like to see your file and deceased Detective White's notes. For your information, I can't picture myself getting involved with anyone or anything while these bad memories haunt me."

"Just let me hold you in my arms, Tina baby. Your problems will all go away. I promise."

"That's exactly what I mean. Holding me might be a temporary fix, but I need more than that."

"I can do that too. Let me prove it to you."

"You're impossible, Jim. I can't seem to get through to you that two years have passed and the pain continues. It does not get better. Someone out there killed my parents. That same someone left me homeless and alone. If it hadn't been, and still is, for Mara, I don't know where I'd be."

"Let me come to Chicago this weekend. If you insist, I'll bring my notes. We can go over them and then go on from there."

"Promise?"

"What choice do I have? You drive a hard bargain."

"What time will you be here, Jim?"

"There's a flight that gets in at two o'clock. Is that okay with you?"

"All right, but remember you've made a promise and I expect you to keep it. This will be a business, not a social, meeting."

"You know what they say about all work and no play…I'll take a cab to your place."

"Wait! You need my address. Mara found a new apartment for me while I was away."

"You did say you were going to move."

"Come to think of it, how did you get this unlisted number?"

"Have you forgotten, my sweet? I'm a policeman, and know everything. By the way, I've just been promoted to Detective."

"Congratulations. Then you probably have my address as well."

"Now that you mention it, yes I do."

"How about everyone else in St. Louis? Do they all know where I live? I moved, you must remember, because I was being harassed."

"Someone of authority would have to put through a request for personal information. It's my case. Therefore I have all your files in my desk. It's helpful since I also have a very special interest in you."

The phone conversation continued and Tina felt herself becoming increasingly defensive. Realizing that it would not be in her best interest to continue to show annoyance, she changed her tone.

"I guess I'm still jumpy from the long return trip, but should be adjusted by the time you get here on Saturday. Let's continue our discussion then."

Mara had been in the room while Tina and Jim talked. She could hear only one side of the conversation, but it was clear that Tina was about to lose her cool. That was not the way to go if a person expected cooperation from an opponent. Fortunately Tina also came to that conclusion and ended her conversation with Jim before erupting.

Although Tina would have liked their meeting to be on neutral ground, there was little chance of that happening. Jim expected to be at Tina's apartment and planned to give her his special "welcome home" treatment. The friends knew that holding Jim at bay would present a challenge.

"You'll have to be on your toes, Tina. Your friend Jim moves fast. Do you think you're up to the test?"

"Half the battle is knowing that I'll have to be on guard. Maybe I can borrow your German Shepherd."

"That's not a bad idea, Tina. Suppose I leave Toro with you the morning of the day Jim is expected. We'll pretend that you are dog sitting for a few days. I'll arrange to be down the block in my car when Jim gets to your apartment and will give him an hour. That ought to be enough time to get through the business part of his visit.

"Good! Then you can come by to pick up Toro and hang around making a nuisance of yourself until Jim gives up on any other ideas he might have. What if he asks me out to dinner?"

"You're on your own then, Tina. Eat and run! Get sick. Have a headache or something! Under no circumstances let him back in your apartment."

"I really don't want to encourage any more visits from Jim. Hoping to get my hands on the files is the only reason I'm letting him come here. The papers could help me decide where and how to proceed—or if I should give up in my search for answers. When I'm satisfied that I know what Jim knows, I'll get rid of him."

"And how do you expect to do that, my friend?"

"I'll tell him that I've fallen in love with someone."

"May I ask who that someone might be?"

"That reminds me, I must call Stan. He doesn't know I'm home or how to reach me."

"I'm hoping that means what I think it does."

"It means that I can't wait to see him, Mara. However I can't make plans with Stan until after my Saturday meeting with Jim."

Mara knew not to be too pushy. From where she stood, it was beginning to look very likely that she and Tina would end up sisters-in-law as well as best friends. Happy with that thought, Mara left to do some food shopping.

Tina immediately picked up the phone to call Stan. He was at his desk and it was as though he was in the room with her. His voice was such a comfort—almost an embrace.

"You're back, my love! Do you have an active imagination? Let's pretend I'm giving you a big kiss. Mmmm that was good, but just a preview of what's to come. I've missed you, Tina. Please don't ever go away again. The worst is that I won't be able to get to Chicago for a while. There's a super hot job I have to finish this weekend and then, next week, it's meetings with the big brass. Best I

Gerda Osiecki

can hope for is the weekend after next. We're talking about Christmas Eve. Would that be okay?"

"Terrific! Can't think of anything better than spending Christmas with you," replied Tina knowing that she'd be busy until then and that the time would go quickly. First would be her meeting with Jim. After that, she together with Mara, were planning to do some serious sleuthing.

"I've missed you too Stan. It was a great trip, but I'm glad to be home. Got in yesterday. My head and stomach are still in a time warp, but I promise everything will be back to normal by the time you get here."

"I have a zillion questions, Sweetness, but they will keep until I see you. These six weeks, knowing you were so far away, were the longest I've ever endured. Can't tell you how happy I am that you're home. I only wish your home was here with me. There's entirely too much distance between us and I've decided we have to do something about it. How would you feel about my asking for a permanent transfer to the Chicago office?"

"Could you Stan? Would you really do that to be with me? That would be wonderful."

"Do you mean it, Tina? Are you telling me that you wouldn't mind my being underfoot?"

"The idea is looking better all the time. Let's give it some serious thought. As you know, there are still a lot of skeletons in my closet. You might not like having to share me with ghosts and problems."

"I want to share everything with you, Tina. Oh there goes my red phone. It's a conference call. There's a deadline and I've got to hang up, but I'll call back tonight. Can't wait to see you a week from Friday. Look for me around seven. We'll have dinner out."

"You make me feel very special, Stanley. I'm beginning to think that I'm falling in love with you."

"Those are the most beautiful words I've ever heard, Tina. All I need do now is persuade you to drop that word 'think'. Be ready for an all out crusade when I get to Chicago. It's no secret, Sweetheart, that I love you. I've always loved you. Darn! The phone is beeping. I really must go. Please leave your number with my secretary. I'll call you tonight."

Considering all Tina and Mara had planned in the interim, Christmas Eve and Stan's visit would come quickly.

It was Saturday afternoon. Jim had arrived. Tina's challenge was about to begin. Taking a deep breath, she opened the door to his knock. Mara's German Shepherd, Toro, stood protectively at her side. In her hand Tina held a large bottle of seltzer water.

"Tina, baby," said Jim as he stepped briskly into the apartment and then froze in his tracks at the sight of the huge animal. The bottle, also, was an obstacle. How could he lift Tina off the ground and bombard her with kisses? These encumbrances had not been expected or planned for.

"Come in, Jim. How've you been? It's good to see you. How about a drink? I was just checking my inventory."

"Where did that monster come from? You've got a big kiss coming, Tina, but between the bottle and the mutt, I'm having a little problem with the logistics. Let's put that bottle down on the counter and we'll start over. I've been waiting a long time for this moment."

Tina couldn't think of any way to intercept his kiss, but managed to extricate herself when Toro, being playful and wanting to be included in the embrace, jumped up reaching Jim's shoulders.

"When did you get a dog, Tina?" asked Jim as Tina tried to hide her amusement.

"He's real friendly and only wants to play, Jim."

"So do I, but not with him."

"His name is Toro and he belongs to Mara. I'm dog sitting. Isn't he a beauty?"

"The only beauty I see in this room is you, Tina. Come here! Let's try that kiss one more time. Like me, you must be ready for more."

"Hold on, Jim. We have to talk."

"First things first," said Jim as he again stepped forward to pull Tina close.

"No, Jim," Tina said backing away. "First we talk. That was our deal. Bring me up to date on what's been happening. For instance, did you and Officer McCarthy learn anything from your meeting with John Jacobs? I have lots of questions, and after you've filled me in, I thought you might be interested in hearing about my travels in New Zealand and Australia."

"We can get to all that later, Tina. First I really need a little encouragement from those luscious lips," said Jim as he made a move to corner her in front of the refrigerator.

"Hold on, Jim. Toro would be only too happy to rescue me, but I don't think we want him to get involved. Don't look at me like that. I made it very clear that we had to talk and you promised we would. I'll make you a drink or would you rather have coffee?"

"You don't make things easy, but okay, baby—you win. As per your request, we talk! I'll have that drink though. Make it scotch and soda, please."

While Tina fixed drinks for them both - her's was an extra mild screw driver—Jim made himself comfortable on the couch and beckoned for her to sit beside him. Instead, drink in hand, Tina positioned herself in a chair. Tina, obviously, wanted to keep distance between them and Jim, by this time, knew better than to force the issue.

"So tell me about Australia and New Zealand. Anything exciting happen?" asked Jim although he really didn't care.

Knowing Jim wasn't interested in anything other than pursuing his own agenda, Tina gave an abbreviated version of her experiences. "The first trip was mostly routine," Tina began. There was no eye contact while she spoke about the beautiful scenery, the animals and her tourists.

Jim knew Tina was holding him at arm's length. "What is it Tina? Speaking with you on the phone the other day and being with you now—you seem different. Is something wrong? Has someone been tormenting you again?"

"I guess now is as good a time as any to tell you, Jim. While on the second tour, I had quite a shock. Would you believe I saw Larry in New Zealand? I saw him with my own eyes."

"Larry was in New Zealand? That can't be. Are you sure it was Larry or someone who looked like him."

"Yes, I'm sure. He was in a cable car coming down from a restaurant in Queensland."

"Did you talk to him?"

"No. I was in a car going up to the restaurant. He was headed in the opposite direction."

"Could it have been your imagination? What would Larry be doing in New Zealand?"

"It was him. Our eyes met. He recognized me. I tried to catch up with him, but he disappeared. My driver and I searched everywhere. He obviously didn't want to be found and certainly succeeded. If only I could have talked to him. All I want is to have him explain his involvement in what happened to my parents. Maybe I'm crazy, but it's hard to believe that he'd murder anyone even though he certainly appears to be responsible for the theft of all my family's assets. Can you understand that there will be no closure for me until I know how involved he was and with whom."

"No wonder you're not yourself, doll. What a coincidence - you running into Larry in New Zealand. They told me he was in Brazil." No sooner were the words out of Jim's mouth when he realized he'd made a big mistake.

"Brazil, South America?" Tina asked, stunned. "I was led to believe no one knew where Larry was. That's what you and Detective White told me. How long have you known this, and why was it kept a secret from me? Whose side are you on, Jim?"

"Now calm down, Tina. It was a rumor. You know how it goes. Someone says something and the next minute everyone is repeating it as fact," said Jim, hoping to retrieve his slip of the tongue.

Tina was not buying Jim's explanation. She let it pass however, as it gave her the opportunity to turn the tables and put him on the defensive.

"Okay, Jim, now it's your turn. Tell me exactly what happened when you and Officer McCarthy visited John Jacobs. On the phone you said he was of no help being too young at the time to be in the confidence of those in control of the gangs. I'd like to talk to Jacobs myself—privately. Maybe you guys intimidated him. I might be able to get him to remember things he forgot or was reluctant to tell you."

"I've got the greatest respect for your feminine charms, Tina, but I'm convinced they won't produce anything in this case. It worries me, also, that you might be making waves that could be unhealthy. I wish you'd let it go."

"Jim, I'm home for the winter and I intend to put my time to good use. I need to talk to Officer McCarthy and want you to give me his phone number."

"Aren't you getting a little carried away, Tina? Are you planning to visit all the gangs operating in the Chicago area? They might not like you poking around. Take my advice and leave it alone."

"I will never be able to leave it alone—not until I know why my parents were murdered and by whom. Are you going to tell me how I can reach Kevin McCarthy or do I have to go over your head?"

"That could be a dangerous move on your part."

"Are you threatening me, Jim?"

"Tina, my love, you're over-reacting. I'm not threatening you. Remember, we discussed the possibility that there might be leaks within the police department. I'm trying to protect you."

"Where does Officer McCarthy live, Jim? I want to talk to him."

"You're behaving like a child, Tina, but I can see you won't give up until you get your way. He lives in Bakerstown, outside of Chicago - 105 Radcliff Drive. I'll go with you."

"No. I want to go by myself."

"I'm not the enemy, Tina. Have I given you reason to be angry with me?"

"Not angry, but I am losing my patience. You and your precinct have come up with nothing in over two years. I've simply decided to take matters into my own hands."

Trying to pacify Tina, Jim made a move to embrace her. Backing up and turning a cold shoulder, Tina abruptly asked him to leave.

"Did we have a fight?" asked Jim perplexed.

Moving toward the door, Tina said, "I need some time alone, Jim. Please go. I'll call you after I've seen Officer McCarthy."

Tina's attitude left him no choice. She opened the door and Jim had to leave. The reunion had not turned out as he had anticipated. Walking to the car, Jim asked himself, "What happened to that sweet, docile little girl who was going to be a pushover? This new Tina was feisty—all strength and determination?

Tina surprised herself at the outcome of the meeting. When Mara arrived a short time later to pick up her dog, prepared to rescue Tina from the clutches of Jim, she was happy to learn that her friend had already sent him packing. Without any help, she had maneuvered Jim into revealing Officer McCarthy's address as well. They could now, finally, contact him personally.

"I'm proud of you, Tina. Staging that fight was sheer genius. When did you come up with that idea?"

"It just happened. One word lead to another and the next thing I knew a confused and bewildered Jim was out the door. Having Toro here shook him up right from the start. It worked so well I'd get a dog myself if it wasn't for my job."

"You could leave the dog with me. Toro would love having a brother or sister to run around with. So, tell me, what's the plan? What is our next move?"

"Tomorrow we see Officer McCarthy. I'd like our visit to be a surprise and hope our frustrated friend doesn't get to him first. It would be real helpful if the shock of Jim's hasty departure lasted a few days."

"At least we can expect him to be licking his wounds for a while."

"Can you be ready to leave by ten tomorrow morning, Mara?"

"No problem, Sherlock. I had planned to scrub floors and polish silver, but a day with you is much more invigorating."

The next day found the two friends in the suburbs, on retired Officer Kevin McCarthy's doorstep. It was a brisk sunny day in mid-December and the drive had been pleasant. Tina did not want to warn him of their coming and knew they were taking a risk that he might not be home. The surprise visit was planned in hopes of witnessing his reaction to a face to face encounter. A brief moment and a distinguished-looking gentleman of about sixty, answered their ring.

"Would you be Kevin McCarthy?" Tina asked.

Gerda Osiecki

"Yes, and you are?"

"Tina Cappo and this is my friend, Mara Konigswahl."

"You're the young lady whose parents were murdered in their hotel in St. Louis two years ago. Officer McDonald told me about you. Together we've been trying to track down some clues. Come in! Now," he said, after inviting them to sit down, "what can I do for you?"

Tina wanted to thank Kevin McCarthy for the assistance he had given Officer McDonald in locating and visiting John Jacobs and Enrico Gomez, two ex-members of the local gangs. In addition, not satisfied with McDonald's brief accounting that nothing had been gained from their visits with the two men, Tina hoped McCarthy would have something to add. She also wanted to pressure McCarthy for the addresses of the two men. It was important to her that she speak to them directly.

"I need to see their faces when I ask questions," Tina explained. "Officer McDonald is discouraged and about to give up, but it's my parents who were murdered and I can't let go without having checked out every lead."

"What makes you think, Miss Cappo, that you'll succeed where the police have failed?"

"You didn't fail, but maybe you missed something or perhaps McDonald is trying to protect me by not telling me everything. My instincts keep bringing me back to the 'Uptown Boys.' Gomez and Jacobs were members of some local street gangs at the time. I need to talk to them and am asking you to help me. McDonald does not approve and won't tell me where Jacobs and Gomez can be reached."

"You could be asking for more trouble than you need, Miss Cappo."

McDonald had made McCarthy aware of Tina's strange phone calls. She, obviously, was being harassed. Someone was trying to scare her off.

"You know I've changed addresses and phone numbers several times, but they always find me—every move I make. I'm scared, but cannot spend my life looking around every corner. I really need your help, Officer McCarthy."

"Okay, you've convinced me, but let me go with you when you see the guys."

"You've already given up so much of your time, Officer. Truthfully, I would prefer meeting with these men alone. They might not object to Mara accompanying me, but seeing you again, could be intimidating."

"Perhaps two pretty ladies would have more success than two grumpy officers. I'll give you that, but you must get back to me if your meetings result in anything new."

Promising she would, Tina's final request was that McCarthy not tell Officer McDonald of her intentions. When asked for a reason, Tina explained that she suspected Officer McDonald was holding out on her. "In addition," she said "someone is leaking information about me. Being responsible for my case, Jim has access to files not available to others. It could be the cause of the leaks.

"Jim insists that his records are kept under lock and key but, either innocently or by design, information about me is getting out. My life has become an open book and I'm suspicious of everyone. It could be a co-worker calling and harassing me. It's possible someone at police headquarters has a grudge against me. Whoever or whatever it is, I want it to stop."

Gerda Osiecki

"I don't blame you for being upset, Miss Cappo, and will do what I can to help. Now how about a cup of coffee while we go over my notes. They should match what Jim has already told you."

"Could we start with your recollections of the group you refer to as 'The Uptown Boys?'"

Officer McCarthy explained that he and his partner referred to the new kids as the "Uptown Boys," for lack of an official name. They appeared to be of a different breed than the local gangs.   While the locals would fight among themselves, and get into trouble, it was mostly kid stuff. They'd hang around the malls and sometimes try shoplifting. Maybe they'd do drugs. When the 'Upton Boys' came on the scene, things were different. Suddenly there were break-ins.   Houses and condos were looted and trashed. People were beaten and robbed. The local kids were questioned, but had alibis. Some of us officers began to put the blame on the new kids from uptown and reported our suspicions to headquarters, but nothing ever came of it.

"It's those rich kids," the local gangs insisted. "One time I heard a boy say, 'those rich kids have friends in the police department and that's why nobody brings them in.' I mentioned this to my captain. It wasn't long after that when I was offered an opportunity to retire."

"You mean 'persuaded?' How could they convince you to retire if you didn't want to?" asked Tina.

"They have ways," replied Officer McCarthy "First they took away my squad car and partner. Then they had me walking a beat in a different neighborhood. When I questioned the moves, they gave me a desk job and said I was getting too old for the streets. Having enough time in, I signed my retirement papers. Need I tell you, in back of my mind, there was always the feeling that I should not have heard or repeated the accusations of the local kids. That's why I was happy to help Jim when asked."

218

"What about your visits with John Jacobs and that Gomez person, who I understand is in jail?"

Explaining that they didn't get much out of Enrico Gomez, McCarthy confirmed what Tina already knew. He added, however, that Gomez remembered getting into a fight with one of the kids from uptown who had been referred to as "Tony." When speaking with John Jacobs, currently a fire fighter, McCarthy learned that he also had heard the name "Tony" and that he appeared to be the ring leader of the intruders from uptown.

McCarthy informed Tina that Jacobs had seen Tony once. Being the youngest in his gang, he was often excluded from things that were going on. He had big ears and learned to snoop. One day, while hiding behind a fence, he saw Tony with another member of his group. The boy called Tony by name. They were discussing a hit being planned by the "Uptowners."

John told us that he had been picked up by the police that night, but was later released. "I liked the kid and knew his mother really tried to look after him. One day she saw me on the street and told me they planned to move away. The move, apparently turned John's life around. There's nothing more I can add, but that we visited him and he's doing great."

"You've been a big help Officer McCarthy and I appreciate it. Now please tell me where and how I can reach these two men."

"You can have my notes, but be careful. Get back to me if you learn anything additional."

"It's been a long time since I've been so optimistic. Thanks for your time and patience. It's been a pleasure talking with you."

Tina and Mara went to see Enrico, but learned little. He was angry with the world and would probably always be in trouble with the law. His fight with someone by the name of Tony about ten years ago was still fresh in his mind and caused him to use some colorful language. Otherwise, he added nothing to what they already knew.

Then Tina and Mara went to see John Jacobs. Jim had told Tina little had been gained from interviewing him, but Officer McCarthy had mentioned that Mr. Jacobs remembered hearing the name "Tony" and that John had actually seen Tony on one occasion. Although much time had gone by, it was possible John Jacobs could give them a description.

"Thank you for seeing us, Mr. Jacobs. I'm Tina Cappo and this is my friend Mara. I realize you've already had a visit from officers McDonald and McCarthy, but wanted to meet and speak to you. It was a long time ago, but is there perhaps, something additional you remember— anything about that Tony person you saw that would set him apart? Could you describe him?"

"There is a picture in my mind. I remember he was very angry at the kid with him. He was shouting, calling him names and cursing loudly. His voice was high pitched— sounded like a teenager whose voice was changing. He had long, dark hair that was pulled into a pony tail. His eyes were piercing. They were almost black. He wore an ear ring and had a peculiar way of walking."

"What do you mean, peculiar?"

"Well he walked, swaying his hips, like a girl. And his hands—he talked with his hands. There was something feminine about his mannerisms. Actually, if I hadn't known better and heard the kid call him 'Tony,' I'd have thought he was a she—a girl with very vulgar vocabulary."

"Anything else you can think of?"

"No that's it! I was just a kid and bless Officer McCarthy every day since for having saved me from myself. Thanks to him I'm looking at a nice promotion at the end of the month."

"Mara and I are happy for you and want to thank you for taking the time to talk with us. Please call Officer McCarthy if you think of anything after we've gone. I move around a great deal. Otherwise I'd ask you to call me."

The friends had to admit the last two days were very interesting. While there was nothing definite, they had learned more on their own than they had from Jim.

"I'm convinced Jim's holding out on me, Mara."

"He's certainly not telling you everything he knows."

"This Tony that both Jacobs and Gomez spoke about—why didn't Jim mention his name when I asked if he'd learned anything while with McCarthy? There are lots of Tonys in this world, but I remember it was someone by the name of Tony Luppo that had talked to my father about buying another hotel."

"It could be coincidence, Tina, but Jim should have mentioned it when you asked if he'd learned anything from his interview with the boys."

"How would you feel about going to St. Louis with me over the weekend, Mara? Detective Jim must have a private life. It would be interesting to know more about him. We might be surprised at what we learn if we can observe him in his own environment."

"We'd have to go incognito. Any suggestions as to how we can convincingly do that?"

"First, we'd better try not to be seen and certainly never together. That would be a dead giveaway. We'll rent a car and take turns following him. Jim mentioned that he would be on duty this weekend."

The girls put their heads together and figured out ways to look different. They would change their hair styles by wearing wigs. Dark glasses were a must. Getting into the spirit, Tina decided that she would go blond whereas Mara would masquerade as a brunette. "Wonder where Dolly Parton gets her hair pieces," said Mara. "Maybe I could duplicate her body while I'm at it."

"That's a joke" laughed Tina. "Imagine you, flat chested Mara, emerging with the curves of an hour glass. You could put three padded bras on top of eachother. It's a little late for plastic surgery."

"The bras might work for me, but what about you, Tina? How do you plan to disguise that perfect figure? One thing I know for sure is that there's nothing I can do about my height. No matter what I do, I'll always be tall. As for you, my friend, even with stiletto heels, you'll still be short."

"Bottom line, we'll do our best not to be seen. That's the safest approach."

The next day found the two conspirators getting their disguises in order. While their preference was not to be seen at all, there was always the possibility that Murphy's Law would come into play. They worked, therefore, very hard at changing their appearances and, when the day was over, had done a reasonably convincing job. Even Mara's husband would have had doubts were he to come home unexpectedly. After much laughter and some good natured teasing, they retired. In the morning would begin their weekend adventure in St. Louis.

Mara sat in the rented car outside police headquarters a good three hours before there was any sign of Jim. The shift ended at four p.m. and a little later began the exodus of uniformed men and women. Most seemed to be in a jovial frame of mind. She spotted Jim leaving with two other officers—one of whom was an extremely attractive woman. They, together with what could have been half the off-duty force, went straight to the local watering hole. From the looks of things, Mara felt secure that Jim would be going nowhere for a while. She called Tina at the hotel to come and take over.

Tina's cab only took a few minutes to get there. Relieving Mara and slumped down in the seat of the car, she waited for Jim's next move. About an hour later, he and the lady officer left the pub apparently to have dinner. Tina carefully followed them to Luigis, an Italian restaurant a few blocks away. The couple were seated near the window allowing her to observe them without herself being seen. Watching as they enjoyed the wine, food and each other, Tina came to the conclusion that Jim and his companion were more than just friendly co-workers relaxing.

Continuing to follow them after they left Luigis, Tina found herself at an apartment building not too far from the hotel Tina's parents had owned. She was reminded of happier days, but pulled herself together. Tina was on a mission and this was not the time for reminiscing.

Watching Jim and friend retreat, hand in hand, into the building, confirmed her earlier suspicion that this was not a platonic relationship. Whose apartment were they going into? Was it his or hers? When it was safe, Tina checked the names on the bank of mail boxes in the lobby. It turned out to be Jim McDonald's apartment.

"I'd say the evening was a success," said Tina to Mara when returning to their hotel room that night. "We now know where Jim lives and that he's romancing one of his co-workers - a female police officer."

"Do you think it's serious with them?"

"From my viewpoint, yes I do. Sure would love to find out who she is."

"Why? You should be glad he's got other interests, or do I detect a little jealousy?"

"I don't care what he does with his personal life as long as he stays out of mine, Mara. However, if she is cozying up to Jim, there could be more than romance as a motive. She might know about me or about my parents' murders and that he is working on the case. A clever woman could find out where I live, my phone number or anything else she might want to know. Maybe that's the answer to the mysterious phone calls and the leaks."

"Are you suggesting that we follow her tomorrow? It might not be a bad idea and should be easier than following Jim. At least she doesn't know us. We won't have to be as careful."

"Let's sleep on it. One thing I know for sure— Detective Jim is a lover. If he thinks he's going to seduce me, forget it pal."

"Well it's morning. We slept on it. So what have we on the agenda today? Do we hang out at the precinct again? Do you think she spent the night?"

"Just for kicks, I'm going to call and find out if Detective McDonald made it to work this morning," said Tina.

"And if he didn't?"

"We'll camp out in front of his apartment again. They'll have to get up some time. At the very least, she'll need a change of underwear. That's when I'll start tailing her. Are you ready, Dr. Watson?"

"I'm ready when you are."

The telephone call revealed that Jim was taking a sick day. Mara and Tina parked the car across from his apartment and waited. At about noon there was the first sign of life. The pretty police officer emerged from the building looking a little worse for wear. Leaving Mara the car in the event Jim made an appearance, Tina nonchalantly followed the lady.

After a walk of about five blocks, she watched her subject enter one of the numerous brownstone houses in the area. Continuing her watch and not too long afterward, she saw the lady "cop" leave the premises dressed in what appeared to be a fresh uniform—destination, the precinct. Apparently she was going to be late, not sick like Jim.

Knowing she'd be occupied for a while, Tina went back to the brownstone to check out the names of the residents. There were three—Alexander, Olsen and Lombardo. Taking a wild guess, Tina called headquarters asking for Officer Lombardo. She was right and now had a name to connect with the face.

Meanwhile, Mara held to her "stake out" at Jim's place. He eventually emerged dressed casually in sweats. Following him at a discrete distance to the liquor store down the street, she observed him stocking up on wine. Then he went to the local supermarket where he bought, at the deli counter, salads and barbecued chicken.

Looks like he's getting ready to entertain someone. I wonder who, thought Mara as she, when he left, asked the clerk to make sandwiches for a lunch she would probably be sharing with Tina in the car. My guess is his lady friend will be back before long.

How right she was. Following Jim in the car as he walked back to the apartment building, she again settled down to watch. Soon after Mara could see the female police officer approaching. Casually strolling about a block behind her was Tina who had accomplished her mission. The friends now knew where Jim lived and learned that he had a girlfriend—a lady "cop" whose name was Lombardo. Mara and Tina had no idea where this information would take them. Before they could tie Officer Lombardo into leaking information about Tina's whereabouts, they'd have to know a great deal more about her. That would have to keep for another day. As of now, all they could do was take their new-found knowledge back to Chicago where it could be digested at leisure.

.

Mara's husband had unexpectedly returned from South America and was surprised, on entering the condo, to find a dog sitter in charge. When told that Mara and Tina had gone to St. Louis, he was concerned. It was with great relief that he heard a key turning in the lock. Who was that stranger in the doorway? After his initial shock at seeing Mara still in disguise mode, he pulled her close and kissed her soundly. In the process, her dark wig fell to the floor. The vision of his heavily padded wife, made up to look like a hooker and wearing weird clothes, was too much. Even though she was back to her own hair color, the rest of her didn't fit the picture. Alex stepped back and howled with laughter. Toro, confused, found it puzzling that his mistress looked strange while his master appeared to be having a fit. He had to do something. Forcing himself between them, he decided to fix everything by giving them his own version of a "welcome home" kiss.

"Thanks, Pal," said Alex as he led Mara to the kitchen where he washed Toro's slobber off both their faces. He then poured them each a glass of wine. Sitting on his lap, Mara gave Alex an abbreviated account of her weekend adventure with Tina. She cut it short because both were eager to get into bed where they made up for all the lonely nights with some much needed loving.

Hours later, holding close his contentedly sleeping wife, Alex was awake thinking about Tina and Mara's trip to St. Louis. While wanting to help Tina, he was not comfortable with the risks the two of them were taking. Judging from what had happened to Tina's parents, his precious wife and Tina could end up hurt. From Mara's account, he was convinced that there was at least one person in the St. Louis police department who was not on the up and up.

Could there be connections to the mobs in Chicago, he asked himself? If so, Mara and her friend Tina were amateurs bucking an organization not known to fool around. As I see it, he continued thinking, Tina's obsession with tracking down the murderer of her parents can only lead to more trouble and I'm worried. If only I could find a way to divert her attention elsewhere. I'd enlist Mara's help except that those two are thick as thieves and seem to enjoy playing detective. It wouldn't be an easy sell. Maybe, if we put our heads together, Stan and I can come up with some ideas when we're together at Christmas.

14

It was the week before Christmas. Both Tina and Mara were racing against the clock. In addition to last minute shopping for gifts and holiday meals, there was the need to clean and decorate apartments. Having vowed, temporarily at least, to put problems aside, Tina was determined that all would be perfect upon Stan's arrival on Christmas eve.

Except for Stanley, shopping had been easy. Festively displayed merchandise encouraged her to purchase even some surprises for herself. Wandering through the mall, she hummed along with Christmas music coming from speakers everywhere. The pet store entrance, she noted, had been converted to look like a giant Christmas tree. Welcoming her inside was someone wearing a poodle mask, but dressed as Santa. Tina laughed aloud and quickly found some extra treats for Toro. She felt good and realized that it had been over two years since she'd allowed herself to look forward to the holiday season.

The problem of finding a gift for Stan was solved when she saw a relaxed mannequin posed in front of a glowing fireplace. Matching pajamas, a robe and slippers, she decided, would be perfect for Stan when traveling to

Chicago. Knowing he'd be warm and comfortable might prompt him to visit more often, Tina hoped. At the very least, having sleep-over clothes available, would save Stan time and space when packing his suitcase.

On Monday Tina had a call from Alan who was again driving tourists around Great Britain. While continuing to ask about any plans she might have to accompany him on another trip, both sensed that the fire had gone out. Absence, in their case, had not made the hearts grow fonder.

Alan asked about the murder investigation. Tina told him about her almost encounter with Larry in New Zealand. She also shared her suspicions regarding the recently promoted Detective McDonald and the St. Louis Police Department. Alan warned her to be careful. "I think about you all the time and it worries me that I can't protect you from here," he said.

"You were very important to me, Alan, and I'll never forget you."

Alan picked up on the word "were" and understood their romance, necessary at the time, was over. While remaining a happy memory, he knew it was being replaced with a comfortable friendship.

It was Christmas Eve. Stanley was expected momentarily. Tina's first Christmas in her own apartment, and everything was as perfect as she had wanted it to be. Decorations, lights and poinsettias were everywhere. Even the pictures on the walls were covered with foil and ribbons. They appeared to be gifts not yet opened.

Tina was a bundle of nerves as the doorbell rang. Stan had insisted they go out for dinner. "After we eat we'll have the whole night to ourselves," he had said when last they spoke on the phone. Mara's advice, Tina remembered as she opened the door, was to relax and go with the flow.

In front of her stood a big man whose face was hidden behind a monstrous blooming Christmas cactus. In front of the plant, this mystery person held about a dozen unbalanced boxes threatening to topple to the ground. "You must be Stan," Tina said as she retrieved the top three packages in the nick of time. Two had escaped and were already on the ground. "I hope those didn't contain eggs," Tina said, laughing.

"You won't think it's so funny when I get this stuff on the table," Stan answered. Quickly doing so, he pivoted and caught Tina in his arms. Lifting her overhead, she squealed, "Put me down, Stanley. I'm not a ballerina." Stanley obeyed, but then maneuvered her to a nearly couch where he kissed her. Then, still captive in his arms, he whispered, "Now that we've taken care of the preliminaries, what's next pussycat?"

While Tina remained immobile, still savoring the kiss and working on a response, he added, "Whatever you're thinking, it will have to wait. We'll save the 'what's next' for later. First let's find us something to eat. I'm famished."

Dinner was at a nearby German restaurant Mara had recommended. Since is was Christmas Eve, the establishment had few diners. To the background of Christmas music, they looked around and admired the festive holiday decorations. The Victorian tree in the corner was, in itself, a work of art. Mara was to be congratulated for having suggested the perfect setting for two people who had started out a little uptight. The atmosphere was relaxing. Any insecurities they might have felt, were quickly overcome.

Stanley was anxious to hear about Australia and New Zealand and that, of course, brought the conversation around to the cable car incident. "You really saw Larry and he knew you did?"

"It's hard to believe, I know. We, our bus driver and I, spent hours trying to find him, Stan, but he vanished into thin air."

"Does McDonald know?"

"Yes, but when I told him he seemed shocked and said something very strange. He said that he understood Larry was in Brazil. It was a slip of the tongue and Jim tried to cover it up as soon as he said it, but it convinced me that I'd been lied to by all who claimed to have no knowledge of Larry's whereabouts."

"Maybe Larry got bored with South America and decided to take a little vacation. Whatever brought him to New Zealand, I'm sure he didn't plan on running into you, Tina. I'd advise him to think seriously about being more careful. If he was instructed to get lost in Brazil, they, whoever "they' are, won't be happy knowing you found him even temporarily."

It was late. The restaurant had already closed it's doors to all but those still seated. "I think we should let these people go home to their families," said Stan signaling for the waiter.

Tina gladly moved on to a different subject. She didn't want to talk about her weekend in St. Louis with Mara. It would be hard to explain and she had a feeling Stan wouldn't approve of their spying on Jim and his lady friend. Having satisfied Stan's hunger for food, she would rather go back to her apartment where they could explore the "what's next" question that had been left open.

Taking his coat and leading him to the lounge chair beside the beautifully decorated Christmas tree, Tina gently kissed him on both cheeks. Stan quickly took the initiative kissing her fully on the mouth. It was a prelude to more, but Tina was fast and managed to free herself. With authority, she instructed Stan to sit down and close his eyes.

"Stay right there, Stan, and don't open your eyes until I tell you to. I've planned a surprise, but it will take a few minutes."

Doing as he was told, but curious, Stan asked, "What are you going to do to me?"

"You'll find out," Tina promised.

First Tina turned on the TV—a channel she knew would be playing soft Christmas music. On the screen was a burning Yule Log. Hurrying, she went into her bedroom to change into a sheer pink nightgown covering it with a see-through matching peignoir. After releasing her long dark hair from it's many hairpins, she retrieved a pitcher of chilled eggnog from the refrigerator. Setting it beside the two glasses already on the coffee table and standing before him, she said, "Okay! Ready? Now open your eyes or have you fallen asleep?"

After a long pause, appearing to be transfixed, Stan finally said, "You are a vision, my love. Simply looking at you, I'm breathless and speechless. Have you any idea what you and those misty blue eyes do to a person? Pulling her onto his lap and kissing her passionately, Stan added, "It's going to take more than will power to keep me here on the couch when I haven't yet seen your bedroom."

"Before we move on," Tina replied seductively smiling, "I have something Santa brought just for you. On the box it says you're to open it first."

"Sounds like a camera. Cameras always come with instructions to 'open me first.'"

"You'll see."

It was an eternity before Stanley made it to the inside of the box. Teasing her, he first removed the ribbons and bows winding them into a ball. Then, while making wild guesses about the contents of the box, he slit each piece of tape and carefully folded the wrapping paper. Impatient, Tina threatened to explode.

"Will you hurry up, already," she said as Stan finally opened the box and asked, "What have we here?"

Inside the box were the pajamas, robe and slippers Tina had purchased. Teasing, but at the same time hoping for the intimacy the gift suggested, Stan said, "No fair me being all dressed up while you stand there in your nighties. I think you and I need to have a little talk."

Again on his lap, Stanley smothered her with kisses. "You must know that I love and want you, Tina. From the first day we met, I knew you were the only one in the world for me. There is so much love I want to give you, but I need to know that you are serious about me and willing to make the commitment I've been looking for."

"I love you too, Stan, and am sorry it took such a long time for me to figure it out. I'd like to prove my commitment, but it's difficult to seduce you when you're so formally dressed. Please won't you go and make yourself comfortable? I'd be happy to help you."

"Not so fast, Sweetheart. It's time now for you to cover those baby blues. Two can play this game."

Taking a little black velvet box out of his jacket pocket, Stan picked up Tina's left hand and ceremoniously slipped a beautiful diamond ring on her fourth finger. Bringing her hand to his lips, he whispered, "Now, my darling, you may open those eyes."

"Oh my God, Stanley! It's beautiful. Yes and when?"

"When and yes what?"

"When are we going to get married?"

"Hey! What's this about getting married? I don't remember asking you. Do I get to try before I buy?"

Tina undid the ties of the sheer lacy covering over her flimsy see-through gown. Then she loosened his necktie and began working on the buttons of his shirt.

"Hussy," Stanley said as he removed her sexy negligee and carefully sat Tina down on the sheepskin rug that was conveniently located in front of the couch. "Don't move," he said as he rummaged through the boxes of Christmas presents just received, pulled out the new pajamas and retreated to the bedroom presumably preparing to get comfortable. When he returned wearing only the tie of his pajamas, Tina laughed and said, "Now I've seen everything."

"Well, I haven't," Stan answered. "There's still your nightie for me to contend with, but we're making progress."

On his knees, beside the love of his life, Stan stopped clowning and became very serious. Taking Tina in his arms, he kissed her passionately. The kiss quickly escalated to where Stan and Tina gave in to all the desires that had been building. In their excitement, neither was aware that they had risen from the carpet and were now standing face to face. The flimsy gown Tina had worn was on the carpet. Except for the tie around Stan's waist, both were completely naked. For a moment Tina was self-conscious, but Stan came to the rescue by breaking the silence.

"You are perfection, my darling—more beautiful than I could ever have imagined." Lowering themselves again to the soft white carpet, Stan kissed her again and again. There was not a part of her body that he missed. Their passions overflowing, Tina demanded equal time. It felt natural to explore and caress the man she wanted to spend her life with. No longer embarrassed or self conscious, Tina felt no shame. They were soulmates—he Adam, she Eve.

Eventually the two lovers moved from the floor. Turning off the television and the lights, they went to the bedroom where they made love off and on until nearly daylight. Sleeping for a few hours, they awoke in each other's arms. The night, in addition to the passion experienced, had been one of tenderness, honesty and love. They were meant for each other and knew the commitment made would last a lifetime.

"Should we elope?" asked Stanley over breakfast Christmas morning. Tina had made pancakes and sausages. In addition there were muffins and lots of hot coffee.

"Mara and your family would never forgive us."

"How long does it take to put a 'proper' wedding together, Tina? I'd like us to get married immediately, if not sooner."

"Me too, Stan, but there's much to think about and do."

"I'm going to ask my boss for a transfer to our Chicago office, but if it can't be worked out, would you consider living in Boston?"

"Mi casa es su casa," replied Tina. "Let's plan for a date in June. We'll want a honeymoon. Can you get a vacation then? I want to show you Yellowstone Park and you've always wanted to see the Canadian ROCKIES. The roads are often closed until late June."

"You're right, Sweetheart! It would make sense to wait for warmer weather. I'd like to do some hiking in the Tetons and take a whitewater raft on the Green River."

"And I want to be married in church, in a white gown, with a Maid of Honor—Mara, of course."

"And my brother, Alex, the Best Man."

"Mara and Alex will be so surprised when we break the news. It will be a Christmas surprise they'll welcome."

"My guess is that Mara and my brother have suspected this happy ending from the beginning."

"Yes, and they've probably already hired the hall, the band and addressed the wedding invitations."

"Well, this rock on my finger will stun them no matter what bets they've made regarding our future. Oh, Stan, I'm so happy you never gave up loving and wanting me."

"And I'm happy that you're happy, my Princess."

Mara and Alex had invited Tina and Stanley for Christmas dinner. Tina was bringing the appetizers and dessert and Stan had bought wine. Having packed the gifts, a plant and the promised food contributions, Tina and Stan took a cab to the condo.

As their driver wormed his way through traffic, Tina thought about her ring and wondered how long it would take Mara to notice it. As though reading her mind, Stan said, "Bet you sneaked to the phone and have already told Mara about our engagement."

"Are you accusing me of having a big mouth? You know very well that I haven't been out of your sight since Christmas Eve."

"Oh! Was that you who was all over me while I was trying to get some sleep last night?"

"Yes and it was me who, at your request, ate breakfast while sitting on your lap this morning."

"I still don't believe you made me do the dishes just so your ring wouldn't get dirty."

"Didn't I make up for it by letting you soap me down in the shower?"

Tina and Stan were still teasing each other as they reached the door of Mara and Alex's condo. "Ho, Ho, Ho! Merry Christmas," they all shouted as the door opened. After setting down shopping bags and a huge red poinsettia, everyone hugged and kissed. Toro, not to be outdone, went from one to the other licking their faces while his tail wagged furiously.

"You look radiant," said Mara to her friend. Tina was all in red and white. Stan was adjusting a Santa hat and had donned a Christmas tie. Alex couldn't resist asking if they were impersonating Mr. and Mrs. Santa Claus.

"We're just Santa's helpers," said Tina as she waved a very conspicuous finger under Mara's nose.

Mara's face illuminated as she spied the sparkling ring. "You did it," she said and then repeated, "You really did it. Let me see that rock." Grabbing Tina's hand as she lead her to the window for a better view, everyone proceeded to talk at once.

Congratulations were in order. Alex kissed Tina and hugged his brother. Then both couples danced around the room. Stan had Tina up in the air. Toro, not to be outdone, jumped up and down. When all stopped to take a breather, Alex said, "We're happy my older brother finally decided to make a move. Didn't we tell you that Tina was a good catch waiting to be caught?"

It was at least half an hour before the excitement died down. That's when the questions began. "When, where, what, how?" asked Mara and Alex almost in the same breath.

"Soon, in Boston, a real wedding in a church wearing a white gown with a Maid of Honor and Best Man," responded Stan. "You and Alex our first choice."

After comments from Stan that he should have made a bet about Tina's not being able to keep her ring a secret for more than five minutes, the ladies threw up their hands and retreated to the kitchen to look after dinner. The men went to the opposite end of the condo where the conversation took a different direction.

"Big Brother," said Alex playfully slapping Stanley on the back, "I'm delighted that you and Tina are getting married. You are good together and I couldn't imagine either of you with anyone else. However, there's another reason why I'm so enthusiastic about your news."

"You want to see us settled down just like you and Mara."

"True, but more important, I've been trying to figure out a way to keep my adorable wife and your soon to be lovely bride out of trouble."

"What kind of trouble, Alex?"

"Did Tina tell you about their recent escapade?"

"We talked about her encounter with Larry in New Zealand. Imagine them being in the same place at the exact same time. Too bad their cable cars were moving in opposite directions allowing Larry to disappear again."

"The episode left Tina quite shaken, Stan. Understandably she is now even more determined to get answers to her questions. Not that I blame her, but truthfully I'd rather she let go and went on with her life."

"Agreed, but put yourself in her position, Alex. Her parents were murdered. Only answers will bring closure."

"I know, Stan, but all those strange phone calls—obviously Tina's making waves and that could be very dangerous. Are you aware that our ladies think of themselves as Sherlock Holmes and Doctor Watson reincarnated?"

"That's news to me, little brother. Go on!"

In the family room, secure that the girls were out of earshot, Alex brought his brother up-to-date. He told him, in addition to the continuing mysterious phone calls and hang-ups, there had been a call from Officer McDonald on her first day back from New Zealand—that Tina was in a new apartment with an unlisted number she herself had not yet memorized. When asked how McDonald had gotten the number, he told Tina that there were no secrets from the police.

"The remark," Alex said, "started Tina thinking and suspicious that leaks regarding her comings and goings might be coming from the St. Louis police department itself."

"Tina could be on to something, Alex. Someone in the department might want to scare her off."

"Well it's working. Tina is frightened, Stan, but more than that, she no longer trusts McDonald. She's convinced he's holding out on her."

Alex explained that Tina had asked McDonald for the results of some interviews he'd arranged with two ex-gang members retired Officer McCarthy had put him on to. McDonald told her that the meetings had been of no help. Insisting on meeting with Gomez and Jacobs herself, Tina learned that there was someone known as Tony who had been an important member of the Uptown gang—that the name had been given to McDonald and McCarthy.

"Needless to say, Tina was furious that McDonald had chosen not to share this 'Tony' information with her—especially since her father had been introduced to someone known as 'Tony Luppo.' when looking to buy another hotel in Chicago."

"Adding what you've told me to McDonald's slip of the tongue that Larry should have been hiding out in Brazil, I can understand why Tina would suspect the police and lose confidence in McDonald."

"True, but I really believe the ladies went overboard doing what they did last weekend."

"Sounds serious. What did they do?"

"Would you believe they went to St. Louis—to spy on McDonald? They rented a car and followed him around for two days. They discovered there was a girlfriend—a fellow police officer and tailed her as well. Found out her name is Lucy Lombardo. Time ran out and they came back to Chicago, but I'm sure the girls have every intention of continuing their stakeout. Somehow Tina feels there's something to be learned by tracking down that Uptown gang."

"Are we talking about a mob connection, Alex? That's not good. You've got my attention. How do we put the brakes on our ladies?"

"Planning for your wedding ought to help, Stan. It should keep them out of trouble for a while."

From the kitchen, they heard a loud crash and then, what sounded like, laughter. "What's going on in there? asked Alex. "Do you need help? Should we call 911?"

"It's just the turkey, Honey, but don't panic. There's a spare in the freezer."

As the men raced each other to the kitchen, Alex said, "Hope you're not too hungry, pal. Sounds to me like we won't be eating before midnight. Think you can hold out?"

Stan assured him that he'd live, but suggested they help clean up whatever mess the girls were in. Cautiously entering the kitchen, fully expecting to see Toro wrestling with their turkey, the brothers were surprised that the floor was spotless and everything was in order. Dinner appeared to be safe and sound.

"What was all that noise about?" Alex asked.

"Nothing, darling," answered Mara.

"All that clanking could not have been nothing, Mara."

"If you must know, we kicked around some pot covers pretending a disaster to get your attention. We missed you. Anyhow, it's time to carve the bird. Incidentally you were awfully quiet in the den. Might I ask what you two were plotting?"

Eager to change the subject, Alex turned to Stan suggesting that he toss the salad. All doing their respective jobs, it wasn't long before the two couples were seated in front of a sumptuous meal. It was their first Christmas dinner together. Needless to say, the conversation moving from one subject to the other, was lively. There was a great deal of teasing from the brothers, but Tina and Mara were a good match for them. Much of the talk centered on wedding and honeymoon plans.

Alex thought Tina and Stan might want to settle on the East coast and cautiously said, "After all the work Mara went through finding Tina a place near us, you wouldn't move away. Tell me you wouldn't leave us again, Tina."

Everyone knew Mara would be devastated. With Alex traveling the world, she was lonely. Tina was her best friend and life saver. Seeing the sad faces, Stan told them of his plans to ask for a permanent transfer to the newly opened Chicago satellite. "I'm going to check out the possibilities with my boss. There may be something for me here, but, of course, don't plan on it happening overnight."

"Do you really think there's a chance?" asked Mara, her face brightening just a little.

"There'd better be," Stan answered, "if I ever expect to see happy smiles from you all again."

Tina had been quiet, but got their attention when she said, "Don't forget I have things to settle in this neighborhood and am not going anywhere soon."

The brothers exchanged knowing looks. They really wanted Tina to back off. The never ending phone calls, intended to scare her off, had not worked. By now, everyone including the callers, must have figured out that they were dealing with a woman on a mission. While Stan and Alex understood Tina's need to keep the promises made to herself, they also knew she'd be in grave danger if she actually did find Larry or the truth behind the murder of her parents on her own.

Having lost confidence in Detective McDonald and the St. Louis police precinct, Tina was determined to find Larry—and Tony as well. What if McDonald or his lady friend had seen Tina and Mara in St. Louis following them around? It was no wonder the brothers were concerned and anxious to have Tina give up.

"Perhaps the preparations for your upcoming wedding will help push Tina's crusade to a back burner," said Alex when again finding himself alone with Stan.

"My plan is to persuade her to spend time with me in Boston."

"Could you get her to move in with you until and if your transfer becomes a reality?"

"Fat chance, Alex. I can hear her already. First she'll remind me that she's just gotten settled in her new apartment. Then she'll argue that it's me who should do the moving—unless, of course, I can't work out a deal with my boss. In that case, any moves would be put on hold until we get married."

Stanley fully expected to convince Tina to spend the remaining holidays with him in Boston. He wanted to surprise his parents by showing up on their doorstep with his bride to be. They would spend New Years eve and day at the farm. "I trust you and Mara have not told Mom and Dad that we've been seeing each other," Stan said.

"Not a word," replied Alex. "We didn't want to build their hopes up in case you chickened out."

"Not me! You know I've had my eye on Tina since the day you brought her to the family home. Can't wait to see Mom and Dad's faces when we knock on their front door. Imagine what they'll say when we tell them we're going to get married. They like Tina and have often hinted that I should find someone nice and settle down."

"What about Tina's job? Is she ready to give up traveling around the world?"

"Do you really think she'd want to continue escorting tourists when she's got a hunk like me waiting for her at home?"

"I guess you're right, Stan. Tina's still a novice, but I know I've had it with traveling and will be happy when I can come home to my darling wife every night," Alex answered thinking about all the lonely nights he'd spent in hotel rooms."

The last of the dishes were done and it was time to leave. All had eaten too much and were ready to call it a day. Thanking their hosts for a very special Christmas, Tina and Stan found a cab and were soon back at her apartment. Opening the door, Tina bent down to pick up an envelope lying on the floor. Inside was a single sheet of typing paper. Centered on the page were the words:

"LEAVE IT ALONE"
LEH

What had been a beautiful day, ended abruptly.

"That louse—he's found me again," said Tina as tears started to roll down her cheeks.

"It's time to contact the police, Tina. We'll go in the morning. Then you're coming with me to Boston. You must get out of here."

"I just got here, Stan. It's a great apartment and I'm not going to move again—not until we're married."

Softening his tone as he took Tina in his arms, Stan said, "These people are not fooling around Sweetheart. Right now they only want to scare you, but I shudder to think of what might happen if you don't, as the note says, 'leave it alone.'"

"Don't you understand, I can't leave it alone. My parents were murdered. I'm finally getting somewhere—otherwise they wouldn't be bothering me. You know the police have been of no help. They might even be the problem."

"Why do you say that?"

"Well, someone is leaking information. Supposedly only Detective McDonald knows where I live, work and my unlisted phone number. Yet they always find me—no matter what precautions I take."

Not knowing that Alex had already told him, Tina owned up to the fact that she and Mara had gone to St. Louis over the weekend—that their purpose was to spy on Detective McDonald. "We followed him around and found that he was cozy with a female officer formerly from Chicago. Instinct tells me that she might be connected somewhere and getting information about me through him. Her name is Lucy Lombardo. I intend to find out more about her."

"It's Christmas, Tina and we've just gotten engaged. We should be happy and celebrating."

"Tell that to the coward who left a note under my door."

Tina was angry. Holding her close, Stan calmly said, "You're taking chances with your life, Honey, and I can't allow that. Come to Boston with me. I know it's difficult to walk away, but you're not safe here. The more you dig, the more threat you are to whoever they are. We'll live in my apartment until we get married. I'll work on my boss for that transfer and we'll be back with Mara and Alex before you know it. We'll get another apartment and you'll have a new name. You'll be Mrs. Stanley Turner and out of sight. They'll lose interest in you."

There was no response as Tina continued to stare at the paper in her hand. "All you have to do is lay low for a while," Stan continued. "They'll forget about you. It's true you may never find who murdered your parents, but you won't become another victim either. Need I remind you that you are very important to me. We can't bring back your parents, but you and I have the rest of our lives. Please, Tina, listen to me. I love you so much. I want you safe. Come with me to Boston. We'll spend New Years with my parents. They haven't a clue that we've been seeing each other and will be surprised when we tell them of our engagement."

Sighing, Tina finally spoke. "I'd be letting my parents down, Stan, but perhaps you're right. It's over two years and there's been little progress. The questions keep coming, but the answers continue to elude me. Let me think about it. Okay?"

"Great! Now, let's you and me turn out the lights and see what develops."

"That's not how I do my thinking," said Tina allowing just a speck of humor in her response.

"You can think tomorrow. Meanwhile you know sleep isn't instantaneous. If you'll allow yourself to relax, I've got some great techniques I'd like to experiment with."

Tina awoke early the next morning. The note, which was on the night table, was still very much on her mind. Picking it up and re-reading the warning, the initials

"L E H" jumped off the page. "Stan," she said shaking him out of a sound sleep.

"What? What time is it? Is something wrong? Are we evacuating?"

"Those initials on the note—L E H—that's Larry E. Hermano. It was Larry who slid the note under the door. He was here at my apartment. How did he find me and is he warning or threatening me?"

"If you're right and it was Larry, he's putting his life on the line, Tina. You can be sure, whoever it was that paid Larry to disappear, will not tolerate his reappearance or his trying to make contact with you."

"Then you think the note was not meant as a threat?"

"I didn't say that. Why would he, or someone else, risk running into you at your very own apartment?" Reminding her that Larry had gone all out to avoid a face to face encounter in New Zealand, Stan added, "It doesn't make sense. Remember, the person leaving the note under the door managed to get your address. Others could have it as well. Come with me to Boston, Tina. You're not safe here."

Tina agreed to go for a week or ten days. It would make Stan feel better and give her time to think. Seeing Stan's parents again and telling them of their good news would be exciting. As for idle hours while Stan was at work, she planned to visit her travel agency, explaining that she would be leaving to get married. While there she'd gather travel brochures allowing her to come up with an itinerary for their honeymoon. Ten days would go quickly.

There was no question that Tina loved Stanley and was prepared to spend the rest of her life with him.

However, she was also determined to keep her apartment at least until they were married.

"Just so you know, Stan, I'm going back to my apartment after ten days. I'm sure it was Larry who left the note which means he's in Chicago. He may want to contact me again and I must be available. He's the only one who can put my ghosts to rest. Please don't be angry with me. I promise that nothing will interfere with our wedding in June. In the meantime, I'm sure we can work it out to be together on weekends. I'll come to Boston one weekend and you to Chicago the next. Okay?"

Stan was disappointed that Tina wouldn't give up her ties to Chicago and move in with him, but he couldn't be angry with her. All he could do was worry and warn her to be careful.

"I promise there will be no more sleuthing, Stan. And if Larry doesn't contact me within the next several weeks, I'll let it go like the note says. Meanwhile there is so much to do. The first thing we'll have to settle on is a date for the wedding. I'm assuming you'll want to be married in your family's church. The date, of course, will depend on availability. We'll check that out when we're with your parents. Your Mom will also want to start on a list of people to invite. I only have an aunt and a few friends, but we'll need to know how many guests to prepare for."

"My head is spinning already, Sweetheart. Maybe we should consider eloping. On second thought I wouldn't want to miss seeing my beautiful bride walking down the aisle. It's a once in a lifetime opportunity."

Deciding that the deal Tina was proposing would buy some time and the best he could get, Stanley called the airlines. Luckily there was an available seat on his flight. They would have ten days. Once in Boston, Tina might be persuaded to stay longer.

Mara and Alex came the next morning to help Tina pack and close the apartment. There were some tears, but even Mara was convinced, after learning about the note under Tina's door, that it was time for her to get out of town. As for Tina, her plans were to spend only ten days in Boston. She treated the departure as just another one of her tour assignments.

15

Stan's apartment was in a very quiet suburb outside of Boston. It was almost midnight when the newly engaged couple reached the door.

"Wait just a minute! Close your eyes," said Stan, setting down the luggage and relieving Tina of the parcels she was carrying. Picking her up in his arms, he carried his bride-to-be over the threshold.

"Stop, you nut! Put me down," shrieked Tina.

"Quiet—you'll wake the neighbors," said Stan covering her lips with a kiss before setting her gently down on the bed.

"Isn't this supposed to be a wedding night ritual? I think you're jumping the gun," Tina said, laughing at Stan's imitation of someone with a broken back. "And what happened to the rest of your apartment? Did you leave last month's dishes in the sink and your dirty socks on the floor? You whizzed me through the rooms with my eyes closed and I didn't see a thing. I'm in bed and not even tired."

"Imagine that! Suppose we take care of us not being ready to sleep first. Haven't made mad passionate love since yesterday and you're mighty tempting lying there like that. The grand tour of my apartment can wait."

"Have I possibly unleashed a sex maniac? Should have known what would happen if I let you lure me to Boston."

"Let's discuss the pros and cons of this later. Right now I want to hear you say that you love me."

"I love you Stanley and I know you love me. Can't wait to marry you. We'll have babies and a dog. Do you like cats? Maybe we'll have one of those as well. I'll have a family again. Thank you, Stan, for being in my life."

Tina did not see the remainder of Stan's apartment until the next morning. Waking to the delicious aroma of freshly brewed coffee and frying bacon, she was a sight to behold as, on her toes, she responded to his warm kiss. Not having done any unpacking the night before, Stan had left a heavy white bathrobe on the bed for Tina's use. Her long, almost black, hair hung over the robe. It was a challenge for anyone to find the petite body wrapped in the oversized garment trailing on the floor.

"As always, you are a vision, Tina. You would be, that is, if I could find you under that outlandish costume you're wearing. Let me help you to a chair before you trip over your train."

"Very funny, Stanley."

"It's you that's funny, Honey. How'd you sleep last night, by the way. Was my being next to you a distraction?"

"I slept like a log and don't remember a thing. Exactly what did happen after you carefully put me down on your bed?"

"Sorry Tina, I haven't enough time to refresh your memory right now. For some reason my boss expects me to make an appearance at work today. I do have a few minutes for a quick tour of the apartment before I leave. You might want to prepare a cozy dinner for us tonight and will need to know where the pots and pans are hidden."

"Always thinking ahead, Stanley, but I love you anyway. Don't know why it took me so long to give in to your charms."

"The important thing is that you did," Stan said as he walked her through the rooms she'd missed the night before.

From the expression on Tina's face, it was evident that she was impressed with the apartment. The decor was manly and done in excellent taste. From her observation— after all he had not expected, when he left, that she would be returning with him—Stan liked things neat and orderly. This realization was another plus for him since Tina was of the same mindset.

"Guess you're not marrying me because you want a cook and housekeeper. You've done a great job with breakfast and the apartment is clean as a whistle. Were you maybe expecting company?"

"In my wildest dreams, Tina, I didn't anticipate you'd be such a pushover. Why you literally jumped into my lap when I proposed. You didn't even wait for me to get down on bended knees."

"That's because I was afraid you might not be able to get up."

"Always the last word! The only way I know to quiet you is to cover your big mouth with mine," Stan replied, skillfully catching her as she tried to escape.

"I wish you didn't have to go to work today, but will use the free time taking myself over to the tour agency. I'll flaunt my beautiful engagement ring, and at the same time turn in my resignation. The people at Cartrite have been very good to me. They helped me through some bad times and I'll always be grateful to them."

"It's you and me now Sweetheart, and I won't allow any more bad times."

"I am looking forward to the good things ahead, Stan. There's the wedding and our honeymoon for starters. I plan to pick up some brochures while at the agency. Although some ideas are already floating around in my head, I'll want reference material."

"It appears you have your day pretty well taken care of. As for me, I'm going to the office to boast about my beautiful fiancée. Then, if I can get to my boss, I'll sound him out about a permanent transfer to our Chicago plant."

"Do you think he'll go for it?"

"If he could see your pleading eyes, he'd melt on the spot," replied Stanley as he gathered his things and prepared to leave for the day. Tina, still in Stan's oversized bathrobe clearing the table, went with him to the door. Kissing her as though about to leave for the north pole, Stan said, "I'm off. Keep the home fires burning."

"Hurry back, Stanley! I'll miss you." Closing the door behind him, Tina hoped that Stan's boss was in a good mood. That his wife had been nice to him the night before. There was a satisfied smile on Tina's face as she remembered what her night had been.

The news of their engagement was received with much enthusiasm at the Cartrite Travel Agency. Tina's co-workers surrounded her admiring the new diamond. They showered her with questions including the where, when and how of the wedding plans.

Explaining that she and Stan had only begun to work out the details, all laughed realizing that they were being premature. When Tina told everyone that she had come to turn in her resignation, there was disappointment but they understood. Her manager had planned for her to guide some Italy tours in the spring, but was happy that she'd given enough notice to find a substitute. Although Tina had been with the agency only a short time, it was plain that she would be missed. The office staff wanted to meet the lucky man, and insisted that a party was in order. A date was set for the following week.

Stanley, upon arriving at his office, asked for an early appointment with his boss. Mr. Yoakum had a reputation for being firm, but was well-liked by all for being fair in his dealings with employees as well as business associates.

Yoakum pretends to be stern, thought Stanley, but he's always been willing to listen. Look how great he's been about letting me fly back and forth to Chicago even though he must suspect my motive for wanting to go there.

The appointment was granted for two o'clock. As Stan watched the clock, Mr. Yoakum was deep in thought. "I'm sure Stanley wants to see me about a permanent transfer to Chicago. I don't want to lose him here, but perhaps I can get the best of both worlds. Maybe I can convince him to do a reverse commute. He could be here in Boston one day each week and stay in Chicago the other four."

"Come in Stanley. How's it going? Did you have a good Christmas? What's new in Chicago these days?"

"What's new is she said 'yes.' Would you believe it, Mr. Yoakum, the most beautiful, wonderful girl in the world is going to marry me in June." Having said that, Stan nervously wondered how soon he could approach the question of a transfer to the Chicago office.

"That's great, Stanley. She's a lucky girl. I must say, however, that I've seen the handwriting on the wall for quite some time. Now tell me, exactly when do you plan to take over as manager of our Chicago office?"

"What was that you said?" asked Stan, almost falling off the chair. What his boss was offering, so spontaneously, was a promotion as well as a relocation that would make him, Tina, Mara and his brother very happy. Unbelievably he hadn't even had to ask for it.

"I do have one condition, Stan. If it wouldn't be too much of an imposition, I want you to give me one day a week in Boston. Do you think you and your bride-to-be could handle that?"

"You've got a deal, Mr. Yoakum. I'm getting the best of both worlds. How can I thank you?"

"No thanks necessary, Stanley. The promotion's overdue. You've been with me a long time and have done a great job for the company. Business in that Chicago office has been picking up since you've been spending time there. With a manager in residence, I expect it will really take off. It's your job to prove me right. Now, however, I believe congratulations are in order. I can't wait to meet your special lady and hope you will have dinner with us at our house tomorrow night. Muriel will want to join me in celebrating both your engagement and the new promotion. By the way, Stanley, the name is Dennis. I think it's about time you called me by my first name."

Stan left his boss's office in a state of shock. Almost at his desk, he found himself surrounded by the office staff. Everyone was congratulating him. How quickly news travels, he thought. Tempted to call Tina, Stan decided to wait until back in the apartment. He wanted to see her face when he told her the good news.

Tina had stopped on her way back to the apartment to buy groceries. She planned to surprise Stan with a home cooked meal. The menu called for a salad, porterhouse steak, potatoes and fresh broccoli. Entering the apartment, Stan looked at a beautifully set table. Tina had found the best china and cloth napkins. There were lighted candles everywhere and a bottle of Merlot was cooling. She'd gone all out.

"Please uncork the wine," Tina said as she attempted to direct Stanley to a chair.

"Can't I have another kiss, and I need to wash my hands?"

"By all means, but hurry. I've been slaving in the kitchen all day and don't want to overcook anything."

A few more kisses and hands washed, Stan sat at the table and poured the wine. Raising glasses, Stan toasted his bride-to-be and was ready for food. "I'm a hard working man and very hungry," he said.

The steaks were done to perfection—medium rare as he liked them. The main course was followed by ice cream, coffee and home made brownies. "How lucky can a man get?" Stan asked as he patted his now satisfied stomach. It had been the best home-cooked meal he'd had since leaving his parent's farm. "Not only are you beautiful, Tina, but you're a terrific cook."

"One steak isn't much of a test, Stanley. If that's your reason for wanting to marry me, you'd better see what I do for an encore."

"I've already seen what you do for an encore, and like it very much. As far as I'm concerned, you've passed the test with flying colors. Now let's hear about your day at Cartrite," said Stanley wanting to save his special news for last.

"They were all very happy for me even though I told them that I was leaving. The staff wanted to know if we had set a date. They plan to take us out to dinner next week. How about your day? Did you get to talk to your boss?"

"I did, but..." said Stan hesitating. There was a downcast expression on his face.

"Oh Stan! He wouldn't go for your idea of a permanent transfer. Trying to hide her feelings, she said, "I'm so sorry, but don't feel bad. We'll work something out."

Taking pity on her, Stan held Tina's hand and said, "You won't believe this, Sweetheart, but before I had a chance to ask..."

"He told you not to even think about it," interrupted Tina.

"Right! He'd already decided I'd make a good manager for the Chicago office and was throwing in a salary increase to boot."

"You're kidding! I don't believe it. You've known all day and let me think he'd turned you down. You're mean, Stanley." Smothering him with kisses regardless, her next words were, "Was it really that easy."

"Well there was a little condition attached. I had to promise my boss that I'd spend one day each week in Boston. Think you can handle that?"

"Watch me! Oh Stan, I'm so excited. Wait until I tell Mara and Alex. When do you think this will come about?"

"Probably not for a couple of months, but certainly before we get married. Can you believe it, Tina? Everything is falling into place. It all started when you said 'yes' to my proposal. You're my good luck charm. Did I mention that Mr. Yoakum wants to meet you and has invited us to his house for dinner tomorrow night?"

"I'd like to meet him too. For what he's done, your Mr. Yoakum is my hero. He's made me very happy, but I know it wouldn't have happened were it not for your hard work and talent. Mr. Yoakum is lucky to have you."

Overjoyed, Tina suggested that they call Mara and Alex. Then they would call Stan's parents. "I have a better idea, Sweetheart. We'll spend New Year's Day at the farm with my parents. They have no clue that we've been seeing each other and I'd like to surprise them."

"I wouldn't want to shock them, Stan, but if I remember correctly, they do like me and might welcome your surprise. Do you think they would let us stay overnight? We could celebrate New Year's Eve with them. Your Mom and I will have much to talk about. It's never too early to start thinking about wedding preparations. Your father will want to hear about your new job as well. We'll need an overnight to cover everything."

Tina and Stan agreed that a few days with his parents were long overdo. Having satisfied their appetites, Stan and Tina were ready to tackle the dishes and make phone calls. "Following our calls, Tina, I have a proposition to make. I'd like to get another look at that sexy nightie you unceremoniously threw on the floor Christmas Eve. Here's the deal. If I promise to give you a big kiss, will you try to keep it on a little longer this time."

"That could be arranged if you keep your hands in your pockets."

Chuckling, Stan retorted, "Do you know what I like best about you, Tina?"

"Tell me!"

"That you're never at a loss for words. Now be quiet and give me a kiss. I love you and like what kissing leads up to."

"And do you know what I like best about you, Stan?"

"Your turn. Tell me!"

"That you don't learn to quit when you're ahead."

Tina called Mara with Stan's news that he would be relocating to Chicago. Mara, as expected, was delighted. When Stan called his parents, he was very secretive only willing to tell them that he'd be coming on New Year's Eve with an important guest. Try as they might, they could not coax additional information out of him.

"You'll just have to be patient and wait a few days," was all he would say before hanging up.

Tina and Stan had dinner at the home of his boss the following evening. Muriel had been anxious to meet and entertain the soon-to-be manager of their Chicago branch office. She was a gracious hostess delighted that Tina's bubbly personality allowed for easy communication. The Yoakum's children, Meg, three and Matthew, four, were awake when Tina and Stan arrived. They had brought presents—games suitable for their ages. Hardly had the cocktail hour begun when Tina found herself on the floor explaining the simple rules of Meg's new game. There was an immediate bond between her and the children.

"It's difficult to know who's having more fun," said Dennis, laughing as he brought Tina a drink to go with the appetizers all were eating. "Are you sure you're not robbing the cradle, Stanley?"

Stan's bride-to-be had made a hit and Stanley was very proud as he said, "I've had my heart set on this young lady for a long time. Now you know why."

While it was too soon to discuss definite dates and plans, there was no mistaking that Dennis had big ideas for Stan and the Chicago office. By the time Tina and Stan left the Yoakum's house, they were elated. The evening could not have gone any better.

"And the best is still to come, my love," said Stan as he ushered Tina into his bedroom.

On Friday of that week they took off for Stan's family home in Vermont. It was a beautiful drive. The roads had been cleared, but the snow-covered trees and landscape made it feel as though they were in a painting by Currier and Ives. Stan's parents were so excited about their son's planned visit that they were pacing the floor when the leased car finally pulled up into the driveway. Mom and Dad Turner almost tripped each other racing to open the door. Stan was bringing a guest and they were beside themselves with curiosity.

"I don't believe it," said Mrs. Turner. "Could that be Tina? No one else that I know is so tiny and has such long dark hair."

"You don't suppose our boy has finally come to his senses," replied Stan's Dad.

"It is—it is Tina. Did you know about this, Dad?"

"Not me. I'm innocent. Nobody ever tells me anything."

"That's because you can't keep a secret for longer than a minute."

By now, the happy couple, carrying all kinds of packages, had made it up the walk and into the arms of the welcoming committee.

"This is the nicest surprise I've had in a very long time," said Stan's Mom hugging Tina and kissing her son.

"Couldn't have come at a better time. It was getting lonely around here," came from the mouth of Stan's Dad as he hugged his son and kissed Tina on both cheeks.

After the packages and outer clothing were taken from them, Stan picked up Tina's hand and held it up for his Mom and Dad to see.

"You two are engaged? Another surprise! How wonderful! Are you getting married soon?"

"That's one of the reasons we couldn't wait to get here. We're thinking about the end of June, but have to work it out with the church and any plans you might have."

Everyone began talking at once. Stan's Mom was so excited that her words were coming out backwards. Stan's Dad insisted they all have drinks to celebrate, and then didn't get around to fixing them. He kept interrupting himself. Finally, Mom brought the wine and some snacks "to hold them over until dinner." There were endless questions. Stan's folks wanted to know when the lovebirds had again started seeing each other. They were eager for the smallest detail including when and how Stan had proposed. Tina and Stan dared not tell them.

"Why are you waiting until June to get married and where do you want to have the wedding?" There were other questions. Where did the young couple plan to live? Would they have a big wedding? Had they decided on a church and reception hall? What about Stan's job? The questions continued until someone remembered it was almost midnight.

"Happy New Year everyone," said Stan's Dad. "With all this good news and excitement, I'd say we're off to a good start."

While at the Turner farm, Tina and Stan inquired and learned that the little church, where the Turner boys were baptized, was available on June 30. Arrangements were made with the minister to reserve the day. The reception would be held at the only hotel in town. Other than her aunt, and she was too frail to travel, Tina had no family meaning guests from her side would be limited to a few friends and co-workers. Stan had many relatives and, having lived his life in the same town, there were friends he'd want to invite. His mother promised to begin working on a list.

"I'll get my suggestions to you as soon as I can, Tina," she said as the couple departed after having spent a wonderful and productive two days. "As for you, Stanley," she continued, pretending to be angry, "tell Alex and Mara that they'd better have a good explanation for being so secretive about you two."

"I'm sure they didn't want to build up any false hopes, Mom. After all Tina isn't everyone's cup of tea and I might have changed my mind."

"Now cut that out, Stanley. You and Alex are always teasing your women."

"Just like Dad, who still gives you a hard time—and look how it's broadened you," said Stan gently patting his Mom on her well-rounded rump.

Back in Boston meant back to work for Stan. It was the start of a new year that promised to be exciting. Preparations for transfer were already underway since Dennis, having made the decision to put Stanley in charge of the Chicago operation, was anxious to get the ball rolling. With time on her hands Tina began the search for "the perfect wedding dress." Some nights, at Stan's insistence, they would go out, but most of the time Tina had dinner ready when he entered the apartment.

"Makes me feel like we're already married," she said greeting him at the door in an apron and not much else.

"How do you expect me to concentrate on food when you look like that?"

"You've had all day to concentrate. Now it's time to relax, my love."

On Wednesday they went to dinner with Tina's Cartrite associates. It turned out to be a kind of wedding shower for both of them. Since Tina and Stan already had two apartments which would be combined, it was difficult to decide on appropriate gifts. Aside from the usual comedians, some decided to pool their resources. Holiday china was on sale it being after Christmas allowing them to purchase fifteen place settings.

"What a perfect idea," said Tina. "We'll expect you all for dinner at holiday time next year."

"Love the Christmas tie that plays Jingle Bells and the Santa Claus socks," added Stan as he and Tina made the rounds to thank everyone.

"I hate to spoil a beautiful day," said Tina as they returned to Stan's apartment later that night, "but we have to talk about my going back to Chicago. If I plan on being in my apartment by Tuesday, I'll have to call for a flight reservation tomorrow."

"I don't want you to leave, Honey—not until I can go with you. You've spoiled me. Who can I trust to have dinner ready for me at night and what do I do with the extra pillow in my bed?"

"You know I must get back, Stan. There are things I have to do and others that I want to do."

"What could be better than being here with me?"

"Can't think of a thing that beats being with my favorite man, but there's someone out there that might want to get in touch with me and I've got to make that possible. I promise, Stan, not to get into trouble. No more Sherlock Holmes. You've convinced me that it's more important to stay alive. You and I have a great deal of living to do. It won't be long before you're settled in your new job and then we'll be together forever. In the meantime, if you can't get to Chicago, I'll catch a plane for Boston. Do we have a deal?"

"I'd rather you stayed with me, but what can I say? Promise you'll call me the minute anyone tries to contact you and that you and Mara will give up spying on people anywhere, anytime. Just for the record, I don't plan to get much sleep until we're together again. Not only will it be awfully empty in bed, but I'll worry knowing there are bad people out there."

"I made a promise, Stan, and I mean it. I won't do anything stupid. With you in my life, I have too much to lose."

By Tuesday afternoon Tina was again in her Chicago apartment. It had been difficult leaving Stan in Boston, and he certainly did not want to let her go, but promising to fly back every other weekend helped with the good-byes. Her apartment, on entering, was cold and very empty. Tina checked the mailbox and the telephone answering machine. There were a few hang-ups, but no messages, and there was a note from Jim.

"Are you still mad at me, doll? Don't know what I did to set you off, but decided I'd better not call until you cooled down. Hope you're missing me by now. Let's get together soon. I'll call on Wednesday."

Let him call, said Tina to herself. Can't wait to tell him I'm engaged to a wonderful man who treats me like a princess and doesn't think of me as a doll or a baby. Except for any new developments regarding the murder of my parents, I'd be happy never to hear from Jim again. He's not been straight with me and I don't trust him any more. For all I know, he could be the enemy.

After settling herself in, Tina called Mara to let her know she was back. There was some exciting news. "You're going to be an aunt, Tina."

"You're pregnant? That's terrific. Why didn't you tell me?"

"Alex and I are very happy about becoming a family, but I've been feeling lousy. I did want to tell you of my suspicions on Christmas Day, but wasn't sure. I certainly didn't want to jinx things. Even Alex didn't know until I confirmed it with a doctor visit. Can we count on you and Stan to be Godparents?"

"Take a breath, Mara. Let me say 'congratulations' and we'd be honored to be Godparents. Are you getting fat yet?"

"The baby isn't due until September. It's a little early to be getting fat. Actually, I've lost some weight. Even the smell of food is turning me off right now, Tina, but having you back will help get my mind off myself. How about coming over here for a cup of tea after you get your bags unpacked? You can tell me all about your week in Boston."

"Okay, but first I want all the nitty gritty details about your exciting news. How could you get pregnant without telling me? I'm supposed to be your very best friend."

"It was easy. All it took was a few nights at home with Alex. I hate to say this, Tina, but much as I love you, you had nothing to do with my getting pregnant."

"Can't I take some credit for not being around during the holidays bothering you both? That should count for something."

"For your information, this baby got started before the holidays, Tina."

"Whatever! Anyway it's the best news I've heard in a long time and I can't wait to see if you look different. I'll be over in a little while. Is Alex home or do we go out to dinner? You've got to keep up your strength if you want that baby to grow big and strong."

"Alex had to leave this morning for Portugal. We'll go out and I'll give eating a shot. Plan to stay overnight. We'll need lots of time to catch-up."

"Sounds good to me. My apartment without Stan is awfully lonely right now. Guess I've had too much of a good thing lately."

Tina took care of a few chores and then was happy for an excuse to leave her quiet apartment. A smiling but pale faced Mara welcomed her with open arms. Morning sickness was lasting throughout the entire day and had left it's mark.

It was difficult to believe that only a few days had elapsed since Christmas. There was so much to talk about. After exhausting the subject of Mara's pregnancy, Tina spoke of Stan's expected new job. Mara was happy that the promotion would mean more money, but mostly because Tina and Stan would continue living nearby.

Before getting back to the expected baby, Tina talked about her visit with Alex and Stan's parents. The date, time and place of the wedding had been determined while with them and could now be marked on their respective calendars. Then she went into detail about the dinner at the home of Stan's boss and the bridal shower given by the Cartrite employees.

"I'd say you and Stan accomplished a great deal and were quite busy while you were away."

"Obviously not as busy as you and Alex. I come home after a few days and find out my friend is going to be a mommy. A baby! How did this happen? Tell me."

"Well, there's the obvious answer to your question, but we have been anxious to start a family. Neither of us wanted to be 'old folks' sending kids off to kindergarten. Besides, a person needs young legs to keep up with those little guys."

"Or gals," responded Tina. How would you feel about one of each? Any chance of twins? I always thought 'twofers' would be fun."

"You never know. But, speaking of twins, the condo will be too cramped for us once the baby comes. We're thinking of buying a house in the suburbs."

"Terrific! Maybe we can take your place. We'll need more space when we get married. Stan has so much stuff which, when added to mine, would have us tripping over each other if we stay in my apartment."

"Then I'd better get a place in a hurry. It takes time you know to find the perfect dreamhouse. Then comes negotiating over price, the contract and closing, not to mention renovations needed. Alex and I want an older house, with character. There must be big windows and open porches."

"How about a picket fence? I can see you now, sitting on the porch rocking babies all night after having washed windows all day."

It promised to be an exciting few months ahead for both Tina and Mara. By the time Tina turned the key of her apartment the next day, she had all but forgotten about Larry and the possibility that he might try to contact her. Perhaps she could finally get on with her life and forget the past.

There was a flashing light indicating a message on the answering machine. Expecting the usual hang-up, Tina was surprised to hear a man's voice.

"I'll be at Cafe Rio on Jacob Street tonight at 8 p.m. If you're interested, be there," was the message on the tape.

What was that all about, thought Tina. Probably a wrong number. No way am I going to check it out. A wild goose chase is all I need right now. Thank you very much, whoever you are, but I have better things to do with my time. Until I see Stan this weekend, my priority is to start making plans for our honeymoon. I'll want to have a partial itinerary ready when he gets here.

Surrounding herself with travel brochures, maps and books, the days went quickly. Knowing of Stan's desire to see the Rockies and Yellowstone National Park, Tina looked for a tour beginning in Denver, Colorado and ending in Calgary, Canada. They were planning on a three-week honeymoon.

After going through the material available, Tina found there was no such packaged tour. She wasn't enthused about sharing their honeymoon with a busload of tourists either. She came to the conclusion that it might be best to rent a car and do their own thing—plan an itinerary from scratch. This would allow them to explore sights off the beaten track. At the same time, they would not be held to a strict time schedule.

When Stan called that night, Tina was in high gear. As she enthusiastically outlined preliminary ideas, she was delighted that they met with Stan's approval. On the phone over an hour, Tina neglected to mention the message that had been on her machine. There were so many more important things to think about—there was the love they had found, the wedding and planning for a honeymoon and there was Mara's news about having a baby and wanting to buy a house. After saying "goodnight," Tina found no difficulty sleeping.

It was not until the next morning that Tina remembered the message of the night before. *I wonder if anyone met someone at Cafe Rio last night,* she thought. *Would you believe that I put it out of mind until this minute. There's hope for me yet, I guess.*

Mara walked to Tina's apartment the following afternoon and found her friend buried under papers, books and maps. Together they made lists of places to visit, hotels to stay at and then estimated distances between destinations chosen. It was Tina's intention to include all the scenic wonders between Rocky Mountain National Park in Colorado and Jasper in Alberta, Canada. By the end of the day, she had come up with a workable plan.

"Better keep careful notes, Tina. Some day I'll have Alex to myself long enough to follow in your footsteps. It all sounds exciting."

"I wish you could come with us, Mara."

"Since when do newlyweds invite in-laws to tag along on the honeymoon?"

"You're right! I guess, that's not such a good idea. However, Stan and I promise we'll take care of your baby anytime you want to run off and take that honeymoon you were cheated out of."

"Thanks for the offer. You never know, we might want to take you up on it some day."

"Three weeks might just about make it," Tina said to Mara looking over her tentative ideas. "Stan and I will go over the material this weekend. If he likes what I propose, I'll start making reservations."

"The itinerary has lots of variety and looks great, Tina. I wonder why others would not have thought to package a similar tour. I'm sure there would be many seasoned travelers interested in something different."

"It's strange that you and I are thinking along similar lines, Mara. The idea of putting together and marketing a tour package like this has been in back of my mind since beginning this project. There's nothing like it available to the general public at the present time. If my itinerary could be cut down to two weeks, it's very possible it would be attractive to touring agencies throughout the world. Deals would have to be made with hotels, restaurants and transportation companies, but I think it could be done. Would you help me if I decide to pursue the idea? I know you'll be busy with a baby, but I really would like you in this with me—any time you could give."

Believing that Europeans with their love of health spas, as well as senior citizens, would be interested in a leisurely two-week bus tour through beautiful scenery not yet invaded by tourists, Tina and Mara almost forgot that they were primarily working on the details of a honeymoon. Out of nowhere a career opportunity had presented itself. The friends, increasingly caught up in the idea, were startled when the phone rang.

It was the promised call from Detective Jim McDonald. "Hi doll! Hope you're over your temper tantrum. When do I see you. It's time to make nice-nice."

"Forget it Jim. We can talk, if you have anything worthwhile to say, right now on the telephone."

"Tina, I'm sorry. I don't know what I did, but if it makes you feel better, you've got my apology. Let's get together on Saturday. I'll come to Chicago and we can spend the whole day talking and making up."

"No Jim. All we need to talk about is business. So far you haven't been very informative on that score. Have you lost interest in finding the murderer of my parents or are you simply holding out on me?"

"Why would I want to hold out on you? I'm on your side, Tina. I've been promoted and am now a detective. The new job has more responsibility and I've been very busy. You won't believe the cases that are on my desk demanding attention. I'm doing the best I can with yours, but you know, there isn't much to go on. You met with Officer McCarthy. Did he tell you anything you didn't already know?"

"Only that he was more or less invited to retire by pressures put on him from his superiors and that Enrico Gomez got into a fight with someone by the name of Tony," Tina answered sarcastically. "He also said that John Jacobs had actually seen this Tony and remembered him as appearing to be effeminate in his mannerisms and movements. I'm an amateur Detective McDonald, but to me it fits that the Tony, remembered by both Gomez and Jacobs, could be the same Tony Luppo that was introduced to my father at the hotel. Officer McCarthy's information also confirmed Detective White's theory that Larry might be homosexual."

"My, my, Miss Cappo, you have been busy. But what does it mean? Where does all this so called information lead the investigation? Nowhere! That's where the trail ends."

"Then why do I continue to feel hot breathing on my neck? Something I'm doing must be making someone nervous."

"That's the very reason I want you to drop it, Tina. You're asking for trouble—especially if you insist on poking your nose into things. Let it go. Torturing yourself won't bring your parents back. I'm sure, even they, would want you to go on with your life. From the moment we met I had hoped you'd have let me help you do that. Don't close the door on us."

"Listen to me, Jim! There is no 'us' and there never was an 'us.' For your information I'm getting married in June to a wonderful man. I've known him for a long time."

"You're getting married? I must say you are full of surprises. I guess I should say I'm happy for you and wish you good luck. Truthfully, I had other plans, but maybe you'll let go of the past now and get a life. Believe me, it will be healthier for you."

With those words, Jim thought it best to end the conversation. Saying he was sorry their short relationship had not worked out, he added, "I think we could have made sweet music together, but it's your loss, baby-doll."

The phone back on the hook, Tina turned to Mara, puzzled. "What did Jim mean that I'm asking for trouble? Was he warning me of things he knows or things he suspects? The more I talk to him, the more confused I get. I do believe he's threatening me. Is someone putting pressure on him to do so? Well I promised Stan to play it safe. If Larry himself contacts me, I'll listen. If he doesn't, I'm prepared to let go of the promise made to my parents. Sometimes even the best of intentions can't be worked out."

16

Although Tina's primary reason for leaving Stanley in Boston was to be available should Larry try to make contact, there had been no word from him. Her days were fully occupied, however, and by Friday, Tina was eager to go over tentative honeymoon plans. Unfortunately Stanley's boss had scheduled a Saturday afternoon meeting making it impractical for him to fly to Chicago. Lonely and missing each other, although it had been only a few days, it didn't take much to persuade Tina to pack up her honeymoon ideas and fly back to Boston.

"Wait until you see what I have planned for us," Tina said.

"Sounds ominous, Sweetheart. Are we talking about our honeymoon or do you have something more provocative in mind?"

"Our honeymoon, of course. I've found the most beautiful pictures—things to see and places to stay. If you agree and if I can get reservations, I'd like us to stay at hotels and lodges located in the national parks."

"Sounds like the way to go."

"There's a 4:30 flight, Stan. We'd better hang up and save the conversation for my arrival in Boston." Moving into action, Tina was in Stan's apartment by 9:30 that night. They had eaten dinner and were now comfortably sprawled on the floor going through the material Tina had brought. There were pictures taken at Jackson Hole Lodge, Old Faithful, Mammoth Motor Inn, Glacier Park Lodge, Many Glacier Hotel and Prince of Wales Lodge—all set in beautiful surroundings. Holding Tina close, Stan said, "You've convinced me. Early reservations are necessary or we'll be disappointed. I'm sure hotel rooms are booked solid in season."

It was quite late when the couple went to bed. Although Tina wanted to tell Stan about the new career opportunity she was considering, it would wait until morning. They were both ready to put aside the catalogs in favor of a little action.

On waking the next morning, after an encore of the previous night, they showered and had breakfast. Happily sated, Tina could no longer restrain herself. "I've been thinking, Stan, and have a great idea." Stan put down his coffee cup waiting patiently for Tina to continue. He sensed that this was not going to be an ordinary, everyday, idea.

After several deep breaths, Tina began. "As you know, Stan, I no longer have a job. While I plan to be a lady of leisure until after our wedding and honeymoon, I do want to work when things settle down."

"Okay, Sweetheart! Now tell me about that great idea of yours. With all the preliminaries and the worried look on your face, it must be a whopper. You've got my undivided attention."

"I've been thinking about starting my own business, Stan."

"There's nothing to stop you, my love, but what do you have in mind?"

"Our honeymoon itinerary."

"Now wait a minute. You want to take people along on our honeymoon, Tina? I don't think so."

"Not our honeymoon, Stan. That's one of many times I want you all to myself, but why wouldn't a similar tour interest people who, like us, are looking for something different?"

"Maybe, but how would a person get started on what you are proposing?"

Tina had given much thought to the subject and was prepared to explain. Summarizing, her plan was to speak directly with hotel managers when making their honeymoon reservations. She would tell them about her idea to market a similar tour to the public offering to meet with them if they were interested.

Tina planned to put together a reasonably-priced fourteen-day tour. Hotels would be asked to set aside a given number of rooms during the months of June, July and August. Depending on the itinerary, tourists would be staying at each hotel anywhere from one to three nights and be served two meals a day. Bus transportation would be arranged between Denver, the starting point, and Calgary, the end. An attractive flier would be printed and circulated to travel agents responsible for promoting, selling, and making reservations.

"What do you think, Stan? I believe it's doable."

Trying to digest all Tina was proposing, Stan thought carefully before responding. Taking her hands in his, he said, "You're amazing. I leave you alone for a few days and you've got your whole future figured out. I can't imagine what you'd do with an entire week. Seriously, I think you might have something. It will be a lot of work, but right down your alley."

"Not for me, but for all of us, Stan. If it works out, I see a business that Mara, if she's interested, and I could handle without taking too much time from our husbands and families. You and I will want to have children after we're married and it would be great to work out of our home. The tours will take care of themselves once we get going, but I do expect there will be a great deal of running around in the beginning. Are you with me?"

"All the way, Sweetheart. Knowing you're wearing my ring, I can handle anything, but try to save the weekends for us. Did I tell you my transfer to the Chicago office becomes effective on February 28?"

"No more commuting between our apartments? That's great news."

"Remember, my boss wants me in the home office one day every week. Maybe you could coordinate your out of town appointments with my being in Boston."

"I'll do my best to work around your schedule, Stan. Changing the subject, have you thought about where all your stuff will go when you move here? There's not much empty space in my apartment, as you know."

"Just a few things are coming with me. Clothes and a toothbrush is all I really need. Everything remaining will go into storage until we figure out what we're doing. We might even find a larger apartment before our wedding."

"You'll miss your lounge chair, Stan. Perhaps we can squeeze it in."

"Even though we've managed nicely so far, Tina, I think our first priority should be to trade in your single bed for a double."

"I thought you liked being all tied up in knots, Stan. Why would you want to ruin a good thing?"

"We're talking about the long haul now, Tina. For the money they're going to pay me, I think they'll expect me to come to work with my eyes open now and then."

The weekend behind her, Tina was again opening the door to her apartment. On entering, her eyes focused on a now familiar envelope. Tearing it apart, she read, "I'm not your killer. The hotel was all I was after. Murder was never part of the deal. I'm sorry, but please let it go. Bad things will happen to everyone if you don't. LEH"

"Larry was at my door again, Mara," said Tina when they later spoke on the phone. "He must have known I was away and felt secure in coming. Where does he get his information and why won't he just come and talk to me?"

"He can't risk it, Tina. If his associates discover he's in town and leaving messages, there's no telling what could happen. Frankly, I wouldn't be surprised to find his name in the headlines one of these days."

"Do you think he'll try to contact me again?"

"Not if he values his life. I really believe this is the last message you'll get. He's said all he wants you to know."

"This is so infuriating, Mara. It's as though there's always another shoe waiting to drop. I was almost ready to concede that my parents' murders weren't the end of the world, but the threats and messages keep bringing it back.

Instead of notes, why doesn't Larry pick up the phone and say what he has to say?"

"Maybe he's afraid your phone is tapped."

"Could it have been he who left the message asking to meet at Cafe Rio?"

"Cafe Rio? When was that?" asked a startled Mara since this was the first she'd heard about it.

"Right after my holiday stay with Stan in Boston. I slept at your place that night. The message was on my machine the next day. A man said, 'Meet me in Cafe Rio at eight o'clock tonight if you're interested.' It didn't make sense. I told myself that the call might have been meant for someone else, and ignored it. Planning our honeymoon was uppermost in my mind at the time."

"You did right by ignoring it, Tina. Larry, I believe is gone for good. He doesn't want to be confronted by you knowing you'd ask questions that might be hard for him to answer. You were out of town and he felt secure leaving a final warning. He wants you to let go and get on with your life. As for that Cafe Rio call, if it was meant for you, it was probably your phone stalker, not Larry, wanting to lure you out into the open. Have you told Stanley and what does he think?"

"Stan doesn't know about the latest note or the Cafe Rio invitation. He'd worry and it wouldn't help any to tell him. We'll be together soon. Hopefully, then, all this will go away."

Since Alex was in Portugal and not expected back until the beginning of March, Mara suggested that Tina stay with her. "We could console each other," she said "and at the same time begin seriously collaborating on the new business you're thinking about. Oh! Did I tell you that I registered with several real estate agencies last week?

279

One called this morning wanting to show me some houses. Could I coax you to come with me? As you know, the sooner I find a house, the sooner you and Stanley can have this place."

"Enough, Mara! You've sold me. I'll be your house guest until Alex returns. Traveling much of the time seeing hotel people, I shouldn't be too much of a nuisance."

"You could never be a nuisance, my friend. Tell me, though, what happened? I didn't expect to win you over so easily."

"What did it, Mara, was the invitation to go house hunting with you. Some day Stan and I will be in that position and I'm curious. For me it will be a learning experience."

"With us under one roof, it will be much easier to start working on your new idea as well, Tina. I really want to help in any way I can."

"I'm glad to hear you say that, Mara. I'd like you to go into this project with me—as my partner."

"Me a partner in your business? Are you sure? There's nothing I'd like better, but only if you think I could handle my end."

"It's all settled then. We're partners starting now."

Tina briefly outlined her plan. She would attempt to sell five two-week tours beginning in July and ending around Labor Day. Hotel managers would be asked to set aside rooms. Bus companies would be contacted for suitable transportation. Since tourists would be starting from various locations, air travel would be up to each individual. The tours would begin in Denver and end in Calgary. "Details will have to be worked out," Tina said "but be prepared that the months ahead will be busy ones—especially in view of my wedding and your pregnancy."

"What was Stan's reaction when you told him about your entrepreneurial plans?"

"He's all for it. Thinks it's a great idea. Stan's transfer will be finalized at the beginning of March and he'll be moving in with me. Whatever traveling is necessary I'll try to do while he's at work."

"It appears you've thought about everything, Tina, but there will always be glitches and surprises. For one thing, we haven't talked about tour guides."

"In the beginning that will be my job. After the tours catch on, we'll hire someone. The biggest problem I see at the moment is marketing. I'd like you to prepare an attractive brochure or pamphlet for distribution to travel agencies. They need to see that we are offering an alternative to the restricted tours presently available. How soon, could you have something ready? The brochure should include pictures—particularly of the hotels at which the tourists would be staying."

"Give me a week for some rough drafts."

"Tour agencies may help defray the cost of printing eventually, but for now, it's on us. You do realize that we're talking about a first tour beginning, not this year, but the following July. We'll need time to get the word out. People usually plan vacations a year in advance."

"If it wasn't for our having a baby and wanting to buy a house, I'd like to help financially, Tina. It's going to cost quite a bit to get this project underway."

"All I ask is that you help me physically, Mara. I need your talent and support. Stan and I have some savings. We'll be cutting our expenses in half when Stan gives up his apartment in Boston. If my idea turns out to be a disaster, we'll know soon enough and have to bail out."

Tina joined Mara in her condo the next morning and immediately went to work refining the honeymoon plans. After satisfying herself that mileage covered would allow Stan to see all the 'musts' on the list, she began calling hotels. Speaking directly to hotel managers when making her reservations, Tina followed up with a well-prepared sales pitch.

"I'm convinced it's an idea waiting to happen," she said to each manager. "I've been a tour guide and know seniors would welcome an alternative to excursions presently available. Many have traveled extensively and been on tours illustrated in brochures. They are ready for something new and different. Foreign travelers love mountains and would be interested in continuing north into the Canadian ROCKIES where they'll find the most beautiful scenery in our hemisphere. We will emphasize that our tourists will be staying in the best hotels—some near mineral hot springs, a favorite among Europeans."

When Tina put down the phone that first day, she had successfully lined up a series of appointments. Mara was taking notes and the women were surprised to find that Tina would be devoting quite a few days in March meeting with interested hotel managers. Mara assured Tina that a pamphlet would be ready for her first appointments.

"Stan and I will be checking out the hotels when on our honeymoon, Mara, and that's good. We'll know from personal experience that accommodations, food and service will meet tourist expectations."

Stan arrived on Friday night and was impressed that Tina and Mara had interested so many hotel managers in their project. Tina's first appointments were to begin the following week.

It was the day before Tina's departure that Mara had a call from her realtor. He had a promising new listing. Alex was away, but Tina was happy to have a look with her. The house was located in the suburbs of Chicago easily accessible to Alex's home office and O'Hare Airport. This was important in view of his frequent flights out of town.

The house had been vacant for some time and needed major overhauling, but there were interesting features which were appealing. Outside porches surrounded the house leading to gardens that had once been lovingly cared for. A beautiful two sided fireplace serviced both the living room and all purpose den. There was a sizable eat-in kitchen, but it was outdated. It needed everything. Separate from the kitchen was a large dining room. There were three bathrooms. They all needed help. The one on the main floor was very small and a disaster. It could be expanded by moving a wall that was now a mud room. The upstairs bathrooms had potential, but would require sprucing up. These second floor bathrooms serviced four large bedrooms. There was much unfinished space on the second floor which Mara visualized as future walk-in closets.

Attached to the house was an adequate two-car garage. The exterior of cedar shakes had been kept in good repair, but all trim required scraping and painting. The grounds of the half acre on which the house stood were neglected. Because of its condition, the agent felt that an attractive settlement on price could be negotiated. Mara liked the house enough to put a binder on it, but Alex would have the final say. He wasn't expected back for another two weeks. While the agent was anxious to make a sale, it was obvious the house was not going to disappear overnight. Exerting pressure to make an offer would have been non-productive.

"I'll call you the minute my husband gets back," Mara said. "Try not to show it to anyone in the meantime."

Knowing that she had other things going, the agent left the scene confident that the house would remain on the market for a while.

"What do you think, Tina?" asked Mara when they were alone in the car.

"If it's an older house with character you want, I'd say that's it. The only thing missing is the character that left the place without trying to shape things up before putting on a 'For Sale' sign. Seriously, if you get it for the right price, I'm sure you'll end up with a treasure."

"The agent told me that the house was occupied by an older man who had to be moved to a nursing home. His only child, a daughter, lives in another state and is anxious to unload it. The house has been empty for about six months. She's been paying the taxes, worrying about pipes bursting and vandalism. There's potential in what I see and I hope Alex agrees. Our offer, of course, would have to be much below the asking price in view of the repairs needed. Perhaps we can agree on a price that will take care of some renovations as well."

"There's no problem with the house that money won't fix, Mara, but you're going to need lots of that green stuff before you're through."

In addition to the obvious repairs and renovating, Mara knew she'd want to do some remodeling. Enlarging the main floor bathroom would be expensive. As for the front entrance into the house, Mara would want it to be more impressive. She knew major changes would require permits, and perhaps variances. "Fortunately, Tina, everything doesn't have to be done at once."

In the car, after leaving the agent, the friends canvassed the area. They learned that the house was considered to be in a good neighborhood. Surrounding homes appeared to be well cared for. The school district had an excellent rating. Churches and shopping were convenient. Pleased with their survey, Mara was prepared to make a bid if Alex was similarly impressed.

Upon Alex's return, they immediately called the agent who eagerly met them at the house. As Mara hoped, Alex was satisfied with her find. He could visualize a dream house inside the walls and was eager to get to the drawing board. An offer was made and, after some negotiation, was accepted. All agreed they had struck a good bargain. They would go to contract in two weeks and, hopefully, close by the time Tina and Stan were married.

Alex drew up plans which Mara, elected to be the contract coordinator, would submit to sub-contractors for bids. This, in addition to the new travel business and preparing for a baby, would be a challenge, but Mara was well organized and up to the task.

March first was moving day for Stan—not only to his new job and office, but into Tina's little apartment. The soon to be married couple had no problem adjusting to the close quarters since they were busy, happy and in love. Stan had vacated his Boston apartment, stored most of his belongings at the home of his parents, and in accordance with the commitment made to his boss, made arrangements with a hotel for a weekly one night stay in Boston.

Mara had arranged Tina's travel plans. Her friend would leave on March fourth covering appointments made in Colorado, Wyoming and Montana. The week after would find her in Canada.

"You should apply for a passport," Tina said when Stan returned from his first day at the new job.

"You're right. I should and will have some pictures taken tomorrow. You never know when some beautiful female will want me to run away with her. It's good to be prepared," teased Stan.

"The only female you're going anywhere with, Mr. Turner, is me, but get that passport anyway."

Tina's appointments in the States went well. Hotel managers were enthusiastic and quoted rates, dates and deals that she brought home to evaluate. After reviewing Tina's planned itinerary, all had voiced surprise that others had not already thought of packaging such a tour.

While Tina traveled, Mara, armed with plans Alex had drawn, was getting quotes from contractors. Alex expected to have much of the renovation done before their baby arrived. Mara's priority was the kitchen followed by the first floor bathroom. Stan's' major concern was the front entrance and the need to replace windows.

For Mara there was never a dull moment. By the time Tina finished with her appointments, she had narrowed the field of contractors down to half a dozen estimates. She then proceeded to check references. On her return and when available, Tina accompanied Mara and was fascinated by her expertise and efficiency. Mara had a gift for organization and made things happen. Her talents would be a great asset in Tina and Mara's joint business venture.

By the time Alex returned from a short assignment, Mara had gathered enough information to hire two contractors. One would be responsible for the outside work and the other inside. Both confirmed that building permits would be needed before work could begin.

Early on Monday morning, blueprints in hand, Mara was at the Department of Planning and Development in Chicago for the necessary building permits. The door to the elevator had already closed, but reopened when Mara pressed the "up" button. Stepping in, she noticed a very attractive young woman standing in the rear. She looked familiar.

It took Mara a few seconds to realize who the woman was since she would not have expected to see her in Chicago much less out of uniform. Then it registered. The woman at the back of the elevator was Officer Lombardo. She was Detective James McDonald's St. Louis girlfriend. Instantly recovering, Mara followed Lucy Lombardo as she left the elevator and found herself at a door on which was stenciled, in gold letters, PLANNING COMMISSIONER—ANTHONY LOMBARDO.

Lombardo? Well, what do you know, said Mara to herself as she casually followed the woman through the door to see where it would lead. Officer Lombardo doesn't know me from a hole in the wall, she thought. No other way would I be doing what I am right now.

"Why hello Miss Lombardo. Was your father expecting you? I'll buzz and let him know you're here."

"If he's alone, let me surprise him."

"Of course—go right in." Then, turning her attention to Mara, the receptionist asked, "May I help you?"

"I'm here for a building permit," replied Mara pleased with her discovery as well as her fast thinking.

"You're on the wrong floor. Take the elevator down one flight to room 601."

"601? Thank you!" Mara left. The coincidence of this encounter was unbelievable, but what did it mean? Obviously Jim's girlfriend had a very influential father and he was in Chicago. Someone in his position could carry a lot of weight. Is Mr. Anthony Lombardo a good guy or a bad guy? Whatever he is, thought Mara, Tina will faint when I tell her of my discovery.

After completing the required forms and attaching the plans, Mara placed everything in an envelope leaving it with a clerk to be processed. Returning to her condo all she could think about was the coincidence of having seen Lucy Lombardo. It was about six o'clock when Tina's phone rang.

Not taking the time to say 'hello' Mara asked, "Is Stan with you?"

"Yes! We're just about ready to eat. Come join us."

"Thanks but I have leftovers that need attention. I'd like to stop by later, however. There's something important I can't wait to tell you."

"You sound excited. Don't keep me in suspense. Can't you give me a hint?"

"No! I want to see the look on your faces when you hear what I learned today. I'll be there in about an hour."

"Okay but you've peaked my curiosity and I can't wait for you to get here. We'll hold off on dessert." It wasn't like Mara to be so mysterious. While waiting for her, both Tina and Stan were on edge.

They both jumped on her when she arrived. "What is it Mara? We've imagined all kinds of scenarios. Is there a problem with the house or the permits? Are you feeling okay? With the baby coming, maybe you're doing too much."

"None of the above, but you'd better sit down." Tina and Stan were barely seated when Mara, no longer able to contain herself, blurted, "I saw Officer Lombardo today."

"You saw who?" Stan asked, puzzled.

"Detective Jim McDonald's girlfriend."

"No kidding! Where?" asked Tina.

"At City Hall when I went for our building permits. Officer Lombardo was in the elevator with me. When she got off I followed and found myself in the office of Chicago's Planning Commissioner. Would you believe Officer Lombardo is the daughter of the big honcho, Commissioner Anthony Lombardo?"

"What was that you said? He's the Building Commissioner? You're right. I don't believe it," said Tina turning to Stan. "Why a person in that position could have his hands into almost anything."

Dumfounded, but slowly getting the picture, Stan said, "Good thing you never took your problems to the Chicago Police Department, Sweetheart. It's bad enough you're persona non grata in St. Louis.".

Recovering from the shock, Tina said, "Let's recap! What conclusions can we draw from Mara's discovery? How does Jim fit in this picture and where do we go with our new information and suspicions? Is there someone we can trust?" Tina then answered her own questions.

"As I see it, we have a female police officer in St. Louis who turns out to be the daughter of Anthony Lombardo, Planning Commissioner in Chicago. We have the 'Uptown Boys' club in Chicago. That gang appears to have been protected. There was Detective White working for the St. Louis Police Department. He was killed while doing some investigating in Chicago regarding the murder of my parents. We have a retired police officer who was demoted because he made waves regarding the Chicago 'Uptowners.' Then we have Officer Jim in St. Louis who has recently been promoted to Detective and who is having an affair with Officer Lucy Lombardo, the daughter of Chicago's Planning Commissioner. I do believe we've just gone full circle."

"Don't forget Larry," Stan added. "He fits in there somewhere."

"Yes, there's Larry who disappears and then reappears. He is alleged to be homosexual and knew Tony Luppo who is also thought to be gay. Tony Luppo just happens to have the same initials as Anthony Lombardo. Coincidence? The only thing I see wrong with this picture is that the Planning Commissioner is too old to be Tony Luppo. We'll probably find an explanation for that somewhere down the line."

"You're building up quite a case, Tina," Stanley said, aware that his precious Tina could be walking on very thin ice. "What do we do with this information, my love? Chances are the Planning Commissioner has friends— obviously in more than one police department. I'm afraid, if this ends where it appears to be going, they'll be out to get you. You won't be safe anywhere."

"I have to tell someone, Stan, and there is one person that will listen to me. We can trust him."

"Who might that be?"

"Retired Officer McCarthy. I'll call him and ask if he'll see us. We can't ignore this and I know he was sincere when offering to help."

"I'll go with you, Tina. Try to arrange a time after hours or on the weekend when I'm off."

"You'll like McCarthy, Stan. He's on our side."

Calling Officer McCarthy, Tina told him that there were new developments that needed to be explored. "I'd like your advice," she said and asked if she could bring her fiancée. "Stanley and I are getting married in June."

"Congratulations! By all means bring Stanley. I'd like to meet your young man. Since I'm retired, and home all day, you pick the day and time."

"Is tomorrow evening too soon? Stan gets off at five. We could start out for your place as soon as he leaves work and should be there by seven. We'll take you out to dinner, but you'll have to suggest a restaurant."

"Tomorrow at seven is fine."

They ate at a diner. It was the only eating establishment open near McCarthy's house serving customers at that hour. After the introductions and being seated in a comfortable booth, Tina proceeded to synopsize the events of the last several weeks.

When done with her story, Stan said, "I'm afraid my girl has irritated some powerful people by insisting on answers regarding the murder of her parents. I hope these same people aren't aware that Tina knows what she knows, but I think it's time that someone be told of her suspicions and summations. Do you agree?"

Retired Officer McCarthy owned that Tina's concerns regarding Detective McDonald were well founded. "You don't have any proof, and it is possible that he's being manipulated by that Lombardo woman, but if there is corruption in both Chicago and St. Louis police departments, it certainly would not be a good idea for Tina to go to them with her theories."

"Agreed,' said Stan as he protectively took Tina's hand.

"Larry is in great danger if he makes any more appearances and I don't think he will.   Regarding McDonald's recent promotion, it may have been a bribe encouraging him to change sides.   One doesn't usually go from officer to detective so quickly.   If anything, the promotion should have gone to Miss Lombardo.   She's the one with the seniority and connections."

"The pieces of the puzzle are coming together, Officer, but I need someone to prove or disprove my theories.   Stan and I are about to be married and begin a life together.   I'd like it to be a life that lets me pick up a phone or walk down the street without fear.   I was thinking about abandoning the promise made to my parents, but these latest developments make it impossible for me to let go.   Have you any thoughts as to where I can go for help?   I need someone who will be on my side—someone I can trust."

"Let me tell you about something that happened to me after I last saw you, Miss Cappo.   It appears I rubbed someone the wrong way.   Wanting to help Jim McDonald, I had asked one of my remaining friends in the department to look into some old files…"

"Which prompted you to visit Enrico Gomez and John Jacobs who told you about the Uptown Boys and the neighborhood gangs. Were there repercussions?"

"You might say that.   Shortly after seeing Enrico and John, I had a visitor.   He introduced himself as an inspector from the Planning Department.   Apparently he didn't like a patio I had added to my house ten years ago. The next thing I knew, there was an order from the building department to destroy it.   Ordinarily I'd have been asked to pay a fine, but these guys wouldn't let me off the hook that easily.   Nothing would do but for me to tear up the concrete and have it hauled away."

"Like I've been telling Tina, these guys don't fool around. We're not here to get you further involved, Officer McCarthy, but hoped you'd know who would be interested in Tina's discoveries."

"There is a friend in the FBI who might be able to help. Maybe it's out of his jurisdiction, but I'll give you his name and you can take it from there. Other than that, Miss Cappo, I suggest you lay low. You're not Sherlock Holmes and should leave the detective work to the professionals. Get married. Move out of town. Take on a new identity if you can."

Thanking retired officer McCarthy for his time, Tina and Stan said 'good-bye,' promising to keep in touch.

17

The earliest appointment Tina and Stan could arrange with Mr. Stone, McCarthy's FBI friend, was the following Friday. There had been no messages or phone calls in the interim causing Tina to have second thoughts. Was she opening Pandora's box? She was tempted to cancel, but Stan thought they had gone too far to back out.

Agreeing that they'd better keep the appointment, they found themselves being ushered into Mr. Stone's office. "Nice to meet you, Miss Cappo, Mr. Turner." Everyone seated, the agent got to the point immediately.

"Officer McCarthy tells me you have a theory that might be of interest to the bureau. He has piqued my curiosity and I'm anxious to hear what you have to say."

"It's a long story, Mr. Stone. I assume Officer McCarthy told you that my parents were murdered about two years ago and that I have been on a crusade to find the assassins."

"Yes, and that you are being harassed with phone calls, strange messages and threats. I'm sorry for your loss and know it's been difficult for you. People can be cruel and ruthless when someone stands in the way of something they want.   I trust you've documented whatever has occurred."

Tina told Mr. Stone that she had kept a log of everything she could remember, and that it had not been difficult to reconstruct the annoying events since most could be traced to before, after or during her overseas tours. "I've also recorded, for your information," Tina said, "events of the last several weeks which led me to suspect that my problems could be tied to Chicago's Planning Commissioner."

"So I understand. Tell me what happened."

Having lost confidence and trust in Detective McDonald, Tina confessed that she and her friend, Mara had disguised themselves and gone to St. Louis to spy. "While there we discovered that Detective McDonald, who was supposed to be looking into the murders of my parents, and a fellow officer, Lucy Lombardo, were a twosome. It occurred to us then, being so close, that they might have shared information and that Lucy could be the one responsible for the leaks concerning my whereabouts."

"A possibility unless it was McDonald himself."

"True, but a few days ago Mara stumbled onto something that really shook us up. Going for a building permit in downtown Chicago, Mara found herself in an elevator with Lucy Lombardo. Aware that Lucy would not know her, she followed her out of the elevator to the office of Anthony Lombardo, Chicago's Planning Commissioner. Lucy Lombardo is his daughter."

Trying to digest what he had heard, Mr. Stone's phone interrupted.   He was needed at a meeting. Apologizing for having to run off, Mr. Stone asked Tina to leave him with all the backup material she had. "I'll go over everything and get back to you in a few days, but I do want you to know that the bureau has been interested in Anthony

Lombardo for several years. We know he has influential friends, and it's no secret, they help each other. Some of these friends may have found their way into police precincts and may be mob connected. We haven't been able to prove it, but your input, Miss Cappo, may help put some of these people away."

"Is there any way you can keep Tina's name out of this?" asked Stan concerned for her welfare.

Mr. Stone gathered together the papers needed for his meeting and walked them to the elevator. "Miss Cappo's parents were murder victims. That's why they keep close tabs on her. We'll do whatever we can to protect her."

"It's hard to figure how it's done, Mr. Stone, but someone is always one step ahead of Tina. Even this latest move—someone had Tina's number even before she'd unpacked her toiletries. We're getting married soon and would like to think we could keep our next address a secret. Any suggestions?"

"For one thing, get your marriage license out of state."

"We've already worked that out, Mr. Stone.

"Good! In addition, Miss Cappo, you should immediately apply for new credit cards and licenses under, what will be, your married name. If and when you move, do not leave a forwarding address. When you give up your present apartment, try to change your appearance. Pretend you're in a witness protection program." Noticing Tina's look of despair, Mr. Stone said, "It's not the end of the world, Miss Cappo. They claim blonds have more fun. Here's your chance to prove it.

"As for you, Mr. Turner, you must avoid Miss Cappo, her apartment and even your brother since he is married to Miss Cappo's friend, until you find new living quarters. When Miss Cappo takes on her new identity, becomes Mrs. Turner and moves again, she'll be out of sight, and hopefully, out of mind. They'll eventually forget about her. In the interim, Miss Cappo, stay with your friend or you might want to sign up for another European tour."

With these final words, Mr. Stone left them to go down the hall to his meeting. Tina, turning to Stan, was visibly upset. "You heard what he said. We're not allowed to be together until all is ready for us to go into hiding. It's not fair—not to you, me or anybody."

"Don't worry, Honey. We'll work it out. Mr. Stone is right. We mustn't be seen together. The bad guys don't know me. I've only recently come to Chicago and, even then, as a commuter. If anyone has noticed me in your building, I could have been a tenant or visitor in another apartment. At least until we're ready to make a move, we have no choice but to avoid each other."

Tina had mixed emotions. She hated having to avoid Stanley and leaving her apartment again. The thought of giving up her identity didn't sit well with her either. On the other hand, she was happy to have found an ally in Mr. Stone and that he had taken her seriously.

"I really had hoped we could stay in this apartment until we were ready to buy Alex and Mara's condo. It would have been ideal for us, Stan, but it looks like we'll have to abandon that idea. According to Mr. Stone, until you find a place where I can become a brown-eyed blond, all bets are off. We couldn't buy that condo even if it were available since my enemies, aware that Mara and I are friends, would quickly see through my disguise.

"It's going to be tough staying away from you, honey, but I'll start looking for a place in the suburbs immediately. Meanwhile, you'll be safe with Mara."

"That's okay for me, but you will be alone and isolated just when you're about to start a new job."

"All the more reason for me to find an apartment quickly, Sweetheart. Personally, I can't wait to move in with that brown-eyed blond recommended by Mr. Stone."

"It isn't funny, Stan. I want to be with you."

I've been thinking, Tina. Our plans are to be married in June. Would you consider going to Vegas for a civil ceremony now? We could follow it up with a formal church wedding in Vermont as scheduled."

"Las Vegas won't be necessary, Stan. There's no reason to wait until we're married to begin our new life. All we need is a location away from here and I hope that won't take too long. I'll stay with Mara and Alex for now, but you realize, neither of us will be able to see even them when we go into hiding—not until they also disappear into the house they've bought."

Mr. Stone had promised to call, and true to his word, reached Stan at his office several days later. "Miss Cappo's notes have created quite a stir in the department, Mr. Turner. I've gone over them with my superiors and all agree that her theories, as outlined, have merit. It's true that the Commissioner is of the wrong age to fit the picture of Tony Luppo, but Commissioner Lombardo has a son. He is Lucy Lombardo's brother. He could be the missing link. I have a picture of Mr. Lombardo, taken with his son, and would like to have Miss Cappo look at it."

"Tina told me she never saw Tony Luppo. Neither did she see any of Larry's friends or family members."

"Tony Luppo may have been using another name. I'll have the picture sent to your office, Mr. Turner. You can let me know if it rings a bell after Miss Cappo looks at it."

Before hanging up, Mr. Stone confided that the FBI was making plans to move one of their men into Detective McDonald's St. Louis precinct. "We think the Lombardo family has influence there and in other cities as well. It will take time, but thanks to Miss Cappo, we're optimistic about building a case against the Commissioner and his entourage."

Stan cautiously entered Tina's apartment that night making certain that he had not been observed. Tina was packing. "I feel like a refuge, Stan—someone without a country. Every time I think I'm settled, I have to move again. Will it ever end?"

"We're getting closer, Honey. Don't give up now. Mr. Stone called today and said all concerned are impressed with the information you've given them. The FBI is working on placing one of their men into the St. Louis police department. His job will be to determine who's giving and taking orders, as well as where McDonald and Lucy Lombardo fit in. Apparently the FBI feels that there is a mob connection—not only in St. Louis precincts, but in other city police departments. By the way, Mr. Stone is sending you a picture. It appears Commissioner Lombardo has a son. He felt you might recognize him. Maybe he'll turn out to be Tony Luppo."

"I don't hold out much hope of that since I never saw the man."

"You've started packing?"

"Yes! I stopped at the condo today and told Mara about our meeting with Mr. Stone. She's happy to have me, but I'm concerned about where you will go."

"I've been thinking about that, and have an idea. However, you'll have to call Detective McDonald as soon as possible. Tell him that you're giving up the apartment and staying with Mara. Make some excuse."

"He knows I'm getting married. Thankfully he doesn't know who you are or that you're related to Mara's husband. I'll tell him we met in England and that we plan to live in Europe after we're married. To assure that he leaves me alone, I'll tell him that I'm escorting a final tour for Cartrite leaving next week. They'll back me up if I alert them."

"That sounds plausible. I'm sure no one will want to follow you overseas. Now, getting back to my great idea. How would it be if I sublet this furnished apartment when you leave? That way, all you have to do is move your clothes and personal things. We should be able to accomplish that, inconspicuously, in a few hours. Too bad my car is in my parents' garage, but Mara won't mind helping you."

"When did you get a car, Stanley? You never mentioned having one."

"The car is about five years old. Public transportation in Boston is good while parking is impossible. It's been stored at my parent's farm. Not that it helps now, but I'll drive it to Chicago next weekend. We'll definitely need wheels when we move to the suburbs."

"You're right, but getting back to your idea about sub-letting. Why didn't I think of that? It's a wonderful idea, Stan. Having a strange car around here will be all the more reason for people to expect to see a new face coming out of this apartment. Better get new plates though."

When Stanley returned from work the next night, Tina was packed and ready for the move to her friend's condo. Mara would be coming for her after dinner. Tina was sad knowing there would be no more shared dinners in what had been her apartment. "I know, Stanley, that it's necessary to avoid eachother for the time being, but I don't like it."

"It's only temporary my love. We'll be married soon and then we can both disappear. Oh, I almost forgot. That picture Mr. Stone promised to send. It arrived at my office today." Taking it from his attache case, he handed Tina a picture of Commissioner Lombardo standing next to his son.

Prepared to be disappointed, Tina stared at the picture and said, "Dear God! I do know that man."

"From St. Louis? Was he at your hotel?"

"No! Not there! He's that young man who was such a pain on our Egypt and Greek Island tour. His name is, or was, Jason Thomas. Remember my telling you that he was very unfriendly and didn't mix with anyone? He left the tour early and at considerable expense to himself. He was one of those well enough to go into the pyramids with me when all the lights went out."

"The day you were shoved and fell? You said it was pitch black dark. It might have been he who pushed you. It could have been a deliberate assault."

"I don't know. Maybe it was an accident. Everyone panicked in the total darkness and it's possible that someone lost their footing and ran into me."

"I don't think it's accidental that the Commissioner's son was on your tour, Tina."

"Now that I know he's not Jason Thomas, but Anthony Lombardo, Jr., I'm afraid I have to agree with you."

"I saw you off in New York when you left for Egypt. Looking back, there were two men suspiciously staring at you when we walked to the departure gate. Could they

301

have been with your unfriendly tourist?" Noticing that Tina had turned very pale, Stan asked, "Are you okay, Sweetheart?"

"Not exactly! What you're suggesting is frightening. Thank God I'm no longer on my own. With you, Mara, Alex and the FBI in my corner there's comfort, but we'd better waste no time converting me into that blond bombshell we've talked about. Promise you'll recognize me when we meet on the street or in a restaurant."

"Do you have to cut your hair, Tina?"

"Yes! A wig over all this hair was a little hard to deal with when Mara and I were in St. Louis, but I'll try not to take off more than necessary."

Mara arrived and Tina reluctantly went with her leaving Stan in the apartment she was deserting. Tina planned to live as inconspicuously as possible until she and Stan could be reunited. The following week would take her to Canada where she had appointments with four hotel managers. She welcomed the diversion knowing Stan would be working and apartment hunting. Maybe he'd get lucky and find a suitable place quickly.

Prepared to tell some lies, Tina called Detective Jim the next morning. "Hello Jim. Thought I'd check in with you. Do you have anything new for me?"

"I'm afraid not, Tina. It's been very busy here, but nothing to do with you. Didn't you tell me you were getting married? Did the guy dump you, I hope?"

"That's not nice, but no such luck, Jim. We're getting married in June."

"I don't think you ever told me who you were marrying or where you met this Mr. Wonderful?"

Having decided to tell Jim that they had met on her Great Britain tours, Tina said, "He's originally from New York, but likes London and so do I. We're going to live there. You'll get my new address when we're settled. Meanwhile, until our wedding day, I'm staying with Mara. I've vacated my apartment. No sense paying rent there when I've agreed, as a favor, to run a tour for my agency starting next week. It will keep me out of the country until just before the wedding."

"Good of you to let me know. I'll leave a message with Mara if there's anything to report. I guess there's not much left for me to say other than I wish things had worked out differently for us. We could have had a blast." Preparing to hang up, Jim added, "Have a good life, dollface. See you around."

Tina and Stan managed to sneak in a few short lunches near his place of business before Tina left for Calgary. Her appointments with hotel managers went as well as those on the American side of the border. All were cooperative, enthusiastic and eager to make deals. Tina left promising to review all the facts and figures presented and reminded them that she would be returning shortly with her new husband to test the facilities. She expected, after the honeymoon, to distribute the brochure describing her new tour entitled,

THE GREAT ROCKY MOUNTAINS
UNITED STATES AND CANADA

Stan flew to Boston for his weekly meeting. Arranging to be there on Friday, he was able to pick up the car at the home of his parents, visit for a while and then drive back to, what had been, Tina's apartment.

While Tina was away, Mara talked to her realtor and learned of an apartment that Stan and her friend might

303

find to their liking. Checking it out on his return and knowing Tina would be pleased, Stanley signed a lease and paid the required rent and security. It was two weeks later that neighbors watched a handsome young couple move in. According to observations and descriptions, the woman was pretty, blond and very petite. "Too bad she hides behind those thick glasses," said the neighbor across the hall.

"What glasses," responded her husband, smirking. "I saw just a beautiful body. I'd give it a perfect ten. By the way, the gentleman introduced himself as Stanley Turner. It appears the couple are newly married."

"One thing about Mara, she always finds great places for us to move into," said Tina when back in town. "Unfortunately, my acquaintance with them is always short lived."

"I promise, Sweetheart, there will be no more moves until we're ready to buy a house of our own. It's going to work this time. Those bothering you will lose interest in the daughter of Mr. and Mrs. Cappo when they learn you've married and are living in England. We are known here as Mr. and Mrs. Turner. Having been careful, there's no way for anyone to make the connection."

"It's so good to be together again, Stan. I hope we'll soon be able to ditch the disguises. Having to stay away from Mara and your brother is hard and I really miss them. Mara calls and we talk on the phone, but it's not the same."

"It shouldn't be much longer, my love. When Alex and Mara get into their new house, everything will be better. I only hope no one traces them to their address."

Tina assured Stan that Mara and Alex had been and would continue to be cautious when checking on their house. "When the house is ready, they plan to move in the middle of night just like we did. Remember Stan, it's me they want. McDonald knows that I plan to live in Europe and that I'm presently on a tour. He won't be interested any longer in what happens at Alex and Mara's condo."

Stan called Mr. Stone with the news that Tina did recognize the man in the picture with Commissioner Lombardo. She knew him as Jason Thomas, who had been on her tour of Egypt and the Greek Islands.

"Oh, yes! In her notes, Tina explained that he had left the tour ahead of schedule and was with the group when she fell in the pyramids—that he kept himself aloof from the tourists throughout the trip."

"I'm convinced, Mr. Stone, that this man had a reason for being on that tour and not because of the sights. Maybe he had instructions to get rid of Tina somehow. Or he might have been there to check up on her. Whatever his purpose, I don't think it was in Tina's best interest."

"My guess," replied Mr. Stone, "is that he was on the trip to observe and perhaps frighten her. If his purpose had been to do harm, you can be sure he'd have succeeded. Anyway, thanks to Miss Cappo, we now know that Jason Thomas and Anthony Lombardo, Jr. are one and the same. Perhaps, using another alias, he will also turn out to be Tony Luppo, Larry's homosexual friend."

Before hanging up, Stan told Mr. Stone that he had found an apartment and that they were living happily in a community away from the city. Tina had gone into disguise mode. They were known to their neighbors as newly married Mr. and Mrs. Turner from Florida. Mr. Stone added to his notes details of where he could reach them and was assured that they had carefully covered their tracks. It was Tina and Stan's intention to remain incognito in this apartment until given the word that it was safe to do otherwise.

About a week later, Mr. Stone called to inform Tina that they had succeeded in getting an FBI man into the St. Louis Police Department.

"Our man will have to move slowly. It won't happen overnight, but he'll be watching Lucy Lombardo and Detective McDonald very closely. We expect they will lead him to those in the department who might be taking orders from Commissioner Lombardo. I'll get back to you with developments as they occur," he said.

18

.

The months leading up to the wedding went quickly. Tina and Stanley were content in their new surroundings. Stan had taken his possessions out of storage and together with Tina's belongings, their larger apartment was again filled to capacity. Some of the overflow had found it's way to Mara who would soon be furnishing an entire house.

Tina's wedding gown was ready for a final fitting. She had chosen an off-white Chantilly lace dress that was form fitting from the demure neckline to below the hips where it flared until reaching the ground. Iridescent beading outlined the flowers that were patterned into the lace. The sleeves, also lace, were long and tapered. Tina's perfect figure was accentuated due to the bias cut of the dress. Modeling for the dressmaker and Mara, all agreed that further alterations were not needed.

On her head, Tina planned to wear a wreath consisting of tiny ivory and pink roses. Flowers in her bridal bouquet, matching those in her wreath, would be larger in size.

The seamstress out of earshot, Tina turned to Mara and whispered, "The wig comes off on our wedding day. I might have to hide the photographer's pictures for the rest of my life, but Stan is going to know it's me he married."

Since the ceremony was to be far removed from Chicago, Tina felt safe in wanting to be herself. Stan's folks would not recognize her as a blond with brown contacts and ask for an explanation.

Tina and Stan's wedding day was to be in two weeks. The men had been measured for tuxedos and were all ready. As for Mara, the Maid of Honor, she was quite pregnant and relieved that her friend had not scheduled a later date to be married. Having anticipated her condition, she'd wisely chosen a high-waisted, full-cut gown. It was shocking pink. Modeling before Tina, both agreed that the color and style was perfect for the shape she was in.

"I still can't believe you're pregnant," Tina said as she studied her friend from every angle.

"Being tall has it's advantages, Tina. The added pounds get spread out over a larger surface."

"I guess that means I'll be in trouble when it's my turn to get pregnant."

The friends laughed at the picture Tina described and then changed the subject to talk about Alex and Mara's new house. The closing was scheduled for the coming Friday. They expected to move in before Tina and Stan's wedding day.

Time was flying. Only ten days remained until the big day. Renovations on Mara and Alex's house had begun. Periodically checking, they were careful not to be followed. Like Tina and Stan, whose apartment was about ten miles from their new house, they planned to disappear in the dead of night.

It had rained for two days, but June 30, when it finally came, could not have been more perfect. The sun shone brightly, and it was not hot or humid. The bride and groom, attended by Mara and Alex, beamed as they met at the altar and exchanged vows. Although Tina and Stan had already been living together, there was something magical about the words, "I now pronounce you man and wife" spoken by a minister in a small town church where all in attendance were eager to offer best wishes and congratulations.

Stan's parents, although aware that Tina's mother and father had been murdered, did not know their sons, together with Tina and Mara, had found it necessary to go into hiding. Telling them would have caused needless anxiety and all had agreed that nothing should come between them and a perfect day.

The ceremony went smoothly as did the reception at the hotel. Everyone had a wonderful time eating, drinking and dancing. Then it was over. Friends and neighbors went home. Tina and Stanley had reservations at a hotel near the airport since they would be flying to Denver early the next morning.

Alex had business in Toronto and started his drive in that direction. Expecting to be away for three days, it was a good opportunity for Mara to visit with his parents. On his return Alex would pick up his wife. Together, they'd fly back to Chicago. With everyone but Mara gone, the Turner house was very quiet. It would become even more so when Mara left. Mr. and Mrs. Turner announced their plans to visit both sons and daughters-in-law upon the arrival of the new baby. It would be their first grandchild.

The honeymooners were on their way following the itinerary Tina had arranged. They expected surprises, but not the very first day. Stan went to pick up the rental car that would be their transportation for the next three weeks.

It was almost identical to the car Stan had brought back from the farm - a yellow convertible that would barely accommodate them and the small cooler containing snacks. Amused, Tina asked, "Are you sure we need such a big car? Any idea where we'll put the luggage?"

"It's the only convertible they had, Sweetheart. You may as well know now that I have a thing about convertibles. You're going to love the sun on your face and the wind blowing through your hair."

"How about sunburn and windburn? Do you have a thing about that too?"

"Not necessarily, but think about the snapshots we'll get. There will be nothing between us and the magnificent scenery surrounding us."

"Or the big black bears as they climb in to get out of the rain that comes down in buckets."

The words were hardly out of Tina's mouth when it started to rain. At first there were only a few sprinkles. Then came the deluge. Before either of them could figure out how to unconvert the convertible, they were soaked to the skin, and in the mountains of Estes Park, very cold. Fortunately the rain stopped almost as quickly as it had begun. The sun came out again, drying them off, and the drive through Rocky Mountain National Park proved to be even more spectacular than Tina had remembered.

The days loafing around Glenwood Hot Springs were a honeymooner's delight. Each morning the bed was made only to find it in disarray half an hour later. Tina and Stan were constantly changing clothes as they prepared to swim in the pool, use the sauna, have a massage or go for meals. Their naked bodies were always a temptation to take time out for playful wrestling.

"It was clever of you to arrange a stay here for a few days, my Darling."

"I knew you'd expect more than nature walks and scenery on our honeymoon, Stan."

"What would give you that idea? You know I love nature and beautiful scenery. I love you, and in my opinion, you're right up there with the Grand Tetons and anything else you've planned for us. Nature made you and you're the best there is."

"It's good to know where I stand, my love, but wait until you see what's on the agenda for tomorrow."

"Promises, promises!"

"I'm talking about our itinerary, Stan. Tomorrow we go to Dinosaur National Monument. The park is spread over 210,000 acres. First we'll go to the quarry where tourists can actually see prehistoric dinosaur bones being carefully excavated from the huge rock wall that is one side of the visitor center. In the afternoon we'll drive to the other end of the park and take a long hike on one of the trails leading to a peak high above the Green River."

The day at Dinosaur National Monument was as exciting as Tina had promised. "Why have I never before heard of this place? Are they trying to keep it a secret? I know your tourists will love it and how about Mara? She'd love to see what goes on here. It's right down her alley."

"She'd be in her glory," agreed Tina. I can see her hanging on the wall chipping away with the best of those paleozoologists guys."

Before leaving the area, Tina and Stan signed up for some whitewater rafting. It turned out to be more exciting than Tina had planned, but Stan thought it was terrific. The rubber raft hit a rock causing it to nearly capsize. While all were already wet, they were now drenched and very cold. Tina made a mental note to adjust the tour she was planning to market. Her itinerary for the public would be changed from rafting to a gentle float trip and barbecue lunch. Whitewater was not for everyone and would be offered as an option, but only for the brave and adventurous.

The Grand Tetons were Tina and Stan's next destination. It wasn't long before they saw moose and deer. Fearful of running into a bear while hiking on the trails, they sang and made loud noises. That bear were present could be seen by their tracks and droppings. Tina was relieved when reaching Jenny Lake and Hidden Falls. Just beyond, they could wait for a boat that would return them to the lodge.

At the dock, they met a young mountain climber who was visibly shaken. He explained that his companion had just been airlifted from the area having fallen from the snow-capped mountain above them. "When I heard his scream as he lost footing and bounced his way to the bottom, I thought he was done for, but he survived. The medics told me that he'd broken his leg and probably some ribs. He was lucky. The bones will heal in time."

Asking if he would climb again, the young man's response was, "Certainly! I'll be up there tomorrow, but won't be telling my parents about this incident."

Leaving the beautiful Tetons, Tina and Stan were ready for Yellowstone National Park. Although it was July, weather enroute to Old Faithful Lodge, where they had reserved a cabin, was threatening. "The rustic cabins look so romantic in the brochure," had been Tina's words to Stanley when planning the trip.

Anxious to see Old Faithful blast off, it was their first stop on arrival. Within minutes, right on schedule, the mighty geyser put on her display before the audience sitting in awe. Tina and Stan would see it again, but now they were hungry and went into the lodge for dinner. To their dismay, the rapidly approaching storm had caused a power outage. No hot meals were available. They had to settle for the last two bowls of lukewarm chile.

When Tina and Stan went to their cabin, they discovered not only the lodge was affected by the storm. The entire park was without heat and electricity. It was very cold in their cabin. Having nothing better to do, they went to bed.

"I guess some people would consider going to bed so early a hardship," said Tina.

"Luckily we're honeymooners, but 'Baby It's Cold Outside,' sang Stanley."

"Inside too," echoed Tina. "Did you remember to pack our longjohns?"

"No, but come into my arms, Sweetheart. I'll keep you warm as toast."

It was not enough being in Stan's arms. The Storm brought frigid air to Wyoming, and before the night ended, Tina and Stan had layered whatever clothing they could find in their luggage. The cabins were equipped with bunk beds. They took the mattresses from both bunks, stacked one on top of the other, covered them with all the towels and bedding they could find and then went to bed. Although huddled together, they were still cold. Even love couldn't keep them warm. It was a night they would never forget. Welcoming daybreak when it finally came, they longed for a cup of hot coffee. If only there was some to be had. As for a shower, forget about it. Even a wet wash cloth was out of the question. Water from the tap was the closest thing to ice. Shivering, they joked about their predicament and had left-over muffins for breakfast. Then they walked around the geyser basin and again watched Old Faithful erupt.

The freak storm continued to blow for another twenty-four hours, but didn't stop nature from doing what Tina and Stan had come to see. Geysers were bubbling and shooting off steam everywhere. Tina and Stan marveled at the fragility of the ground beneath their feet. Even in the lake there were geysers. It brought to mind a park ranger's story told on her previous visit. He said that fishermen would catch fish in the lake and then cook them by lowering the line into the steaming geysers.

There was sleet by the time they arrived at the Paint Pots and Black Caldrons. Not deterred, they carefully walked on the protective boardwalks. Yellowstone Park, from south to north extends over one hundred miles. Heading north, the weather began to improve. Their next reservation was in a lodge—not a cabin. Power had been restored and the honeymooners were assured of a comfortable night. Again Tina made herself a mental note. Cabins were out. Her tourists would have reservations only in lodges and hotels. Needless to say, in this case it would not have made a difference since there had been no power anywhere in the park.

It was Tina and Alex's third day in the park and all was back to normal. They stopped to see and take pictures of Yellowstone Falls and what is known as "The Grand Canyon of Yellowstone." Their day ended at Mammoth Hot Springs. "It's the furthest north in the park and another one of it's wonders."

"I don't believe I've ever heard of it, Tina. Do people go in the waters like we did at Glenwood?"

"No! You'll have to see it for yourself. It's hard to explain. Mammoth Hot Springs is wet and slippery. It looks like a pastel-colored glass mountain. Some describe it as a cave that's inside out. Minerals keep layering on top of what is below always changing and growing.'

Tina's Promise

As they slowly approached, Tina pointed to the left and said, "Believe it or not, Stan, the last time I was here, that icy looking stuff was a roadway. The mountain changes from day to day. We'll walk around the boardwalk after we get settled in at the hotel. I know you'll be fascinated."

"I can understand why you've always been excited about this part of the United States, Tina. Do you realize we've been away from home over a week and not once have you mentioned our other life?"

"I haven't thought about it at all, Stan, and it feels really good to be free from fear. I know we'll soon have to go back to being that other couple—the nice tall man with the little blonde wife—but I hope the disguise won't be necessary much longer. Tell me! Has the trip, so far, met with your expectations, Stan? Did I exaggerate?"

"It's everything you've led me to believe and I'm really happy to be seeing it with you."

"From here on everything will be new to me as well. According to what I've heard and read, the best is yet to come, Stan."

"Every day with you gets better than the day before, Sweetheart. Don't know how much more I can stand, but I'll keep trying."

In Montana they stayed two nights at a lodge in Glacier National Park. The drive on Going to the Sun Highway was not only beautiful, but exciting since there remained a great deal of snow on the switchbacks leading higher and higher through the mountains. "It's as though the road ahead falls off the face of the earth," said Stan.

"That's probably why they call this 'Going to the Sun Highway'," answered Tina.

315

Another two nights were spent in Many Glacier Hotel where the waiters and waitresses were all students of music working summer jobs. During the day, instrumentalists could be found outdoors practicing. After serving dessert at the end of the dinner meal, the entire staff would gather around the piano to perform for the guests. For Tina, having studied piano and violin, this was a special treat.

"You never told me you play the piano," said Stan shocked that there were still things that he didn't know about his wife.

"My parents gave me a baby grand for my sixteenth birthday. I'd been taking lessons for a few years and was doing quite well. Regretfully, the piano disappeared along with our hotel."

"You'll have one again, Tina—and that's a promise."

"Forget it, Stan. An instrument that size would never fit in our apartment and we'd be forced to move again."

"Well, it's the first thing we'll buy for our house when we're ready to take that step."

"It can wait. When we get home, I'll be busy putting this tour package together. There wouldn't be time to play piano, even if I had one. How about this hotel, Stan?" Tina asked, changing the subject since the piano had been an important part of her life and was bringing back memories of her lonely childhood. "Do you think my tourists will find it as enchanting as I do?"

"Between the location and the wonderful staff, they won't want to move on. Except that I know there's more to come, I don't want to leave either."

"Tomorrow we stay at the Prince of Wales Hotel in Waterton Lakes, Alberta, Canada." Tina explained that the hotel was situated at the edge of a beautiful lake. They had reservations for two nights allowing for a leisurely boat ride. "Then we head for Jasper National Park. I understand it's a very scenic drive. According to the brochure, every turn in the road presents another photo opportunity. After Jasper we go to Miette Hot Springs. Are you ready for a repeat of Glenwood? We'll be there for three whole days. There will be time to relax, swim, go into the sauna and make mad passionate love. What could be better? We might even take a long walk in the woods. This time of the year, there's daylight until almost midnight."

Like all good things, even a honeymoon has to end. They would have a few more days in Banff and Lake Louise and then leave for home from Calgary.

Most everything had gone according to plan, and except for some weather problems, was a vacationer's delight. There had been scenery, variety, good food and hotels with character. Tina was convinced that a fourteen day version would be appealing to the traveling public.

"I hope the tour agencies will see it that way, Stan. That's the first hurdle we'll have to cross. If they are interested, I know people will come."

Back in Chicago the real world awaited them. Tina was again a brown-eyed blond. There was a message from Agent Stone on the answering machine. "Got your message, Mr. Stone," Tina said responding.

"Glad to have you back, Miss Cappo—I mean Mrs. Turner. From the sound of your voice, I'd say your vacation was a happy experience."

The small talk behind him, Mr. Stone proceeded to tell Tina that the agency had successfully placed one of their FBI operatives into McDonald's St. Louis precinct. "His real name is Ronald Tate, but down there they know him as Robert Taylor."

"Mr. Taylor wasted no time befriending Miss Lombardo and Detective McDonald. The trio are already good drinking buddies. It appears McDonald couldn't make it one night, leaving Miss Lombardo and Taylor to themselves. After a few beers, Lucy confided that she had a brother in Chicago's Mercy Hospital dying of Aids. 'I try to see him as often as I can,' Lucy told our man, adding that it was depressing having to make the trip alone. Mr. Taylor took it as a hint and volunteered to keep her company the next time she planned to visit her brother."

"Why would he want to do that?" asked Tina.

"It could be an opportunity to meet Lucy's father, the Commissioner. Lombardo might make him an offer he couldn't refuse."

"You're losing me, Mr. Stone. An offer to do what?"

"To join their operation, perhaps. There's no telling what could turn up if our man makes an impression on Lombardo, Sr."

"Do you really believe Mr. Lombardo could be conned by an imitation police officer?"

"He's a good actor. Robert Taylor has been trained to play many parts. He'll ask tough questions, Mrs. Turner, and be on the lookout for anything out of the ordinary. If he meets the Commissioner, he'll do everything he can to gain his confidence."

"What about Detective McDonald? I thought it was Lucy Lombardo and McDonald who have a romance going."

"They do. Taylor hangs out with them, but that's it. As for Taylor going to Chicago with Miss Lombardo, I believe she wants her father to meet him. We hope it will happen."

"Lucy's brother is in a bad way," Tina said. "I don't want to make judgments, but his diagnosis fits in with the homosexual theory. If Larry was involved with him, he too could be having problems with his health by now. Could that be the reason for the notes under my door? If he has symptoms of Aids, he might be regretting his involvement with those that destroyed us."

"You could be right, Mrs. Turner. I'm encouraged that there have been no recent disturbances in your life. It looks like you've succeeded in eluding your harassers by disappearing, but don't give up that blond wig or get careless until we're sure. I'll get back to you if there's anything new to report, but call me if you need me."

Mr. Robert Taylor, known to the FBI as Ronald Tate, was a clever man. His dossier had been planned and rehearsed so that no one could trip him up. Having been extensively interviewed by both the police Captain and his first assistant, they sized him up as potentially "one of them." This meant he could be bought and trusted to be loyal to their cause. Once accepted into the inner sanctum, it didn't take long for Officer Taylor to confirm that Detective McDonald and Officer Lombardo were part of the in crowd.

"Play your cards right," said Officer Lombardo as the trio were relaxing one night, "and you'll go far."

"How about you, Lucy? What's holding you back? Any promotions in the foreseeable future? I see you, Jim, made detective recently."

"I'm not as ambitious as our buddy," answered Lucy. "It's different with you macho guys. Right Jim?"

"I repeat, Taylor, all you've got to do is learn to play the game. Don't be a hero. If they tell you to do something, don't question them. Do it. Our bosses know what's best for us and for the guys running the show."

"Yes, I know, Jim, and I'm all for getting along. Let the mavericks stick their necks out."

Mr. Taylor made sure that there would be no mistaking his relationship with Lucy Lombardo. The last thing he wanted was a flirtation and the green-eyed monster. He and Lucy were simply friends and Jim had no cause to feel threatened. Everyone knew it was Jim McDonald who Lucy spent her nights with.

Lucy was a very persuasive person. She needed information about Tina and knew Jim was on the case. Hinting that a promotion might be imminent if he shared information, Jim gave her free reign. He didn't know why Lucy was interested in Tina, but he did get promoted to detective and was now considered to be 'one of them'. As a detective, he was no longer a nobody 'cop', and ripe for a sell out.

It was shortly after his first meeting with Tina that Lucy began asserting herself. She insisted that Jim keep her current on all Tina's moves which allowed her to arrange for annoying telephone calls. While Jim surmised that Lucy was behind Tina's harassment, he had made a deal. From that point he was prepared to close his eyes and take the rewards or punishments that followed.

When, a week later, Officer Taylor accompanied Lucy to see her ailing brother in Chicago, Tony Lombardo, Jr. no longer looked anything like the young man in the picture that had been in FBI files.

Speaking to Agent Stone, Robert Taylor—or Ronald as he was known to the FBI—said, "Lucy's brother is very sick. I suspect he won't be around much longer."

"You're probably right, but what about Commissioner Lombardo? Did you meet him?"

"Not this time. He was away on business. I did get into the family residence though. It's a mansion and very well guarded. There's quite an elaborate security system, and I'll make a bet, there are hidden cameras around. On the wall of the study were many group pictures of kids. I studied them while waiting for Lucy to change. The pictures appeared to be of the same children taken year after year. Except for the vast differences in ages, I'd have thought they were annual school class pictures."

"Perhaps they were of relatives or friends of the family," suggested Mr. Stone. "Or could they have been those 'Uptown Boys' we're heard about?"

"Lucy and Anthony, Jr. were in the center of every picture. There were no other females."

"Do you expect there will be another opportunity to meet the Commissioner, Ronald?"

"I only know that Lucy was disappointed her father was not available. She appeared anxious for us to get together, but when, where and how has to be her call. I can't push it."

"I know, Ron, and I'm not pressuring you. I'm sure there will be another opportunity. Keep me posted."

About to move into their house in the suburbs, Alex and Mara had gradually been taking things from the condo they were vacating. It was now their last day. To move the balance of their furniture and belongings, they rented a U-

Haul. Wanting to disappear, like Tina and Stan, they waited to load the truck until it was dark and quite late. Streets and roads, by the time they left the condo, were deserted assuring them that they'd gotten away unnoticed. They left no forwarding address.

A few days in their new home, they dared to resume a relationship with Tina and Stan. There had been no phone calls and both couples could assume that they were successful in their escapes. Apparently Tina had satisfied her harassers with the story that she'd moved to England and that she'd given up her search for her parents' killer. Tina continued to wear her wig, but otherwise their lives were getting back to normal.

Mara's due date was nearly upon her. Alex had planned his schedule to be in the neighborhood, but babies are not always cooperative. Tina had been recruited as a back-up just in case. It wasn't necessary. Being a perfect little boy, Stephen Michael made his appearance right on schedule. What had been a huge watermelon unbalancing Mara a few hours before was now an adorable eight pound one ounce baby boy with a very healthy pair of lungs.

"Congratulations, you two," said Tina who had been pacing the floor in the waiting room while Alex helped Mara take deep breaths during the delivery. Unfortunately, Stan was in Boston missing all the excitement. He would have loved to see Tina's face as she gently squeezed the baby's cheeks saying, "He's beautiful. And would you believe it? He's already got three chins just like Grandma Turner."

"Speaking of Grandma, I must call the folks. They've been on the phone every day for a week. Mom wants to be here to help when Mara and the baby come home. I understand their bags are packed and standing in the hallway. All they need is my phone call announcing that Stephen Michael arrived."

While waiting to move into their house and to have the baby, Mara had used her time well. A very attractive four-page brochure was ready to be presented to travel agencies. Tina's initial contacts were impressed with the scenic pictures and descriptive copy. All were eager to promote the new tour, but she had only contacted local agencies. Exposure had been limited. To reach the larger, franchised tour agencies, she would need to do bulk mailings and advertise.

"When ready," Tina said to her partner, "we'll want to invite representatives for a preview of what we have to offer. It will be expensive, but necessary. The rewards will be worth the cost. There's nothing like the recommendation of someone who's been there and done that."

Like Mara, Tina had also been busy. She had contacted bus companies and made deals with hotel managers allowing her to price the tour package attractively. Tina was optimistic. "I believe in this idea and in us, Mara. I couldn't do it alone, but with you as my partner, I know we have a winner."

"Yes, we're partners—sink or swim. We're up to our ears in great ideas and not a spare dime in our pockets, but I believe in us too."

"Perhaps I can persuade some nice bank to back us. Remind me, Mara, to think about that tomorrow."

Stan and Alex were proud and supportive. What more could anyone ask? They were married to wives who were lovable, creative, ambitious, and content.

19

Officer Robert Taylor, or Ronald Tate as he was known to the FBI, was with the St. Louis police department about four months when he had his first break. Anthony Lombardo, Jr., in spite of the Commissioner's power and influence, was dying. His father wanted Lucy home and asked that she bring Officer Taylor.

"So this is the Robert Taylor I've been hearing so much about," Commissioner Lombardo said as he was introduced in the crowded hospital waiting room.

"It's an honor to meet you at last," said Robert impressed by the size of this man who was Lucy and Tony's father. A quick guess would put Mr. Lombardo at six and one-half feet weighing approximately three hundred pounds.

Turning to Lucy, Mr. Lombardo said: "I'm glad you're here, Lucy. Tony's been calling for us. The doctors tell me he's running out of time and I think it's best if we go right to his room. Come with us Taylor! Okay if I call you Bob?"

"Sure, Mr. Lombardo."

"It's Commissioner Lombardo. I've worked hard for that title and like the way it sounds."

The scene in Tony's hospital room was depressing. Lucy rushed to her brother's side and embraced him hoping he wouldn't notice her worried expression. An oxygen mask covered Tony's mouth and nose. Only his eyes were able to express his feelings. There were tubes feeding him intravenously, countless monitors and a catheter to eliminate waste. His color was almost gray and his body pencil thin. Tony, Jr. looked like a victim of the holocaust.

While Lucy held and fussed over her brother, Anthony Lombardo, Sr. stood rigidly at the foot of the bed. Aside from "hello" he had said nothing. Keeping a one-sided conversation going was difficult and Lucy tried to get her father to respond to things she was saying, but her father, after fifteen minutes, left with the excuse that he would bring back coffee and donuts. It was as though he'd done his duty by simply being in the room for a few minutes. Officer Taylor was perplexed.

"Forgive Dad," Lucy said to her brother. "You know he doesn't handle sickness well. Some men are like that. If you remember, he acted the same way when Mom told us she had cancer."

Noticing that her brother seemed to be staring at Robert, Lucy suspected that he might not have recognized him from their previous visit. "Remember Robert Taylor, Tony? You met him before. I told you then that he's a police officer like I am and that he hangs out with Jim and me. Jim couldn't make it today but sends his best. Did I tell you that Jim was promoted? He's now a big shot detective."

Anthony made an attempt at a smile, but was too weak to respond. It was good to have visitors. His friends had been loyal in the beginning, but as his condition deteriorated, they gradually found other things to do.

Tony's immune system was collapsing, and while hoping for a miracle, it was obvious even to him that the end was near. He did not want to die alone and knew Lucy was the only one he could count on.

Lucy and Robert had been at the hospital about an hour when they decided it was time to leave. Knowing Lucy would be back in the evening, she was able to persuade her brother to close his eyes and rest. The Commissioner was just returning with the coffee he'd gone to get. "Well, I'll be stopping by tomorrow," he said. "Might as well go back to the house now. Bob can stay with me while you visit your brother tonight, Lucy. As they walked to the car, Lucy's father said, "I'm sure he'll find it more interesting talking to me than sitting in a room with someone he hardly knows."

The Commissioner had no tolerance for sickness, and in truth, had abandoned his son when learning about the life style that caused him to become HIV positive.

When back in St. Louis, Bob called his FBI boss. "I had quite an interesting experience in Chicago this weekend, Mr. Stone."

"Did you get to meet the commissioner this time?"

"I sure did! He's unbelievable—a cold fish. With a son near death, one would think he'd have some compassion. On the contrary, he was impatient and annoyed. I find it hard to understand a person like that."

"It takes practice, but tell me what you learned from those private talks with the Commissioner. Were there any hints about inviting you into the family business?"

"Not specifically, but he asked questions about my background, both work-related and private. He seemed to be impressed with the answers I gave. I had to let him set the pace you know. At this point in our relationship, it wouldn't be prudent to come across as pushy."

"I understand, but you can't blame me for wishful thinking. We really want to nail this guy."

"So do I and am doing everything possible to help you."

Taylor explained that Lucy had spent most of the weekend at the hospital giving him and Lombardo, Sr. plenty of time to get acquainted. Commissioner Lombardo spoke of his family and how proud he was of his children. "They were trained," he said, "to run the family business, but with Tony sick, it will be up to Lucy to carry on when I'm gone."

What kind of business?"

"I'm afraid he brushed me off when I asked, but I got the impression that he has his fingers in many pies."

"Are there more Lombardos?"

"Children? No, just Lucy and Anthony, Jr. Mrs. Lombardo died almost ten years ago, but the Commissioner hinted that there were influential relatives and friends. I suspect many are involved in his business dealings."

"I assume you have reasons for your suspicions."

"Yes, I do. Curious about the many group pictures Lombardo had on the walls of his study, I asked whether they were annual class pictures taken at school. Lombardo told me that the families of his friends socialized throughout the year. It seems a new picture of all the children was taken each year at the Lombardo Christmas party.

"Calling attention to the fact that Lucy was the only female in the photographs, Commissioner Lombardo explained that his daughter was a tomboy whereas girls were usually more interested in dancing and piano lessons.

He said Lucy and the boys formed a club and that they met regularly in the Lombardo house."

"Could that have been the club we think of as 'The Uptown Boys?'"

"That would be my guess. Lombardo did say they sometimes got into trouble, but that it was 'kid stuff.' 'Mischief,' he called it."

"I'm willing to bet they were into more than mischief and that the Commissioner was their inspiration and teacher. There's a world of opportunity out there waiting for talented delinquents and we know from retired Officer McCarthy that these Uptown Boys were no angels.

"And we know that someone was always there to hush up any 'mischief' the kids got into."

"Did you get the impression that Lombardo might want to recruit you, Ron?"

"I believe he's still checking me out. He did mention that my Captain was impressed with me and that I had made some good friends in St. Louis. He hinted at a bright future down the road and said he'd be watching my progress. My instructions, when leaving for St. Louis, were to keep in touch. I tried getting feedback from Lucy, but she was, understandably, preoccupied with her brother's critical condition and only confirmed that her father liked me.'

"You're doing fine, Ron. Sorry, Bob! I keep forgetting you are Robert in St. Louis. Keep up the good work, but be careful. Lombardo is no dummy. I'm sure he's watching you like a hawk. Get back to me if there's anything I should know. Good luck!"

With all the information in front of her, Tina had come to the conclusion that some help in starting her new business would be needed. She made an appointment to see the loan officer of her bank. Prepared with facts, figures and arguments as to why her idea would be a good investment, Tina introduced herself and said, "Thank you for seeing me, Mr. Long. I am in the process of starting my own business and am here asking for a loan."

"What kind of a business do you have in mind, Mrs. Turner?"

"It will take a little explaining. Do you know anything about the travel industry?"

"I've been on a few cruises with my wife, but that's about it. Tell me!"

"You've probably seen the racks of brochures displayed in travel agencies. Many of those brochures contain tour packages that have been negotiated and marketed by someone promoting a particular itinerary. Depending upon their customers' interests and tour availability, agencies recommend trips. I've been a tour guide and have a pretty good idea of what people want. They want good food, clean accommodations, safe transportation, an exciting itinerary and an experienced, well versed tour guide."

"Sounds good so far, but what do you have that's not already on agency shelves?"

"My husband and I have recently returned from a trip through the United States and Canadian Rockies. I planned the itinerary because there was no such trip currently on the market. The scenery was magnificent and our three weeks were more than we could have hoped for. It occurred to me that a similar tour could be marketed to the general public.

"Condensing our itinerary to two weeks, I talked to hotel managers and contacted bus companies. Their reaction to my idea was positive—as a matter of fact they were surprised that the tour had not already been available. I believe, Mr. Long, that my proposed itinerary is special. It will be the answer for travelers who are looking for something new and different. Aside from scenery that is the best to be found in North America, there are first class hotel accommodations. Included are stops at mineral hot springs, a favorite of Europeans.

"I've already contacted travel agencies who agree that it's a tour experience waiting to happen. People will come if it is properly advertised and marketed. That's where I need some help, Mr. Long. My partner and I have prepared a beautiful four-page brochure. As you can see among the papers submitted, it's ready to be circulated. Printing and mailing is expensive."

"It sounds like you've done your homework. What kind of money are you looking for?"

"My husband and I have set aside about $25,000 and would like you to consider a like amount. Literature should go out by the end of November and I'll need money for printing, advertising and postage. Some of the larger agencies, I'll want to see personally. Hopefully they will eventually help subsidize the printing and mailing expense. We want to be ready for our first tour to begin in July, a year from now."

"In addition to your $25,000, do you have any collateral and how do I know you'll succeed?"

'My husband has a good, steady job and I know I'll succeed by the enthusiastic reception I've received from the hotel managers who have given me commitments as well as the agencies I've already spoken to. I've listed everything in my proposal and hope your bank will see this opportunity as I do and back me up. We'll be offering some gratis tours to representatives of franchised agencies and realize these complimentary trips will eat up any profit the first year, but word of mouth is important in the travel business. We'll also be arranging some in-person seminars. Eventually we hope to branch out into the European markets as well."

"I'm impressed, but of course, would want to take everything you've given me to the head of our loan department. I assume your husband is willing to sign on with you."

"Having recently returned from our honeymoon favorably impressed by a similar itinerary, he thinks it's a great idea. The price for a two-week trip has been negotiated and is reasonable. We are confident that the tour will catch on quickly."

"I assume you'll be getting deposits from tourists as they reserve space and then require full payment a month before departure. What about insurance and refunds? Have you thought about air transportation?"

"It's all in the file I'm leaving with you. People will make their own air travel arrangements and can purchase trip insurance. As to liability, we would, of course, have to add that to our cost of doing business."

"Well, Mrs. Turner, I believe that's all I need for now. Give me about a week to get back to you. I might have difficulty corralling the committee that makes final decisions, but if they agree with my thinking, we'll have ourselves a deal."

Tina made a detour to see Mara before going back to the apartment. Not only did she want to tell her of her morning, but she wanted to spend some time with little Stephen Michael.

"He's getting cuter every time I see him. Is he sleeping through the night yet?"

"Not exactly. He's a heavy weight and wants his Momma to feed him every three hours. Considering he takes an hour to be fed, burped and changed, it's a never ending process."

"Why don't you take a little nap after the next feeding. I'll stay here and play with Stevie. Neither Stan nor Alex will be home for dinner tonight. I'll raid the refrigerator and cook us a meal which we'll have when you wake up."

"That sounds heavenly. You're an angel. I feel guilty not helping you knock on doors, but really could use a break today. When Stevie is a little older, I'll make it up to you."

Lucy, Jim and Robert were having drinks when the call came announcing that Lucy's brother had passed away. This time it was Jim who had the weekend free. They made arrangements with the airlines and were packed within the hour. Robert drove them to the airport and then went to work.

"Would you come into my office, Robert?" asked Captain Steiner.

"Sure Captain! What can I do for you?"

"You are friendly with Detective McDonald! Did he ever talk to you about the Cappo murders?"

"I remember him saying something a while back. It was an unsolved case."

"Yes! McDonald was looking into it, but I told him to drop it."

"Could I ask why?"

"The case had whiskers and he wasn't getting anywhere. There were more recent problems to focus on. Did he ever mention the daughter, Tina Cappo?"

"Not that I recall."

"She was pretty pesty, but seems to have quieted down lately. McDonald tells me she got married and moved away. I'd like to have you verify that for me. It's not that I don't believe McDonald, but I'd like to finally put this case to bed."

"It shouldn't be too difficult to find out what Miss Cappo is up to, Captain. I'll check around and get back to you."

It was interesting that Captain Steiner should be concerned with Tina's whereabouts. Even more interesting was a call Officer Taylor received a few days after Tony Lombardo, Jr.'s funeral. The call was from Commissioner Lombardo.

"Bob! It's Anthony Lombardo. Do you have a minute?"

"I'm so sorry about the loss of your son, Commissioner. Wish I could have been there with you and Lucy, but we're short staffed and I couldn't get away."

"I understand. Thanks for trying and for your sympathy. Right now, though, I have a favor to ask."

"Anything!"

"My son had a friend. His name is Larry Hermano. I'd like to find him. He used to work for the Carillion Hotel in St. Louis. I've checked, but he's not there anymore. Since you're working in the neighborhood, you might be able to track him down for me. Just one thing—don't let on to anyone that I'm looking for him."

333

"I understand, Commissioner. It's best that you tell him about your son personally."

"It's really important that I find him, Bob and I'll take care of your expenses."

The time had come for Officer Taylor to call his FBI contact, Agent Stone.

"Things are heating up around here, Mr. Stone."

"Glad you called. It's been some time and I was getting concerned. What's up?"

"For starters, Anthony Lombardo, Jr. died. I couldn't get away, but Lucy and Jim McDonald went to the funeral. Jim is back to work, but I haven't seen him. Anyhow, while they were gone, I had a summons from our esteemed Captain Steiner."

"You're moving up in the world."

"You might say that! He wants me to confirm Detective Jim's story that Tina Cappo is really gone and no longer going to make waves. I plan to wait a few days to get back to him. Is there anything you want me to say?"

"Tell him Tina married someone she met while conducting tours in England and is now, as far as you know, living in London. If he wants proof, Tina can give you the name of someone who will back her up."

"That probably won't be necessary, but good to have in my back pocket."

"Always be prepared. That's my motto."

"Mine too, but now let me tell you about another surprise. I had a call the other day from Commissioner Lombardo. You won't believe it."

"Try me!"

"Lombardo wants me to find Larry Hermano. The reason he gave was to inform him about his son's demise."

"You're right, Ron. I don't believe that he'd expect you to buy that story. How do you plan to deal with this assignment?"

"I haven't figured out where to begin with this one, boss. The Commissioner suggested I start at what was the Cappo's hotel. I think our friend has heard some rumors and is on a fishing expedition. Any ideas?"

"You could quiz Detective McDonald. He probably hasn't told the Commissioner everything he knows."

"That's one of my problems. I was told to keep my investigation secret. No one is to know that Lombardo is conducting a man hunt. I'm to report only to the Commissioner himself. What's your take on this, Mr. Stone?"

"If Commissioner Lombardo is aware of the Larry sightings, it won't be a good thing to be found. Larry was paid to live in exile after the Cappo murders. His coming back to Chicago would be a real problem for the Commissioner. If located, you can be sure, Larry's next disappearance will be permanent.

20

It is true that Larry could cause the Commissioner and his associates a great deal of trouble if he were to come forward.

That Larry was one of a large family, as he had often told the Cappos, was fact. Thereafter, however, his story went from truth to fiction. The Cappos had been led to believe Larry's family was supportive of him, and that they had pooled their meager resources to send him, the youngest and last hope, to college believing it would result in a better life.

In truth, Larry was a troublesome child. Where his parents and older siblings were successful career people, Larry was lazy—always looking for shortcuts. He refused to apply himself and dropped out of school at the age of sixteen. The family reacted and he retaliated by running away from home. Although his parents hoped he'd come back, when he didn't and made no attempt to contact them, they wrote him off as "the black sheep" of the family. "Every large family has one," they rationalized.

Larry, after knocking around a little, ended up in Chicago. A grandparent had left him with a bank account on which he lived high for a while. One day, purchasing funny cigarettes from a street vender, he met Anthony Lombardo, Jr. who was immediately attracted to the tall, good looking, seemingly independent young man. Finding they had something in common, Larry invited him into his furnished studio apartment. Larry told Tony that his parents had died and that he was on his own having run away from an abusive uncle who was his guardian. The two boys became friends and it wasn't long before Tony brought Larry home to meet his family.

Larry knew that his money wouldn't last forever. His aim was to cultivate the rich and famous. In Tony he had a find for it was obvious his new friend was wealthy. All Larry needed to do was be on his good behavior and work on the family's sympathy. An abused orphan, they would surely feel sorry for him.

Having a well rehearsed sob story, Tony's family fell for it. When Larry's money ran out, he found himself welcomed by the Lombardos and moved into their life. Tony's father saw something promising in him.

The Lombardo children were enrolled in a private high school and Mr. Lombardo insisted that Larry join Lucy and Tony. "Some day," said Mr. Lombardo, "you'll find a way to pay me back, but you won't amount to anything or do me any good unless you get a good education."

Larry didn't have to be told that the Lombardo's would expect something in return for their hospitality and generosity. He was street smart and expected there would be strings attached.

Tony, Jr. was the first to call in the IOU. Although unknown to his father at that time, Tony was gay. He made no secret that favors were expected in return for the welcome mat offered. Introducing his friend to the alternative life style, Larry found it strange but not repulsive. As a matter of fact he rather liked the idea of being so important to Tony after a while.

Soon after moving in, Larry was invited to join "The Club." Here he learned to drink and experiment with drugs. Cocaine appeared to be the drug of choice. "The Club" had rules and new members had to be initiated. Any new recruit was put to the test. He had to meet a challenge dictated by the majority of it's members.

Larry's challenge was to break into a neighbor's house. Proving that he had carried out the assignment, it was required that Larry bring back to "The Club," six place settings of the family silverware. The owners were away and the task shouldn't have been too difficult to carry out, but Larry was caught by a police officer. When Tony's father got him off without so much as a reprimand, Larry began to realize that "Papa" was a man of influence.

"Glad that's over with. So much for a life of crime," thought Larry. However that was not the end of it. Larry soon learned that "The Club" was in reality a training ground, run by the Lombardo children, but orchestrated by the father. There were weekly meetings at which they played "let's pretend" games.

For example, Tony, Jr. would address the kids at a meeting and say, "Pretend you want to appropriate a car. Tell us how you'd go about it. Club members were expected to share ideas which would be evaluated and critiqued. After suggestions based on experience were made by Tony, Jr. the kids were encouraged to go out and try their luck stealing cars. Other challenges could be purse snatching or an apartment burglary. Those successful could expect recognition and rewards from the Commissioner.

Larry found it frightening at first, but discovered that the club members were rarely apprehended, and if they were picked up, never found themselves in real trouble. If there was a problem for the members, it was the local street gangs who wanted to fight when finding themselves unjustly accused of crimes the "Club" boys had committed.

"We've had it with youse guys gettin us in trouble. Jus cause yer rich aint no reason you should git away wid everyting. De cops keep pullin us in. We din't do notin," was the mantra of the local kids as they fought with the boys from uptown. Tony Lombardo's kids were street fighters having been trained from an early age and it was the local kids who usually ended up on the wrong side of any argument.

As "The Club" members matured and graduated from High School, they were encouraged by Commissioner Lombardo to give up the kid stuff and move into more sophisticated business enterprises. The Commish was always ready to give a helping hand and advice, but it was understood by all that he would eventually want a fair share of profits realized. He always called in his IOUs.

"And what do you want to do with your life?" asked Mr. Lombardo when it was Larry's turn to graduate.

"I've heard some of the guys talk about investing in night clubs or restaurants, but I think I'd like to work my way up in a hotel with the idea of eventually owning one."

"You'll need to learn about the business, Larry, and I'm willing to stake you a little longer. There's a catch, however. You can reach your goal and manage—perhaps even own a hotel some day—but remember, I own you. It's called pay-back. I've got the same deal with the other boys and their chosen careers. You'll always make a good living - more than you could ever achieve on your own—but you answer to me. Do I make myself clear?"

"I have no quarrel with that, Mr. Lombardo. You've always been fair with me and the other guys."

"Tony, Jr. and Lucy are my eyes and ears, Larry. Their job is to check up on you and your progress. They do the same with all the enterprises the boys and I have invested in. You may not always like what has to be done to achieve my goals and sometimes I'm ruthless. If you've got a problem with that, tell me now and we'll go our separate ways."

"No problem, Sir."

Larry was ambitious and could only see the plus side of Mr. Lombardo's proposition. He planned to get a license of some kind and then get into an established hotel where he could make his mark. Endearing himself to the owners, he would work his way into their confidence. Trusting him, there would be no problem cheating them as he had been taught at Club meetings. True the hotel, technically, would end up with Mr. Lombardo calling the shots, but Larry would be the owner and very well compensated. In his opinion, this was not a bad deal. While it would take time to realize his ambition, Papa Lombardo had assured him of his patience and cooperation.

With a little more help from Mr. Lombardo, Larry received a crash course and phony certificate in Hotel Management. He sent out his resume and Tina's grandfather was willing to take a chance "on the young fellow fresh out of what he called 'hotel school.'" The price was right and the hotel was ready for some new blood. Larry's youth and seemingly gracious manner sold Tina's parents as well. They recognized the need for extra hands and fresh ideas. Larry was on his way - he had his foot on the first rung of the ladder to success.

From time to time Larry was faced with giving a status report to Mr. Lombardo—Planning Commissioner Lombardo was his new title. As for Tony, Jr., they met secretly as often as it could be arranged between them. Larry was a one-man guy and faithful to Tony—his ambition was more important to him than his sex life, and he believed that his relationship with Tony was that of a couple committed to each other. Unfortunately for Larry, Tony was more adventurous in his liaisons. His job was to see that all the club alumni were looking out for his father's interests. Since he had recruited several of the members for the same reason as Larry, he had no difficulty satisfying his need for variety which, to him, was the spice of life.

In addition to his promiscuous behavior, Tony had another serious problem. He was a compulsive gambler and had run up hefty gambling debts. As his father's enforcers, Tony and Lucy were expected to check on all the businesses run by 'Club' members to see that they were living up to whatever bargains had been negotiated. Like most parents, the Commish was blind to the faults of his own children and not aware of Tony, Jr.'s weaknesses. He assumed his children could be trusted to look out for his interests. He had no reason to suspect his son would be skimming money off the top to pay gambling debts.

As for Larry, his plan was going forward nicely. The Cappo family, owners of the Carillion Hotel in St. Louis, had welcomed him with open arms. He came to them with many new and innovative ideas that were immediately implemented with the result that their Carillion Hotel was rated well above competing newcomers. Larry was personable. Everyone liked him. The hotel profited and the Cappos rewarded him by treating him as one of the family. He was taken into their confidence about everything including personal financial matters, and knew of Spencer's dream to, some day, open a second hotel.

As the years went by, Tina's parents were delighted that Larry took an interest in their only daughter. They pictured a future with Tina married to Larry. Having two hotels, one would be managed by the young couple. With a little luck and hard work, the two Carillions might end up as a chain.

Larry was aware of Tina's teenage crush. Although he was not interested in female relationships, he could picture her as an insurance policy if needed. She was a pretty little thing and it wasn't difficult to play "let's pretend", the game he'd learned so well in "The Club" years before. He'd often share meals with her. He teased and flirted a little. Then, one day, he really looked at her. Tina was all grown up and about to go away to college. She was a beauty. Larry began to worry about her exposure to other men who would surely find her desirable.

When Tina came home from her first school break, Larry decided it was time to capitalize on her "crush" and make a move. He started to romance her in earnest. Before long there was talk of an engagement in Tina's senior year. Larry had it made. To insure his success, he needed only to marry the boss's daughter - someone who already worshipped him.

It was not that simple, however. There was that commitment made to Commissioner Lombardo who had a very different plan in mind. That plan did not include Spencer, Terry or Tina.

When told of Larry's plan, The Commissioner said bluntly, "They have to go, Larry. The hotel and everything they have in assets must be invested into some deal that goes sour causing them to default on their debts. That's when we'll foreclose and take the hotel. The details will have to be worked out, but it's been done before with some of the other enterprises run by my boys. I'll help you, but you have to do your part."

Larry didn't object to the challenge and knew better than to upset the Commissioner. Knowing of Spencer's interest in expanding his holdings, he immediately began pressuring him to look beyond the St. Louis area for a suitable hotel.

"I believe there are already enough hotel rooms in this area, Spencer," he said thinking it would be easier to pull a scam in Chicago where he could use the resources of Commissioner Lombardo. Being in Chicago would, at the same time, make it easier for him to see his lover, Tony, Jr.

Concentrating all his energy toward the new goal of getting Spencer interested in Chicago real estate, Tina was put on a back burner and almost ignored. "You could call me more often," she said when he did reach her at school, "and a letter now and then reminding me that you love me, would be nice too. All you ever say is that you're tired or that you are expected somewhere. You're never there for me, Larry."

Larry was a smooth talker and managed to deal with Tina's complaints most of the time. It helped that she was away at school during the year and that the distance involved prohibited frequent trips home, but she expected that he'd want to be with her when on school breaks. His excuse was always that Spencer needed him on the road looking for hotel properties.

It had been a long time coming and Commissioner Lombardo was beginning to taste the rewards for his patience and investment in Larry. He came up with a plan that would facilitate matters.

"I'll have my son arrange to stay at the hotel for a few days," he said. "You'll pretend not to know each other. We'll give him a different name. Tony Luppo sounds good. Let's say you pretend to meet by chance at the hotel bar. He'll tell you about some Chicago hotels he and a partner own. He'll mention that the partner wants to sell because the hotels need updating requiring a large investment of cash—money they don't have. You'll fix him up with Mr. Cappo who, you tell him, is anxious to buy. There you have it. It's the perfect setup for a con.

"I'll take care of the accountants and the legal people who will make sure everything looks legitimate on paper. When we're through the Cappos will be hopelessly in debt to us. Then we'll call in our IOUs and take over. All you have to do is talk Spencer into giving you Power of Attorney over his bank accounts and other assets. I'm sure he'll understand the need for collateral in event of default."

"Why would he give me Power of Attorney?"

"That's for you to figure out. He's not well, you said."

Larry, as planned, met Tony Luppo at the bar shortly thereafter. He introduced Tony to Spencer and the scam was underway. By the time Tony left the Carillion, he had convinced Spencer that Mr. Luppo's hotels might be a good investment and worth a look. While waiting for an appointment with his doctor, and although he was not feeling well, Spencer made a quick trip to Chicago. Taking a cursory look at the properties in question, he was satisfied that, together with Larry, they could turn the run-down hotels around and make a profit if a satisfactory deal could be arranged.

"I can't risk not having someone in charge if the doctor suggests an operation, Larry. You know what I'm looking for having done much of the legwork for me. You also are aware of my financial situation. I am interested in those hotels and would like you to find a way to get them. Check out the details. If the deal looks good to you and you think I can afford it, get the paperwork started. In case I find myself suddenly incapacitated—and you can never predict what's going to happen—I don't want your hands tied. I've called my lawyer to prepare a Power of Attorney which will enable you to proceed no matter what happens to me."

"It was so easy, Commissioner. I still can't believe it. Before I had a chance to mention a Power of Attorney,

344

Spencer told me that he had his attorney drawing up the papers. It won't be long now."

"What do you plan to do about Tina, Larry?"

"I don't think I'll have to do anything. When she finds out that I've been responsible for defrauding her and the family, she'll want no part of me."

Commissioner Lombardo called in some favors from his friends. Between his attorney and his accountant, they took care of all the paperwork. The Power of Attorney allowed Larry to convert the hotel and all other assets of the Cappo's into a paper purchase of Tony Luppo's hotels. Mr. Luppo did not exist, however. Neither did the two hotels Spencer looked at belong to him or his fictitious partner.

Tina and Mara were in Capetown as promised and Spencer was preoccupied with his deteriorating heart problem making it easy for Larry to begin implementing Commissioner Lombardo's scenario. The deal that Larry had supposedly worked out was a partnership with the existing owners who would be bought out by Spencer in two years.

While Tina, learning of her father's impending surgery, cut short her vacation, it was too late to interfere in the matter of the hotel. Her main concern was the scheduled surgery which, fortunately, went well. School was about to begin again and Spencer was recuperating. Knowing there was nothing more she could do, Tina began her Junior year hoping for a visit from Larry. Seeing him, she felt, would reassure her and do much to end the nagging feelings of insecurity and disappointment.

Two weeks later it was all over. Tina, overnight, had no parents, no home and was penniless. There was nothing left of the comfortable life she had known.

The Cappos did not yet know it, but Larry's plan to wipe out the family assets was successful. With the help of the Power of Attorney, everything was mortgaged and now, officially, belonged to Anthony Lombardo, Sr. Larry had been in Chicago when the final papers were signed. He was to meet Tony, Jr. that night at a run down motel located west of St. Louis. It would be their last rendezvous for a while since Larry would then begin his temporary flight into obscurity. He knew it would be only a matter of time before the Cappos understood what had happened and he wanted to be long gone by then.

However, unknown to Larry, his friend and ring leader of "The Club," had his own agenda. Tony Lombardo, Jr., otherwise known as Tony Luppo and Jason Thomas, called it "unfinished business."

While staying at the Carillion those few days several months before, ostensibly to interest Spencer in his phony hotel scam, he had become aware of the vault hidden behind the reception desk. Believing the safe contained not only cash, but valuables belonging to guests of the hotel, he was determined not to overlook this source as a means of giving himself a bonus.

Tony was a high roller and had always been one to run up sizable IOUs with his bookie. For a while he had succeeded in staying afloat by skimming off some of the proceeds from his father's interests in the operations run by "Club" members, but with computers now keeping tabs on things, it was becoming more difficult and he was again in over his head. Threats from his bookie were getting serious. Having already suffered one beating, he preferred avoiding another encounter with the muscle-men. He needed cash. The contents of the hotel safe promised to solve his problems.

In passing, Larry had told him that the safe could be opened only with a special key always on Spencer's person.

If out of town for some reason, the key was entrusted to a bonded representative who would be on the premises. To get to the key, Tony knew he'd have to break into the Cappo's apartment while they were sleeping. It was risky, but his life was on the line. Just in case there was trouble, he brought a gun and a silencer.

There was no problem getting into the apartment. The "let's pretend" games of Tony's youth paid off. An obvious place to begin searching for the key was in the bedroom. Since the business suit Spencer had worn that day was neatly arranged on the clothes valet, it made sense to look first in his jacket. Unfortunately, just as he had his hand in the pocket, Terry woke up. It was a mistake she should not have made. Tony couldn't afford to have her scream nor could he have witnesses, so he shot both her and her sleeping husband, retrieved the key and left to finish what he had started.

It was a little difficult getting the night clerk away from the desk long enough to loot the safe, but Tony faked an emergency—a power failure—and bought himself fifteen minutes while the breaker panel downstairs was investigated and reset. That was all the time he needed to clean out the contents of the safe and make his exit. No one, except Terry, had seen him come or go and he had silenced her forever.

When morning came and the bodies and empty safe were discovered, he and Larry were far from the scene. They had met as planned, but at Tony's insistence did not stay at the hotel. Following Tony's car, Larry drove for hours not knowing where his friend was leading. They only stopped when needing gas and by then they were in Tulsa, Oklahoma. Deciding to leave one car behind at the station, Larry took over the driving. Together they would look for a suitable place to spend the night. No longer having the responsibility of staying alert, Tony pulled out a flask and began drinking. Adding some potent pills, he was soon out cold. By the time Larry found what looked like a motel, he had a real problem maneuvering Tony into bed. Drunk and stoned was not the way Larry had planned to spend the night with his lover. Disappointed and still angry the next morning, Larry was quite vocal. It was then that Tony confessed to what had taken place in St. Louis the night before.

"She shouldn't have woken up," he said. "It was her own fault. I had to kill them when the old lady saw me go for the keys."

Larry couldn't believe what he was hearing and, for the first time, was really afraid. Until now everything had been child's play.

"Stealing is one thing," he shouted at Tony. "Murder is another. They'll think I did it. Everything points my way. They don't even know you exist. I was supposed to lay low for a while and then come back to take over in the hotel, but what you did was stupid and changes everything. Your father has to be told and had better have some ideas about getting us out of this mess."

"Send my boy back to me," said the Commissioner when informed of what had happened. "You two must separate immediately. Tony Luppo is a fictitious person. They can't find someone who doesn't exist. You're right, Larry. They will be looking for you. The theft of the Cappo's properties would have died down eventually since we made sure they'd find no proof of wrong doing, but murder changes everything. I hate to say this, Larry, but running away from the Carillion has made you a prime suspect and the police will stop at nothing to find you."

"So where does this leave me?"

"You've done a great job. Everything is in our hands just like we planned and no one knows of my involvement. The dummy corporations set up by my attorneys are foolproof. You were to have come back to St.

Louis after things had calmed down and then take over the hotel for us, but you must realize that doing so is no longer an option."

"You're telling me that my dream of owning the hotel are over because of your son's greed?

"You've got to get out of the country fast, Larry. I know you're disappointed, but I'll take care of you. Go to Mexico. There will be travelers checks waiting for you at the post office in Matamoros under the name of Henry Lopez. From Mexico find your way to Rio de Janeiro and call me. You must never be seen in the States again. Do you understand?"

"I understand, Mr. Lombardo, but you'd better understand that I'll need lots of money if you expect me to hide out indefinitely. I really don't like the idea of spending the rest of my life looking over my shoulder because of your son's stupidity."

"Yes, he was stupid, but he's my son. I adopted you into my family and you're my son as well. I'll take care of you, but you must promise to stay away from us and keep your mouth shut. If you do that, you'll live well no matter where you end up. You'll never have to work again, and in these times, that's pretty good. Did I mention you'll have an account in a Grand Cayman bank to which money will be transferred every month? All you have to do is pick it up and forget about your other life in St. Louis."

Tony returned to Chicago and was given a stern reprimand from his father. "How dumb could you be - breaking into the Cappo's apartment? What were you thinking?"

"I thought there would be jewelry and valuables in the safe and wanted to bring it to you as a bonus. I was mistaken. The safe was empty," lied Tony. In truth he had stopped on his way home with the loot to take care of his debts. The thought of what might happen to him if he didn't, took top priority in his mind.

Not realizing his son was lying, the Commissioner rationalized that the safe at the reception desk might have been a smoke screen for the real thing—that valuables were kept elsewhere and that the famous key was nothing but a ruse to fool anyone with ulterior motives.

Having gotten away with his neck this time, Tony went about his business but soon found himself in debt again. In addition, he began having problems with his health. At night there would be periods of sweating while during the day there were severe headaches accompanied by dizzy spells. Having had a cough and sniffles for weeks, he finally decided to have a medical checkup. That's when he learned the shocking truth—Tony had Aids. His promiscuity had caught up with him and no amount of influence on the part of his father could spare him from a diagnosis that was irreversible.

Tony had successfully hidden his homosexuality from the commissioner for years. Now his secret would come out. Not only that, but he was going to die. Perhaps the doctor was wrong. There was a second opinion and a third and all resulted in the same diagnosis. Tony was sick and going to get sicker. Angry, Tony resolved that he would live the time remaining to the fullest. While continuing to collect from "Club" members for his father, the drinking, drugs, sex and gambling remained a part of his daily routine. He did now allow his partners to practice safe sex, but for some, he knew, it might already be too late. Those he would not worry about. No one, after all, had offered him a choice.

Tony's debts soon piled up again. New threats were made by hoodlums and they'd already given him samples of what they could do. It was not to his liking. To get the collectors off his back, he had killed, robbed and burned out the Milwaukee family Tina had read about. They had been managing one of Commissioner Lombardo's many enterprises and known to keep large sums of money in the house.

Unfortunately for Tony, there had been a witness. Officer White had seen and confronted him. He was about to make an arrest, and now would have to be eliminated as well. Tina was scheduled to have met Officer White the night Tony shot him dead.

"It's not hard to kill if you've done it before and are going to die anyway," was Tony's rationalization.

21

The Commissioner of Planning and Development, Anthony Lombardo, Sr., was furious when he finally learned the truth. That his son was homosexual was bad enough. That he was a gambler was worse. That he stole from his own father was unforgivable.

He had brought up his son and daughter to be like him—devious, deceitful and dishonest, but warned them always to be careful to stay within the limits of the law. The law, of course, was interpreted by him and his associates and their ability to bend it. By having a few friends in strategic positions, he didn't need to be a member of the Chicago mobs that were always under suspicion. He had "The Club" working for him. One might say he was in command of his own mini mob.

The kids, now grown, were all doing well and expanding into areas that would be lucrative to them and, therefore, to him. The deal was that his kids could take over and own whatever they wanted, but he had invested in them and, therefore, owned them. Over the years Commissioner Lombardo found himself in control of many businesses. There were apartment complexes, shopping malls, liquor stores, even cemeteries and mausoleums. His boys tried to stay clear of gambling, entertainment and enterprises that were already in the hands of big city mobsters.

"It's best you find your own opportunities—those that are not already considered private property," was his advice to the boys.

In his back pocket the Commissioner had lawyers, accountants and some union bosses—most of them parents of the boys—but his greatest assets were those planted in various police departments. They made it possible for his boys-in-training to stay out of trouble and also gave protection to them when they were out on their own. All the bases were covered and he was proud of himself for having built up such a lucrative after hours business. It was a business that allowed him, during the day, to be the important and respected Commissioner of Planning and Development.

Where did he go wrong with his son who should have known better than to kill those Cappo people? Surely Tina would not have been such a pest if it was only the hotel and money that were taken from her. Killing her parents was the thing that got her so ticked off and unreasonable, thought the Commish when alone at dinner that night.

Tina was a real thorn in his side. Yes, he had instructed his son to give her a hard time on the phone hoping she'd be frightened and go away, but the girl was stubborn and persistent. Too bad Tony didn't finish her off while on that Egyptian trip.

Detective White snooping around was a nuisance as well. It's a good thing my boy took care of him. Good also that I was able to move Lucy to St. Louis where she managed to bribe Jim into giving her information about Tina's comings and goings. Looks like we've scared her off. I understand the girl is getting married and planning to live overseas. That should be the end of our problems with her, but then there's still Larry to deal with. McDonald told Lucy that Larry was in New Zealand recently and almost collided with Tina. He managed to get away, but not before she saw him. I always liked the boy, but he knows too much and that spells trouble—especially if he has guilt feelings. He might want to unburden himself. As it is we have the FBI poking around all the time. A word from Larry and they'll come down on us. We've got to find him and make sure he's silenced for good.

22

After a decent interval, Officer Taylor, the FBI plant, reported to his supervisor.

"Getting back to you and your question about Tina Cappo, Captain Steiner, it is true she married someone she met in England and is living in London. I contacted her tour agency and learned that she guided a last tour as a favor and then left for her wedding. Do you want me to check further? I could go to Boston and meet with some of her former co-workers. They might have a name and address."

"No reason to do that. Actually I need you here. Lucy is moving back to Chicago and the work is piling up."

"Lucy's leaving St. Louis? What happened?"

"I don't really know. Something about being needed by her father. With the death of her brother, I guess it's understandable."

"What about Jim? I mean, Detective McDonald?"

"What's he got to do with it?"

"Nothing, I guess, but you must know that Lucy and Jim were seeing each other."

"That's their problem. I've got plenty of my own. Although I'd have liked more time for evaluation, I want you to get together with Lucy and have her clue you in to what she does around here. It looks like you'll need a crash course to fill her place, but I think you can handle it. If you have questions or problems after you've seen Lucy, get back to me. Good luck!"

Robert Taylor didn't quite know what to make of this conversation, but thought he would soon find out. The FBI had sent him to get information and, at last, he could see the door opening a crack. The order to get together with Lucy, who had taken another bereavement day, was a sign of trust. Knowing she was in her apartment, he called.

"Lucy, it's me, Robert. Are you okay? I'm so sorry about your brother and wish I could have been with you. Anything I can do?"

"No thanks, I'm fine! Did Captain Steiner tell you I turned in my badge earlier today? Now that Tony's gone, my father needs me in Chicago."

"Yes, he did and I'm sorry to see you go. Jim will be even sorrier, but maybe you've already discussed your leaving with him."

"He knows, Bob. Don't waste your breath worrying about him though. He'll soon find something else to do."

"Probably, but I'll miss the three of us bullshitting over drinks. By the way, Captain Steiner had me in his office this morning. He wants me to get together with you. You're supposed to clue me in on the way things are done. I'm not sure what he means, but that's what he said."

"Steiner trusts you and so do I. Apparently my father does as well. Otherwise he wouldn't be asking you to find Larry. How are you doing? Any sign of him yet?"

Bob Taylor was surprised that Lucy was aware of the assignment her father had given him. "Then you know your father asked me to find Larry. I guess he didn't mean you when he asked me not to tell anyone. Actually I haven't found him but haven't given up the search. I did, however, verify for our Captain, that Tina Cappo has left the States. She's married and living with some bus driver in London."

"A bus driver? I'd say that's a come down, but who knows what turns a person on. It's nice to know we won't have to worry about that trouble-maker anymore."

"So tell me what you know about Larry. It would be helpful if I didn't have to start from scratch. Why does your father want him? Since he ran away, I can assume he was responsible for Tina's problems, but what has that to do with the Commissioner?"

"It's a long story that I'd rather have my father tell you when and if he sees fit. Let's just say my father knew Larry from a long time ago. They sometimes had business dealings."

"What kind of business dealings?"

"I really don't know, but if you're wondering whether my father had anything to do with the murder of Tina's parents, he didn't. Police records and Jim's early research proved that Larry was given Power of Attorney by Tina's father. With that he had carte blanche. Apparently he planned, eventually, to come back as the hotel's owner."

"But why would he kill them, Lucy? With a murder wrap hanging over his head, there is no way Larry can ever come back here. Right now he could be anywhere in the world."

"The last I heard he was supposed to have gone to South America. However, Jim said that Tina had almost collided with Larry in New Zealand a few months ago. I don't know what he would be doing there, but he ran from the scene. Tina never got to speak to him."

"It's been a couple of years since Larry disappeared. I'm wondering what he's using for money. Someone must be bankrolling him. What about the hotel? Is it closed down or is someone running it these days?"

"I understand some consortium has taken over the operation of the Carillion, but I haven't had occasion to check it out."

"Whoever is in charge might talk to me. I'll make it a point to go there tomorrow. Now, however, you're supposed to be giving me 'how to' lessons, Lucy. Our leader wants me to take over your job and you've been elected to clue me in on the inner workings of our prestigious precinct."

"I'll do my best, Bob. Although recently hired, you must have wondered why I seem to get special treatment in the department and why I'd have left Chicago, where my father could have set me up in a cushy job."

"The thought had crossed my mind, Lucy."

"My father sent me here because he has business interests that need to be protected. What better protection could he have but that provided by the police department. Captain Steiner looks out for his interests, but to keep the Captain in line, he's got me. Dad has a similar set-up in Chicago. My brother was overseer, but with him gone, he needs me there. Apparently he now feels the Captain, you and Jim can handle things here."

"I must admit being curious about some things that were condoned in our precinct. Being new and low man on the totem pole, I thought it best not to ask questions. It's beginning to make sense now."

"A person would have to be blind not to notice that we overlook a great deal of what goes on in this town. Drugs, prostitution and other lucrative, but illegal, activities are thriving here because our Captain is warned whenever there is to be a raid. My job is to see that our friends have ample time to go underground until the coast is clear. When I leave, it will be your job to alert the captain. Think you can handle it?"

"Sure, but what about this Tina Cappo person? Why is Captain Steiner so interested in her whereabouts?"

Lucy explained that the Captain had assigned Jim to the Cappo case because Tina wouldn't give up on her crusade and was causing him grief. He wanted Tina's actions monitored, but when Jim's interest in her became more personal than professional, Lucy was recruited. "Perhaps it was all the questions I asked, but Jim became suspicious and then resentful. I needed his cooperation and had to do something. Arranging to have him promoted, I won him over. He became my informant. It wasn't such a bad deal for him. He got a promotion and some good sex with me. What more could a guy want?"

"Were you involved in the murder of Tina's parents?"

"Not me and not my father. Anyway it wasn't murder. The deaths were accidental."

"What kind of an accident kills two people?"

"Maybe it's why my father needs the protection of the police. That's all the lessons for now, Bob. Captain

Steiner will give you instructions as needed. Be a good boy and you, too, might soon be a candidate for promotion."

Robert Taylor did get to the Carillion Hotel and found a man of about thirty in charge. At first he appeared to be receptive to questions.

"Are you the new owner?" asked Robert.

"Let's just say, I'm in charge," was the answer.

"How long have you been in charge?"

"About a year."

"Did you know the previous owner?"

"No! I understand the place was privately owned - some people by the name of Cappo."

"What happened to them?"

"From what I was told, they died and the place was sold."

"Anyone still here who worked for the previous owners?"

"The staff was replaced when I took over."

"Why wouldn't you keep on experienced help?"

"Come on, Mister! Why all the questions? I really don't think it's any of your business and, if you'll excuse me, I have work to do."

The new manager, or whatever he was, refused to answer any more of Mr. Taylor's questions and, not too politely, ushered him out the door.

Don't know how he got that job—certainly not because of his great personality, thought Bob. Well, I'll just have to tell the Commish I tried to find Larry and failed. He might want me to look further, but I doubt anything would come of it. They say "follow the money," and unless someone is willing to tell me who's financing Larry's disappearance—and I suspect it's the commissioner himself—he's not going to surface until there's a good reason.

Robert Taylor and his boss at the FBI had not communicated in about three days. During that time Robert had covered a great deal of territory and was anxious to share his findings.

"There's been so much happening here, Mr. Stone. Briefly, Lucy is leaving the department to work for her father in Chicago. With her brother dead, he needs her. I'm to take over her job in St. Louis. Lucy was told to clue me in on how they do things here and I met with her. It was a very interesting meeting."

"I'll bet it was. Anything we haven't already suspected?"

"Lucy confirmed that her father has interests in the buying and selling of drugs and guns in the St. Louis area. Being illegal, the Commissioner often needs the support of the police. It was Lucy and the Captain's major responsibility to see that things went smoothly. Having sold out Tina, Jim McDonald got his promotion and is now included in the inner circle. Since I'll be taking over for Lucy, and presumably have everyone's trust, I'll be privy to what's happening as well."

"Looks like you've wormed your way into a very good spot, Bob."

"At least until I stop playing ball. For now, though, it looks good. I did try pumping Lucy about Larry, but all she said was that her father and Larry occasionally had business dealings."

Bob Taylor then talked to Agent Stone about his visit with the new people at the Carillion hotel. "Apparently all the staff was newly hired. The manager was not very pleasant. After a few questions, he escorted me to the door. He probably didn't like being interrogated—or maybe he didn't like me. Anyhow, that was a dead end. I'm FAXing my full report. If you have questions or want to give me further instructions, call me. I plan to stay in tonight. Maybe I'll pull a blanket over my head. Still can't get over Papa Lombardo and his reaction to Tony's illness and death. He really is a piece of work."

"Read your report, Bob. You've been busy and, whether you know it or not, are making progress. When you talk to Commissioner Lombardo, be sure to tell him about your reception at the Carillion. I suspect he already knows how it went since he must have some of his own people in there. As to his request that you find Larry, the Commish has been financing him all along and would know, better than anyone, where to find him. If Larry has gone underground, you can be sure there's a reason. He's probably beginning to fear for his life."

"I wouldn't doubt it, Mr. Stone."

"When you talk to the Commissioner, tell him about your discussion with Lucy—about the drug and gun business and the need for police protection. Listen carefully to what he says and let me know how he reacts. We'll play along for now, but will sabotage Lombardo when the time is right. I find it interesting that Lucy confirmed our theory that her father has infiltrated the Chicago police department. I wonder where else we'll find him. Keep up the good work,

Bob. We'll get this guy one of these days and put an end to his empire."

"Hi, Commissioner! Robert Taylor here. Don't want you to think I haven't been working on it, but so far, no luck finding Larry Hermano. I understand the police here have been trying for some time and are equally frustrated. Lucy volunteered that he was supposed to be in South America, but had recently been glimpsed by Tina Cappo in New Zealand. If true, that chance encounter would make him more cautious than before. He's probably taken on a disguise and gone underground."

"You're telling me you have nothing at all? I am disappointed."

"I tried—even went to the Carillion hotel. New people are in charge and, I might say, they are not very friendly. To put it another way they, unceremoniously, showed me the door. Lucy did tell me you knew Larry and had business dealings with him over the years. It would help if you filled me in. Something might click."

"Yes, I knew him through my boy Tony. He brought the kid home. He was an orphan and I felt sorry for him. We took him in for a couple of years. He was bright and ambitious. I helped him where I could. The boys were friends. He's going to feel terrible when I tell him that Tony died."

"Lucy said there were business dealings. Could I ask what they were?"

"He did favors for me sometimes. Until he went to St. Louis, he was at our house quite often. Then we lost touch, but I know Tony saw him on occasion. You know Tony died of Aids. I don't know how close Larry was with my son after he left Chicago, but he should be checked and I want to warn him about that as well."

It was clear that Commissioner Lombardo was not going to elaborate any further. "Do you want me to go on with my search? Larry must be getting money from someone. I could try the banks. South America is a big place, but I'll do what I can if you want me to continue."

"No, Bob! Forget it for now."

"On another subject, I understand from Captain Steiner that Lucy is leaving the department. He wants me to take over for her and has asked that we get together. He said she would fill me in on the procedures around here. I'm just back from her place. She told me about the gun and drug business and why it was important to have good people in the precinct—people that could be trusted to sound the alarm if there was any trouble brewing from the FBI. It pleases me that you and Captain Steiner have taken me into your confidence and, I assure you, I'll do whatever you need done."

"I don't usually get guys off the street to work with us, but I like you. Lucy brought you to me and I trust you. For now all I ask is that you keep your eyes and ears open and do your job. If Steiner has anything special, he'll let you know. Welcome Aboard, Bob!"

While all this activity was going on in the life of Robert Taylor, Tina and Stanley as well as Mara, Alex and little Stephen Michael were living their lives. Tina was still in disguise mode, and had gotten accustomed to being a blonde. At night, when alone with Stanley, she could let her hair down and be herself, which was always a consolation. As long as Stan loved both versions of his lady, she was happy. There had been no more strange calls or messages. Apparently those responsible had gotten the word and were satisfied that raven-haired Tina was married and living overseas. The thought that she was safe was comforting to all.

Mara and Tina were as close as ever and visited back and forth. The baby was growing and a real joy to everyone. Stevie had two mommies and two daddies. Soon would be his first Christmas. Grandma and Grandpa Turner were coming to spend the holidays and all were looking forward to a family reunion. The contractors had finished their work and the dream house was just as Mara and Alex had envisioned.

"Some day we'll be able to afford a house like this," said Tina as she and Mara were having lunch. "First things first, however. Right now every cent has to go into the business. Even with that nice loan from the bank, we've got to be careful with our finances. Once deposits start coming in, and they'd better, we can begin to relax a little. Feedback from the agencies who have been circulating our literature and talking up the tour, is encouraging, but people usually wait until February to make vacation commitments. I'm confident the trip will sell—so confident that I've reserved a block of thirty rooms at each hotel that has signed on. The tour bus seats fifty-four passengers. For starters, we'll be reserving eight seats per tour for agency representatives. The remaining tickets, if sold, should cover the expense of those freebies. Obviously we won't get rich the first year, Mara—we'll be lucky to break even—but with proper marketing, we should do okay eventually. Word of mouth from those who sign on for the early tours will be our best advertisement."

"In addition to the mailings, the correspondence and the bookings, is there anything more I can do to help, Tina?"

"You're doing all you can and more than your fair share, Mara. I'm always thinking and plotting, but plan to cut down on the road trips soon. Stan has been busy with his new job and hasn't complained, but things are settling down there and I want to have some time with him before the summer when our tours get underway. By the way, Mr. Yoakum his boss, tells me I'm the best thing that ever happened for his business. How about your Alex? Any chance that he'll get to stay put one of these days?"

"I hate to even mention it, Tina, but there are rumors about a promotion soon. The present Engineering Coordinator is planning to retire and it's as though the job description was written just for my dear husband. Pray that it happens. It would mean no more traveling. We'd sure like to have our man home with us at night."

"Do you know how lucky we are, Mara? We have loving husbands who are happy in their chosen professions and moving up the ladder. At the same time, the business we've started, while allowing us ample time for our families, has all the indications of becoming a success. As of this moment, I have only one regret."

"And what would that be, my friend?"

"That I still haven't been able to keep the promise made to my parents. Stan doesn't know, but there are many nights that I wake up in a cold sweat thinking about them in those coffins. It's like having a nightmare. When it happens, there's no way to get back to sleep and I'm tempted to get up and do the laundry or begin vacuuming. I would, too, except that then there'd be two of us wide awake."

"Have you heard from Agent Stone lately?"

"Oh yes! I meant to tell you as soon as you walked in the door. He invited Stan to have lunch yesterday so as to bring us up-to-date. For one thing, Tony Jr. died and, for another, Lucy is back here in Chicago. Apparently her father, the Commissioner, needs her now that Tony is gone. Jim McDonald and Agent Stone's man, Robert Taylor, are to take over for Lucy in St. Louis. That should enable the FBI to get evidence against Lombardo. Mr. Stone promised to keep us informed."

"I wonder where Larry is these days," questioned Mara as an afterthought.

23

Yes! Where was Larry? Larry's intention in coming back to the States was to meet with Tony. Knowing his hangouts, it wasn't too difficult to catch up with him. Needless to say, Tony was shocked to see him.

"I don't want to make any trouble, Tony," Larry said, "but I need you to get a message to your father."

"My father told you to go away and stay away. What are you doing here?"

"Your father also told me he'd take care of me. I didn't kill the Cappos. You did. Except for that stupid act, instead of hiding out depending on handouts, I'd be owner of the Carillion today. You and your family are reaping the rewards while I'm taking the heat. True, your father doles out money each month, but it's hardly adequate. I want what's due me—what I worked for all those years. Living in some God-forsaken place is not what I bargained for. Tell your father I want my life back."

"You've got a life and you're being compensated."

"But not nearly enough for the sacrifices I've had to make because of your greed."

"It's my father's decision. What do you want from me?"

"I'm not happy and don't like what your father has done to me. You guys are living it up while I'm trying to stay clear of the police. If your father doesn't find a better way to deal with my problem, I'll have to look for another remedy."

"Is that a threat, Larry? If it is, I don't think you're being very smart. Father wouldn't approve. My advice is that you take what you're given, get out of town, go back to wherever you were and be grateful my dad hasn't written you off completely. You're expendable and if my father learns you've been hanging around here, it could cost you. It's bad enough we've got Tina Cappo hounding us. Remember, we don't need either of you in our lives."

Larry was furious. He'd been betrayed and didn't appreciate Tony's attitude or his threats. What a fool he'd been. He could have married Tina and, by now, been sitting pretty. Of course Papa Lombardo didn't give him much choice at the time. It was the Lombardos who had brought him to meet the Cappos in the first place and it was clear he had sold himself to the devil when accepting Commissioner Lombardo's favors years ago.

I can't forget the sight of Tina that day as we passed each other in the cable cars, thought Larry. Imagine her being a tour guide for Cartrite. I almost booked that tour myself. What a situation that would have been. She wasn't a bad kid and I really should warn her to stay out of Commissioner Lombardo's way. However infuriating, Tony's threats were not to be taken lightly.

Through some clever investigating, Larry learned where Tina lived and, being careful to choose a time when he knew her to be out, arranged to slip the warning notes under her door. He was temporarily living in an out-of-town rooming house. While there he contacted an acquaintance—one of the members of "The Club" who had chosen to break away and go it alone. From him he learned that Tony was sick. He had Aids. Could he, too, have contacted the dreaded virus? A checkup several days later confirmed that he was indeed HIV positive. Extremely depressed, Larry returned to Rio to await his fate and think about his options. He sincerely wanted to make amends.

24

Arrangements were made for Jim McDonald and Robert Taylor to take over for Lucy's duties in St. Louis. The drug operation was going well. Captain Steiner and Lucy had kept the dealers in line and profits were finding their way into the pockets of Commissioner Lombardo. The new gun laws, however, were causing some problems which the commissioner, together with the captain, were working on.

Robert's duties, at the moment, were routine. He was catching on and doing well. It occurred to him that a retirement party for Lucy would be interesting and fun. Catching up with his captain in the men's room, he made the suggestion.

"Great idea, Bob. You get the place. Try to set it up for Friday night, but you'd better check it out with Lucy first. She might have other things to do."

"It would be nice if it were a surprise, but I guess you're right. She's probably busy getting ready for her move to Chicago. Since the gang hangs out at Pete's place, I'll see what I can arrange there. Meanwhile help me spread the word. We'll need to know how many people to plan for."

371

Almost everyone not on duty came to the party. Robert had arranged for a D.J. knowing some would want music. There was plenty of liquor, great food and girls. Spouses were not invited. Since there were not many women on the force, the local escort service, which also came under the protection of the police department, sent willing hostesses. A party wasn't a party without women.

Lucy arrived looking beautiful in a long red chiffon dress. She went immediately to Bob, kissed him and asked him to dance. Then, drink in hand, she made the rounds. Embracing and kissing everyone of her colleagues, she seemed to be having a good time, but where was Jim? Why hadn't they come to the party together? It was Lucy's last night in St. Louis and all knew she and Jim were inseparable.

About two hours into the party, Jim finally made an appearance. From the way he walked, it was obvious that he had already been drinking. Ignoring everyone, he headed straight for the bar and immediately latched on to a long-legged voluptuous redhead. Stunned, Bob watched him down two double scotches. Then he raised himself from the barstool and prepared to leave—the redhead in tow. For Lucy there had not been a hello, good-bye, good luck or even a look in her direction.

Puzzled, Robert caught up with Lucy and asked, "Did you two have a fight or something?"

"Not that I know of. But you know Jim. He's always got one waiting in the wings, just in case. In this case I'm leaving and he's got the promotion he wanted. Why would he need me anymore? Truthfully, whatever we had going was gone anyway. Yes, he could have said good-bye and wished me luck, but I'm not devastated. Let's dance!"

"Wish you'd have told me sooner. I could have moved in had I known the coast was clear," Robert responded, flirting.

"Don't make jokes, Bob. Believe me there were times when I wish you had."

"How about we drink up, Lucy, and say goodnight to the gang? I'll take you home."

"Okay! I guess the party's just about over anyway. Come on! Let's go! We'll have a nightcap at my place. Maybe I can coax you to sleep over so that you can kiss me good-bye in the morning."

Robert had been hoping for such an invitation. What better way to learn her innermost secrets, he thought, remembering how well the method had worked for Lucy when she went through Jim's files to get information about Tina. Robert was not a prude and Lucy surely had the looks and the body to tempt any red-blooded American male. Like James Bond, he was more than willing to go that extra mile.

"What's your pleasure, Bobby?" asked Lucy in her most seductive voice. She turned the lights and stereo very low and, with an inviting smile, moved slowly toward him.

About to take her into his arms, Robert noticed that the top buttons on her blouse were open. The view was spectacular. Pretending to close them, Robert unfastened the remaining buttons instead. Lucy laughed as Bob said, "I think we've had enough to drink. Let's check out the bedroom."

"Sounds good to me." Taking him by the hand, Lucy lead the way. In the room, between open-mouthed kisses, Lucy pulled down the zipper of his pants. Robert, aroused, quickly went into action. While otherwise fully clothed, they made love. Robert could not remember afterward, how or when he had managed to get past Lucy's scanty silk panties. The urgency of the moment had been a driving force.

After the initial frenzy, they managed to remove the remaining obstacles—their shoes, her hosiery, her bra, his shirt, socks and underpants. Their first passion satisfied, they could now proceed at a more leisurely pace. It was a long night. Lucy was insatiable—a hungry tigress—and Robert had no problem cooperating. It was nice to know there were perks that went with the job he was doing for his country.

"Where have you been hiding yourself all this time?" asked Lucy when taking time out to catch her breath. "Look at all the fun we've been missing. Promise you'll come and visit me in Chicago. It would be a shame to have this magic end here. You're good—really good."

"I am? Say it again," said Robert as he rolled over Lucy one more time.

Momentarily satisfied and comfortable in Robert's arms, Lucy said she'd work on her father to find something for Bob to do in Chicago. "I usually get my way," she said.

Robert didn't mind mixing business with pleasure. Lucy was sexy and she was also the answer to many questions the FBI was looking for. It was a good deal all around.

Robert spoke to Agent Stone a few days later. Leaving out the intimate details, he reported that Lucy was back in Chicago and that her romance with Jim was over. "Looks like I've taken his place in her heart," he said.

"That's what I like," teased Stone - "a man who uses all his assets. Seriously, if you get in solid with the Lombardos, it would probably open other doors. I'm convinced St. Louis is only the tip of the iceberg. When we move in to make an arrest, I'd like to have the whole picture. Keep working on your relationship with Lucy but be careful. We've got the momentum and don't want to scare them off. Now tell me, what's the latest on Larry?"

"I think Larry's in trouble. The Commissioner wants him badly. He knows too much and could expose all their shady dealings. Larry's daring visit to the States, leaving those notes for Tina, proves his boy is getting restless and threatening. I suspect that Larry's purpose in surfacing was, not only to warn Tina, but to give voice to his frustration at being exiled."

"I have to agree with you, Robert. We know Larry took early retirement under duress. The Commissioner probably assured him that he would be well taken care of, but my guess is Larry's idea of compensation and the Commissioner's are not the same in terms of dollars and cents."

"I'd really like to know what arrangements were made regarding the transfer of money," interrupted Robert. "Obviously the system worked out has made it possible to keep Larry's whereabouts secret even from the Commish— otherwise he would not have asked me to find him. I'm working on Lucy. Finding me irresistible, there's a good chance she'll succeed in convincing her father that I'd be an asset to him in Chicago."

25

The calendar on the wall indicated it was the first of June. Although deposits from travel agents only began to trickle in toward the middle of February, by now, all tours for the summer season were fully booked. Final payments were due two weeks prior to trip departure and there had been no cancellations to date. Favorable evaluations from the first group of returning tourists would insure Tina and Mara's success as entrepreneurs. That was the good news.

The bad news wasn't all that bad—just discouraging. Tina found that she had to remain in disguise because the Lombardos were still on the loose. Agent Stone called periodically to keep in touch, but nothing was happening. Tina felt they needed Larry's input and Larry, unfortunately, was nowhere to be found. For all anyone knew, he might be dying or already dead.

Lucy, meanwhile, was busy doing all the chores that were previously the responsibility of her brother. The Commissioner had gotten several new accounts in neighboring states. Call girls, escort services and modeling for pornographic films had become new enterprises his "boys" were branching out into. "The Club" members were always coming up with new ideas. Papa Lombardo was amenable to all suggestions, gave advice, promised protection and, as always, took his cut. Anonymous bank accounts in Switzerland were steadily growing and waiting for the day when he might need them.

Although Lucy was doing a better job than her brother of keeping everyone honest, there were not enough hours in the day if the Commish expected her to get around to everyone. For assistance, and for other more personal reasons, she campaigned to have Robert brought to Chicago. While Lucy's father knew there was an ulterior motive, he had to acknowledge that another pair of hands would be beneficial to all. If it would solve the problem and make his daughter happy at the same time, he preferred not to quibble since, in truth, he liked Bob and thought him worthy.

When relating the good news to Robert, it was Lucy's suggestion that he, at least until finding a place of his own, share her apartment. When Robert left St. Louis to move in with Lucy, Detective Jim McDonald became the Captain's right hand man giving him more prestige and everyone was happy.

By summer's end, the Turners—all five of them— were settled and happy. Tina had escorted the first two "ROCKIES" tours herself to be sure there were no glitches. Everything went beautifully. The weather was perfect and her tourists were ecstatic. Agency representatives, who were invited to accompany the groups, had only good things to say and felt certain there would be increased demand making it necessary to run more tours in the future. That would require booking additional rooms—something to work on in the fall and winter months ahead. If the prestigious hotels she had contracted with for this year couldn't accommodate all their future needs, Tina would have to enlist other hotels in the area—perhaps setting up a second price structure. Tina and Mara were on their way. Word had reached across the Atlantic to European agencies, and calls for additional information were coming in. Tina planned to go overseas with proposals when things quieted down.

The brothers, Stan and Alex, were content and doing well in their chosen careers. The Chicago satellite office was expanding under Stan's efficient management and Alex's imminent promotion promised to put an end to his travel assignments. He, Mara and the baby, who was growing like a weed, were looking forward to being a normal family.

Before stepping into his new job, Alex was asked to take whatever vacation days that had been accumulated. It appeared to be a good time to implement their long delayed plans to visit Mara's family in Capetown. Mara's parents were delighted and quickly began preparing for the promised, belated wedding celebration inviting family, friends and neighbors. All were anxious to meet Alex and welcome the new baby.

Some time that summer, Larry began to have the first noticeable symptoms of the disease that would ultimately take his life. His one remaining contact in the States had written to tell him that Tony had died. Although realizing his problems were of his own making—his greed and his ambition to get rich quick on the sweat of other people—he blamed Tony, Jr. for his illness and Tony's father for having betrayed him.

Yes, he had betrayed the people who trusted and befriended him, but he regretted having done so and wanted to make amends. Tina had to believe that he was not a murderer. In addition, before leaving this world, Larry wanted to see Commissioner Lombardo in jail. He was determined to put an end to "The Club" and the "let's pretend" classes. He wanted to be sure that there would never be other trainees brought into the Lombardo rec-room.

Reluctant to go directly to the authorities believing it would lead to his arrest—he did not want to spend his remaining time in prison—he decided to write to Tina. I'll tell her that I'm dying, he thought, and that I want to make amends. I'm sorry for all the bad things I've done. She loved me once. Perhaps she can find it in her heart to forgive me even though I know I don't deserve her compassion. I'll ask her to meet me somewhere. We'll talk. It will be good for her as well, he thought. If she's still causing trouble for Mr. Lombardo, she might be persuaded to drop it when I tell her how dangerous he can be.

Larry did write and mailed it to the address where he had last left the notes. The letter was returned marked, "No forwarding address." There was only one recourse. Larry would have to go back to the States. His illness was progressing rapidly, and travel would soon be impossible. Before that happened, he was determined to find Tina and explain his involvement in what had changed her life. That accomplished, he would settle the score with Commissioner Lombardo.

I'll go to that agency she worked for, he thought. They should be able to tell me where Tina is. If that doesn't work, I'll try the college she and Mara attended. They may have had some contact with her. There's Mara's boyfriend if all else fails. He came to the hotel one summer. As I remember, he went to the same college. His name, I think, was Alex Turner. I remember him saying he was brought up in Vermont. Whatever it takes, I'm going to find Tina and tell her the truth.

26

As it turned out both Larry Hermano and Robert Taylor were making moves at exactly the same time—Larry, looking for Tina, from his current hideout in Mexico and Robert from St. Louis into Lucy's Chicago apartment.

The Cartrite Agency, Larry thought, would have the most recent address for Tina. He knew she had worked for them and might still be in their employ.

"Miss Cappo? I'm sorry, Sir. She no longer works here," said the receptionist at the desk responding to Larry's inquiry.

"Could you give me an address or phone number where she can be reached?"

"Sorry! It's against company policy to release personal information concerning employees," was the courteous response.

Disappointed, Larry's next attempt would be St. James College in Vermont. He was tired and had come down with an upper respiratory infection. Having spent the night in a nearby motel, he drove his rented car to the college. It was raining when he arrived. Having had little sleep, he looked like a ghost. The desk clerk was one of those people who have a mortal fear of germs. While sorry for him, she wanted him out of the office as quickly as possible.

"Can I help you, Sir? You really shouldn't be running around in the rain with such a bad cold."

"I know, but I'm looking for someone who attended school here. She's no longer living at the last address I had and it's very important that I locate her. The name is Tina Cappo."

"Without written authorization, I can't release information about our alumni. I'm very sorry."

"It's an emergency—a medical emergency. I have to have a bone marrow transplant and it has to do with tissue type," Larry lied hoping the clerk would be sympathetic. "Please help me."

Panicking that his germs would get near her, she went to the Rolodex. "The last address we have is the Carillion Hotel in St. Louis."

"I've been there. She's moved. Don't you have anything more recent?"

"That's all we have, Sir."

"Maybe you have something on Mara Konigswahl. She was her roommate."

"I really don't think it's my place to give you that information."

"You must help me. Can't you see I'm desperate? I'll die unless you help me." Larry was red in the face and sweating profusely. Becoming more alarmed, the receptionist answered, "The best I can do is give you the phone number of Mara's parents in Capetown. You can tell them your story and if they see fit to give you their daughter's address, it will be their decision."

"Okay! I understand your predicament and appreciate the fact that you've been so patient with me. Thank you! I will do as you suggest."

Larry did call as soon as he returned to the motel. After what appeared to be a long time, Mara's mother answered the phone.

"You don't know me, Mrs. Konigswahl," he said. "My name is Larry Hermano. I'm a friend of your daughter, Mara. I've been trying to locate her. Would you be so kind as to ask her to call me at this number."

"That won't be necessary, Mr. Hermano. If you wait a minute, I'll get Mara to the phone."

"Mara is there with you?"

"Yes! She and Alex arrived yesterday. We're getting ready for a big wedding celebration. Mara," she called. "There's a gentleman on the phone for you—says he's Larry Hermano."

"Larry? Get Alex on the other phone, Mom. Hurry! Larry? What is it? How did you know I was in Capetown with my family?"

"I didn't! All I wanted was that your mother give you a message to call me back. I can't believe I'm actually talking to you. You've got to help me, Mara. I've been trying to find Tina and sent her a letter, but she moved leaving no address."

"For good reasons, Larry. She's afraid for her life and has gone into hiding. Do you have any idea what kind of hell you've put her through these past years? Suddenly you want to find her. What were you thinking leaving those stupid notes under her door? You didn't even have the guts to face Tina one on one. What do you want from her now?"

"Please, Mara, listen to me. I didn't kill Mr. and Mrs. Cappo. I do know who killed them and want Tina to hear the truth."

"Why should she believe you?"

"I have nothing to gain by lying. I'm dying, Mara. There's not much time left. I have Aids."

"After what you've done, I hope you don't expect sympathy from me or from her."

"No, I don't deserve anyone's sympathy and am not looking for pity. Some might think I'm getting what I deserve and I wouldn't blame them."

"Where are you, Larry?"

"Right now I'm in Vermont near the college. I pleaded with St. James to give me this number."

"Stay where you are, Larry. What's the phone number there? I'll call Tina. She'll probably get back to you."

"Thanks, Mara! Believe me, I mean Tina no harm."

Mara had to compose herself before calling Tina. She and Alex tried to come up with an easy way to minimize the shock, but found there was none.

"Tina, it's Mara."

"Hi! How's it going? Everyone all right? Party in full swing?"

"Tina, you'd better sit down for this one. It's a shocker. Would you believe I just had a call from Larry?"

"Larry Hermano? What's he doing in South Africa?"

"Not South Africa. He's in Vermont at the moment. St. James gave him my parent's telephone number. He's been trying to locate you since your last move and hoped my parents could lead him to you. Needless to say, he didn't expect to find me here with them. Larry is waiting for you to call him back, Tina. He's dying and wants to talk to you." Giving Tina the number to call, Mara asked that she get back to her. "I cant wait to hear what Larry has to say."

Shaking internally, Tina waited to pull herself together before dialing the number Mara had given her. She'd often imagined a conversation between herself and Larry—one that would explain his part in the murders and theft of the Cappo properties. It was about to happen. What would he say? How would she respond? There was so much anger and hurt and resentment in her. Could she keep the conversation civil?

"Larry," was all she could say before Larry jumped in.

"Tina—I'm so sorry. I sent you a letter, but it came back stating you'd moved. I have to talk to you."

"Well, here's your chance. Talk to me."

"Can't we meet somewhere?"

"I've gone to great lengths to hide my whereabouts. Why should I come out in the open for you when we can just as easily talk on the phone? Why did you do it Larry? My parents trusted you. You were like a son to them."

"I didn't kill your parents, Tina. It's bad enough that I ruined them financially and used you, but I'm not a killer."

"Why should I believe you? Everything about you has been a lie. We treated you like family. I loved you. You led me to believe we were going to get married."

"I was involved with the wrong people, Tina. It's no excuse, I know. Admittedly I wasn't much good to begin with, but I didn't kill anyone. You must believe me."

"If you didn't, who did?"

"It was Tony. Your father knew him as Tony Luppo. Tony Lombardo was his real name. His father, Commissioner Lombardo, took me in many years ago and I was in his debt. You might say, he ended up owning me. Together, we devised a way to get the hotel and money from your parents. It's a long story and it would have worked—I'd have the hotel today and Tony's father would have gotten his share—but it wasn't enough for young Tony. He was in trouble with his bookies and wanted the keys to the safe hoping he'd find enough cash and jewelry to pay them off. When he approached the bed to get the key from your father's pocket, your mother woke up. Tony panicked and went crazy with the gun."

Tina couldn't say a word. Breaking the silence, Larry continued, "You're not the only one in hiding, Tina. Everyone's looking for me too. The Commissioner has a contract out on me because I know too much and the law wants me because they think I'm responsible for the killings as well as embezzling. It doesn't matter anymore. What matters is that you know I didn't murder your parents. You must believe me."

"I never did believe that you killed my mother and father, Larry, but you must come forward and tell what you know."

"I want to. I'd like nothing better than to put an end to Lombardo and his operation."

"Then why don't you? What's holding you back?"

"I'm really sick, Tina. They tell me I have full blown Aids. There's not much time left for me and I don't want to live out the rest of my life in a jail cell. I think you could understand that."

"Maybe something can be worked out. Let me see what I can do. I'll call you back after I've made some inquiries."

"Give me a number where I can reach you. I can't stay here much longer."

"Give me twenty-four hours, Larry. Then call Mara again. I'll leave a message with her for you," said Tina who was not about to turn over her unlisted number to anyone. Then she called Stan at work to fill him in on everything that had transpired.

"I can't believe Larry has surfaced again - this time via Mara who happened to be visiting her family in Capetown. This guy really gets around," was Stan's amazed response.

"Let's meet for lunch, Stan. Larry was in Vermont when he called and I'd like us to talk over what he said before contacting Agent Stone. Larry wants some assurances that the FBI is amenable to making a deal and I promised to check it out. He's planning to call Mara tomorrow for Stone's decision."

"Good thinking, Sweetheart. I'm glad you didn't give him our number. How this plays out will have to be up to Agent Stone."

While all this was happening with Tina and Larry, Robert, or Ronald as he was known to the FBI, was having quite a time for himself. He had become Lucy's main man and, as such, was increasingly welcomed into the inner sanctum of Lombardo's business enterprises. One of the first things he learned was that "The Uptown Boys" were in reality known simply as "The Club" and that members of "The Club" were recruited mostly through close business associates of Commissioner Lombardo. In some cases they were related to his friends. The children of these families had grown up together, and like their fathers, were eager to make their marks in schemes that would result in overnight riches. To Robert, "The Club" appeared to be a training ground for junior mobsters or racketeers.

"This bunch is not, and has never been, connected to the organized Chicago mobs," said Robert to Agent Stone when calling. "The boys operate independently in projects they choose and find lucrative. Graduates of "The Club" stay away from areas already controlled by existing mobs, but get involved with hotels, shopping malls, food chains, apartment complexes, condominiums, escort services, mortuaries—in some areas even guns and drugs.

"The career choices belong to Commissioner Lombardo's graduates. He helps them get started with seed money. There is always a price, however. Payback time starts when the operation begins to show signs of success. That's when the Commissioner takes his cut. In exchange for promises of protection, he demands a high percentage of any profits. To make sure there are profits, he has key people entrenched in police precincts where 'Club' members operate."

"In making the rounds with Lucy, have you met any of Commissioner Lombardo's powerful associates?" asked Agent Stone. "Before proceeding with indictments, we've got to assemble a foolproof case."

"Lucy has been introducing me around. Rather than have her catch me taking notes, I'm secretly running a tape recorder. I also keep a diary describing people I meet. It's written in code understandable only to me. I'll get the tape to your office. You may want to send people to investigate. As to the Commissioner's business associates, I haven't met any of them yet. There's supposed to be a big party tomorrow night at Lombardo's place. Lucy has asked me to take her. I'm counting on making some important connections at this affair and will let you know what develops."

"We should meet soon, Ron. Do you think you could tear yourself away from luscious Lucy for a while—after the shindig? I think we need to put our heads together."

"It might be difficult. The lady is hot for my body. I'll try to convince her that we need to come up for air."

Agent Stone hung up the phone. It immediately rang again. "Mr. Stone. It's Tina. You won't believe this, but I just spoke to Larry Hermano."

"He found you again?"

"It's okay. He doesn't know where I live or my phone number. It's a long story, but he got to me through my friend Mara's parents. Coincidentally, Mara and Alex had just arrived in Capetown for a visit with them. She took his number and had me call him back. At the time, he was in a motel in Vermont."

"What did he have to say after all this time?"

"To make a long story short, Larry has Aids. He wants to come forward with what he knows, but needs assurance that he won't have to spend whatever time he has left in prison. According to Larry, it was Tony, Jr. who killed my parents. He wants to meet with me and explain all, but I told him I'd have to think about it. Larry will call Mara tomorrow for my decision. It appears he's on the run not only from the law, but from Commissioner Lombardo as well. He wants to talk and I do want to listen. Is there a chance that he can cut a deal? What should I do or tell him?"

"Do you really believe that he's dying and that he didn't kill your parents?"

"As you know, I never could visualize Larry as a killer. Regarding his claim that he's dying—yes, I believe he has Aids. Remember he was very close to Tony who just died of the disease."

"You must not meet him alone, Mrs. Turner. Our agent, Robert Taylor is in Chicago right now and will go with you. You can introduce him as your husband."

"Okay, but what's Mr. Taylor doing here? I thought he was helping Jim in St. Louis."

"Lucy Lombardo has convinced him to move in with her. She's working on her father to get him involved in their business operations. She doesn't know he's doing undercover work for us."

"What do I tell Larry? Can I give him any assurances that he won't have to go to jail if he comes forward?"

"If he's told you the truth about Tony, Jr. and is really sick, you can tell him we'll give him protection and immunity from prosecution provided he makes a full statement detailing all he knows about Lombardo and his operations. Also that he is willing to take the stand when the case comes to trial.

"I'm going to suggest that the meeting take place in Milwaukee, Mrs. Turner. There's no point in any of you being seen together in the Chicago area. When Larry calls tell him you and your husband will meet him in the Townsend Hotel Lobby on Saturday at six p.m. I'll prepare my man Taylor."

27

The party given by Commissioner Lombardo was an elaborate affair. Black tie and long gowns were the order of the day. Lucy looked terrific in a slinky blue strapless dress and all eyes were on her as she entered the hall, fashionably late, on Robert's arm. Waiting for them were most of "The Club's" active members.

In attendance, eager to go into action, were many recently trained new recruits. Robert was particularly curious about these. From what source were "Club" members lured into this world, he wondered. Were they family or friends of friends? Suspecting a tie-in to the Commissioner, Robert hoped the party would give him an opportunity to meet his many associates. To his surprise, however, Mr. Lombardo's contemporaries had not been invited. Of the older generation, only the Commissioner was to be seen. After introductions and greetings, even he left to attend another function. Robert was disappointed, but felt there would be other opportunities. In the meantime there was plenty of food and lots to drink. He would have a good time.

Lucy, apparently, was also determined to have a good time. Quickly downing two scotches straight up, she left Robert's side to circulate. Watching her as she flirted with all the males in the room, Robert thought it amusing. Lucy's in rare form tonight, he thought. It's almost like she's out to prove something to someone. I know she's ignoring me, but that's okay. It gives me an opportunity to do some networking. There's much to be learned by keeping one's eyes and ears open.

The witching hour came and Robert went to claim Lucy. She had her arms wrapped around one of the young men and made it clear that she didn't want to leave. It took considerable coaxing to pry her loose. Ushering her into a cab, it was evident that she was giving him the silent treatment. Was she angry at him? In an attempt to break the ice, Robert said, "I expected to meet some of your father's friends tonight."

"Who needs those old farts?" she responded. "I had a great time until you rudely interrupted and it seems to me you were doing okay yourself."

"I don't consider your father old and really would have liked to meet his friends. Guess I'm curious about 'The Club.' I've often wondered how it got started and if there is some connection between the boys your father recruits and his associates."

"Just what kind of a connection are you looking for?"

"Well, I got the impression they all know each other. They act like one big, happy family. Are the members related in some way? Is that what makes all the enterprises they get involved in so successful?"

"You know what, Bobby Boy? You ask too many questions. What difference does it make? Why do you insist on trying to fit round things into square boxes? It's none of your business. Get off it."

Robert knew enough to let the subject drop. Instead, aware of her mood and quick temper, he tried humoring her. Gently picking up her hand, prepared to kiss each fingertip - a tactic that usually caused her to giggle—did nothing but aggravate her further. She looked daggers at him and moved to the furthest corner of the cab. Closing the gap between them with the intention of taking her in his arms, didn't work either. She turned her head and rigidly stared out the window. Robert next tried sweet talking her—something she'd repeatedly accused him of being a master at—but nothing he said or did made a difference in her mood. If anything, with each attempt to fix things, Lucy became more hostile. By the time the taxi dropped them at the building, there was no doubt in Robert's mind that she had it in for him.

They entered the apartment in silence. Lucy threw her expensive coat on the floor, kicked off her shoes, said something about a headache, and slamming the bedroom door behind her, invited Robert, unceremoniously, to sleep on the couch. There was not even a mention of blankets or a pillow.

Trying to figure out what had set her off, Robert mentally went through the events of the evening. Yes, he had danced with several of the lady guests at the party and he had engaged some of the men in conversation asking about their business ventures. It all seemed harmless enough to him, but something was definitely wrong. Something had triggered Lucy to be very unfriendly.

What Robert didn't know was that Lucy had come across his coded diary just moments before leaving for the party. The Commissioner had trained her to be suspicious and the strange notebook, together with Robert's interest in the guests and colleagues of her Dad, set off a warning signal somewhere in her brain. She wanted to be alone to sift through her thoughts and take a second look at this person she had invited to live in her apartment. Had she perhaps been premature in trusting him? Was it woman's intuition? Whatever it was, she planned to watch Robert very carefully and perhaps mention her suspicions to her father. At the moment she was very tired and knew it was impossible to be rational having consumed so much alcohol. She'd think about it tomorrow.

Lucy had difficulty falling asleep and finally gave in to taking tranquilizers. They knocked her out and she slept until almost noon the next day. By the time she awoke, Robert had made a call to Agent Stone telling him about the evening and his disappointment. That he had not met anyone of importance at the party was one thing, but Lucy's rejection of him concerned Robert even more. Was she on to him? Had he done something to give himself away? Lucy had been weird all evening and he couldn't figure out what had happened to cause her behavior.

Agent Stone listened and warned him to be on the alert. After suggesting that Robert get out at the first sign of further trouble, he told him about Tina's call and the meeting he'd scheduled for Saturday.

"I would like to be with you and Tina when meeting Larry," he said, "but Larry is skittish. He's looking for assurances that there will be no arrest. He might be reluctant to talk in front of me. Going in my place, you can pose as Tina's husband. He'd understand that she would want him present. Do you think you can get away from the apartment without Lucy becoming more suspicious than she already is?"

"You know me. I'll think of something."

Robert had just returned to the apartment, after having called Agent Stone, when Lucy woke up. As a peace offering, he had stopped at the delicatessen for bagels and lox. At the neighborhood florist, he also bought one red rose.

"Good morning, Gorgeous," he said although it was already just about noon and Lucy looked anything but gorgeous. Presenting her with the rose, he continued, "Did you miss me, my sweet?"

Ignoring the rose, and without a word, she reached for the coffee pot. Obviously the mood of the night before was still with her.

Trying again to win her over, he said, "Sit up, my love. I'll prop your pillows. Let me fix your coffee. I brought bagels and your favorite—cream cheese and lox. We'll have breakfast and then you and I can take a little nap. We both had too much party last night, but I promise you'll feel much better after we spend a little time under the covers."

Looking into her eyes, Robert could see that Lucy was not pacified. As a matter of fact, storm clouds were gathering and he sensed she was about to explode. Why? He'd obviously slipped up. Where? He reached to take her in his arms hoping to soothe her with a kiss, but she pulled away shouting, "Get away from me, you creep."

"What's wrong, baby? Please tell me what's wrong."

"You tell me! Who the hell are you?"

"Why I'm your man, Lucy—your slave, admirer and protector. Don't you remember? Come on, Sweetheart. Move over so I can remind you."

"Forget it, Bob! This isn't a joke and I'm not interested in whatever you're selling. Looking at you now, it's like I'm seeing you for the first time and there's definitely something wrong with this picture. You are not who you pretend to be. I don't trust you."

"Why? What have I done? Where have I failed you? Tell me! I'm always with you and I thought we were a great team. Yes, I do ask a lot of questions, but that's because I'm still learning. Come on, doll face, give me a break. It's time we kissed and made up," said Robert again attempting to encircle her in his arms.

A rigid Lucy pushed him aside and said, "Maybe that's the problem. You're learning too much too fast. How about explaining, if you can, what it is you want from me—besides my body, of course."

"You've lost me, Lucy. I don't know what you're talking about. You've had this tremendous chip on your shoulder since yesterday. Up until then I thought we had something special."

"For your information, Mr. Taylor, I stumbled on to your secret last night—just before we left for the party."

For a moment Robert thought she'd found out about his FBI connection, but then she went on to say, "That notebook didn't disturb me too much until I realized nothing written in it made sense. Everything was in code or a foreign language. Why would you want to do that if you have nothing to hide?"

"Come on Lucy! There's a good reason. You've introduced me to so many people since I came to Chicago and I like to remember their names and what they do so that I don't embarrass myself by asking stupid questions. My handwriting is terrible. It's a kind of shorthand."

"Why not simply write, 'John Brown, the Butcher, Alex Adams, the Florist or Robert Taylor, the two-faced rotten spy.'

"Wow! You really are off the wall today, Lucy. Hopefully this isn't your way of showing me the door although, I understand, it's a tactic used when terminating a relationship. I really would hate us to be over so quickly and hope it's only that you need some time to cool off.

Maybe we should take a vacation from each other for a few days."

"Good idea. Where do you intend to go? Come to think of it, I never really knew where it was you came from."

"I have family in Milwaukee—a sister. Haven't seen her in a while and I'm sure she'd like it if I spent the weekend with her. A change of scenery will do us both good, and when I get back, we can try again to recapture what I thought we had here."

"Suit yourself!" retorted Lucy again retreating to the bedroom.

Robert packed a few things and left. The fight, or whatever it was, had worked out to his advantage. It was now easy for him to go along with the arrangements made by his boss to meet with Tina and Larry in Milwaukee. As to Lucy's growing suspicion, that was another matter—one he'd have to concern himself with in the future—but only if he dared come back at all.

Lucy spent the remainder of the day nursing a severe headache. Although it eventually subsided, her concerns about Robert's loyalty did not.

I'm a bitch when I get like this, she acknowledged, but my instincts tell me there's something wrong. If I still feel this way tomorrow, I'm going to have a talk with my father. He'll help me sift through my feelings and know what to do.

Tomorrow came and the bad vibrations persisted. I'll call and tell him I'm coming for lunch, she said as she picked up the phone.

"Sorry, Miss Lucy! Your father is out of town. We don't expect him back until Sunday night."

"Do you know where he's gone?"

"He only said he was going to meet with some new clients and that you'd be able to handle anything that came up in his absence."

"No phone numbers where he could be reached?"

"None—I'm sorry. Is there an emergency?"

"No! It will keep. I'll call him on Monday. The problem, if there is one, won't run away."

It was Saturday in the lobby of the old Townsend Hotel. Tina and Robert had arranged to meet earlier so as to become acquainted and were seated when Larry walked in at precisely six o'clock. Introducing Robert as her husband, the three sat down for a few minutes of small talk. For privacy, Agent Stone had reserved a room on the third floor. They were just about to leave the lobby for Room 304 when Commissioner Lombardo, who had made an appointment with a newly acquired account, entered the hotel. As Robert and Larry rose from the deeply upholstered chairs, the Commissioner became aware of the animated group.

Well I'll be damned! That's Larry—and Robert. What the hell are they doing here together? And who is that pretty little thing with them? I've seen her somewhere before. Why that's Tina Cappo. Her face was all over the newspapers for a while. She's supposed to have gotten married and I was told she had moved to London. What's she doing in Milwaukee? And how about Larry? He's supposed to be in South America. I'm paying him good money to be there. Instead he's here with Robert, my newest protege. Lucy and I were grooming Robert to come into the business. Obviously, he's not who we thought he was. None of this is making me feel very comfortable. I've got to think, but I'd better get out of here first. Fortunately the three of them are too preoccupied to have noticed me.

Later, having registered at another hotel, the Commissioner sat down to evaluate the situation. It wouldn't take a rocket scientist to know he was in trouble. Tina, Larry and Robert together meant the authorities were, or would soon be, looking for him. The Lombardo empire was crumbling if not already crumbled.

The party is over, Commissioner Lombardo thought. I always knew it couldn't go on forever. Too bad Tina wasn't in that apartment and wiped out along with her parents that night. She's been a thorn in my side since the beginning. That's why we're in this mess. And Larry? I should have gotten rid of him when he and my son botched that Carillion takeover. I might have known he'd get restless. As for Robert? Both Lucy and I were taken in by him. That was a major mistake and I'll have to take the blame for it. Well, it's the day of reckoning. It's time to think about my options.

Yes, I have influential friends, but they won't be helping me this time. It's no longer a case of a bribe here or there. We're talking murders, and even though my son committed them and is dead, I'm in deep trouble having condoned and covered up for what he did. This means jail time—maybe life imprisonment. Under the circumstances, you won't find my associates sticking their necks out for me. They'll have problems of their own. At the very least, their lucrative operations will be shut down. FBI people have been nosing around for years, and now that they have something, you can bet it isn't going to be a picnic for any of us. I'd say my only recourse is to salvage what I can and get out of the country while there is still time. The first thing I must do is call Lucy.

"Dad! Where are you? I wanted to have lunch with you today, but they told me you were out of town. I'm so glad you called."

399

"Hold it Lucy. We've got problems. First answer one quick question for me. What is your friend Robert doing in a Milwaukee Hotel with Larry Hermano?"

"What did you say?"

"You heard me. I just saw the two of them together. What's worse, they were with Tina who's supposed to be living overseas. How could they have gotten together and why isn't Robert with you in Chicago?"

"Are you sure it was Tina, Dad?"

"I've seen enough pictures of her. Yes, I'm sure, and even if I wasn't, how do you explain Larry—and what happened between you and Robert?"

"We had a fight and decided to take a weekend off from each other. I wanted to discuss it with you, but was told, when I called, that you were out of town. What happened was that I came across a mysterious notebook Robert was hiding."

"Mysterious? What do you mean?"

"It was written in code, Dad, and looked suspicious to me. I accused him of being a spy."

"After what I've just seen in that hotel lobby, my bet is you're right, Lucy. Fortunately none of that trio saw me. They have no clue we're on to them, giving us a slight advantage. I've thought it through thoroughly and we've got to leave. It's important that we move quickly."

"Leave? Where will we go?"

"Over the years I've managed to accumulate a sizable bankroll—just for such an occasion. It's safely stashed away in Switzerland. America's been a great place for us and we've enjoyed a good life here, but there's no question in my mind that it's over. The FBI won't be far behind and it's time to cash in our chips. We must get out of the country at once—before the authorities miss us."

"What do you want me to do?"

"Listen to me carefully, Lucy. I'll get the plane tickets and do whatever is necessary with the banks here. You get our passports and clean out the wall safe. We'll meet tomorrow at two p.m. I'll be waiting at the Lufthansa Terminal, Newark Airport. Don't worry about clothes. We'll buy new. We've got less than a day, Lucy, to make our getaway."

"What about your associates and the operations of 'The Club' members? Shouldn't we warn your friends?"

"They are all big boys and will have to fend for themselves, Lucy. Nothing lasts forever and it's good that I had the foresight to plan ahead. If my friends and associates were smart, they'd have done the same. Let's not waste our time and energy feeling sorry for them. We have a lot of territory to cover before meeting tomorrow and have our own backs to worry about."

The meeting between Tina, Larry and Robert went well. Larry was remorseful and obviously very ill. He confessed to his involvement in the scam that impoverished the Cappos and agreed to go with Robert to FBI headquarters where he expected to sign a statement that would incriminate the Lombardos. He told them about his introduction to the Lombardo family, "The Club" and the numerous lucrative enterprises of it's graduates. His statements, together with all the information Robert Taylor had amassed would certainly enable the FBI to begin the process of closing down the Lombardo empire. This was a major coupe for the Agency and Mr. Stone. In large part, it was Tina's persistence that had brought about the downfall of a clique that had been under surveillance for many years.

Larry was assured of protection from the law as well as from the Commissioner who would be sent to prison. He was grateful that Tina could find it in her heart to forgive him for his participation in the fraud and was pleased to know that she was happily married. When learning of Tina and Mara's successful business, he was reminded of the wrong choices he had made.

Tina could at last see light at the end of the tunnel. There would be no more hiding out. Commissioner Lombardo and friends would soon be in the hands of the FBI. Those guilty would be brought to trial, convicted and sent to prison. She would dispense with her disguise and once again be the real Tina. In addition, having kept her promise, she would find peace.

Unfortunately, Tina was not entirely out of the woods. Yes, Tony Jr., the murderer of her parents, had suffered a cruel death. And Larry, who had been responsible for defrauding her family, could not escape the sentence imposed by his serious illness. However, although Agent Stone moved quickly to have the Commissioner and Lucy arrested, he found they had eluded him leaving no trace as to where they had gone. Agent Stone would never know that a chance encounter in a Milwaukee hotel lobby had tipped off "The Club's" originator, Commissioner Lombardo.

Others of their associates were not so fortunate. Thanks to Larry's testimony and sworn statements, the FBI rounded up the operators and closed down their many diversified enterprises. Included among the indicted were those who had taken over the Cappo's hotel. Tina's friend and family attorney had offered to look after her interests and felt certain the Carillion would ultimately end up in her possession. As to other family assets that had disappeared, he was not so sure, but promised to give it his all.

Agent Taylor's tapes and notes made it possible to bring in for questioning even the most recent "Club" inductees. While many of Commissioner Lombardo's attorney and accountant friends were identified and would be brought to trial, some of his associates managed to fall through the cracks.

Police precincts in St. Louis and Chicago cleaned house resulting in the arrests, among others, of Captain Steiner and Detective Jim McDonald. Chaos prevailed for quite some time.

However, safely out of the country, there remained Lucy and her father. He was now ex-Commissioner Lombardo. Although financially able to live comfortably on the money the Commissioner had squirreled away, they were already bored and beginning to look for new ways to fleece the innocent and unsuspecting. According to Lucy, Canada had possibilities. Surely they could find and train another group of ambitious young people.

Tina and Stanley moved one more time. The success of Tina and Mara's tour package enabled them to buy a house not very far from Mara and Alex. Tina was herself again. There were no more disguises and no more Sherlock Holmes imitations. All her energy now was centered on Stanley, her wonderful patient husband, and the business she and Mara had built. While their "ROCKIES" tour was already becoming popular among Europeans in England and Germany, it was Tina's intention to visit agencies in Italy, Spain and Switzerland at the end of the current tourist season. She expected to make new and interesting contacts. Perhaps she'd run into the Lombardos some day. Stranger things have been known to happen.

THE END

ABOUT THE AUTHOR

With a view to sharing her love of travel, this retired Human Resources Director has combined fact and fiction to create TINA'S PROMISE, another exciting murder mystery. Her first book, VEGAS CROSSROADS, was published in 2001.

Always eager to inspire readers to explore the wonders of the world, the writer uses her settings and experiences as background for creating murder mysteries. Her characters are fictional. Some are good and inspirational while others are bad and evil. There are always twists and turns in the author's plots making for suspenseful reading.

Ending TINA'S PROMISE, the author has left the door open for a possible sequel. Gathering material as she continues globe trotting, she expects there will be one.

Printed in the United States
1337400001B/4-12